GOODNIGHT, VIENNA

ALSO BY MARIUS GABRIEL

GOODNIGHT, VIENNA

MARIUS GABRIEL

LAKE UNION
PUBLISHING

Text copyright © 2022 by Marius Gabriel

Published by Lake Union Publishing, Seattle

www.apub.com

Amazon, the Amazon logo, and Lake Union Publishing are trademarks of Amazon.com, Inc., or its affiliates.

ISBN-13: 9781542035231
ISBN-10: 1542035236

Cover design by The Brewster Project

Printed in the United States of America

To my children

Prologue

You had to be careful where you walked, not just because the pavements were smashed and the streets blocked here and there by tons of rubble that had yet to be bulldozed away, but because the zones of the four Occupying Powers – American, Russian, British and French – were marked only by hand-lettered noticeboards; and it could be dangerous to wander into the wrong zone without the right permit.

The Russians, in particular, were unpredictable. They might give you a swig of vodka, if they were in the mood. They might take you round the back of a bombed building and rape you. There was no way to know.

She had been warned that women who walked alone in Vienna were kidnapped sometimes at checkpoints. They vanished into the cellars and were never seen again, even if the paltry ransom was paid.

But she could not let fear hold her back. She had experienced many years of fear, and she knew that if you gave in to it, you stopped moving altogether. So she let her feet go where they willed.

As in a dream, nothing was the way she remembered it. But things were half-recognised sometimes. You saw a marble statue you had once known, ghostly against the dark ruins; but the horse and rider had both lost their heads, and they now stood among a scattering of cracked masonry, like ice floes in a half-frozen sea. Or you looked down a street that seemed familiar somehow, except there was nothing for the memory to catch hold of, because the buildings you might have known were hollowed out and the coffee shops you might have sat in were empty caverns filled with debris and foul water.

Weeds grew between the heaved-up paving stones, some of them in flower, dirty purple or bloodless white, rank life reclaiming the places where once carefully tended roses had bloomed.

And as in a dream, the streets were deserted. If you did see another person, it was a silhouette that flitted like a shadow at the end of a once grand *Hauptstrasse*, and was gone; or an old woman plodding with her head down, scavenging for God knew what; or children clambering on the distant hulk of a burned-out tank.

Vienna was a city that belonged to the dead and their ghosts. And to soldiers. The soldiers who congregated in odd places were the only presence that seemed really alive. Russians in fur caps and padded coats, negotiating with women who took to the streets in their nightwear to leave no doubt as to what they were selling; Americans with cameras, photographing everything as though it were not all defaced and despoiled; British and French with hard eyes, sporting the thin moustaches made popular by the film stars of the day.

Otherwise, Vienna was desolate and grey.

She walked along the banks of the Danube, and it was desolate too; no longer blue and rollicking, but a flat wash of lead that ran from the Black Forest to the Black Sea, and no more belonged to Vienna than did the flat, leaden wash of the sky overhead.

She walked the broken streets, remembering, yet not really sure what it was she remembered. It had been so long ago, a lifetime ago, though only a scattered handful of years.

She came at last to St Stephen's Cathedral. But it was not as she remembered it. The American bombs and the Soviet artillery had seen to that. The rich swathes of stained glass were gone, leaving gaping holes. The wooden trusses of the roof had burned to charcoal. The stone skeleton of the great building was blackened by fire. The ranks of saints and bishops were mutilated. A heavy price had been paid.

She stood looking at it for a long time before she had the will to go in. She picked her way over the rubble and through the doorway.

The bare interior of the cathedral was being cleared by old men with handcarts. But candles had been lit in the heavy wrought-iron candelabra, as though God still lived here, and still cared about such things. Their small flicker led her on.

An old priest made his way towards her, hurrying as fast as his arthritic limbs would allow, his red-rimmed eyes anxious. He took her arm, and pointed a finger upwards to warn her of the danger of falling rubble; men were up there, working on the roof, black spiders against the grey sky. She nodded to show that she understood. He pointed to the wooden collection box. She found a few schillings in her pocket, and dropped them in. They landed inside with a hollow rattle that reverberated around the nave. Gutted as it was, the cathedral conserved its aural space. There was a hush between these walls, an echo that was somehow holy, despite everything. Every sound you made, every cough or scuff of the shoe, was returned to you in a whisper, as though by a legion of phantoms.

She made her way slowly to the altar, trying to remember how she had felt, what it had been like, before the war. She stopped at last and looked up. The Gothic choir stalls were buried in ash. One night before Christmas, long ago, a choir had sung here, jewelled

3

voices supported by the deep hum of an organ. Here she had stood and listened, entranced. She strained her ears now for the ghost of that music. But it had fled.

If she was looking for something, it was no longer here. She would have to find it somewhere else.

It was time to go back.

She turned at last, and made her way back through the ruined city to the concert hall.

Chapter 1

In the autumn of 1937, Papa sold the last Fabergé egg.

It wasn't one of the most extravagant ones. Those, encrusted with pearls and emeralds, had all gone long ago. But it was the one that Papa had treasured most. The Tsar himself had given it to Papa before the Revolution. It was made of engraved platinum, and when you popped it open, there was a silver model of the royal carriage inside. And if you looked in the windows, there were enamelled portraits of the Imperial Family gazing placidly out – the Tsar and the Tsarina, the grand duchesses and the poor little Tsarevich.

When the collector came to pick it up, barely hiding his glee, Papa burst into tears. But then Papa always burst into tears, so Katya wasn't all that sympathetic. The Romanovs were dead in any case, murdered by the Bolsheviks, as lost as the world they'd once inhabited; and holding on to such things was bad luck.

Besides, the money was needed. Money was always needed. Papa's ill-conceived business ventures had all failed, one after another. Selling the jewellery they'd smuggled out during the Revolution had barely kept them afloat.

They could have cut back, of course. Lived more economically. But that hadn't occurred to either Papa or Mama. Living economically wasn't their style. Their style was grand houses, grand hotels, grand clothes, grand gestures. They still insisted on consorting with dukes and princesses, in whose company such things were de rigueur, as though Lenin and Stalin were figments of the imagination, and any day now they would all go back to St Petersburg and resume the wonderful life they had once had.

Katya had been a child when they'd left Russia. She remembered the panic of their departure, the coachman hoarsely shouting, 'Quick! Quick! The Reds are coming!' and the housemaids and footmen staggering down the marble staircase, loaded with valises. She remembered peering out of the back of the carriage at their house, seeing it recede until the whirling snow swallowed it up. She remembered the roads filled with retreating soldiers. And then the long train journey to Paris, and Papa crying all the way, and Mama silent and grim, and her with nothing to do but look out of the window at the snow, or play with Mimi, her little white poodle, who had run away as soon as they reached Paris (or been stolen, Papa said).

Of the life they'd had before that, she remembered only parts, except that she had been happy.

After arriving in England, she had been expensively educated at a girls' boarding school in the Cotswolds, and led through the social graces and the mysteries of upper-class rituals at a finishing school in Bournemouth. Mama and Papa were transparently hoping for a marriage that would save their lost fortunes (now being enjoyed by the Bolshevik proletariat) and pay back her expensive education. She spoke German, French, English and Russian, and was accomplished at the piano.

She had been presented to a succession of eligible young men, but either they hadn't been interested in her, or she hadn't been interested in them, or in some cases, both.

After a few less than dignified years of being on the shelf, and a period of maturing from girlhood into womanhood, Katya had announced that after all, she didn't *want* to be married off to some suitable millionaire – even if such a creature could be found. And when she'd further announced that she had decided to go to university and train to be a doctor, Mama and Papa had been horrified.

'But Katinka!' Papa had exclaimed. 'We've already spent so much on your education!'

'I'm in my twenties, Papa. I can't sit around forever.'

'And a *doctor*, besides,' Mama had said. 'Such an *unsavoury* profession!'

But Katya had stuck to her guns, had gained entry to medical school in Glasgow, and had passed her first year, and then her second, with flying colours. She was home for the holidays now, in time to see Papa part with the last Fabergé egg.

The egg, however, hatched trouble.

'We've got you a position,' Papa said, by way of opening the discussion.

'What sort of position?' Katya asked, looking up from her textbook of anatomy.

'A job,' Mama clarified.

'As what?'

'A governess.'

'A governess! But I'm starting my third year in a few weeks!'

'There isn't money for that,' Mama said bluntly.

'I can work in the mortuary. They need assistants there. I'll pay my own fees.'

'That doesn't help *us*,' Mama said, even more bluntly.

Papa, who had a gentler way of doing things, interceded. 'We're in debt, my dear. Head over heels.'

'But the egg—'

'The egg didn't even pay off what we owe. The staff. Friends who've lent us money. The wine merchant, the tailors – we still owe them all.'

'Wine merchants and tailors!' Katya exclaimed.

'It's all been arranged,' Mama said.

'And,' Papa added persuasively, 'it's *almost* like being a doctor.'

Katya threw her hands up in the air. 'I don't believe what I'm hearing! What have you two done?'

'He's a widower,' Mama said, 'with one child. A sickly little girl. You'll manage easily.'

'And he's very rich,' Papa put in, before Katya could reply. 'He's paying very highly. Enough to get us out of debt – and more besides. We'll be secure at last.' He took Katya's hands. She tried to pull them away, but he held on tight. 'Katinka! This is a wonderful opportunity. It's the answer to our prayers.'

'It's not the answer to *my* prayers,' Katya said in a tense voice. 'How could you ask this of me?'

'We've never asked you for anything before,' Mama said sharply. 'We educated you without regard for the expense.'

'Sending me to piano lessons and finishing school wasn't exactly an education, Mama.'

Mama shrugged. 'Perhaps if you'd been prettier, you'd have caught the eye of a suitable husband. But you are twenty-six years old, Katya. It's too late for that. This is your chance to make something of yourself.'

'I was making something of myself!'

'You mean you were throwing yourself away.' They had been over this argument a hundred times when Katya had first announced her intention to go to medical school, and she was too

8

disheartened to face it again. In Mama's mind, medicine was a nasty profession, and no real lady would ever enter it. As for working in the poorer city areas – which had been Katya's aspiration – hadn't exactly such people, led by the monster Lenin, stolen everything from them? Why should Katya want to help such *canaille*? 'People don't trust women doctors, and that's a fact.'

Katya rolled her eyes. 'We're in the nineteen-thirties, not the eighteen-thirties, Mama.'

'Nobody will ever go to a woman doctor unless it's positively the last resort.'

'In any case, one never knows what might happen,' Papa said encouragingly. 'In Vienna, in the house of a wealthy man – who knows what opportunities will present themselves?'

'Vienna!'

'Yes, Vienna.'

'But – there's a civil war in Austria!'

'Oh, pooh.' Papa waved that away. 'That was three years ago. A small uprising of communists, swiftly dealt with by the government. All over now.'

'A small uprising of communists? They said that about the Bolsheviks, Papa.'

'Not the same thing at all. A few broken heads, and the rest ran away when the troops arrived. It's the most peaceful city in Europe now. And the most beautiful. The concert halls! The opera! The art galleries!'

Katya pulled her hand away from Papa and folded her arms. 'I'm not going.'

'Do you want to ruin us?' Mama demanded, her eyes flashing. 'Is this the gratitude we get?'

'Of course I don't want to ruin you,' Katya retorted. 'If it comes to that, you've ruined yourselves. Just wait until I'm qualified as a doctor! I'll support you then, I promise!'

'We can't wait that long, Katinka.' Papa managed to secure her hand again. He squeezed it. He had tears in his eyes now. 'Our creditors are ruthless. It's the end for us. You're our only hope.'

'We owe six months' rent on this place,' Mama added. 'We'll be out on the street.'

Katya looked around the drawing room where they were sitting. It was beautifully furnished and hung with fine paintings. The house was a regal residence in Kensington, and visitors were always impressed, but unfortunately, Mama and Papa didn't own any of it. They rented everything: the house, the furniture, the paintings, the carpets, even the kitchen things. They'd always lived in houses like this, rented in the best parts of London or Paris, with butlers and maids to attend to them. And it had always been far beyond their means.

They'd managed to stay one step ahead of their creditors for years. Usually, selling a Fabergé egg, or some other piece of jewellery, had granted them a reprieve. But Katya could tell that this time was different. Mama's handsome face was haggard. And although Papa was prone to tears, this time they were not elegant sniffs, disposed of with a silk handkerchief, but the noisy gulps of a child who had fallen down the stairs.

'You're serious,' she said.

'Of course we're serious,' Mama said. 'Come.'

She led Katya to the window and pushed the curtain aside. Three burly men were standing on the pavement with their hands in their pockets, staring at the house. They looked rough, threatening. 'Who're they?' Katya asked.

'The bailiffs,' Mama said. 'They're waiting to hear what you decide. If you refuse, they've got orders to come in and take away the furniture. And then we'll be bankrupted. We'll lose everything. All our friends. The roof over our heads. Everything. You can't get out of this, Katerina. Not without betraying us.'

There was a silence. An ultimatum had been delivered. Katya looked from her mother to her father, biting her lip. 'You'd better tell me about it,' she said at last.

'You've met him,' Papa said. 'Thorwald Bachmann.'

'I don't know any Thorwald Bachmann,' Katya protested. 'When did I meet him?'

'When you came down at the end of the winter term. He was at the party we gave.'

'*That* party?' Katya groaned. She could barely recall it. She'd arrived from Glasgow on a Friday evening, exhausted after a particularly gruelling term, having caught a cold that made her groggy, to find that her parents were throwing one of their glittering cocktail parties. The house had been full of noise and people. A glass of champagne had been thrust into her hand. She'd stumbled, only half-sensible, through an hour or so of chatter with strangers before her cold, her tiredness and the champagne had overwhelmed her, and she'd crept away to bed.

She remembered none of the people she'd spoken to, let alone someone from Vienna with a name as unusual as Thorwald Bachmann. She was sure she would have remembered that.

'What did he look like?'

'Tall. Distinguished.'

'That doesn't ring any bells. What did we talk about?'

'You were talking about your university studies.'

'Babbling, as usual,' Mama put in.

'Being very interesting,' Papa said. 'He told me he could see your spirit shining through.' Papa raised a finger to emphasise the truth of what he was saying. 'His very words. "I can see her spirit shining through," he said.'

'Oh, nonsense, Papa.'

'He has a single child, a daughter of twelve. Gretchen. She's been unwell most of her life. He needs a governess to take care of her.'

'He doesn't know anything about me. How can he think of trusting a sick child to a stranger?'

'Apparently the child is not so much sick as—' He hesitated. 'Troubled.'

'Troubled?'

'Perhaps *difficult* would be a better word.'

'Nothing you can't deal with,' Mama said, dismissing the digression with a wave of her white, bejewelled hand. 'The work is easy, and two years will soon pass.'

'What do you mean, two years?'

'Subject, naturally, to a probationary period,' Papa said. 'A couple of weeks' trial. And then he will pay your first year's wages in advance. We'll send you something every month, of course. You won't need much money. You'll be living as one of the family. Everything taken care of.' Papa waved his plump hands volubly, a true Russian as he talked. She absorbed only fragments of what he was saying: big house, rich man, princely salary, all the elements that meant most to Papa.

'What's wrong with the child?' Katya asked dully.

Papa stopped in mid-sentence. 'Well,' he said, pinching his lower lip, 'it seems nobody really knows.'

'Hasn't she seen a doctor?'

'All the doctors in Vienna, apparently. None have helped. And some made things worse. She was put in a hospital for a time. She was so unhappy there that she almost died. So now he wants to keep her close to him, at home. She has no mother, poor little orphan.'

'If she has a father, she is not an orphan.'

'Well, poor little motherless creature.' Papa waved the distinction away. 'He wants her to have a woman's touch.'

'I insist on meeting him before this goes any further,' Katya said.

'No need,' Papa replied airily. 'He's already made up his mind.'

'But I haven't made up mine! And how could he possibly have made up his mind about me?'

'He relies on first impressions. Herr Bachmann is a man who trusts his instincts. I've noticed,' Papa went on expansively, 'that many of the most successful men are like that. They take immediate decisions, without reflection. They know that their first impressions are almost always the right ones. It's a gift.'

Mama sat down beside Katya. 'There's nothing to it,' she said in a quieter voice. 'All you have to do is show the girl kindness. Be gentle. Play the piano for her. Amuse her. Get her involved in games. Nothing too rough, mind. Like you did with the Tsarevich.'

Katya thought back to the pale, grave boy who used to be brought to their house in St Petersburg. Five or six years older than Katya, the Tsar's youngest child and only son, Alexei, had been an extremely delicate boy. The haemophilia that he'd suffered from had made it impossible for him to engage in sports with other children. The slightest blow would produce huge bruises. She remembered him unrolling the sleeve of his khaki blouse (the Great War had been raging then, and he was always dressed as a little soldier, complete with medals jingling on his thin chest) and showing her the dark contusions caused by careless childhood misfortunes.

Although the appointments had been ostensibly for Alexei Nikolaevich to 'play with Katya', the boy took no part in her games. He couldn't run or jump as other boys did: his joints would swell agonisingly. She'd been warned not to involve the crown prince in anything that might injure him, even slightly. A nosebleed could threaten his life. He would sit in a chair, his hands folded, watching her quietly as she gave her dolls tea parties or rolled a ball for Mimi to chase. She would pick out tunes on the piano for him. Sometimes he would fall asleep in the chair (even she knew that her amusements were not a very gripping spectacle) but that didn't matter. And they had grown very attached to each other.

Afterwards, the carriage would rattle up to the door and he would be taken home again, and she would solemnly kiss him goodbye on each cheek. She remembered how cold and soft his skin was.

'Herr Bachmann knows all about your kindness to the Tsarevich,' Mama went on. 'He was deeply impressed. It's not everyone who has had the privilege of looking after a prince.'

'I didn't "look after" him at all. I was just a child myself. I played on the carpet while he watched.'

'It was far more than that. They chose you.'

'Because they thought I was too small to hurt him.'

'He loved you.'

'And I loved him. But that doesn't make me a nursemaid.'

'You were a *great* help to the Imperial Family,' Mama said briskly. 'Among my most treasured possessions are notes from the Tsarina praising your gentleness, and thanking me for allowing the Tsarevich to be in your care.'

'And you showed these notes to this Austrian?'

'Of course.'

Understanding was dawning on Katya. 'So he thinks I'm some kind of expert on delicate children?'

'Well, of course he knows that you have a natural gift.' Mama leaned forward. 'This is our last chance, Katya. A golden opportunity for us. And a golden opportunity for you – if you will only use it. And don't take that cross face to Vienna, please! You look like a ruptured frog. You need to be cheerful, gentle and agreeable.'

Used as she was to her parents' duplicities and exaggerations, this was really too much. They'd gone through life spinning tales of their wealth and great connections. It was true that Papa was a baron, had been friends with the Tsar, and had done a lot of business for the Imperial Family. That was why, every Easter, the Tsar had presented Papa with a jewelled egg to mark his gratitude. It was also true that they had once been rich, but those days were just memories. And it was true that the Tsarina had brought the Tsarevich to their house on occasions because children of his own age were considered too risky to associate with. Even the Tsarevnas, his sisters, were occasionally too rough.

But what Mama had told the Austrian was plainly a fabrication. And like so many of Mama and Papa's fabrications, it would puncture like a balloon. Katya had no idea at all how to deal with children, let alone one with a mystery condition. If Herr Bachmann had been told that she had some special experience, or some special sympathy with sick children, then he had been deceived.

'And who is this Thorwald Bachmann?'

'I've checked him out from top to bottom,' Papa said, patting her shoulder earnestly. 'He has a wide range of solid interests with controlling shares in every one. A man of unassailable wealth,' he added, smacking his lips over the words.

'Who cares about that! What did his wife die of? Bludgeoned to death and buried in the garden?'

'This is not a time for facetiousness,' Mama said. 'His wife died after a long illness when the child was very young. Why are you being so difficult? Can't you see what a golden opportunity this is?'

'All I can see is that you've sold me off to a stranger to pay your debts. You'll spend everything, and at the end of the two years you'll tell me you're in debt again, and want me to spend another two years! Or five! Or ten!'

Mama didn't even bother to contradict her, but Papa put on his most solemn face. 'I swear to you, darling—'

'Don't swear anything! You've promised so many times to change, and you never do!'

'It is not your place to criticise your parents,' Mama said in her austere way. 'It's your place to do your filial duty. We have given you everything. Now it is your turn to give something back to us.'

And with that, Mama stalked out of the room.

When they were alone together, Papa sat down beside Katya and took her hands in his. 'Katya,' he said quietly, 'I know how hard this is for you. I wouldn't ask it of you if it wasn't our only hope. We've been bad parents, I know that. I only hope that one day you'll be able to forgive us.'

'Of course I forgive you,' Katya said wearily. 'And of course I won't let you be ruined.'

Papa's eyes filled with tears again. He kissed her hands. 'Thank you, darling, thank you,' he whispered.

The truth was that Katya knew she was beaten. Though she despaired of Mama and Papa's improvidence, she could never leave them to their fate. If she did, they would join that tide of White Russian refugees who wandered the earth penniless, from Shanghai to New York, scraping whatever pitiful living they could find, mocked for their airs and graces, all their pretensions of belonging to the aristocracy shattered forever. Being bankrupted would probably kill Papa. For all her toughness, it would probably kill Mama, too.

She couldn't let that happen to them.

But she couldn't hide her grief, either. The hurt was too raw, the disappointment too sharp. Her dream of being a doctor wasn't just on hold. She knew better than that. It was almost certainly over. Her wings had been brutally clipped, and she might never climb the sky again.

Katya shed no tears, but she mourned inwardly and constantly. She'd had a life of privilege, and had never been happy in it – especially knowing that they could afford none of it. The idea of becoming a doctor, and giving back to society, had given her the greatest happiness she had known.

Out of her mourning a decision eventually emerged: that whatever happened, she would *not* give up her medical dreams. She would fulfil the duty that her parents had set her, hard as it was. But when it was done, she would go back to medical school in Glasgow, and pick up the pieces of her dreams, and put them together once again.

Chapter 2

The train journey from London to Vienna, which took two days, brought back her childhood memories of the flight from Russia. That voyage had marked a momentous change in her life, and now, here was another.

The train steamed out of Victoria station, leaving Mama and Papa waving on the platform (Mama looking sternly satisfied and Papa weeping inconsolably). She was travelling on the Wagons-Lits Orient Express to Paris, Strasbourg, Munich and then Vienna. Her employer had bought the tickets, and she was booked First Class all the way, in a private compartment. Money, as Papa had said, was clearly no object for Herr Bachmann. She was attended to like royalty, her luggage taken care of by cheerful porters. A steward informed her that she could have all her meals served in her compartment, if she so wished. She politely declined. She wanted to explore the rest of the train.

The Orient Express, painted royal blue and gold on the outside, and appointed like a grand hotel on the inside, was undeniably beautiful. The wealth of the man to whom her parents had sold her (that was the way she still saw it) was already starting to envelop her. Her compartment, panelled in exotic woods, was fitted out in the most fashionable art deco style. She had her choice of the upper or lower bunk, a writing desk with a pretty pink lamp, a washbasin, an easy chair, and a bell to summon the steward.

It made her feel slightly suffocated, so as soon as the train had pulled out of Victoria, she emerged from her cabin and wandered down the train. Her fellow passengers were smart and fashionable. She half-expected to see Hercule Poirot sipping a crème de menthe with an American millionaire and a Hungarian count. She'd read the Agatha Christie book a couple of years ago, but never expected to find herself on the train.

She found an empty seat in the bar car, and ordered a cup of tea. It came with petits fours, one of which she ate while watching the drab suburbs of London rattle past.

The memories of that earlier journey from St Petersburg crowded into her mind. She remembered the snow powdering the windows of the carriage, an alien landscape whirling by, her feeling of mingled terror and excitement. Her fingers unconsciously strayed to her lap, where her little white poodle, Mimi, had sat. She remembered her parents' faces, looking as she had never seen them before, shattered. Above all, she remembered the sense of finality, which, even as a child, she had felt so keenly. There would be no going back. There was no longer a home to go back to.

It was odd to feel that her life since that day had been wasted. And yet, that was just how she felt. Mama and Papa had brought her up to think of herself as a wealthy young woman, as though wishing a thing would somehow make it so.

Now, after a bare two years of freedom, she was back in the trap she had tried so hard to escape. She thought of the friends she had made, all those clever, cheerful, interesting young women, all so committed to medicine. She remembered their bright faces, heard the swish of their academic gowns, their laughter, their earnest talk of anatomy, biology, chemistry, politics, art, everything under the sun. They'd all be going back soon. Without her. If she ever met them again, they'd be years ahead of her. They'd be doctors while she was still struggling through her degree. It was a bitter thought.

'May I join you?'

Katya looked up from her thoughts. A smartly dressed woman was standing at her table. 'Yes, if you like,' Katya replied.

'I saw you boarding,' the woman said. 'I'm also travelling alone.' She held out her hand. 'Winifred Brownlow.'

'Katerina Komarovsky.'

'I say, that sounds awfully romantic.' Her new companion smiled, sitting down opposite her and taking off her rather dashing felt hat. She had a narrow, plain but pleasant face.

Over another cup of tea, they quickly warmed to one another, and became Winnie and Katya. Winnie, it turned out, was a secretary, also travelling to Vienna, where she would rejoin the export company she worked for. 'You'll love Vienna,' she assured Katya. 'It's a beautiful city, and so full of culture. And the fashions are beautiful.'

Katya had noticed the woman's foreign-looking but definitely elegant costume. 'So I see.'

Winnie preened. 'I've got an absolutely wonderful boss. He buys me all my clothes.'

'That sounds very convenient.' Katya was glad to have a travelling companion, especially one familiar with the city that would be her home. When she told Winnie the name of her new employer, Winnie looked impressed.

'I've heard of him, of course. He's very rich. A very clever businessman. Lots of interests. Said to be quite a character. Larger than life. I didn't know about the child. But I'd say you've landed with your backside in the butter.'

'My backside doesn't need any more butter, thank you.' Katya laughed. Winnie Brownlow had an enviably slender figure.

A pleasant morning passed. On the ferry across the Channel, they lunched together in the dining car, where the food was as sumptuous as if it had come from a chef in a top restaurant, and in the early afternoon they reached Paris.

Paris was autumnal, cold. The city looked grey and smoky, much as it had done in 1918, the trees shivering uneasily in the wind, smoke streaking from forests of chimneys across a bleak sky.

Their train sat at the Gare de l'Est for a few hours as more passengers boarded. By the time it set off again, Katya and Winnie had shared much of their personal lives – Winnie doing most of the talking, and Katya doing most of the listening. Winnie's life, which included a long-running love affair with her married employer in Vienna, sounded a lot more interesting than Katya's. 'I say, you do draw a person out, Katya,' Winnie said at last.

'Do I?'

'You're a very good listener. I can see why Bachmann wants you for his loopy daughter. You should become a psychologist, or whatever they call them. A mind doctor. You'd be wonderful at that.'

'I'm not likely to become a doctor of any sort at this rate,' Katya replied with a sigh.

Winnie leaned forward. 'I understand why you're angry about being taken out of medical school. But if that's what you really want to do, you will make it happen one day. I hope you won't mind me giving you advice – but don't dwell on the negative aspects of all this. Think of it as an adventure. Whatever happens, it's going to be an interesting experience for you. And in my book, interesting experiences are what make life worth living. Enjoy the job.'

'I'm worried about not being able to do the job properly.'

'Well, I don't have children of my own, but I have nephews. In my experience, even the most difficult children respond to honesty and kindness. And you have a great deal of both. It simply shines out of you. Be yourself, and you'll be fine.'

21

They pulled into Munich station at ten in the evening. It was a vast, rather cathedral-like structure, its vaulted roof supported by a spider's web of steel girders. The building was hung everywhere with rows of swastika flags, making violent splashes of black, white and red.

'That's a sight, isn't it?' Winnie remarked, looking out of the window.

'It's certainly dramatic.'

'Hitler is going from strength to strength. I'm really glad. I believe in strong government.'

'He's an awful bully,' Katya said, having hotly discussed Hitler's persecution of Jews, trade unionists and socialists with her fellow students at Glasgow University. The man with the funny little moustache, the subject of music-hall jokes for years, had come to loom over the world stage.

'He has a vision, if that's what you mean. I like him very much. He talks sense. He's promised to unify Austria and Germany. That'll expand our market immensely. And he'll put paid to the trouble-makers. It'll be wonderful for our business.'

'Really? I'm not sure I'd like to live under Herr Hitler. Germany has become rather a horrible place.'

'You've obviously never been,' Winnie said. 'Hitler has transformed the country. He only wants peace and prosperity. Vienna's still full of communists and agitators. Hitler knows how to deal with those people.'

'By putting them in Dachau?'

'So you've heard of Dachau?'

'I've read about it.'

Winnie was amused. 'In those leftie rags they give out on campus? Surely you don't believe that exaggerated rubbish?'

'I don't believe it can all be exaggerated rubbish. There's obviously a lot of cruelty.'

'Oh, well. Someone has to take a firm hand, or we'll all find ourselves living under Stalin. Don't worry your head about Hitler. He's the best thing to have happened to Europe in a hundred years.' Winnie yawned. 'I think I'm going to turn in.'

They said goodnight. Katya made her way back to her own compartment and changed into her nightclothes. Before turning in, she opened the curtains and took a last look at the outside world. Illuminated by the electric light, the endless ranks of swastika flags did look very dramatic. They had an almost hypnotic effect. Men in military uniform were marching in pairs up and down the platforms. They looked very different from English policemen. Sleepily, Katya shut the curtains again, and climbed into her bunk.

They crossed the Austrian border the next day. The railway ran through a fairy-tale landscape that was infinitely varied. Lush valleys were dotted with quaint villages, each clustering around the spike of a church tower. There were romantic castles, too, where one might expect princesses to be immured, waiting for knights to slay their dragons. Sometimes the train crossed arched viaducts that spanned deep gorges, making passengers gasp as they peered from the windows into the depths below, where no doubt trolls dwelled. Against a deep-blue sky, the mountains were already scumbled with snow along their flanks. Alpine lakes gleamed like steel, winding between forested hills. It was altogether enchanting, and Katya felt her mood begin to lift. Perhaps Winnie was right. Perhaps regarding this as an adventure was the best way to get through it.

Approaching Vienna in the afternoon, however, the reality of her new life started to dawn on her. As the fairy-tale landscape gave way to the environs of a large industrial city, her dreamy optimism vanished. She was a slave-girl being brought to servitude with

23

strangers, not a princess in a bedtime story. Her heart began to thud angrily. Why had she let herself be hijacked?

Part of her anger was directed at herself. She didn't have Mama and Papa's ruthlessness, that steel blade under the velvet cloak. She was soft, yielding. She hated herself for it.

As the train pulled into the station, Winnie Brownlow shook her hand warmly. 'I've enjoyed our time together. My firm's Strauss & Co. Easy to remember, isn't it? Strauss waltzes – Vienna. You can always find me there if you want some English conversation. Good luck, Katya!' She bustled away to get her luggage.

Katya gathered herself and stepped down on to the crowded platform. All around her was the babble of alien voices. She spoke good German, but she swiftly realised that Viennese German was going to take some getting used to. It was spoken rapidly, with a strange accent that she couldn't follow. Clutching her luggage tickets, she tried to find a porter.

'Fräulein Komarovsky?'

She turned to find herself confronted by a small, almost gnome-like man in an olive-green uniform. 'Yes.'

'I am Lorenz, Herr Bachmann's chauffeur,' he said, bowing. He had a nose so long that it hung over his mouth, but his eyes were kindly, like glossy berries, and he spoke English. 'I am here to take you home.'

The car was a huge black affair with a silver star on the bonnet, easily big enough to swallow Katya's luggage and herself and leave acres of leather seating around her. Lorenz drove sedately through the busy streets, keeping silent. Katya, peering out of the windows, saw handsome buildings in an ornate style, which seemed to her, on first acquaintance, to be made out of fondant, like wedding cakes.

As everyone had told her, Vienna was a beautiful city – self-consciously beautiful, like an ageing empress who took great care over her appearance. Indeed, after the foggy drabness of London, there was something almost theatrical about the city, with its grand squares and well-dressed inhabitants, an atmosphere of charming make-believe, as though everyone would suddenly form a chorus line and burst into song.

Her eye was caught by odd details: workmen in lederhosen, double-decker buses plastered with frivolous adverts, a horse-drawn cart delivering barrels of beer. The policemen here looked like characters from a nineteenth-century comic opera, with their funny coal-scuttle caps and huge pistol holsters.

They made their way out of the city and after a drive of some twenty minutes into the countryside, they came to a long, high hedge. Lorenz drove through a pair of tall wrought-iron gates into a cobbled courtyard. Katya could only see the back of the house, but it appeared large, elegant and Italianate. A severe-looking housekeeper in a black and white uniform emerged to greet her. Her iron-grey hair was tied back in a tight bun, emphasising an angular face and a lean neck. She spoke no English, but Katya could follow her German. She greeted Katya unsmilingly, introduced herself as Frau Hackl, and led her into the house. Nervously, Katya followed the lean, ramrod-straight back.

She was led through a big kitchen and up a staircase, seeing nobody along the way. There was no sign of her employer or his daughter, but the housekeeper showed her to the room that was to be hers. Katya walked in hesitantly.

'Herr Bachmann has had the room freshly decorated for you,' Frau Hackl announced, sounding as though she disapproved of such indulgences. 'He instructs me to tell you that you may ask for any changes you wish.'

'I'm sure I'll be very happy,' Katya replied. 'But where is Herr Bachmann? And Gretchen?'

The housekeeper looked frostier than ever. 'You will meet them in good time,' she replied shortly.

'But are they here?' she pressed.

'The master is in his study, and Fräulein Gretchen is in the music room.' She turned abruptly and left.

The woman was plainly not very pleased about her arrival, which made Katya's heart sink. By now, Lorenz had arrived with her luggage. He deposited her bags and left her to unpack. Katya looked around. The room was small but pleasant, and had evidently been got ready with much care. The wallpaper was pale blue with white stripes. The furnishings and carpets were in the same shades. A window overlooked a small orchard, where the apple trees were now heavy with nearly ripe crimson fruit. It was almost a child's room. And it all looked very strange to her.

She thought of her dark little digs in Glasgow, cramped and rather stuffy, where she had talked with friends, toasted muffins on the cracked gas fire, or studied late into the night, and been so happy.

She felt very far from home, like a traveller who has taken an unknown road, and looks at the map, and finds herself hopelessly astray from the course she had chosen when setting out.

Nobody had yet come to fetch her by the time she'd unpacked and refreshed herself, so Katya went downstairs to make her debut. She'd imagined this moment so many times, envisaged how she would behave, what she would say. All of that had gone quite out of her head.

The house was filled with artworks she had only seen before in books – paintings by Klimt and Hoffman marble statues, antique furniture, Oriental rugs and all the other trappings of wealth and taste, the sorts of things Mama and Papa loved. She was reminded of her childhood home in St Petersburg. There was music playing somewhere in the house, one of Bach's *Goldberg Variations*. She moved from room to room in a slightly dreamlike state, almost on tiptoe.

Peering into a doorway, she saw she had found Herr Bachmann's study. It was quite dark, panelled in wood, with a fire burning in a grate. The music was coming from a gramophone in one corner. The man himself was seated at a desk with his back to her, writing busily by the light of the only lamp that was lit in the room.

Katya cleared her throat nervously. He turned and glanced over his shoulder, then rose to his feet.

'Katya!' he boomed. As he strode over to her with his arms spread wide, she realised that he was a huge man, towering over her by at least a foot. He wore a full beard, and was altogether so bearlike that she braced herself for a crushing bear hug. But the arms that enfolded her, powerful as they were, were gentle. He drew her to his broad chest and kissed the top of her head. 'Welcome to Vienna.'

Flushing hotly, Katya backed away as soon as she could. She had never been partial to the abundant embracing and kissing that went on in Russian émigré circles, and this greeting by the stranger who had so ruthlessly cut short her studies was most unwelcome.

'How do you do?' she said stiffly.

He burst out laughing. 'How very English you are!' He had large bright brown eyes, which surveyed her up and down. 'How do *you* do? Did Elise show you to your room?'

'Yes.'

'Is it comfortable enough?'

'Quite comfortable, thank you.'

'And the journey from London?'

'Tolerable.' She could feel her face still hot with discomfort, and wished the heat would subside. She was trying to place him in her memories of that cocktail party. Someone so tall, loud and self-confident should be hard to forget. But nothing stirred.

He put a big fist on his hip. 'You're trying to remember me, aren't you? But you don't.'

'To tell the truth, Herr Bachmann—'

'Please! Everybody calls me Thor. And you don't remember me because these are the first words we have ever exchanged. The evening our paths first crossed, I simply observed you and listened from across the room.'

'It can't have been a very fascinating spectacle. I had a stinking cold that night.'

'Indeed, you were a fine shade of scarlet. Even more so than you are now.' He exploded into laughter again at her expression. 'Forgive me. I shouldn't tease you so soon in our acquaintanceship. I am a dreadful fellow, as you will immediately have gathered.'

'Not at all,' Katya said thinly. His chest was as broad as a cupboard. Above the bushy brown beard there was a broad, prominent nose, those lively eyes surmounted by heavy eyebrows, and a high forehead framed in dark curls. He spoke excellent English, with a rich accent.

'It was a good thing that you were feverish that night,' he said. His voice was deep and vibrant, to go with the rest of him. 'It gave me an excellent chance to assess your character, undistracted by having to make small talk.'

'Well,' she said, recovering her poise after this first encounter, and tiring of this nonsense, 'you summoned me, and here I am.'

'Ah.' Under the beard, his full lips drooped in a melancholy arc. 'You are angry with me.' He looked more closely at her face.

'Furious, in fact. I have torn you away from your studies and inter-fered intolerably in your life. You can hardly bear to be in my pres-ence. It is unpardonable, I agree, my dear Katya. So I cannot ask for your forgiveness. None would be forthcoming, in any case. I ask only that you consider that you are here for a reason, even if it is not immediately apparent.'

'The reason seems to be your whim,' she replied.

He pinched his lower lip, studying her. 'Whim? Yes, if you like. I am very whimsical. Capricious, in fact. I don't deny it. These are words we use to criticise unruly folk, do we not? But I believe that whims are powerful, magical things. By other names, they are instincts, inspirations, impulses. What you English call brainwaves. I have learned to trust mine. Everything you see around you here, everything I have achieved, is the product of my whims. I was not born rich.'

Katya could barely restrain herself from a snort of contempt. As an apology for derailing her life, and taking advantage of Mama and Papa's impecuniousness, it fell woefully short of adequate. It infuriated her to think that this man was to be such a huge part of her future, and take up so much space in her world from now on. 'It must be very nice,' she said, not disguising her bitterness, 'to go through life having all your whims fulfilled and getting your own way in everything.'

'Not in everything, Katya.'

She caught the serious note in his voice. 'Why do you imagine I can be of any use to you, Herr Bachmann?'

He silenced the gramophone, then took her elbow in his big hand. 'Come. Let's sit by the fire for a moment and talk like the old friends I hope we shall one day become.' He steered her to a leather armchair beside the hearth. 'Do you drink coffee?' he asked, looking down at her.

'Sometimes.'

'Good. You and I shall drink it here, often.' He went to a complicated chrome apparatus that stood on a table in one corner of the study, and set it in motion. The room was dark enough to make everything a little mysterious. With a loud hissing and spluttering, a very strong smell of fresh coffee filled the room. He brought her a small white cup, and took the chair opposite.

Katya sipped the brew, and choked. The coffee was boiling hot and almost as strong and thick as tar. 'Good heavens,' she gasped.

'Isn't it wonderful?' he beamed, drinking from his own cup. 'I came across the machine on one of my business trips to Milan. A revelation. Now I import them. Every coffee house in Austria wants one. My whims make money, you see? The Italians truly understand coffee. We Viennese have a very decadent conception of it. Cream, chocolate, and so forth. Here you taste the pure, untainted spirit of the bean, as the desert nomads first knew it.'

She dared not ask for sugar.

He crossed his legs. The flicker of the fire lit half his face, making the tips of his beard glow like red sparks. 'You will meet my daughter, Gretchen, shortly. First, let me tell you a little about her.' He paused for a long time, as though choosing his words. 'Every man wants to see his daughter happy,' he said at last. 'That is something I am denied. She has never been happy.'

'Doesn't she have friends?'

'Gretchen doesn't make friends. She doesn't attract other children. Nor are other children attracted to her.' He put his hands together, lacing his big fingers. 'Children are like those toy magnets. When you throw a box of them together, some stick to others. Each negative finds a positive. Some form clusters. Others form pairs. It's very rare that a magnet remains unattached, as if it had no negative and no positive poles. Gretchen is one of those.'

'I'm very sorry about your wife. When did she die?'

'Five years ago. But the problem existed long before that. From babyhood, in fact. Gretchen seldom smiles or laughs. She doesn't give affection, and she seems to dislike receiving it. She is not stupid, Katya. In some things, she is brilliant. Especially music. Solitary music. She is like a child at the bottom of a deep well.'

'Does she behave badly?'

'At times, yes. Very badly. But harsh discipline doesn't help. It makes it worse.'

'I think that you should consult a psychologist.'

'I have consulted several,' he replied. 'She has even been seen by Sigmund Freud – who, incidentally, is a family friend, and whom you will soon meet.'

'And what did Professor Freud say?'

'He offered psychoanalysis. I declined.'

'Why?'

'I have seen something of psychoanalysis, and the path it takes. I do not want Freud, or anyone else, telling me that I interfered with Gretchen sexually when she was an infant.' Katya couldn't restrain a gasp. He nodded. 'It disgusts you to even hear such words spoken. It disgusts me, too. But that is the path that Freud and the psychoanalysts invariably take. I could see the professor already heading that way. And I assure you, Katya, that whatever is causing Gretchen's problems, it is not that.'

'And the other doctors?'

'We were told that Gretchen has a weakened nervous system. That she lacks mental tension. That the problem lies in the stomach, or in the blood. That she lives in a fantasy world. That she is a narcissist. That she is psychotic. That she will grow out of it. That she will never grow out of it. That she can be cured by sea-bathing. That she is incurable. For each professor, a new useless diagnosis. I am afraid,' he went on, 'that the solution doesn't lie in the hands of psychologists.'

It had already occurred to Katya that Gretchen's condition might have a far less exotic origin than any of these: that she was perhaps simply a very spoiled child, whom her father alternately indulged and neglected. 'I really don't know,' she said, trying to keep her voice level, 'what you are expecting of me. I have no experience with children. My parents may have misinformed you on that score. If they told you that I was some kind of nursemaid to the Tsarevich, then that was completely untrue.'

'I have allowed for your parents' exaggerations,' he replied gently. 'But I don't believe that what they say is completely untrue. The fact that the poor boy's mother chose you as a companion for her very fragile child tells me that she saw something special in you.'

'That's nonsense. In fact, I'm rather bad with children.'

He leaned back so that his face was almost completely in shadow. 'Forgive me for saying this – I have no desire to anger you further – but it is not so long since you were a child yourself.'

'It's many years since I was a child, Herr Bachmann. And my being young does not help in the slightest.'

'I think it does. Childhood is an enchanted kingdom. Once we leave it, we can never go back. We can never understand it again. No matter how we may yearn to. You, Katya, still have some of that magic clinging to you. I saw it that night in London, luminous, like seafoam trailing on the limbs of a swimmer who has just emerged from the waves. I said to myself in that instant, this is the one who can climb into Gretchen's deep well and bring her out into the sunlight.'

Katya was open-mouthed. Was this mumbo jumbo the justification for turning her life upside down? 'So you've decided that the solution lies in *my* hands,' she said incredulously, 'because you think I am childish? Trailing clouds of infancy, or whatever it was you said?'

His voice dropped. 'I've offended you after all. I didn't mean to. I didn't say that you are childish. Only that you are innocent, and closer to Gretchen in many ways than all the learned men and women who have so far been unsuccessful in treating her.'

Katya had started to tremble with anger. 'This is really the greatest nonsense I've ever heard. I shall go back to Glasgow tomorrow and resume my studies.'

'Please don't do that.'

'And you will take back the money you threw at my poor, foolish parents.'

'I don't ask you to perform miracles, Katya. Just to be Gretchen's friend.'

'I can't give up two years of my life being a little girl's friend. I'm sorry.'

Katya had risen from her chair, and Thor rose now, too. 'Meet her,' he said urgently. 'Make her acquaintance. It will cost you nothing.'

'I'm going back to England. This has all been a terrible mistake.'

He reached out to her, as though to take her hands, then stopped himself as he saw her recoil. 'If only I could make you understand how worthwhile this is,' he said in a low, urgent voice.

'Worthwhile to you. But not to me. I have my own life. I never wanted to be here in the first place. I wanted nothing to do with you or your child.'

He was about to retort when he stopped himself, his gaze shifting over her shoulder. 'This is Gretchen,' he said in a quiet voice.

Katya turned. A girl was standing in the doorway.

Chapter 3

Katya was struck by how strange the girl looked. She was thin, with long, dark hair that straggled around her shoulders untidily. She stood motionless in the doorway, staring at Katya. She held a book in one hand, her finger tucked into the page she was reading. Katya got an impression of sad, dark eyes in a pale and pinched face. The girl's empty expression struck Katya to the heart. She wondered how long Gretchen had been standing at the door, whether she had overheard Katya's angry words.

Thor held his hand out to the girl. 'Come, Gretchen,' he commanded.

Gretchen dropped her head and came slowly into the room, her eyes fixed on the ground.

'This is Katya,' he said. The child made no response, but stood mute, her eyes down. 'Say hello to her,' Thor commanded again.

Not raising her eyes to Katya's face, or uttering a word, Gretchen held out her hand. Katya took it. It was small and cool, and withdrawn quickly.

Nonplussed, Katya said, 'Hello, Gretchen.'

Without making any reply, the girl turned and hurried out of the room, disappearing around the door.

'I apologise,' Thor said. 'She was so very excited to meet you.'

Conscience-stricken, Katya turned to Thor. 'I didn't mean her to hear the things we said. I hope she's not upset.'

'Gretchen is used to people dismissing her,' he replied. 'She would be surprised if it were otherwise.'

'I'm not dismissing her! I simply don't think I can be of any use to her – or you.'

Their discussion was interrupted by the sound of a piano somewhere in the house. Katya paused to listen. It began with a few notes, dropping like water, then developed into a complex progression that was familiar to her: it was one of Bach's *Goldberg Variations*, the same piece that had been playing on Thor's gramophone when she'd come in.

'Who is playing?' she asked.

'Gretchen,' he replied, watching her face.

The piece was a very difficult one, but the playing was faultless. 'She's too young to play like that,' Katya said sceptically. 'You must have another gramophone in the house.'

He smiled slightly. 'I ask you to keep an open mind. Come and see for yourself.'

He led her down the corridor. They reached what was clearly the music room Frau Hackl had mentioned, a spacious salon at the centre of which stood a grand piano. The gleaming black instrument was so huge that the little performer almost vanished behind it. But her playing flooded the room with golden cascades of notes.

Katya went to stand close to her. Astonishingly, there was no music score on the stand. Gretchen was playing from memory. Katya watched the pale fingers spanning the keys, moving with a precision and an authority that Katya knew she herself could not achieve. This twelve-year-old played better than she ever would. She played like an adult, a very gifted adult.

She listened for the emotional content in the playing. These Bach variations didn't leave much room for expressiveness. But

35

Gretchen's posture was unusual. She played hunched over the keyboard, as though huddling over something precious, her tangled hair and stooped shoulders shielding the music from any intrusion. It occurred to Katya that her own piano teacher would never have tolerated that crouched attitude, would have called it 'very bad posture'. But who needed good posture when you could play like this?

Fascinated as she was by Gretchen's prodigious musicianship and memory, she was aware of Thorwald Bachmann's eyes, intently watching her reaction. If this was an ambush, it was a very good one.

Abruptly, in mid-phrase, Gretchen stopped playing. Her arms dropped to her sides, and she sat motionless, her eyes fixed on the keys.

'That is as far as she has learned,' Thor said quietly. 'She's listening to the rest of the piece in her mind.'

'How does she play without a score?'

'She can't read music.'

Katya was taken aback. 'You're joking, surely.'

'Not at all.'

'Then how did she learn the piece?'

'From listening to it on the gramophone.'

Katya looked quickly at Thor to see whether he was making fun of her, but his bearded face was serious. 'You play wonderfully,' she said to Gretchen. Gretchen made no response. After a moment, she lifted one hand back on to the keys and began to pick out the next part of the melody, slowly but surely, as though following something she could hear in her mind, inaudible to others.

Thor took Katya's arm and led her quietly out of the room. 'What do you think?' he asked.

'I've never heard anything like that before,' Katya admitted. 'She plays like a virtuoso, without reading a note of music. All those doctors who say she's infantile and so forth – have they heard her play?'

'None of them are able to understand what they are seeing. Freud himself said it was just a parlour trick.'

'A parlour trick? She has a great gift!'

Thor's eyes lit up. 'I'm glad you've understood that,' he said.

'Has she had lessons?'

'She began the piano at three years old. She was already picking out melodies, so we got her a teacher. She's had lessons, on and off, for years. A new professor comes every time, says she's a genius, lasts for a while, then leaves in despair. By now there isn't one music teacher left in Vienna prepared to take her on.'

'Why ever not? What's the problem?'

'There are various problems,' he said evasively.

'Such as?'

'Perhaps the biggest is that she refuses to learn to read music. No teacher will accept that. And then, she refuses to practise. She plays only when she wants to. When the teachers try to show her, she throws a tantrum. They drive one another mad. It's an impasse, every time.'

'And in school?'

'She's not in school any longer.'

'How can she have left school? She's only twelve.'

'For the same reasons. She won't accept discipline. She loathes the teachers, and the teachers loathe her. It's better to keep her out of school than to have constant chaos.'

'But she'll never make any progress staying at home alone, Herr Bachmann.'

'Exactly,' he said meaningfully.

'But how on earth can I possibly—'

'Let me propose a deal,' Thor interrupted. 'Stay with us for two weeks. It can only do her good. Keep an open mind. If, at the end of the two weeks, you're still determined to leave, then you're free to go. I'll come to an arrangement with your parents about the money. They won't suffer any loss.'

'But *I* will. My university term has already started.'

'You'll catch up. You're a very clever woman.'

'First I'm a child? Now I'm a very clever woman?'

'You persist in wilfully misunderstanding me.'

'And you don't understand me at all.'

'Perhaps not. But unlike all the doctors, you know what you are seeing.'

'I can play the piano a little – but I won't succeed where the best music teachers in Vienna have failed!'

'Listen to me,' he said, fixing her with his dark, intense eyes. 'Gretchen stands at a fork in the road. The first path leads towards what you call her great gift, and what the doctors call her parlour trick. The second path leads towards humanity. The first is a road towards increasing loneliness, and eventually, I believe, isolation. The second leads her to achieving friendships and happiness, and a normal life. As her father, that second path is the one that I wish her to take. As for the music, I don't believe anyone can help or hinder her. She'll develop musically at her own pace, whatever we do. But you, Katya, with your warmth and kindness – you can help her develop as a young woman. As a human being. And that is infinitely more precious.'

'If you want a mother for her, you should get married again.'

'I want you to be a friend. That's all. She's on the brink of adolescence. It's going to be a difficult time for her, with no friends and nobody to advise her.' In the music room, Gretchen had begun to play the rest of the Bach piece, the music developing and trans-forming. Katya had the strange sense of hearing it for the first time, although she knew it so well – of hearing it as though it were still being composed. 'Think my offer over,' Thor said gently. 'Then do what your heart tells you to do.'

Tired after the long journey and the emotions of her arrival in Vienna, Katya slept in her little blue room for a couple of hours in the afternoon. In her sleep she seemed to hear the Bach variations, though she couldn't tell whether it was a dream or real.

At around four o'clock, Frau Hackl knocked at her door.

'English tea is served for you, downstairs,' she said sourly.

'Thank you.'

Gretchen was alone in the sitting room, where 'tea' had been laid out – a lavish spread of cakes and pastries. A fire had been lit in the grate and was crackling quietly. There was no sign of Thor Bachmann. She was evidently being put in the lion's den, the lion being Gretchen, who was sprawled on the carpet with a book, and who did not even look up as Katya came in.

Katya poured herself a cup of tea and took a slice of cake, and settled beside the fire. She watched Gretchen. The girl read in the same way as she played the piano, hunched over the book in an attitude of intense concentration, her cheeks cupped in her hands, her tousled locks making a curtain that shut out the world. Besides being tousled, the locks were not very clean; it looked as though her hair hadn't been washed in weeks. Katya found herself itching to take a brush to the tangles.

The book was a lavishly illustrated edition by the Brothers Grimm. Katya realised that Gretchen wasn't reading the text. She ignored the words, focusing instead on the elaborate pictures, her eyes concentrating on them as though following a story in her own mind. The more Katya observed her turning the pages, the more she was convinced that Gretchen was either a very poor reader or couldn't read at all.

It was extraordinary to think that a girl with such manual dexterity, capable of such feats of memory and possessing so much mind power as to play Bach instinctively, could not read music, and seemingly couldn't read words either.

39

She thought of what Thor had said about loneliness and isolation. She could see why Gretchen's genius would fill him with apprehension rather than pride. Gretchen had put a few pastries on the floor beside her book and was using her fingers to cram the food gracelessly into her mouth, spilling crumbs and smearing cream on the Persian rug. The girl was a baffling mixture of great refinement and absolute uncouthness.

Unable to stand it, Katya got up and took a plate and a fork from the table. She put these beside Gretchen, and put the pastries on the plate. The girl flicked a glance at Katya out of the tails of her eyes. Then she picked up the plate and threw the pastries into the fire, where they sizzled on the coals.

'Why did you do that?' Katya asked.

'I don't want your germs,' the girl said in a husky little voice.

'My hands look cleaner than yours,' Katya replied gently.

Gretchen didn't look up from her book. 'I don't care. My germs are *my* germs. I don't want *your* germs.'

'You were making a mess on the carpet.'

'You don't want to be here. I heard you say so. Why should you care about the carpet?'

'I'm sorry you heard that,' Katya said, after a pause. 'I hope I didn't hurt your feelings.'

Gretchen kicked her foot on the floor. 'Please keep quiet. I am trying to read.'

'I don't see you reading. I only see you looking at the pictures.'

There was a silence. The girl looked up at Katya, her eyes glinting behind the tangled curtain of hair. 'What does this say?' Gretchen asked, pointing a finger to the page.

'Can't you read it?'

The girl's face darkened into a scowl. 'I'm not stupid.'

'I didn't say you were stupid.'

Gretchen kicked both feet hard on the carpet in annoyance. 'You tell me. What does it say?'

Katya knelt down beside her and took the book. The ornate illustration showed a skeleton with its bony hand on the shoulder of an old man. 'It's the story of Death's Messengers,' she said.

'Read it.'

'It's not a very nice story,' Katya said.

'I'm not a baby any more,' Gretchen retorted. 'Read it.'

'Very well.' Katya read the short, bleak story, which was only a page long. When she'd finished, Gretchen stayed silent, looking at the illustration. 'Why haven't you ever learned to read?' Katya asked.

The girl's face twisted. 'I don't need to.'

'Learning to read is important.'

The girl shrugged sullenly. 'Why?'

'So you wouldn't need to ask anyone to read to you.'

'It's all nonsense.'

'Reading is nonsense?'

'The words are nonsense. I can't tell one from another.'

'You could easily learn.'

'I can't!' the child snapped. 'Don't you think I've tried? The letters just don't make sense.' Gretchen slammed the book shut. 'You're like all the rest.'

'I'm sorry you feel like that.'

'That's one of the stupidest things that people say. *I'm sorry you feel like that.* It means nothing at all.'

The child, with her twelve years, talked like an adult. An extremely disagreeable adult. 'You're not very polite, Gretchen,' Katya said.

'Why should I be? Nobody bothers being polite to me.'

'I'm being polite.'

'I don't care.' She opened the book again. 'You can go now.'

Katya reflected that there was very little risk of her growing so fond of Gretchen Bachmann that she would change her mind about leaving in a fortnight.

She found herself thinking of Alexei Nikolaevich, the young Tsarevich. Looking back, she had loved the boy in her childish way, and she was certain he had loved her too. The news of his murder – along with all his sisters and his parents – had come as a terrible shock to her. It was her first encounter with the death of someone she had known.

Her mother's death must have had a shattering impact on Gretchen. The loss of a mother in early childhood was not a light blow. One didn't have to be a psychologist to know that. It had clearly left a deep scar, and had almost certainly been affecting Gretchen's development for years. How did one begin to approach such a spiritual injury? Katya had no idea.

'Let's wash your hair,' she said on an impulse.

Gretchen looked up suspiciously. 'What?'

'It must be weeks since it's been washed.'

She turned back to her book. 'I don't care.'

'It's full of germs.'

Gretchen flinched. 'It's not!'

'It is. I know what I'm talking about. I've been to medical school. Even if they *are* your germs, you don't want them crawling all over your head, spreading, multiplying. Next you'll have lice.'

'Leave me alone,' Gretchen retorted. She hunched herself over her book, pressing her fingers into her ears to shut Katya out.

Annoyed, and longing to be out of the oppressive warmth of the room, Katya rose and went out, finding her way to the front door. She walked down a wide flight of stone stairs into the garden.

There was a slight mist as the sun sank low. The garden was extensive, an expanse of lawn extending between formally planted shrubs and trees. Beyond the shrubberies lay a pond, on whose silvery waters a number of black swans drifted. A gardener was raking up piles of autumn leaves that were still drifting from the trees. He touched his cap to her. She walked down to the pond, passing marble statues standing like ghosts on their plinths. The swans, accustomed to being fed, drifted over to her expectantly, arching their slender necks and clicking their beaks.

She turned to look back at the house. It was the first time she had seen it from the front. It was even bigger than she had first thought, dreamlike in the misty evening glow. Her early impression of Palladian elegance was confirmed. The place had been modelled on a Renaissance villa, with colonnades and porticos, crowned with a green bronze dome.

A fantasy palace, she thought, with curious inhabitants: both father and daughter part-genius and part-monster. Gretchen had shown herself to be rude, but that made Katya feel pity, rather than irritation. The child was so determined to remain locked in herself that Katya could understand how it could fill her father with dread for the future.

But why had she let herself be railroaded yet again, half-seduced and half-bullied by Thorwald Bachmann. Why had she tacitly agreed to a fortnight's trial?

The grinding anguish started up in her all over again. Was there anything here worth suspending her studies for?

Katya wandered around the lake, followed by the drifting swans, who didn't give up hope of a titbit, though she showed them her empty hands. The mist clung to her, cold on her skin. She felt her clothes and hair grow damp.

She came across an elaborate rabbit hutch with a solitary occupant, a splendid, silky, white Angora with handsomely tufted ears. The animal was surrounded by tempting vegetables, but sat immobile in its bed of straw, its pink nose twitching slightly. It had round, pale eyes that looked sideways at Katya with a melancholy expression.

'You, too?' Katya said to the fellow prisoner. It closed its eyes, as though crushed by ennui.

At last, she trudged back up through the misty shrubbery to the house. Gretchen was still sprawled by the fire, absorbed in her book.

'I saw your rabbit,' Katya said. 'She's very handsome.'

Gretchen didn't look up at Katya. 'You can wash my hair,' she mumbled sullenly.

'What was that?'

'You can wash my hair,' Gretchen repeated. 'If you want.'

'Gosh, what a privilege,' Katya replied dryly. 'All right. Let's go to the bathroom.'

The bathroom was a palace of marble and bronze, designed more for show than for the comfort of the users. Stripped to her vest, Gretchen leaned over the huge granite tub while Katya shampooed her curls.

Hair was the only thing Gretchen had in abundance, Katya reflected. The girl was painfully thin, almost undernourished, her ribs sticking out and her neck so slender that it looked as though it might snap. To her relief, Katya found no lice, but the thick hair was greasy and knotted, and it took three applications of shampoo to get it clean. It must have been unwashed for months, perhaps years. Gretchen bore it dourly, her eyes shut tight against the foam. Katya wondered what was going on inside this odd skull under her fingertips.

Afterwards, Katya towelled Gretchen's hair dry. 'I'm going to have to brush it,' she said.

Gretchen frowned. 'No! I don't like having my hair brushed.'

'We've come this far,' Katya pointed out. 'We may as well finish the job. Or by tomorrow you'll be looking like a sea urchin.'

'Don't brush hard.'

'I'll try to be gentle,' Katya promised. She found a brush and started brushing Gretchen's hair, which was now gleaming. 'You're lucky to have such luxuriant hair. A lot of girls would do anything to have it. You should look after it better.'

Gretchen, who had her back to Katya, merely shrugged. Her shoulder blades stuck out like the wings of a small marble angel. Katya brushed more vigorously, pleased with the effect. Gretchen looked as though someone cared for her now. Her father couldn't fail to be pleased. Then, unluckily, the brush snagged on some tangles with a sharp jolt.

Gretchen whipped round, and a small palm cracked smartly across Katya's cheek. 'That hurt!' she hissed.

They stared at one another for a moment. Gretchen's expression changed as she saw the look in Katya's eyes. She went even paler than usual.

'If you ever do that again,' Katya said quietly, 'I will walk out of this house and get the first train home. And I will never come back, even if your father goes down on his knees. Do you understand me?'

'Yes,' Gretchen said, suddenly very subdued.

Katya put the brush down. 'You can brush your own hair.'

She walked out of the grandiose bathroom, vibrating with anger.

Katya was lying on her bed reading a book an hour later when there was a very quiet tap on the bedroom door.

'What is it?'

Gretchen sidled in, her hair hanging in her eyes. She had the brush in her hand. 'I can't reach round the back,' she muttered.

Katya sat up reluctantly. 'All right. Come and sit on the bed.'

Gretchen perched on the bed beside her, and Katya resumed brushing, ready this time for any repercussions.

'This used to be my mother's sewing room,' Gretchen said.

'Oh. I didn't know.'

'She used to do embroidery over there, by the window. She had a sewing machine in that corner. And books over there. Papa had it all taken out to make a room for you.'

'I see. I'm sure that upset you.'

'No. She's dead, isn't she?'

'But it's still her room.'

'She stopped coming in here when she got sick. It stopped being her room any more. It was just a room. Now it's your room.' There was a silence, broken only by the crackle of the brush going through Gretchen's curls. 'I'm sorry I hit you,' she said at last, her voice very low.

'Do you often hit people?'

'I only hit back. If they hurt me.'

'I didn't mean to hurt you, Gretchen.'

'I know.' She turned to Katya with a gleam in her shadowy eyes. 'There was a piano teacher who used to smack my knuckles with a ruler when I made mistakes.'

'Did you slap him too?'

'I scratched his face with my nails one day. He ran out, screaming. There was blood on his handkerchief.'

'Gretchen, that's not something to be proud of. Civilised people don't behave like that!'

'I'm not proud of it. But civilised people shouldn't hit children.'

'There are different views on that.'

'You wouldn't hit a child, would you?'

'No, never. *Especially* not during a music lesson.'

'I hated him. Not just because he hit me. Because he didn't understand what he was supposed to be teaching.'

'What do you mean?'

'He used to put a metronome on the piano. As if that was all that mattered.'

'Not everyone understands music the way you do.'

'He was the last teacher I had. He told everyone else what I did, and nobody would come to the house after that.'

'I'm not surprised,' Katya said. That was an incident Thor had failed to mention. 'There, that'll do. Would you like me to tie some ribbons in your hair now?'

'No,' Gretchen replied shortly. 'I'm not a doll.' She got up to leave. At the door, she half-turned. 'Are you going to stay?'

'I haven't made up my mind yet,' Katya heard herself reply.

Gretchen nodded and went out.

Chapter 4

In the hallway the next day, Katya met the towering figure of Thor, who looked down at her from above his bushy beard. 'I note that you managed to get my daughter's hair washed yesterday.'

'Yes. I also offer a trimming service for tigers' whiskers.'

He smiled. 'A less dangerous profession, I agree. Congratulations. You're the first person to have managed that in many years. A very good start. I forgot to mention,' he went on, 'that we're having a dinner party tonight. Just a few close friends.'

'I'm rather tired,' she replied. 'I hope you'll excuse me.'

'Sigmund Freud and his daughter Anna are coming.' His eyes sparkled. 'Even if you decide to go back to Glasgow, surely you won't pass up an opportunity to meet such famous doctors? It will be something to tell your grandchildren.'

Katya grimaced. 'I see. But I have nothing suitable to wear.'

'Oh, this is nothing formal. Wear what you like.' He sailed serenely back to his study.

Sigmund Freud looked old and unwell, his beard completely white and his face heavily furrowed. He was accompanied by his daughter, Anna, who tended to him solicitously throughout the meal.

Katya had been placed on the other side of Professor Freud, a seat of unanticipated honour at the small dinner party that Thor had sprung on her.

As for it being 'nothing formal', the men were in evening dress, the women in silk gowns. The meal was elaborate, and elaborately served on fine china with silver cutlery, candelabra providing glowing light in the room, which was crowded with beautiful things. She felt awkward, to say the least, among the six distinguished guests around the table. She was unprepared, underdressed. But everyone took care to make her feel at ease, especially Freud.

She hadn't expected the great neurologist to pay her any attention, but Freud was courteous, turning to her stiffly and talking in a quiet voice, as though she were a person of great importance to him. He was interested in her childhood memories of pre-revolutionary Russia, as well as the Tsar's family. She told him all she could remember, aware of having very little to say. But he listened carefully, his dark, haunted eyes fixed on her from beneath his craggy brow.

'I'm afraid that everyone is exaggerating the importance of what I did,' she concluded apologetically. 'I was very young. I could only see things through a child's eyes.'

'A child's eyes see many things that an adult's eyes do not,' he replied in his thin voice. 'It is only the ability to communicate what is seen that is undeveloped. You were young, but your experience was invaluable.'

The others at the dinner party were two couples, clearly wealthy and cultured, who were similarly affable to Katya. They had no doubt been invited to welcome her and probably also give her the once-over. Perhaps because she was somewhat overwhelmed by the presence of Freud, it took Katya a while to realise that the men were famous musicians, the composer Franz Lehár and the tenor who had sung some of the most famous roles in his operettas, Richard

Tauber. Their wives were handsome and talkative. Thor sat at the head of the table, his large presence and rich laughter colouring the evening. The conversation was cultured and witty, for the most part, but then turned to politics, and the looming shadow of Adolf Hitler, and his vows to annexe Austria and bring it into the German Third Reich. Lehár was inclined to hope that this might not be such a bad thing.

'Hitler has great vision in some things,' he said. 'Austria can't risk falling into the hands of the Reds again. Nor can we continue to exist as the curious vestige of an empire that was destroyed by the Great War.'

'I fought in that war,' Thor said grimly. 'I saw my generation destroyed beside me. We were dragged into it by Germany. In 1918, I swore I would never allow that to happen again.'

Lehár shook his head. 'That was twenty years ago, Thor. Right now, all logic tells us we should join with Germany.'

'Perhaps,' his wife Sophie said. 'But not *this* Germany, Franz.'

'We're not Germans!' Tauber protested. 'And we're certainly not Nazis. My father was a Jew.' He nodded towards Lehár's wife. 'And so is Sophie.'

'I became a Catholic when I married Franz,' Sophie said, 'as you very well know.'

'That won't pacify the Nazis. As I found out to my cost. My father also converted to Catholicism, but the Brownshirts still beat me up in Berlin – outside the Kempinski, in front of everyone!'

'We've all suffered from anti-Semitism,' Lehár said, shrugging. 'If so many Jews hadn't joined the Left, it would have been much easier. Once the communists are broken, the anti-Semitism will fade away, you'll see.'

'It's got nothing to do with Left or Right,' Tauber retorted. 'Jew hatred is endemic here. And Hitler will fan the embers until there is a blaze to the heavens. I don't see how it's so easy for you to admire Hitler.'

'I don't admire him. But he's the coming man, there's no doubt about that.'

'Yes. He's coming, and we'll be going.'

'The Viennese will never accept Hitler's interference.'

'Are you kidding?' Tauber demanded. 'Austria is full of Nazis. They'll welcome him with open arms.'

'Well, we can but hope for the best.' Lehár turned to Freud. 'What do you think, Professor?'

'There will be no end to anti-Semitism in our lifetimes,' Freud said. 'It will only get worse.' This brought a chorus of protests, which only died down when the next course was brought in on silver salvers.

'Hitler is a bully,' Thor said, as the roast goose was served. The cook, Bertha, had surpassed herself with a magnificent meal. 'The only answer to bullies is to face up to them. Running away is never the solution. We have to stand together.'

Katya felt both admiration and anxiety for Thor's stance. She was already being drawn into the life here, a hapless traveller who had not only taken the wrong road but had stepped into quicksand.

After the meal, they retired to the music room, where Lehár accompanied Tauber singing arias from *The Merry Widow* and *Gypsy Love*. After two or three songs, Freud announced his intention to have a cigar in the smoking room, possibly because the sentimental, light music was not to his taste. 'Perhaps you care to risk suffocation and accompany me,' he said to Katya.

She obeyed the summons and went out with him. The smoking room was panelled in oak, and attended by a footman who had lit a fire, and who offered a selection of cigars from a rosewood humidor. Freud refused the hospitality and drew one of his own cigars from a small leather case in his pocket. He sat in an armchair, crossing his thin legs with care, scraped a match and got the cigar lit to his satisfaction, surrounding himself with fragrant smoke like some ancient deity.

'My doctor tells me these little fellows will kill me,' he said, examining the glowing tip of his cigar. 'Which will grieve my tobacconist. I have patronised him for half a century. But I am sorry for the smell that will cling to your dress.'

'It's an old dress.'

'I wouldn't have travelled so far in life without cigars. They have served me as protection, weapon, inspiration and consolation.'

'I don't think,' Katya said, smiling, 'that I've ever seen a photo-graph of you without a cigar.'

The old man nodded approvingly. 'Then I have not lived in vain.' The butler poured them each a glass of brandy from a decanter. Freud waved the cigar in his yellowed fingers. 'I wish you success during your time with Gretchen,' he said, 'however brief or extensive that time may be.'

Her smile faded. 'I really don't believe I have anything to offer Gretchen.'

'My young friend Thor has a certain genius, as you will find out.' Freud paused for a moment. 'He has asked you to make a great sacrifice – suspending your studies and setting your feet on a different path. But it is likely that this path will lead you to some interesting places. High places, from which you will gain perspectives you would not otherwise have known.'

'I don't know about that. The task seems beyond me. I notice that Gretchen doesn't seem able to read,' she said. 'I admit I was a little shocked. She's twelve.'

'Gretchen suffers from dyslexia,' he replied. 'A disorder first noted some fifty years ago.'

'Is the condition curable?' she asked.

'It is not so much a condition as a refusal. I recommended psychoanalysis, but her father would not hear of it.'

'A refusal?'

'A rebellion. Painful childhood experiences, even hatred of one or both parents cause it. The child cannot openly rebel. So it punishes its parents by refusing to learn to read.'

'But – forgive me, Professor – her mother died when she was very young.'

He nodded. 'The mother dies. She feels rage towards the father for allowing it to happen. She sees it as a kind of psychic murder. She punishes him for his crime.'

Katya hesitated, unconvinced, but afraid to argue with the great psychoanalyst. 'I have the impression that the problem is almost like a kind of blindness. Gretchen told me she has tried to learn, but that she can't distinguish the letters from each other.'

'In the course of a long career, I have come across every possible physical ailment, all of which had roots exclusively in hysteria. Including blindness.'

'But she *wants* to read. She's frustrated that she can't. Bitter. And she has an exceptional musical ability. Have you heard her playing Bach?'

'Yes.'

'Isn't it astonishing? A girl who can memorise the *Goldberg Variations* would learn to read in an afternoon if she could.'

'Or if she wanted to.'

'I don't think Gretchen wants to punish her father. She is the one who suffers far more than he does. I think the problem must lie somewhere else.'

Freud glanced at her through his heavy spectacles. 'Interesting.'

'What is interesting?'

'The genius of my young friend Thor.'

The sound of new arrivals could be heard outside the smoking room, trooping through the hall. Numbers of after-dinner guests were arriving. There was a burst of laughter from the music room, followed by a chorus of singing. 'Thor seems to know everyone in Vienna,' she said.

'How do you like the city?'

'I've only just arrived, Professor.'

'Were you not afraid to come to the eye of the cyclone?'

'The eye of the cyclone? I don't think I like the sound of that,' Katya replied. 'Everyone's been assuring me that the troubles are over, and that everything's going to be peaceful from now on.'

'Ah. You will learn that Vienna is the fulcrum of Europe at this moment. Not Paris. Not London. Not even Berlin. Everything revolves on this city.'

'Do you think Germany will annexe Austria?'

'The world cannot allow Germany to annexe Austria. The governments of Europe have to prevent it, at all costs.' He drew on his cigar. 'If Hitler annexes Austria, he will add nearly seven millions to the population of the Third Reich. Not to mention a nation's gold reserves. When he simultaneously seizes the Sudetenland – as he surely will – he will add a similar amount. This will bring the population of Germany, at a stroke, to over eighty millions. It will be by far the largest nation in Europe. And it will be led by a narcissistic personality who sees himself as a demigod, who believes that he alone is the arbiter of what is right and what is wrong, what views may be held, what destiny civilisation must fulfil.' Freud exhaled smoke pensively. 'A man, moreover, who holds the unconscious of the German people in the palm of his hand. What do you think is the result of all this?'

'I don't know,' Katya replied.

'In one word – ruin. It is ruin, my dear. That is why I say the governments of Europe will not allow it to happen. There is no reason to panic.' Freud threw his half-smoked cigar into the fire and took a fountain pen and a notepad from his pocket. Uncapping the pen, he wrote something on a sheet of paper and tore it out. He handed it to Katya. 'This is the name of a doctor at the University Paediatric Clinic. He is young, but one hears good things about him. They say he is clever with children such as Gretchen. Gretchen's father has an aversion to doctors, unfortunately. So does Gretchen. But this fellow may be useful to you.' Freud capped the pen. 'Don't tell him that I made the recommendation. I've heard he is not over-fond of Jews.' He looked utterly drained. 'And now it is time for me to retire. Would you be so kind as to help me out of this chair?'

Gretchen sat on the stairs, in the dark spot she knew so well, between one lamp and the next. It was where she always sat when there were dinner guests. As long as old Frau Hackl didn't come snooping up here to check that she was in bed, nobody noticed her.

She'd sat here when Mama was alive, and the parties had been happier, and there had been lots of Mama's friends in beautiful clothes with beautiful jewels, and laughter and music.

Now the parties were different. There were still lots of people, lots of noise, lots of food; but the happiness that had been there when Mama was alive – *that* was gone. The pure joy, *that* was gone. It was somehow false now. It was like pretending, like when you were little, and you put your dolls and teddy bears in a circle and made them talk to each other, except that it was you saying everything for them.

She shrank further back into her pool of darkness as she saw Fräulein Katya cross the hall down below, with Professor Freud leaning heavily on her arm, murmuring to each other quietly. She caught that sharp whiff of cigar smoke that was always around him.

Gretchen was a little bit afraid of Professor Freud. He asked such strange questions, and sometimes his black eyes burned into you, making you feel he knew everything wrong you'd ever done.

She couldn't hear what he was saying to Fräulein Katya, but she was sure he was telling Katya how wicked Gretchen was. Gretchen, who refused to learn. Gretchen, who was bad inside. Gretchen, who flung her books across the room, or tore the pages out in fistfuls and threw them on the ground and stamped on them.

Oh yes, old Professor Freud had seen her do all those things, and he thought he knew why she did them, but he didn't. Nobody knew why she did them. They all thought she did them because she was wicked. They didn't know that she did them because she hurt so much.

And there was Papa, meeting them at the door of the salon. Papa, always so handsome, so strong and big, always knowing what to say and do.

Did Papa think Katya was pretty? She was certainly not as pretty as Mama had been. But Mama had been as pretty as angels and ghosts are pretty, and like angels and ghosts, she had faded away and vanished.

Katya was solid and real, and the pink colour in her round cheeks and round arms came and went all the time in little flushes. You could watch it come and go. If you said something nice, there it would be, glowing just beneath the pale skin. And if you said something cruel, you could see it sink again, hurrying back to wherever it lived in her round, solid body.

Her hair was soft and brown, and fell over her forehead in a wave that wouldn't be obedient. Her eyes looked at you from under it sometimes with an air of alarm. As though she were waiting for you to be horrible. Or something.

She *had* been horrible, she supposed. Nasty Gretchen, who said nasty things and was a brat. Who slapped grown-ups in the face.

She cringed as she thought of Katya's expression when she'd slapped her in the bathroom. She'd felt bad. So bad. Why had she done it? She would never do it again.

She prayed that Katya wasn't going to run away back to London just yet, the way so many others before her had run away.

'I see you up there!' It was Frau Hackl, carrying a tray of glasses across the hall, peering up the stairs. 'Go to your bed at once – if you don't want me to come up there with a wooden spoon!'

Gretchen stuck out her tongue, and plodded back to her room.

As Freud and his daughter departed, yet more friends of Thor's were dropping in. Katya would gladly have followed the Freuds' example, and excused herself from the festivities, but it was plainly Thor's intention to introduce her to as many of his circle as possible. The house was now crowded and noisy, champagne flowing and jazz music playing. The Lehárs and the Taubers also soon left, the staid older generation giving way to a younger set of a far more glamorous type. The women wore daringly low-cut dresses and smoked brightly coloured cigarettes, the men two-tone shoes and evening suits in the American style.

Thor himself was at the heart of the party, his height and larger-than-life presence dominating. Taking Katya's arm, he propelled her into the crowd, making introductions on all sides. She was swiftly surrounded by strangers eager to ask questions. Unwisely, she drained the succession of champagne glasses that kept being put in her hands. Soon, her head was swimming. The effort of speaking German was compounded by trying to follow the swift Viennese version of the language flowing all around her. It didn't seem to matter; everything she said was greeted with smiles and laughter.

The music swelled louder, and couples began swaying. Several men pushed forward to ask her to dance. She found herself being twirled in dances that were a long way from the stately waltzes of her imagination. The volume of music and chatter rose deafeningly. The room was spinning, the atmosphere growing hot, dazzling.

After withstanding an hour of this, Katya started to feel overwhelmed. The journey from London had been long and tiring, despite the luxurious appointments of the Orient Express. The emotions of the day had battered her – Gretchen's rudeness, the dire warnings of Richard Tauber and Freud, the strangeness of the world she had been decanted into so violently. She felt that she was a very long way from anything familiar. She was even missing Mama and Papa.

She broke away from her current dance partner, and pushed through the crowd out of the room. Making her way blindly to the door, she threw it open and went outside.

The garden was illuminated by night, but the mist was intensifying, making the cleverly placed lights blur into nimbuses. The cold, damp air enveloped her. Her head was spinning madly, sickeningly. She had drunk far too much. To her annoyance and dismay, she found that she had started to cry.

She stood there, alone and miserable for a while. Then she felt a hand touch her shoulder.

'I apologise,' Thor Bachmann's voice rumbled. 'You're exhausted, and I should have left you to rest.' He passed her an outsize handkerchief. She used it to dry her eyes, angrily wishing he hadn't found her in this state.

'I'm not usually like this,' she said shortly.

'I was thoughtless. I wanted you to feel at home. I've achieved the opposite.'

'I'm fine.'

'Freud took to you. He doesn't usually like young people these days. How was your conversation with him?'

'Rather terrifying.'

'Yes, I know what you mean. The good professor can be intimidating. He and my father were friends. They both tended to think the worst of human nature.'

'Is that what psychology is? Thinking the worst of human nature?'

'Sometimes it seems so. But then, human nature isn't always so pretty.'

Katya had got the better of her tears by now. 'Professor Freud gave me the name of a young doctor who he said might be able to help Gretchen.'

'I'm not overkeen on doctors,' he said, a wary look coming into his eyes.

'Yes, I know. That explains why you felt no compunction about taking me out of medical school.'

'Ouch. But my dear Katya, you don't strike me as the sort of woman who tamely does everything people tell her. You had a choice.'

'Did I? With my parents facing ruin? As you very well knew?'

'Forgive me – but aren't your parents perennially facing ruin?'

'Yes, and I should have left them to it. But that doesn't excuse the way you took advantage of them. And me. It was unscrupulous.'

He didn't try to defend himself. 'I heard you reading to Gretchen. That was kind of you.'

'She ordered me to. She has her father's imperious nature. Except in her case, the iron fist doesn't bother putting on a velvet glove.'

He smiled. 'Neither of us are as bad as all that. Will you come inside and dance for a quarter of an hour longer? The young men are all asking for you.'

'I have no idea why. There are so many lovely girls here. And I'm not remotely pretty.'

'Well, your features agree with each other. That probably explains it.'

She glanced at her watch. It was coming up for midnight. 'A quarter of an hour. And then I'm going to bed.'

'Agreed. What was the name of this doctor Freud recommended?'

'I can't read his handwriting.' She passed him the piece of paper.

He held it to the light. 'Dr Hans Asperger. At the University Paediatric Clinic. Very well. We may as well make enquiries.' He put the note in his pocket and took Katya's arm in a gentle hand. 'Now, Cinderella. Come back to the ball.'

It was very late when the party ended and the last guests went home. Katya tiptoed to Gretchen's door, which was a little ajar, and peeped in. She heard Gretchen's quiet voice from the darkness.

'I'm awake.'

Katya slipped into the room. 'Why aren't you asleep? Was the music too loud? I saw you sitting on the stairs.'

'No. I just can't sleep sometimes. Things go round and round in my head and won't stop.'

'That happens to me, too. What was going round in your head?'

'I was thinking of Mama.'

Katya sat on the bed beside the girl. 'What about Mama?'

'About her lying in her grave, up there in the mountains, so cold and lonely and quiet.'

'You shouldn't think about things that make you sad.'

'That doesn't make me sad. It's nice, in a way. Her coffin is all lined with white satin, and there's a wreath of cream lilies on her breast. Her eyes are closed with silver pennies, and her hands are folded around an ivory prayer book.'

'Did you see her like that?'

'Oh, no. Papa wouldn't allow it. I wasn't there when she died, or when they buried her. But once, I had nightmares about worms eating her, so Papa explained.'

'What did he explain?'

'That there couldn't be any worms, because her coffin is made of bronze, and worms could never get in. He told me how they dressed Mama all in white, like a bride, and lined her coffin with satin, and put lilies in her arms. And they buried her deep in the ground, and the ground up there is so stony that it took six men to dig her grave.'

Gretchen had recounted all this in a dreamy voice, as though reciting a poem that she knew by heart. Katya reached out in the darkness and stroked Gretchen's hair. 'You must miss her very much,' she said quietly. 'Try to sleep now.' She hesitated for a moment, then bent down and kissed Gretchen lightly on the brow.

After Katya had gone out, Gretchen could still feel that kiss on her brow. It had landed like a butterfly, and she lay absolutely still, in case it flew away.

Nobody had kissed her goodnight since Mama had died, except Papa, and he didn't always remember.

She thought about how Mama had faded away, day by day, week by week, month by month; until one day Mama's door had been closed, and Papa had told her that Mama didn't want to see her any more, in case she caught whatever it was that was consuming Mama. So she used to creep to the locked door and lay her head against the panels, listening to the dim voices that were Mama and Papa talking in the darkened room.

Mama was never coming back. She would sleep there, deep in the stony ground for ever. But Katya had come. And perhaps – if she was very good – Katya would stay.

She went to sleep as she often did, lying as Mama was lying: on her back, legs stretched straight out, with her hands folded around the flowers, long withered on her breast.

Thor was waiting for her outside. 'That was very kind of you,' he murmured. 'She gets restless sometimes.'

'It was nothing.'

'Will you join me for a nightcap before we turn in?'

Although she was tired, Katya nodded. 'All right. Just a small one.'

They went to Thor's study, where he poured them each a glass of brandy. 'What was Gretchen talking to you about?' he asked as they settled beside the embers of the fire.

'About her mother's coffin, as it happens.'

He grunted. 'Ah, yes. One of her favourite subjects. Heaven knows why.'

'I can understand it perfectly. It comforts her to think about it.'

'I always felt it was rather a morbid preoccupation.'

'I don't agree. It helps her to imagine her mother still beautiful, peaceful, almost immortal.'

'I never thought of it like that.'

'Her death must have been extremely difficult for both of you.'

'Karin was always frail,' he said, after a pause. 'We had just become engaged when she was diagnosed with tuberculosis. We had to put all our plans aside. She refused to marry me until she was cured. She didn't want to leave me a widower.'

'How sad!'

'The doctors sent her to a sanatorium in the Alps. I used to go up every Friday to spend the weekend with her. I bought a little house in a village nearby, because only patients were allowed to stay in the sanatorium. It was a very strange time, Katya. My memories of Karin are inextricably bound up with the Alps, with the cold, dry air and the white mountains, and the silence. The waiting. It took two years before they said the tuberculosis was cured. We believed them. We wanted to believe. We got married and bought this house. My business was going well. Gretchen came along. We were very happy. We thought our lives were going to be perfect, and for some years, it was good. And then the tuberculosis came back.'

'Oh, no.'

'At first, neither of us wanted to admit it. We told ourselves that the coughing was a cold, or due to the smoky Vienna air. But soon, there were spots of blood on her handkerchiefs. Spots, and then dark red stains. She began to waste away. We had to face the truth. After that, Karin wouldn't let Gretchen come in the same room as her, because she was terrified of infecting her. It was very hard for them both.' He glanced at Katya. 'Perhaps I shouldn't be telling you all this.'

'No, I'd like to hear it. Please.'

Katya watched his face in the firelight as he went on. 'We took Karin back to the sanatorium. We left Gretchen in Vienna. But the lung doctors said there was nothing to be done any more – the disease had spread too far. We were forced to accept that she was doomed. She was so young, and she was already dying. She loved Gretchen very much. It broke her heart that she would never see her child again. She didn't want to go back to Vienna. She didn't want Gretchen to see her die. She said she would rather face the end in the Alps. We had only a few weeks left together. They passed quickly. During the last few days, she just lay in bed, staring out of the window without speaking. And then, one day, I arrived at the hospital to find her covered with a white sheet. She was gone.'

'I'm so sorry.'

'Karin had asked to be laid to rest up there in the mountains, so I did as she wished. There was a graveyard behind the sanatorium where the patients were buried. I got her a plot there. And when it was all over, I had to come back to Vienna, and explain to Gretchen that her mother wasn't coming home ever again.'

'How did she react?'

'She went blank.'

'Blank?'

'There were no tears, no questions. She just stopped talking. It was as though all her emotions had frozen.'

'But there must have been deep pain.'

'Yes. Too deep to be shown, perhaps.'

'And you?' Katya asked. 'How did you show your grief?'

He shrugged. 'I had to be strong for Gretchen.'

'So you bottled it up, too.'

'I'm not one for weeping and wailing.'

'Grieving doesn't have to be weeping and wailing. It's hard work that has to be done.'

'You are very wise,' he replied gravely, 'and I am a foolish old man. That's why I invited you here. To supply wisdom.'

Katya hesitated. 'And there's been no one since Karin?' she asked.

'I could never take the chance of giving Gretchen a stepmother who wouldn't understand her. That would be disastrous.'

'So you hire governesses.'

He glanced at her. 'It would be more accurate to say that I've searched for a governess in vain. Until now.'

'I am a very reluctant governess, Herr Bachmann.'

'I know. But you are a very good listener.'

'Yes,' Katya said wryly, 'so people keep telling me. Oddly, nobody bothers to listen to *me*.'

'I listen to you,' he said with a smile.

'Well, thank you for telling me all this. It helps a lot to understand Gretchen.'

'Good.' He drained his brandy glass. 'I'm sorry to have kept you up so late. You must be ready for bed.'

'I am,' Katya said, rising to her feet. 'Goodnight, Herr Bachmann.'

He held out his hand. 'Please call me Thor.'

'Then goodnight, Thor.' She touched his hand and went up to her bedroom.

As she drifted into sleep, Katya reflected that a lot had been explained tonight. She had come to a house where grief had been sealed in a bronze coffin and buried deep in stony soil. But as in Gretchen's recital, it remained undecayed, still intact, still not confronted.

Whatever other problems Gretchen had, this was surely one of them.

Chapter 5

When Katya came down to breakfast, which was served from a sideboard by the unyielding Frau Hackl, Gretchen was waiting for her, looking very agitated.

'You have to come,' she greeted Katya. 'Bunny's escaped!' Bunny was the Angora rabbit.

'Can I at least have my breakfast first?' Katya said, eyeing the laden sideboard hungrily.

'No! A fox will eat her! You have to come now. You too, Frau Hackl.'

With a sigh, Katya allowed herself to be led outside into the misty garden, followed by a sour-faced Frau Hackl. 'How did she get out?'

'She left the cage open,' Frau Hackl said. 'She's always doing it.'

'I didn't!' Gretchen snapped.

'Don't tell lies.' Frau Hackl, whose shoes were getting wet in the grass, was in a bad temper. 'You should have your mouth washed out with soap. Damn that rabbit. If I catch it, it goes in the cooking pot.'

'No!' Gretchen cried.

Katya smiled at Gretchen. 'Let's look for her properly.'

The door of Bunny's palatial hutch hung open, showing how the creature had escaped. But finding the rabbit was not an easy task. The garden was huge.

'She's gone,' Gretchen said miserably, 'and a fox has eaten her.'

'Perhaps she's just gone to lay some eggs.'

Gretchen glared at her. 'Rabbits don't lay eggs.'

'Sometimes they do.' Katya's sharp eyes had noticed the mound of fresh earth in the bed of red and black hellebores behind the hutch. She borrowed a trowel from the gardener who was standing by, crouched down, and began to dig.

Bunny had made her way a considerable distance in the soft garden loam. Katya herself had had several rabbits as a girl, and knew their ways. How the animals, born in captivity, retained the impulse to burrow was a mystery to her. In the blood, she supposed. An instinct, like the compulsions that drove all of them to be free.

Gretchen circled agitatedly round Katya as she dug. 'Is she really in there?'

Katya nodded.

'Why does she keep running away?'

'I was just asking myself the same question. I suppose she wants to be free.'

'But she has a lovely house!'

'Perhaps she sees it as a prison.'

Gretchen looked at the hutch blankly.

At last Katya caught sight of a fluffy scut. She put down the trowel and reached into the earth cautiously – she knew that, although timid, a big rabbit was capable of biting and scratching when alarmed – and gently drew the animal out. She restored it to Gretchen, who took it with trembling hands. She scolded the rabbit between cuddles, oblivious of the earth all over its long fur.

'It belongs in the pot,' Frau Hackl repeated. She had watched the process with folded arms. 'Nasty, smelly, bothersome thing.'

'Bunny's not bothersome,' Gretchen retorted, clutching the rabbit, her eyes blazing. 'You are!'

Frau Hackl raised her hand, as though to slap Gretchen. 'Children should not be insolent to their elders!'

'Frau Hackl,' Katya said warningly. She had noticed that the housekeeper was careful to be pleasant in Thor's presence, but when the master wasn't there, her true feelings rose to the surface.

She reached into her pocket and took out a little paper bag. 'I found these in Bunny's burrow,' she told Gretchen.

Gretchen inspected the bag. 'What are they?'

'I told you. Rabbits' eggs.'

Gretchen delved inside and came up with a little pink ovoid. 'They're sugared almonds from the bowl in your room!'

'Well, that's what rabbits' eggs are.'

Gretchen snorted. 'I'm not a baby.' Nevertheless, she put one in her mouth and sucked. 'I don't like nonsense.' She was recovering her poise.

'Nonsense is important in life. Where do *you* think sugared almonds come from?'

'From Herr Böhm, the grocer,' she retorted.

'And where do you think he gets them from? He has thousands of bunnies laying for him every morning.'

Gretchen's sulky mouth quivered into something that was suspiciously like a smile. 'That's a very stupid thing to say.'

'But it happens to be the truth. Normally, they lay white ones. But when you give them beetroot leaves, they lay pink ones.'

For a moment, Gretchen's eyes sparkled, as though she were about to laugh out loud. It occurred to Katya that very few people tried to amuse Gretchen, even with such a childish joke as this one.

'Filling the child's head with nonsense,' Frau Hackl spat. 'She wants discipline, not sweets.'

'That – will – do – Frau – Hackl!' Katya said in a clipped voice.

Frau Hackl retreated into the house balefully.

'Bunny has got herself in a right old mess,' Katya said. 'Shall we try to clean her up?'

Together, they managed to brush off the dirt and comb the rabbit back to snowy whiteness. During the grooming, Gretchen accepted another sugared almond. They put Bunny back in her hutch with some fresh cabbage leaves. The rabbit peered out of the wire mesh with a weary expression in its pale blue eyes, nibbling distractedly.

Gretchen was thoughtful. 'Do you really think it feels like a prison to her?' she asked slowly.

'I don't know whether rabbits think much at all.'

'But she wouldn't escape if she was happy in there.'

'I suppose not. Most creatures want to be free. Being cooped up isn't natural.'

'I know how that feels,' Gretchen said in a low voice.

'So do I.'

Gretchen glanced at Katya quickly. 'Is that how you feel, being here?'

'I didn't mean that,' Katya said.

'Yes, you did.'

Katya sighed. 'I didn't want you to hear those things I said to your father. I said them because there's been a misunderstanding. I'm not qualified to be a governess. I was studying to be a doctor. I should never have accepted to come to Vienna. I let my parents persuade me, but my heart is in medicine. I have my own life to lead. I want to go back to it. I'm sorry, Gretchen.'

'Why do you want to be a doctor?' Gretchen demanded. 'They're so *stupid*.'

'Not all doctors are stupid,' Katya said.

'My mother had lots of them. None of them could stop her from dying.'

Katya was silenced.

'They pretend they know everything,' Gretchen went on. 'Showing off and using big words. But they just make things up. They don't help.'

'You're old enough to understand,' Katya said gently, 'that not every problem has a solution. Not every illness can be cured.'

'They shouldn't *lie*. They kept telling us Mama would get better.'

'You're right. Doctors shouldn't lie. But people sometimes think telling the truth is hurtful.'

'They all pretend they know what's wrong with me,' Gretchen went on. 'They don't. They don't know anything about me.'

'Is there something wrong with you?'

'Of course there's something wrong with me,' Gretchen snapped. 'If you can't see it, then you're a fool.'

Katya was just starting to feel sorry for the girl – even like her. She frowned. 'That's not a very nice way to talk, Gretchen.'

Unexpectedly, Gretchen's eyes filled with tears. 'I know it isn't. I'm wicked. Frau Hackl's right. There's a devil in me.'

'No, there isn't. You just need to control your temper.' She held out her hand. 'Shall we go and have breakfast?'

After a hesitation, Gretchen took Katya's hand, and they walked back to the house.

As they ate breakfast, under the forbidding gaze of Frau Hackl, Gretchen watched Katya's hands.

Katya had good hands. They weren't soft and plump. They weren't thin and grasping. They were just right. And quite strong, really. They had intelligence. Hands could be far more intelligent than brains. Gretchen had always known that. You could read hands, the same as you could read faces. In fact, better. Because hands couldn't be painted, or made to take on false expressions. They were just hands, the truest parts of a person.

If you watched people's hands, you could see what they were really thinking, what they were like inside. And when hands touched you, you felt at once what they really meant.

She'd known people – nurses, doctors – whose hands told quite different stories from their words and faces. Their mouths said, *we care about you, we want to help you*. Their hands said, *you disgust us*.

You always knew, when hands touched you, whether they really wanted to or not. Papa's hands were so big that your own hands vanished in them. When he touched you, you always knew how much he loved you. Frau Hackl's hands really wanted to tear your hair out and scratch your face.

And her own hands, that did what they wanted, while she watched in surprise, wondering who this Gretchen was who could make these sounds. They were the truest part of herself. She didn't really have any control over them. But they were her salvation.

Gretchen said, quite suddenly, 'Please don't go.'

Katya was nonplussed. She put down her knife and fork. 'What?'

'If you stay, I'll be better. I promise.'

'Why do you want me to stay?'

'I'm so lonely!'

'You need to make some friends.'

'You're the only one who's tried to be my friend.'

'I think lots of people have tried to be your friend, Gretchen,' Katya said gently. 'But you drive them away.'

'No!' Gretchen said passionately. 'They pretend to be nice, but they don't mean it. I can't read words on the page, but I can read them when they're spoken. I can read eyes, and faces, and expressions. You are the only one who means what she says.'

'Gretchen—'

'I can't pretend,' Gretchen interrupted vehemently. 'I don't know how to. That's why I can't make friends!'

'Do you have to be able to pretend to make friends?'

'Yes! I see other people do it all the time, but I just can't! If someone is being nice to me, and I can see in their eyes that they're really thinking how strange and ugly I am, I just can't pretend.'

'You're not ugly, Gretchen.'

'I am.'

'You're remarkable and special, and you should be proud of yourself. You remind me of someone I once knew.'

Gretchen looked interested. 'Who?'

'He was a Russian boy named Alexei.'

'Where is he now?'

'He died.'

'How?'

Katya thought it best not to mention the Bolshevik firing squad. 'He was very sick.'

'Do you think I'm sick?'

'That's not why you remind me of him. He was very sensitive. And so are you.'

'Please don't go,' Gretchen begged. 'Please!' She jumped up and ran from the room.

Thor Bachmann came in as his daughter was running out. 'Is everything all right?' he asked, helping himself to eggs and bacon at the sideboard.

'We've had an adventure with the rabbit.'

'Ah. It escaped again?'

'Yes.'

'She forgets to latch the door.' He sat down opposite Katya. He was a late riser, she had learned, in contrast to the conventional picture of the successful businessman who was up at dawn. He was wearing a splendid crimson dressing gown and carrying a newspaper. 'The excursion has put the roses in your cheeks, at any rate,' he commented.

Katya didn't deign to reply to that, but picked up her knife and fork and resumed her breakfast. When she next looked up, Thor hadn't touched his own plate. Instead, he was watching her with a slight smile in the depths of his beard.

'What's so amusing?' she demanded.

'Nothing. I just like to watch you eat.'

'I was taught my manners at one of the best finishing schools in England,' she retorted.

'Oh, one can see that.'

'Then what is so amusing about the way I eat?'

'It's very pleasing to watch. You eat with a good appetite.'

'Is that so strange?' She frowned suspiciously. 'Are you saying I'm too fat?'

'Not at all. You're no waif, of course. In contrast to the boyish figures that are currently fashionable, you are a woman of—' He searched for the word. 'A woman of substance.'

'You're being extremely offensive.'

'I mean substantial in every way. Substantial in form and substantial in character. There's so much energy in you. An appetite for things, which I like very much. Sadly, my liking for you is clearly not reciprocated.'

She sawed at her bacon. 'I don't dislike you.'

'You're very sharp with me. I feel like a boy caught stealing apples.'

Katya snorted. 'Some boy!'

'But you seem to be getting on with Gretchen.'

'She's a very lonely child. She needs far more attention than you give her.'

'Do you feel I'm not managing her well?'

'I think it could be done better.'

'I'm sorry to hear that.'

'I'm just giving you my frank opinion. But you are my employer, Herr Bachmann—'

'Thor, please.'

'—and you may give your opinion of me, but I am not free to give my opinion of you.'

'It's evidently rather a low opinion. But I am ready to hear it.' He folded his newspaper and clasped his fingers, smiling. 'You have my full attention. Tell me the worst.'

Katya took a breath. 'Very well. You neglect your daughter. You bring in music teachers and governesses and so forth, but you give her very little of your own time. You don't show her how to get along with other people. You let her spend days alone with her music while you're busy in your study, or away on business. You don't comfort her when she's sad, or reassure her when she's frightened. You give smart parties, while she sits on the stairs in the dark, watching. You never bring her down. She's hardly a part of your life at all!'

He was no longer smiling. His eyes had widened. 'Am I that bad? Doesn't she have everything a child could want?'

'Being a father isn't just providing material things,' Katya retorted. 'A grand piano and a rabbit don't make up for neglect and isolation. Good heavens, Thor! Surely you must see that! You congratulated me on washing Gretchen's hair, telling me nobody had done it in months. Why didn't you do it yourself?'

He blinked. 'Me? Wash Gretchen's hair?'

Katya pointed at him angrily. 'You take great care of that beard of yours. It's always trimmed and perfumed. But your own daughter goes around with dirty hair and dirty clothes, looking like a ragamuffin. I've seen children in the poorest slums of Glasgow who looked happier and better cared for than Gretchen.'

'I suppose you're right,' he said, rubbing his beard ruefully. 'But that sort of thing is best done by . . .'

'A servant?' she said when he hesitated.

'I was about to say a woman. Frau Hackl is supposed to take care of that sort of thing.'

'Frau Hackl has neither patience nor sympathy with Gretchen. And Gretchen knows it very well.'

'Frau Hackl has been with us since Karin died.'

'What's that got to do with it? Fathers are allowed to care for their children, Thor.' She threw down her napkin. She was angry and upset. 'And making money isn't everything. God knows my father never makes any, but I've always known that he loves me.' She got to her feet, not trusting herself to say any more. Afraid that she was going to start crying, she left the table and hurried towards the door. Thor got there before her, moving with deceptive speed for such a big man, and opened it courteously. She looked up at him. Her eyes were hot. 'As for laughing at my figure, and saying you like to watch me eat, I'm not a pet poodle, Herr Bachmann – although I am sure that is how you see me!'

'Katya!'

They stared at one another. For a moment, she had the extraordinary feeling that Thor was about to take her in his arms. He even moved involuntarily a fraction closer to her, stooping as if he were going to kiss her on the lips.

Katya jerked back, her eyes widening. Then she pushed past him and hurried away as though something were pursuing her.

'I've learned this piece for you,' Gretchen said shyly. 'I know you love Chopin. I hope you like it.'

Listening to Gretchen play the piano, Katya was still emotional. She felt most unsteady. She had lost her temper with Thor. She had made a fool of herself. He would probably dismiss her now, and she would get her wish to go back home.

Oddly, that prospect gave her little pleasure. She felt like a theatregoer who had decided to walk out of a play she wasn't enjoying, but who lingered, wanting to see what happened in the next act.

She watched Gretchen. The girl played with her eyes closed, her strange face rapt. Why was she allowing Gretchen to wrap tendrils around her heart, like a creeping vine? Why had she allowed Thor to provoke her so? And what had happened in the doorway of the breakfast room? The butterflies in her stomach gave a synchronised lurch. She must never allow that to happen again.

She had to master her emotions. It was no use becoming flustered with a man like Thor. That would end in disaster. She had to remain mistress of the situation.

At least, she thought morosely, she had given him a piece of her mind.

She settled back in her chair to enjoy the Chopin.

That evening, at the supper table, Thor had an announcement.

'Ladies! Your kind attention please! We are all going to the Alps next week.'

Gretchen's expression was a mixture of anxiety and excitement. 'Truly, Papa?'

'Yes, truly. We're spending a week in Alpbach. A family holiday.' His bright eyes met Katya's. 'We're going tobogganing and skiing and for all I know, mountain climbing with ropes and ice axes. We're going to have fun!'

'I don't like strange places,' Gretchen said.

He put his hand over hers. 'I know, my dear. But you will have your Katya on one side, and your old Papa on the other side, and you will be as safe as a baby kangaroo in its mother's pouch.'

He spent the rest of the meal extolling the beauties of Alpbach and encouraging Gretchen to see it as something to look forward to. Reluctantly, Gretchen allowed herself to be drawn into some kind of enthusiasm. Katya felt rather the same.

After supper, he said quietly to Katya, 'I hope you approve.'

'Is this your idea of being an attentive father?' she asked.

'Something like that. I have taken Gretchen on very few holidays – not because I am a cruel monster, but because she finds them a great strain. She is seldom happy in new places. This trip is only possible because you are here.'

'After our last conversation, I thought you would be sending me home.'

He raised his hands in horror. 'Good heavens. That's the last thing I want. I've taken what you said to heart, Katya. I will try to be a better father from now on. You have my promise.'

'I'm very glad to hear it.'

As she turned away, he went on, 'Thank you for being honest with me this morning. I'm truly grateful.'

Katya nodded. She felt a mixture of emotions. That Thor Bachmann had listened to her advice was a good thing. On the other hand, here was yet another tendril being thrown around her heart, delicate yet strong, binding her to these two strangers. The more involved she became with them, the more her passionate desire to flee back to Glasgow was ebbing away.

Chapter 6

They set off for Alpbach the next week. It was several hours' drive up into the Tyrol. At Salzburg, their route took them through part of Germany. The border post was heavily manned. On the German side, hulking armoured cars were stark against the white snow. The warlike atmosphere disturbed Katya, but the German guards in their long overcoats were full of bonhomie, wishing everyone '*Gute Reise! Heil Hitler!*'

'They've been ordered to be friendly,' Thor commented dryly.

The scenery became spectacular as the going got steeper, and the snow heavier. After they re-entered Austria, crossing the River Inn, Lorenz stopped the Mercedes to fit snow chains on to the tyres for the last hundred kilometres. Katya strolled along the road with Gretchen, looking up at the white peaks that were their destination. She felt a sense of relief at being out of Germany. Beautiful as this countryside and these Alpine villages were, the atmosphere in the Third Reich was made oppressive by the soldiers and the swastika flags that flew everywhere. There was something vehement in this worship of fascism that had gripped the German people. It seemed like a kind of mass hysteria. That it might infect Austria, too, was a horrible idea.

They reached Alpbach in the afternoon, as the winter sun was lowering. The golden light gleamed across a breathtaking Alpine landscape of mountains and valleys. The village itself was charming, the winding streets paved with cobbles and lined with ancient wooden houses.

Thor had booked them into an old traditional inn that stood at the highest point of the village, with sweeping vistas all around. They had adjoining rooms, with a shared wooden balcony. They all stood together on the balcony to watch the sun go down. The air was as icy and fresh as a draught of champagne. It made Katya's cheeks tingle as though they'd been pinched and brought a flush to her skin.

'You look so beautiful!' Gretchen exclaimed spontaneously.

Katya laughed. 'Now, that is one thing I am not. Even Sigmund Freud could only manage to tell me my features agree with each other.'

'You *are* beautiful,' Gretchen said. 'Anyone who can't see that is blind.'

'I don't really mind either way. But thank you.'

'I don't mean your face. I can't really tell if people have beautiful faces or not. I mean *inside*. That's where I see you.'

Katya put her arm around Gretchen. 'Nobody's ever said anything as nice to me before.'

Thor was watching them. 'Gretchen says what we both think,' Thor said quietly.

Darkness gathered in the valley below, and the twinkling lights of the little towns sparkled into life. They went down and ate in the dining room of the hotel, which was crowded with young skiers eager for hearty dishes of dumplings and *Spätzle* to fill cold stomachs after a day on the slopes. The food was excellent. Their waiters pressed a succession of Tyrolean wines on them, which Katya and Thor drank in unwise amounts. They decided to take a stroll through the village before going to bed.

It was a fine night, though the cold was intense. Snow was heaped on the sidewalks. As they walked around the village, music was being played here and there, and through the chinks in the wooden shutters of the old houses, warm interiors could be glimpsed. The balconies of the houses were piled with firewood. The spicy smell of burning fir and spruce logs was in the air.

Groups of friends were out for a walk, like them, calling greetings. When they had done the round of Alpbach, they turned back towards the hotel and paused at the edge of a snowy meadow to look at the moon, which was now rising over the cliffs on the other side of the valley and beginning to flood the night sky with its pale glow.

'I like this place,' Gretchen said decisively.

Thor glanced at Katya, his eyes telling her what a triumph those four words represented.

They were on the funicular ski lift the next day, gliding up the mountain. The slopes below them were massive and smooth, covering the landscape like a vast eiderdown. Thor had arranged skiing lessons for Gretchen and Katya was to stay with Gretchen, in case of any difficulties. Thor, who was an excellent skier, set off down one of the most difficult runs, promising to meet them for lunch at the hotel.

The ski instructor was a young German named Christoph, who was very tall and blond. He was considerate with Gretchen, and soon had her slithering and sliding down the nursery slopes, though sometimes more on her behind than on her skis. He was also scrupulously polite, and blushed every time Katya addressed him.

'I was concerned at first,' he said to Katya, as they watched Gretchen exploring her newfound skills, 'but now she's picking it up very quickly.'

'Better than I had hoped,' Katya agreed. 'Thank you for being so patient with her.'

'Not at all, *gnädige* Frau,' he replied, colouring to the roots of his cropped blond hair and giving her a little formal bow. 'It is my pleasure. Forgive my presumption – but is she your daughter?'

'I'm her governess.'

'*Ach so.* I thought you were too young to have a child of that age.' His manner changed subtly, as though he felt more at ease with an employee, a person on his level. 'Is the position an agreeable one?'

'It has its challenges,' she said with a smile.

'I can imagine. Mine, too.' He waved his hand at the broad, snowy slopes around them, which were filling with brightly dressed visitors on skis and toboggans. 'Most of the people who come here are rich, spoiled city folk. They don't really come for the winter sports. They come to show off their expensive clothes and equipment to each other.'

'Do you find that irritating?'

'I am an athlete,' he replied proudly. 'I take my sport seriously.' He drew his broad shoulders back and pushed his chest out. 'I was at Garmisch-Partenkirchen in 1936.'

'The Winter Olympics?'

'Yes. I was on the German skiing team. I myself did not win any medals, but my teammates took gold and silver.'

'How thrilling! It must be a bit of a comedown to be teaching children on the nursery slopes now.'

He dusted the snow off his gloves. 'The Olympic Games are a moment of glory. After that, one returns to earth with a bump. There is not a great deal of work for people like me, other than instructing. But so long as I am on the snow, I am happy.' He was a serious-faced, handsome young man, though he had made himself look harsher than necessary with a very short haircut. The tips of his ears and the back of his neck were burned by the winter sun. 'And at least it pays something. In the summer, I often find myself at a loose end. Excuse me, Fräulein.' He went off to help Gretchen, who had got stuck.

Katya tried out her own skis while he was gone. She was a far better skater than a skier, and it wasn't long before she tumbled down a slope that was rather too steep for her. Getting to her feet again was surprisingly difficult. Floundering in the soft snow, she felt strong hands take her arms and help her to her feet.

'Have you hurt yourself?' Christoph asked, looking down at her solicitously with his bright blue eyes.

'Only my dignity,' she said with a breathless laugh. 'Luckily the snow is soft!'

'Injuries are very common, nevertheless,' Christoph said gravely. 'You must be careful.' And it was true that several of the people around them were limping or wearing slings, and watching the fun with wistful expressions. 'Would you like to take part in Gretchen's lesson? There will be no extra charge,' he added with one of his quick blushes.

She accepted gratefully. 'How kind!'

'It's nothing, Fräulein.'

'Please call me Katya.'

It was a very happy morning. Gretchen was excited and she was talkative and giggly in a way that Katya hadn't seen before. Christoph's Teutonic Knight reserve thawed slowly – and he clearly found it no hardship to help Katya to her feet each time she tumbled, brushing the snow off her diligently. Nor was it unpleasant for her to have such a good-looking and athletic young man paying her these considerate attentions.

'You must join us for lunch at our hotel, Christoph,' she said.

'Alas, Fräulein Katya, I will be working here on the slopes all day.'

'For supper, then?' she pressed.

He bowed. 'That would be a great honour. If you are sure it will not be an imposition?'

'No imposition at all,' she assured him. 'Let's say eight o'clock.'

When they informed Thor, however, he did not show any great enthusiasm at the prospect of being joined for supper by Christoph. 'Why must we have the ski instructor at our table? This is a family holiday.'

'But he's very nice, Papa,' Gretchen said earnestly, 'and he was so kind to me and Katya today.'

'Surely that's his job?'

'He really did go above and beyond the call of duty,' Katya said. 'I don't know how many times he had to pull me out of a snowdrift. And he's an Olympic skier. I thought you might find him interesting.'

'Really?' Thor rubbed his beard. 'Well, I suppose we must make him welcome, then, mustn't we?'

There was a small orchestra playing in the dining room tonight, and a space had been cleared for dancing later on. The room was even more crowded than usual, and Katya spotted Christoph coming in and looking around to find them. She rose and waved him over.

Christoph was smartly dressed in grey flannels and a sporty blazer over a Fair Isle sweater. He bent over her hand with scrupulous gallantry, and bowed formally to Thor when they were introduced, all but clicking his heels. They took their seats. Thor had ordered a bottle of champagne as a way of making Christoph welcome, but the young man frowned and put his hand over his glass. 'I never touch wine,' he said. 'I do not profane my body with alcohol.'

The four of them consulted their menus and ordered. Christoph interrogated the waiter at length about his choices, insisting nothing should be fried or served with butter. Thor lifted an eyebrow ironically, but made no comment.

After this slightly uncomfortable start, the conversation became warmer. Prodded by Katya, Christoph told them about the 1936 Winter Olympics, which had been held in Bavaria. It was the first time that Alpine skiing had been included in the Games. 'The Scandinavians were furious,' he said. 'Of course, they are the best at Nordic skiing, and they fought tooth and nail to keep our kind of skiing out. But they were overruled, and we finally got our gold medals. What a wonderful time to be a German! We showed the world the glory of Aryan youth.'

'Except perhaps in athletics,' Thor said quietly, 'where some notable non-Aryans took the medals.'

'You mean the negro Owens and his troupe?' Christoph frowned. 'Men whose antecedents lie in the jungle are primitive. Of course, their physiques are stronger than those of evolved white men – just as their brains are smaller. They have an unfair advantage in that respect. That is why they should be excluded from future games.'

Noting the fury in Thor's eyes, Katya hastily changed the subject. It had not been a good idea to bring the ski instructor to dinner after all – but she wanted to avoid a public scene if possible, despite the young man's loathsome views. 'Is there going to be any new snow, do you think?'

Christoph knew a great deal about snow, and this was his cue to explain in considerable detail the differences between fresh snow and old snow, between fast snow and slow snow, between hard-packed pistes and powder. They ate rather glumly through this recital, which was not, Katya thought, likely to improve Thor's temper.

The band, which had been playing dreamy music during dinner, now started on some more lively dance music. Couples were heading for the little dance floor. Christoph shot to his feet and bowed to Thor. 'With your permission, sir. May I dance with the Fräulein Katya?'

'You had better ask her, not me,' Thor said dryly.

Christoph turned to Katya. 'Will you do me the honour of giving me the next dance?'

Reluctantly, but putting a brave face on it, Katya allowed him to lead her to the dance floor. Christoph took her in his arms, and they joined the other couples.

'Your employer is an interesting man,' he said.

'Yes, he is.'

'Very rich, by the looks of it. You're on to a good thing.'

'I'm not just doing it for the money,' Katya retorted in some irritation. 'I'm very attached to Gretchen.'

'Of course, of course.' He grinned. 'One can see that. She is a queer little creature, though, isn't she? Is there something wrong with her brain?'

'She has some learning difficulties,' Katya said shortly.

'Pity. All that money, too. Still, it gives you a job, doesn't it?' He swung her through the throng before she could respond. He danced aggressively, forcing other couples to move out of their way and using his strength to control her, rather than guiding gently. She was glad when the tune ended, and everyone clapped politely.

They made their way back to the table. Christoph pulled out Katya's chair with typical attentiveness. When she was seated, he bowed to Thor. 'Thank you, mein Herr.'

'You don't need to thank me,' Thor said laconically. 'Katya isn't my property.'

Christoph laughed politely as he took his seat. He looked around. 'This season the resorts are very crowded. It's just a pity that so many of them are Jews. They are ruining the country. I don't know how people can bear to rub shoulders with them, with Europe in its present state.'

Katya was horrified. Thor put his glass down. 'In what way are Jews ruining the country?' he asked.

Christoph seemed not to have noticed the dangerous iciness in Thor's voice. 'Surely you must know that the Jews stabbed Germany in the back.'

'How was that?'

'They almost destroyed the German banking system,' he said earnestly. 'And by doing so, they put millions in one pocket, and the German workers in the other pocket, which suited them down to the ground. Slaves and money – exactly as they wanted.'

'What absolute rubbish!' Thor rapped out.

Christoph raised a finger. 'You may think it incredible, but I'm afraid it is true. I, too, was ignorant until I joined the National Socialist movement. That opened my eyes, I can tell you! The Jews are our misfortune. They would have choked the life out of Germany – just as they are choking the life out of *your* country.'

'That's enough of that kind of talk,' Thor growled.

'You will change your mind, mein Herr, when you feel the Jews' hands around your own throat. We thank God that in Germany, Adolf Hitler was able to break their stranglehold.'

Thor's powerful fist slammed down with such force that everyone jumped, and people at the tables around them turned to stare. 'I will not have that man's name spoken at my table.'

Christoph went pale under his winter tan. He stared at them all. 'I appear to have found myself in the wrong company altogether,' he said. 'I had no idea that you were Jew-lovers.' His blue eyes widened. 'My God. Perhaps you are Jews after all!'

'Get out of here, you damned Nazi,' Thor snapped, 'before I throw you out by the scruff of your neck!'

Christoph jumped to his feet. 'I have no wish to stay, I assure you.' He gave them a stiff little bow, and hurried out of the dining room.

People were craning their necks to see what the disturbance was all about. There were mutters and stares – and not of a friendly sort. Someone at a neighbouring table called out, 'Shame on you!'

Someone else hissed, 'Jews!'

Gretchen was frightened. 'Let's go,' she whispered.

Katya touched Thor's hand. 'She's right. We should go, Thor.'

He nodded. 'Yes. I need to cool off.'

Hostile eyes followed them as they went out. They could hear the murmur of unfriendly remarks. It had been a disastrous end to the evening.

Gretchen had been upset by the incident, and it took some time to calm her down and get her to bed. When she was finally asleep, Katya joined Thor on the balcony, where he was smoking a cigar. She took the precaution of bringing two glasses of cognac with her.

The night was crisp and clear. All around them, the lights of the village sparkled brilliantly in the wintry air.

'I apologise for spoiling the evening,' Thor greeted her wryly, taking the cognac from her. 'I lost my temper.'

'I'm the one who should apologise. I should never have invited him. I should have known he was a Nazi sympathiser. I'm mortified.'

He clinked his glass against hers. 'We're both mortified. Here's to mortification.'

She sat beside him. 'Can I say something, Thor?'

'Go ahead.'

'You should be careful what you say in public. I know how strongly you feel. But in that dining room tonight, I really felt threatened. Those people were on Christoph's side, not ours.'

'Are you asking me to keep my mouth shut about what's happening to my own country?' he demanded.

'I'm just asking you to be careful – even if only for Gretchen's sake. She was frightened tonight.'

'It's precisely for Gretchen's sake that I should speak out,' he retorted. 'I want her to grow up in a decent country!'

'I do understand. But—' Katya stopped herself from going further. It was best, perhaps, to let Thor simmer down on his own. And after a while, he sighed.

'As a matter of fact, I'm rather ashamed of myself. It wasn't just the poisonous rubbish he spouted that got my goat. I confess it didn't please me to see you being courted by a handsome young fellow right under my nose.'

'You're joking!'

'Foolish, I know, to feel jealousy at my age.'

'You have no reason to feel jealous at all. He wasn't courting me, and even if he was, I'm not remotely interested in Christoph. He doesn't compare to you in any way.'

'Thank you for soothing my ego.'

'It's the truth. I've not met any man who compares to you.'

'I have never met any woman who compares to you,' he replied quietly.

There was a silence. The atmosphere between them had changed. It was suddenly charged with electricity, with new possibilities. Katya felt her heart racing.

'I've been meaning to tell you something,' she heard her own voice say. 'I've decided to stay.'

Chapter 7

Christmas was only a week away.

Katya had become so involved with the Bachmanns, father and daughter, the time had raced by. And now here she was, skating with Thor in the great square in front of the Vienna City Hall, which had been turned into an ice rink over the festive season.

The night sky was velvety, so clear that the starlight almost outshone the strings of electric Christmas lights in the trees. It glittered on the powdered ice, making it seem as if they were gliding on a sea of diamonds. The air was icy on her flushed cheeks, their breath mingled in white clouds as they whirled and swooped among the crowd, the hissing of their skates making a counterpoint to the Strauss waltzes being played over the loudspeakers.

'You skate so gracefully,' Thor said.

Katya laughed. 'I may be a poor skier, but I learned to skate before I was three!' But she didn't dismiss the compliment. She felt as light as a feather on the ice, floating in his arms without needing his support at all. 'You're not so bad yourself – for a bear.'

He smiled, looking down at her tenderly. Sailing with Thor around and through the crowd was a delight. The ice was teeming with laughing, chattering Viennese, threading around each other. The older people skated in that old-fashioned way she remembered from her childhood in Russia, hands solemnly clasped behind their backs. The younger ones were in groups, sometimes holding hands as they skated.

'Gretchen has made wonderful progress with you,' Thor said.

'I don't think I've had any influence on her progress at all. I think I'm just a sheep.'

He raised his eyebrows. 'A sheep!'

'When I was a little girl in St Petersburg, we had a stable where the horses were kept. Mama's horse was called Yastreb. He was a thoroughbred, very beautiful, but he was nervous, always kicking his stall or biting the door. So Papa got a sheep, and they put it in with him, and that calmed him down wonderfully. He was just lonely. That's the effect I have on Gretchen. I sit next to her, munching hay, and that soothes her.'

Thor burst out laughing. 'I think you do far more than that. But what a lovely vignette of your childhood.'

'I used to love to go into the stables. I loved the smell of the horses, though I always got into trouble because I invariably got my clothes dirty.'

'You had such a glamorous life in Russia.'

'I suppose it was. I don't pine for it, if that's what you mean. I'm not like Mama. She wants to pretend that it's all still the same. And that's why she's always so angry. Longing for what you can't have is the recipe for unhappiness.'

'So you've found out the secret of happiness? And so young!'

'Oh, I long for things, too. But things that are possible.'

'Such as?'

She met his eyes. 'Such as being a doctor. Such as having my own life.'

'Ah. You're still angry with me.'

'I wouldn't say angry. Simmering.'

'Well, whatever you may think, you've made my daughter much happier. I haven't seen her like this since her mother died. I am eternally grateful. But I know that you will go one day. And you will leave me bereft.' He said the last words with a tone in his voice, and a look on his face, that made her feel very strange.

To shake off the feeling, she spun away from him, and did a twirl before returning to his arms. 'I can't stay here forever, you know.'

'No, I suppose not. Unless—'

'Unless what?'

'Unless you change your mind.'

'I won't do that! What are you hoping for? For Gretchen, I mean?'

'That she can be happy.'

'Nothing more than that?' She smiled.

'What is there more than that?'

'Nothing,' she agreed. 'I shouldn't have been so hard on you at first. You're a good father, Thor.'

'Only because you show me how.'

'Well, she's lucky to have you.'

'Have you ever skated blindfolded?'

'Good heavens, no. Why would I do that?'

'To broaden your mind.'

'By shutting my eyes?'

'It helps you focus on what's inside yourself. Here. Let me help you.'

Before she could stop him, he had pulled the woolly hat she wore down over her eyes. The world went dark. Panicking, she clutched at Thor. 'You brute!'

'Try it,' he said softly. 'Just let yourself go.'

'This is terrifying,' she muttered. But she did as he asked. It was one of the most difficult things she had ever attempted, far more difficult than walking in the dark. At any moment, she expected to go flying, or to crash into someone else. Thor's hands guided for a while, then released her.

'Don't let go of me!' she cried.

'I'm right here,' she heard his voice say. 'Just trust yourself.'

She skated in silence, her teeth clenched and her body tense. Now and then, Thor touched her elbow, guiding her away from a collision. But other than that, she was completely autonomous. At first, the insecurity was choking. Then, all at once, it was gone. She had relaxed. She was flying through the darkness, independent, alone. Everything suddenly became very intense, very physical: the feel of her skates cutting through the ice, the cold air on her cheeks. With crystalline distinctness, she could hear every note of music coming out of the loudspeakers, the chatter and laughter of the people all around her, coming and going past her. Every part of her body felt alive, strong. The blood was singing in her veins.

At last, she reached up and pulled the hat off. The world was dazzlingly bright around her, the glow of the ice rising up to meet the starlight. Thor was smiling at her. 'How do you feel?'

She shook out her hair and it streamed in the wind. 'That was alarming.'

'And exhilarating?'

'And exhilarating!'

They skated for half an hour longer, until her Achilles tendons started to protest at the unaccustomed exercise, and the cold had crept into her legs. They gave their skates back and then went to a *Weinstube* to drink *Glühwein*. The hot, mulled brew was warming, making her cheeks flush. It also went quickly to her head, so that everything seemed amusing. She found herself laughing with a freedom she hadn't enjoyed in a long time.

They bought hot chestnuts from an old man with a brazier, and carried them in a paper cone, peeling them gingerly and blowing on their scorched fingers. The Christmas market was busy. They browsed the stalls and shops, buying festive things and goodies to take home to Gretchen.

They left the square and strolled through Vienna, the music fading behind them, until peace enveloped them. 'Whatever you think,' Thor said, 'Gretchen has made good progress with you. Far more than with all the famous doctors and psychologists put together.'

'I think the credit is all Dr Asperger's,' Katya replied. For the last several weeks, Gretchen had been seeing the young doctor at the paediatric clinic every Monday and Wednesday. Asperger's reputation as an expert on childhood psychology was growing daily. Though Katya found his coldness rather daunting, she respected his brilliance, and felt that he had insights into helping troubled children like Gretchen.

'Dr Asperger didn't teach Gretchen to hug her father. He didn't teach her how to smile. You did that. I don't know how to express my gratitude to you, Katya. But believe me, my heart is full.'

'It's been a joy for me,' she replied.

Mist was gathering in the air, making the ornate streetlamps fuzzy and the far ends of the streets mysterious. They passed inns whose half-open doors showed invitingly cosy interiors, and the Musikverein, through whose windows they heard an orchestra rehearsing a Mozart symphony; but by and large the city was quiet. The gaiety that might be found in London or Paris on a night like this was translated by Vienna into a comfortable and somewhat sleepy peace. Yet the city was so beautiful.

They reached St Stephen's Cathedral. Its spire towered into the glowing mist, and in front, a Christmas tree sparkled with coloured light bulbs.

The door of the cathedral was ajar. They went inside. The nave was almost empty, but near the altar, a choir was singing Christmas hymns, their jewel-like voices supported by the deep hum of an organ. Thor took her hand as they walked towards the music. They stood there together, entranced.

When the music ended, he turned to face her. 'Katya, I care for you more each day that passes. And I feel that you care for me.'

'You know that I do,' she said quietly.

His voice caught in his throat. 'I want you to be my wife.'

She felt a jolt of electricity in her heart. 'Oh, Thor!'

'I fell in love with you the day I set eyes on you. I can't live without you. I cannot bear the thought of losing you. I need you to be mine, Katya. You don't have to answer me now. But promise me you will think about it.'

'Of course I will think about it.'

On the way home, Katya remembered the bitterness she had felt when she'd first arrived in Vienna. In its place was something different now. She and Thor Bachmann had become very close. The differences between them – the twenty-year age gap, the circumstances of their meeting, their different characters – were now far less important than the attraction between them.

Exactly what that attraction was, and what it might become, were issues that Katya hadn't delved into too deeply until tonight. She'd just known that whatever her regrets about putting her degree aside for the time being, she had found life in Vienna full of unexpected magic. She knew with increasing certainty that she was falling in love with Thor.

But Thor's proposal would change the magic into a different reality. What would become of her plans if she took this new avenue, and followed all its logical, predictable turnings – marriage, children of her own? And if she rejected Thor now, might she be destroying her own happiness? There might never be a man to match him ever again. She might be left wounded forever, forever longing for what she had refused.

They reached home to find Gretchen fast asleep on the leather sofa in Thor's study. They had left her in the care of Frau Hackl, the austere housekeeper, who was sitting bolt upright on a hard chair, looking grim.

'She woke up,' Frau Hackl informed them, 'and insisted on waiting for you to return. She has been playing the gramophone for hours. But you were so late,' she added, looking pointedly at her watch.

'I'm sorry, Frau Hackl,' Katya said. 'It was such a beautiful night.'

'Yes, I am sure,' the housekeeper said thinly. 'But now she will cry when you wake her.'

'I'll get her into bed, don't worry,' Katya replied. It was true that Gretchen often got cranky when awakened, despite being twelve and a half – especially when the one who awoke her was Frau Hackl. But Katya was invariably gentle with Gretchen, not least because she had learned to love this mysterious, gifted, delicate child who had been put into her care.

She stroked Gretchen's hair and whispered her name. Gretchen's dark eyes opened. She yawned, and snuggled into Katya's arms as Katya helped her to her feet. This in itself was a major achievement, since Gretchen disliked too much physical contact as a general rule. If Katya had taught Gretchen nothing else, she had taught her to give and seek hugs.

Frau Hackl's face soured even further. 'You are casting your spell over her, *nicht wahr?*' she hissed in a voice too low for Thor to hear. 'Over the child and her father, too. You are clever, Fräulein Komarovsky.'

Katya ignored the comment, although such pointed remarks from the housekeeper were becoming more common, and more annoying lately.

She guided Gretchen upstairs and tucked her into bed. Gretchen was half-awake. She looked sleepily up at Katya from her pillow. 'Where did you go?' she asked.

'We went skating in front of the Rathaus,' Katya replied, smoothing the tumbled hair away from Gretchen's face. 'It was lovely. Daddy made me skate blindfolded.'

'Weren't you frightened?'

'At first, I was. Then I learned to trust myself. Afterwards, we bought some things for you at the Christmas market.'

'What things?'

'Oh . . . gingerbread . . . and *Lebkuchen* . . . chocolates . . . and strudels . . . pastries . . . and candied fruit . . .' She watched Gretchen's eyes closing during the recital. In sleep, Gretchen's face lost the anxious look it so often wore, revealing the delicate beauty of her features. Katya knew that she resembled her mother more than her father, except in her dark hair and eyes. *I will take care of her*, she promised the dead woman silently. *I'll never let harm come to her.*

Gretchen drifted slowly into sleep. The music she had been listening to was inside her, spreading through her like rain in the garden. Soon it would make leaves and flowers, and they would come out of her fingers.

It had been so lovely to be put to bed by Katya. How long had it been since she had felt like this? Not since Mama had died.

And where had Gretchen gone – angry Gretchen, who tore up books and stamped on the pages? Where was she? Was this a new Gretchen? Or had the old Gretchen come back, the Gretchen she could hardly remember, who had died when Mama had died? Had Katya dug her out of the earth, the way she did with Bunny?

Katya rejoined Thor in his study. 'I was thinking of the day I met you,' he said. 'I watched you from across the room. You weren't even aware of me, but I was so aware of you that I couldn't take my eyes off you. You were glowing with life, sweetness, innocence and bravery.'

'Bravery? I'm not very brave.'

'Oh, but you are. I could see it in you. You were ready to face life with all its challenges. The past years had been difficult for me. Karin's illness and death had cast a dark shadow over me. I'd been lonely. I was worried about Gretchen, but I seemed unable to find anyone who could help her. All I seemed able to do was make money, and there was no point to that, because I had no one to share my life with. There were moments when I felt a deep despair. When I saw you in London, I felt as though I had come out of a dark place and into the sunlight.' He kissed her hands tenderly. 'I felt that if you were beside me, I could be happy again – and that you could bring the sunshine back to Gretchen's life. I wanted you in my life. Forever.'

'You are everything I've always wanted in a man,' she replied simply.

'Then you'll marry me?'

'It won't work, Thor.'

He looked as though she had stabbed him in the heart. 'Why not?'

'Because I've surrendered too much of my freedom already. Too much of myself.'

'And have you gained nothing?' he whispered.

'Oh, yes! So much.' She looked up into his face. 'More than I can say. But I've learned that in life, what we lose is what haunts us, no matter how much we gain.'

'Katya—'

'Let me speak now,' she said. 'I came to Austria when you called me. I left behind all my dreams. But I made a pact with myself – that they wouldn't be lost forever. That one day I would get them back. I've learned to love you, and to love Gretchen. But if I marry you, I will never do the things I want to do with my life.'

'My darling, I will support you in everything. You can study here. There is an excellent medical university in Vienna, one of the best in the world—'

'That won't work, Thor,' she interrupted gently. 'I need to study in my own language, in my own country. And although you say you'd support me, I don't think it will be as easy as that. You're used to having me here at home all the time. A husband whose wife is at lectures all day, and studying all night, will soon start to complain. I wouldn't be the kind of wife you want. And I wouldn't be there for Gretchen. I would inevitably change and grow – remember how young I am. And when I became a doctor, it would be even more difficult. I would have my patients, my career. We would soon grow apart. We would be angry with one another, my dear – and that would be the end of our beautiful relationship. And I couldn't bear that.'

'If you were my wife, I would treat you like porcelain, Katya.'

'That would be wonderful. If I was a doll. Unfortunately, I'm not made of porcelain. I'm quite human.'

'So you won't marry me.'

'I can't be your wife,' she replied. 'But I can very happily be your lover.'

He stared at her, his eyes dark. 'What do you mean?' he asked huskily.

'Don't you know?' She took his hand and laid it on the curve of her breast. 'I'm human, Thor. I have a woman's heart and a woman's desires.'

'Are you sure?' he whispered.

'I've never been surer of anything.' And that was the truth of how she felt. She meant all the things she had said to him tonight. She had accepted her own feelings for Thor, and he had declared his for her. What did they have in life except one another? 'Happiness is precious. Let's seize it while we can, now. Let's not wait for tomorrow.'

She reached up and kissed him on the lips. His beard, which looked so bushy, was soft against her skin. His mouth was warm. She felt his arms encircle her, pulling her into his warmth.

'Katya . . .'

'Are you shocked?' she murmured.

'Yes, a little.'

'Then take me to bed,' she whispered. 'And I will shock you even more.'

Chapter 8

They awoke in each other's arms. Katya's head was pillowed on Thor's broad chest, her hair spread out across his skin.

'Good morning, my beloved,' he murmured, kissing her brow.

'Good morning,' she whispered, snuggling against him.

He stroked the hair away from her face. His eyes were tender. 'You are so beautiful, Katya. I can't believe you're mine.'

'Isn't this exactly what you wanted when you kidnapped me?'

'I dreamed. I didn't expect.'

'You didn't ask me whether you were the first. I thought men always asked that.'

He raised one bushy eyebrow. 'Do they? It doesn't matter to me, so long as I am your last.'

'You must know that you were the first.'

'How should I know that?'

'By my virginal innocence. I had to keep myself pure, you know. Mama and Papa were hoping to marry me off to a millionaire. I was strictly warned to save myself for Mr Right. That's partly why they were so upset when I went off to university. They thought I would be besmirched there. But I grew into a withered spinster instead.'

'Very withered.'

'Oh, all the girls in my year at Glasgow got themselves lovers. Except me. I heard some ghastly stories about sex. So I was prepared for the worst. But you didn't fumble, you didn't blunder, and you certainly didn't hurt me.' She looked at him solemnly. 'I hope I wasn't too rough with you? I don't know my own strength sometimes.'

Thor laughed. 'You could crush my heart in your hand, if you wanted.'

'But I don't want.' She clambered on to him and kissed him lingeringly on the lips. 'You seem to know a great deal about women,' she whispered, her face close to his. 'You knew all my secrets.'

'They revealed themselves to me,' he whispered back.

'I'm very glad that they did. I was always anxious about my first lover. Can I tell you something?'

'Please do.'

'I've never felt safe in my life. Until I was with you.'

'But you were so angry with me!'

'Yes. Resentful but safe. Having to flee Russia wasn't a good experience. It left me feeling that no matter how secure you felt, things could change in an instant. And then, Mama and Papa's way of life was always so precarious – I always knew that could change, too. I can't remember a time when we weren't hiding from the bailiffs and the debt collectors. Everything was such a terrible strain. They often couldn't pay my school fees because they'd wasted the money, and the headmistress used to call me in for an explanation. My nerves were always stretched to breaking point, right through my schooldays.'

His face was compassionate. 'My poor Katya.'

'But when I met you, my great big cave bear, I started to feel safe again. It's the greatest gift you could have given me.'

She hadn't expected sex to make such a difference. But it had.

She'd intended to avoid binding herself to him. But she had done the opposite.

Sharing their bodies, sharing their delight in one another, had changed everything. She had committed herself to Thor in a profound way. She recalled the casual way her fellow students at Glasgow had talked about their experiences. She'd felt nothing casual last night. It had been a rite of passage that had carried her, in a single night, into womanhood. She didn't see her body in the same way as yesterday. She didn't see *herself* in the same way. Everything had changed.

Whether she'd been sensible or foolish, time would tell. The change was there, however, and there was no going back. In the meantime, she was floating on a sea of euphoria, as though last night's wonderful lovemaking had changed the very chemistry of her body and filled her veins with fizzing champagne.

Despite the progress Gretchen had made emotionally, there were other areas where Katya could see that she was far slower. She still struggled with reading and writing, and was only able to scrawl her name and recognise a few simple words. Katya had been unable to teach her to read music either; Gretchen regarded it as a torment, since her superb memory held complex scores effortlessly – why, then, should she give herself migraines with sheafs of paper? She preferred to spend hours with the gramophone, playing one recording after another, piling up the sleeves untidily. When she found a piece she liked, she would jump up and go to the piano, and play it as though she had been learning it for weeks.

On the way home from the clinic in the car, Gretchen turned to Katya.

'I try so hard, Katya,' she said in an unsteady voice. 'Really, I do.'

Katya saw that there were tears in Gretchen's bright brown eyes. 'Oh, Gretchen, I know you do!'

'I really want to please you – and Papa – and Dr Asperger. I just can't make sense of the letters. They jump around when I try to read them. They're like wriggling ants. I try to make them keep still, but they won't.'

Katya put her arm around Gretchen. 'It's not your fault.'

'I start at the beginning, and I try to follow the line, but I know none of it makes sense, and I have to go back to the beginning again. And my eyes start to hurt, and my head hurts. There's something wrong with my brain.'

'Don't say that. There isn't.'

'I heard Dr Asperger say there was, and there must be. I just wish there was a magic wand you could wave over me and make me like everybody else.'

The misery in Gretchen's face cut Katya to the heart. 'Even if I had that wand, I would break it and throw it away. You're not like anybody else, and I would never want you to be. You're so special, Gretchen. You're the most musical person I've ever known. I've never met anybody who can do what you do. There can't be one in a thousand people who can play Bach by ear.'

'I would rather be like everybody else,' Gretchen said sadly.

'No! You should be proud to be special.' Gretchen just stared out of the window as Katya went on talking. Katya tried hard to encourage Gretchen to value the wonderful gifts she had, rather than dwell on the ones she lacked; but perhaps that was something that would only come with adulthood. In the meantime, the girl was on a long, hard road.

Katya had a discussion with Dr Asperger on their next visit to the clinic, three days before Christmas.

Hans Asperger was boyish and sandy-haired, with an earnest manner. Despite the gold-rimmed spectacles he habitually wore, he was outdoorsy and pink-cheeked, and one of his most frequent pieces of advice to Katya was to 'get Gretchen out for long walks in the country', a prescription that was of no use whatsoever, as Gretchen detested the countryside and considered long walks a form of punishment.

'If you are serious about Gretchen making progress,' he said, 'then she must be admitted to the clinic full-time for a minimum of three months.'

'She would hate that,' Katya said doubtfully. 'She doesn't like to be away from home.'

'Being at home is part of the problem,' Asperger said sternly. 'Whatever good we can achieve in an afternoon's visit is lost as soon as she leaves. She simply reverts to her old forms of behaviour when she gets home. As an inpatient, she would not be allowed to regress. We would be able to push her to do her best.' He caught Katya wincing. 'Sentimentality is of no use to us here,' he said. 'I repeat – if you want to see real progress, then she must be admitted as soon as possible.'

'Perhaps in the New Year, then?'

'Let me consult my staff. Excuse me.'

Katya waited while Asperger went off to speak to the ward matron. The idea of admitting Gretchen to the clinic was disquieting. Gretchen did not deal well with change, and while she was not an affectionate child, and seldom seemed to welcome – or even need – people around her, she might react badly to being placed in full-time care. And Thor might well be completely opposed to it.

But what if Asperger was right? He was undoubtedly brilliant, and if he felt that Gretchen could make the progress he had promised, then perhaps it was worth subjecting Gretchen to some hardship? The long-term benefits could outweigh the temporary unhappiness.

And after all, this was Austria. Katya had learned that while Austrians could be sentimental about their traditions, or Mozart, or chocolate, they expected children to do as they were told, to be seen and not heard.

Asperger bustled back in. 'Excellent news,' he announced. 'We are shortly to be discharging a young patient who has made excellent progress, and who will now be attending a normal school. We can take Gretchen immediately.'

'Immediately! But it's Christmas in a couple of days!'

'We have a place for her now,' he said firmly. 'If you do not take advantage of this unique opportunity, Fräulein Komarovsky, I really cannot say when it will come again.'

'I wanted to have some time to get her used to the idea!'

'She will get used to it, don't worry,' he replied. 'They all do. And you will be impressed with her development. I guarantee it. Discuss it with Herr Bachmann, and let me know as soon as possible.'

To Katya's surprise, neither Gretchen nor Thor were averse to the idea of a stay at the paediatric clinic. It was a measure of Gretchen's progress that she took the proposal calmly and considered it before agreeing. Katya knew that her earnest desire to improve her reading had much to do with her courageous decision.

They agreed that Gretchen would spend Christmas at home and be admitted to Dr Asperger's clinic before the New Year. The three months proposed by Asperger were reduced to one, after which Gretchen's progress would be assessed. Asperger was insistent that visits be avoided for at least three weeks, so that there would be as few distractions from the therapy as possible.

They spent a happy Christmas together; and on 27 December, Gretchen was admitted to the clinic.

Chapter 9

Gretchen had made a friend. His name was Georg.

He was always in a wheelchair, except for when they put him in his cot.

Georg had been tied in so many knots that you didn't know where to start at first. His hands were knotted together against his chest. His legs were knotted around each other. His face was a knot. His tongue was knotted and the sounds he made were a succession of knots that were jerked out of his throat.

When she made him laugh, he would bang his head against the backrest and let out whoops of delight.

They were the same, she and Georg. Except that her knots were all inside. And if Georg's body would only obey him, he could and would do all the things she couldn't.

The women orderlies didn't like Georg because they said he was surly and rebellious. The real problem was that they couldn't understand what he said.

When the nurses and doctors were away, the orderlies could be very rough. They would get angry with Georg. And when they were impatient, they would hurt him, and he would froth and spit and tie himself in even tighter knots, so they would have to manhandle him like an obstinate tangle of washing pulled out of the tub. He would wail as they threw him on to the bed and Gretchen would choke with grief and anger.

'Can't you understand what he's saying?' she demanded of the orderlies.

'Oh, and I suppose *you* can?' one of them scoffed.

'Of course I can! You must be stupid!'

The orderly's palm smacked across her mouth, not hard enough to really hurt, but hard enough to warn her there would shortly be worse. Her name was Hannah, and she could really hurt when she wanted. 'You hear that, girls? I'm stupid – says Miss Can't-Read-Or-Write.'

Gretchen wiped the lye taste of the woman's hand off her mouth and retreated cautiously. 'He says he doesn't want to go to sleep.'

'He doesn't say anything of the sort,' the orderly scoffed. 'He doesn't say anything at all. It's just babble.'

'It's not!' His words were crystal clear to Gretchen, clear as music, but they couldn't understand. 'Can't you hear? He's talking to you!'

'All right then. Translate for us.' The three women gathered around, grinning. 'Tell us what he's saying.'

Georg was crumpled on the bed on his stomach, where they'd tossed him, one baleful eye glaring at them over his shoulder. He began shouting as loudly as he could, which wasn't very loudly. Gretchen started translating as soon as he stopped for breath.

'He says he doesn't want to be put to bed every afternoon at three o'clock like a child. He says he wants to decide whether he sleeps in the afternoon or not.'

Hannah spat on the floor and rubbed the place with the sole of her shoe. 'He says all that, does he?'

'He says he's sixteen years old and the way you treat him isn't right. He says he's entitled to some dignity.'

The women burst out laughing. 'Dignity! That bundle of bones!'

Georg started shouting again. 'He says he has no privacy,' Gretchen interpreted. 'He says he's a man, and—'

'A man!'

'—and he shouldn't be left naked with women all around to look at him.'

'Who wants to look at *him*?' one of the other women said indignantly. 'It's no pleasure for us to look at *that*, I can assure you!'

'What are you so interested in naked boys for, anyway?' another asked. 'Are you in love with him?'

'He's my friend.'

'You mean you're hoping to get off with him.'

'That's disgusting,' Gretchen snapped.

'We know what you miscreations get up to when we're not around.'

'I don't believe a word of it anyway,' Hannah said scornfully. 'He's not saying anything. It's just *papperlapapp*. You're trying to pull the wool over our eyes. And don't tell us we're disgusting, you little minx!' She slapped Gretchen again, a little harder this time. 'Now get out of our way and let us do our work.' She reached out a brawny arm and grasped Georg by his ankle, hauling him roughly over as though he were an inanimate piece of wood. He cried out in pain as his joints cracked.

Gretchen flew at the orderly in a fury, her fists pounding the broad, strong back. Taken aback for a moment by Gretchen's ferocity, the women scattered. Then one of them grabbed a fistful of Gretchen's hair and yanked hard, so that she lost her footing. Slaps rained on her. She tried to protect her face. It was useless to fight back. They dragged her to the linen closet and threw her into the darkness.

'I'll tell my mother and father!' she screamed.

Hannah thrust her face close to Gretchen's. 'Don't even think about it. Or we'll kill you. Your time will come, you little abortion. You and your friend Georg – you don't deserve to be alive. When the Nazis are here, you'll see. I'll be there to laugh when they put you down. Your precious mummy and daddy, too.'

She slammed the door shut. Gretchen heard the key turn in the lock.

She stood in the pitch blackness, trembling from head to foot, listening to Georg crying out again and again.

The days were magical. There were several spells of heavy snow, transforming the garden into a·collection of soft white mounds. She and Thor went for long walks through the white landscape.

New Year's Eve was now upon them, and along with all the upper class of Vienna, they went to the Hofburg for the ball. They had been here for concerts before, but tonight the chairs had been removed to make a dance floor, and the auditorium was filling with couples in evening dress, the buzz of their excited conversation rising and falling like the sea.

Katya had dressed in pale blue. Thor had wanted to take her to the most fashionable modiste in Vienna, but she had declined, preferring to buy something herself from the tiny part of her 'wages' that Papa sent each month. She'd found an unpretentious gown that hadn't cost too much, but was youthful and flattered her slim figure. There was probably not a woman dressed more simply in the whole room.

The great room, lit by rows of immense crystal chandeliers that hung from the painted ceiling, blazed with light. The evening opened with a performance by the Opera Ballet, all clad in white silk, who danced down the centre of the room, the women carrying sprays of pink cherry blossom. Then the orchestra struck up a waltz, and everyone surged to the dance floor.

Once again, Katya found herself whirling in Thor's arms. She had waltzed more since coming to Vienna than in her whole life before. He was an excellent dancer, for all his size. The swift Viennese waltz, she had decided, was a dance designed to make women light-headed. As you spun in graceful circles, the people around you became a blur; the one focal point was your partner, on whom you were forced to concentrate. His strong arms kept you from flying away, and his masculine face held all your attention. It was an integral part of the Viennese mating game.

And Thor was very masculine as he smiled down at her. It was hard not to let herself be literally swept away. The room was packed to capacity now, the crowd sparkling with the jewellery of the women and the medals of the men. Among the stars and ribbons of the ceremonial orders, Katya caught the occasional swastika armband. The swastika had been banned by the government, part of its desperate attempts to avoid being swallowed up by the Third Reich, but increasingly, one saw it creeping into view here and there. She didn't comment on this to Thor, because she knew it was a subject that was guaranteed to upset him.

They danced until they were both thirsty, then made their way to their table and ordered a bottle of champagne.

'One day,' she called over the music of the orchestra, 'I'm going to make you take that beard off.'

'And what day will that be?' he replied.

'When I run out of patience with it.'

'I grew it after Karin's death.'

'I know you did. I've seen the photos of you before. You're very handsome under all that foliage. Why did you grow it?'

'Perhaps I wanted to hide my face.'

'Out of grief?'

'To withdraw from the world.'

'Like a monk?'

'Something like that. If you really don't like it, then of course I will take it off. But please can I wait until the snow has gone?'

It was a wonderful evening, happy and exciting. As always on these occasions, dozens of people knew Thor, and their table was constantly surrounded with friends. Katya noticed how the women looked at her, whispering and smiling among themselves. As midnight approached, the dance floor filled with people. Katya and Thor joined the throng, counting down the last thirty seconds until an explosion of streamers and confetti rained down on the stroke of midnight.

Katya threw herself into Thor's arms. They kissed on each cheek and then on the lips.

'It's going to be a wonderful year!' Thor said, smiling into her eyes. 'Despite Hitler!'

The orchestra struck up the opening chords of 'The Blue Danube Waltz', and everyone took their partners, waiting to begin. As the majestic music swelled out, a huge banner rolled down, bearing the year that had just begun: 1938.

'They're going to transfer me soon,' Georg said.

They were at the table, and Gretchen was helping him eat, because none of the staff liked to do it. She regarded it as a privilege. She paused with the spoon halfway to his mouth, frightened. 'How do you know?'

'I've heard them saying so. They think I can't understand.'

She put the food carefully in his mouth. 'Transfer you where?' she asked. 'Where will they send you?'

He swallowed. She had to be careful, because he sometimes choked. 'I don't know. But you won't see me again.'

'Please don't say that!'

'After the Anschluss, they'll do what they want with people like us.'

'What do you mean?'

Georg held out a shaky hand, made a gun with it, and brought down his thumb like the hammer. 'That's what I mean.'

'No!'

'It's what the Nazis do. You've heard them talk about it.'

'They're just cruel and ignorant. It's not true.'

'It is true.'

'For God's sake, stop that moaning,' one of the nurses called from across the table. 'It's getting on my nerves!'

'He's not moaning, he's talking,' Gretchen snapped.

'Don't you answer me back, Miss Minx. And make him shut up. Or I will.'

Georg smiled at Gretchen, the secret smile that he only gave her. 'I can't stand it in here any more,' he said in a lower voice. 'I'll be glad when they come for me. Anything's better than this. The only thing I'll miss will be talking to you. Nobody else listens.'

'I won't let them take you away,' Gretchen said, tears filling her eyes.

'They don't think we have anything to say. They don't think we have any future. They don't even think we're people. I just wanted to say goodbye. I love you, Gretchen.'

He unknotted his thin arms and wrapped them around her, holding her tight until the angry orderlies pulled him off.

Chapter 10

Georg was gone. His cot was empty, the mattress stripped. The little cupboard beside it where his clothes had been kept was empty too, the doors standing open.

Gretchen uttered a wail of grief. Hannah heard her, and marched over. 'What now?'

'Where's Georg?'

Hannah smirked. 'I told you, didn't I? I told you what they would do.'

'Where have you taken him?'

'You'll find out. You'll be there yourself soon enough.' Gretchen wanted to throw herself at Hannah, biting and scratching, as she had done before. But Hannah's expression warned her what the cost would be. Hannah laughed. 'That's right. You keep your claws to yourself, or it'll be the worse for you.'

'Georg was my friend,' Gretchen said through her tears.

'Your friend? You lot live here in the lap of luxury, treated better than honest working people, sleeping in feather beds, eating better than we do at home, warm and snug.' Hannah put her fists on her broad hips. 'You know what I'd like? I'd like them to pay my husband to come in here one day with his shotgun, and *do* you lot, like he does the magpies and foxes and the other vermin. Come to think of it, he would even do it for free. And I would watch.' She lifted her skirt and gave Gretchen a mock curtsey. 'And now if you'll excuse me, Your Royal Highness, I have work to do.'

Dr Asperger had been firm about discouraging any visits, but Katya couldn't hold back any longer. Lorenz took her to the clinic. Her reception by Dr Asperger was predictably frosty.

'Fräulein Komarovsky, I asked you to give me three weeks.'

'I know, Doctor,' she said humbly. 'But I'm missing her so much – and I'm sure she's missing me.'

He was unimpressed. 'Did I not warn you against sentimentality?'

'Yes, you did. But I have a woman's heart,' she said, hoping this bit of flummery would soften him.

He frowned. 'Yes. The female heart is a problem with which we psychologists will struggle forever, I think. Very well. You may see Gretchen for fifteen minutes only. After that, I wish to speak to you in my office.'

'Oh, thank you, thank you!' she gushed.

She was taken to the day room, where a young nurse, Sister Rosenbaum, was working with Gretchen on her reading. As soon as Gretchen saw Katya come in, she jumped to her feet and raced to meet her, throwing her arms around Katya and pressing her face to Katya's breast.

'Gretchen!' Katya said. 'I've missed you!' She held Gretchen tightly. Gretchen's displays of physical affection were not common, and had to be treasured.

At last Gretchen loosened her grip, and turned a woebegone face up to Katya. 'I want to come home,' she whispered.

'Oh, Liebchen. Aren't you happy?'

Gretchen's brown eyes glistened with tears. 'No.'

Katya crouched down so she could look into Gretchen's face. 'What's the matter?'

'They took Georg away.'

'Who's Georg?'

'My friend.'

'Darling, patients come and go in hospitals.'

'You don't understand! He'll never come back. They're going to do something terrible to him.'

Katya felt dismayed. She'd hoped to see Gretchen better, not worse. 'Let me speak to Dr Asperger.'

Gretchen clutched at her. 'Don't leave me. Please, Katya!'

Gretchen's obvious distress was upsetting. 'I promise I'll be back.'

Asperger was drumming his fingers on his desk. 'Gretchen's progress has been disappointing,' he said.

'She seems upset about a friend she made here, a boy named Georg. She says he was transferred. She's worried about what will happen to him.'

Asperger frowned behind his gold-rimmed glasses. 'The case of Georg is an excellent illustration. It is critical for Gretchen's outcome that she learns to integrate with other children. This is far more important than her other disabilities – the illiteracy and so forth. We assess children according to their future ability to join the *Volk*.'

'The *Volk*?'

'The national community, if you prefer that term. Their behaviour and family standing indicates whether or not they will ever be useful members of society.'

Katya frowned. 'Is that really all that matters?'

He held up a hand to silence her. 'Allow me to continue. A key indicator is the ability to join in with other children's activities and make friends. In all the time Gretchen has been with us, she has made only one so-called friend – the boy Georg. I say "so-called friend" because this particular boy suffers from a severe neurological disorder that renders him incapable of speech. He is only able to make unintelligible sounds. He cannot walk or feed himself satisfactorily.'

'Poor child.'

'It is indeed a sad case. Yet this boy is the only child Gretchen has chosen as a friend. She claims to understand his vocalisations. She criticises the staff because they will not participate in her delusions that he is capable of speech. She has even attacked staff members physically while they are caring for him – because she mistakes their diligence for cruelty.'

'I'm sorry to hear that. But isn't that at least a sign that she's loyal to a friend?'

'I'm afraid it's a sign that she rejects normal relationships,' Asperger retorted. 'It is a sign that she wilfully chooses the most atypical individual around her to associate with. It is nothing less than antisocial.'

'Antisocial is a harsh word to use about a child, Dr Asperger.'

'I don't use it lightly. I'm afraid that I see little hope of improvement for Gretchen. I believe the problem lies in the structure of the brain itself.'

Katya was taken aback. 'But Professor Freud said it was an emotional issue,' she ventured.

Asperger gave a scornful little grunt. 'Professor Freud belongs to an emotional race,' he replied. 'His so-called science is fundamentally a pandering to hysterical self-indulgence. The Jews are often said to be cleverer than other races. This is not so. They are good at exploiting the weak-minded. They excel at music and the other persuasive arts. When it comes to logic, they are weaker. I'm afraid that Professor Freud is on the wrong tack altogether.'

Katya ignored the anti-Semitic remarks. 'Then – you're saying that Gretchen can't be helped after all?'

'This condition is rare in girls,' he replied. She wasn't sure what condition he meant. Before she could frame a question, however, he went on. 'The reason is that the male intelligence is superior to the female.'

'That's rather insulting.'

He adjusted his spectacles. 'Then perhaps we can say that boys and girls have different cognitive capabilities. Boys have the capacity for logic, mathematics, science. Girls—' He raised his finger. 'Girls are suited to the nursery, the kitchen, the family.'

'Dr Asperger, these ideas went out in the nineteenth century!'

'I don't think they will ever *go out*, as you put it. Girls lack the capacity for abstract thought. They rely far more strongly on their emotions and impulses.'

Katya was starting to simmer. 'I beg to differ. I was at university for two years with a generation of women who showed every capacity for abstract thought!'

He cocked his head. 'Yes? Yet here you are, having abandoned your studies, focusing on a child who is not even your own. And, if you will forgive me for saying so, allowing emotion to dominate logic in your thinking.'

'That's not fair.'

'You are very affectionate with Gretchen. Too affectionate, in my view. A little more discipline, and a little less indulgence, would have gone a long way.'

Katya was silenced.

He smiled thinly, and went on. 'I repeat that the condition is far more common in boys. It is an extreme of the male thought process. It is not common in girls because they lack these intellectual powers. That is my finding. The symptoms they display – like Gretchen's – are in my opinion due to hormones. And although there are remedies against hormones, they are drastic ones. Together with the dyslexia, this presents grave challenges for Gretchen. However, we can console ourselves in that it is not necessary for her to be able to read and write in order to fulfil a woman's destiny.'

'Then, Dr Asperger,' she said, rising, 'I think it's best I take Gretchen home now.'

He turned the smile off. 'If that is your wish.'

'It is.'

'Very well. You may keep bringing her back as an outpatient, if you so desire.'

'Even though you say there's no hope of helping her?'

He shrugged. 'One does what one can. Who knows? We can at least continue to observe her progress.'

'I'll speak to her father about that.'

Angry and confused, Katya went back to the day room. 'Don't cry, Liebchen,' she said to Gretchen. 'It's all right. Go and pack your bag. We're going home.'

'Oh, thank you, thank you!' Joyously, Gretchen hurried off to start packing.

Sister Rosenbaum came over to Katya. 'You look upset,' she commented.

'Dr Asperger has just told me that girls are incapable of logical thought,' Katya replied.

Sister Rosenbaum shrugged at Katya's indignant tone. 'He's a very good doctor. You have to forgive his little prejudices.'

'I'm not sure I want Gretchen to be treated by a man with *little prejudices* like that. I feel that with him, she's beaten from the start. He seems to think that she's fit for nothing but to wash dishes.'

'Dr Asperger is very conservative. He's a staunch Catholic, and you know how *they* feel about women. *Kinder, Küche, Kirche.*

Children, kitchen, church. He thinks that a woman's destiny lies with one of those – preferably all three. He's much more progressive with the boys.'

'Unfortunately, Gretchen is not a boy.'

'I understand that you don't like Dr Asperger's attitudes,' the young nurse said, lowering her voice, 'but he's a remarkable doctor.'

'In my experience, children respond to kindness, not bullying. But Dr Asperger says I'm too sentimental.'

'You're wonderful with Gretchen. You show her love. In Austria, it's not as common as you would think to be so affectionate with children, especially if they have learning difficulties. If you keep supporting her, she'll be able to get through the work here.'

Katya sighed. 'All right. Perhaps I'll keep bringing her back twice a week.'

Gretchen was silent on the way back home.

'Was it really awful?' Katya asked.

'I missed Georg so much. And I just felt so—'

'So what, Liebchen?'

'So *stupid*.' Gretchen began to cry.

'You're not stupid,' Katya said, putting her arm round the girl.

'I am! There are children years younger than me, and they can read and write better than I ever will. Some of them are still wetting the bed every night, but they know their alphabet. Why am I so *stupid*?'

'Is that what Dr Asperger says? That you're stupid?'

'He says I'm lazy and disobedient, and I don't do what I'm told. But I can't help it.' She wiped her eyes. 'I can't help being the way I am. I try so hard to do what he wants, but I always get everything wrong. Then he makes me do it again, and it just gets worse. So I try and guess the answers, but I get that wrong, too, and then he says I am dishonest and a cheat.'

Katya's heart sank as she hugged Gretchen. Freud's recommendation had not turned out well. 'You don't ever have to go back, Gretchen. We'll find somebody else to help us.'

Gretchen shook with a sob, then looked up. 'No. I want to go back.'

'But why, if he's so harsh with you?'

'I *want* to be able to read. I want to show him that I *can*, that I'm *not* lazy or stupid.'

Katya felt a wave of love and respect for the girl. She took out her hankie and blotted Gretchen's tear-stained face. 'All right, Liebchen. If that's what you really want. I'm so proud of you for saying that.'

They got back to the house to find Frau Hackl and the cook in the kitchen, listening to the radio, which was turned up loud. The guttural voice that was rasping from the loudspeaker was unmistakably that of Adolf Hitler. It filled the kitchen with dark emotions – rage, bitterness, threat. The two Austrian women were listening with rapt expressions on their faces, but to Katya, it felt as though the broadcast had made the atmosphere of the house foetid, toxic.

'Turn that off,' she snapped.

Frau Hackl turned to her with a hostile expression. *'Ach, so.* Are you now the mistress of this house?'

But Bertha the cook quickly switched the radio off. The copper pans hanging over the stove seemed still to be ringing in the silence. 'Beg pardon, Fräulein Katya. We didn't hear you arrive.'

'As you can see, Gretchen's back,' Katya said. 'Please lay two places for lunch.'

Bertha beamed. 'Of course, Fräulein. Welcome home, Gretchen!'

The women fussed over Gretchen, but Katya felt there was an atmosphere of resentment now. Thor was away on business in Switzerland, and in his absence she felt very young compared to the three household staff members. Giving them orders did not come naturally to her. Even Lorenz, although a gentle person, was old enough to be her father.

Gretchen raced joyfully to her piano, and was soon filling the house with Chopin, which drove away the lingering menace of Hitler's tones, cleansing the house.

She sat quietly to listen to the recital. The nocturne she played now was so affecting that Katya's eyes filled with tears. There was genius in Gretchen – if only the world could be got to see it.

Gretchen had plunged into a sea of music. It surrounded her, floated her off the jagged rocks, took away the pain. It surged around her, through her, into her and out again. She was so grateful for it. She had missed it so much.

When Gretchen had stopped playing, Katya got up and stroked the girl's curly hair gently. 'How do you do that, Gretchen?'

Gretchen looked up at her with dark eyes. 'How do you read and write?'

'That's much easier.'

'Not for me,' Gretchen retorted.

'You're right. I'm sorry. I just can't imagine how you hold such long pieces of music in your memory for so long.'

'Oh, I played it every day in the hospital.'

'On that funny old piano?'

'No. They wouldn't let me play the piano. They said it distracted the other children. I played it here.' She touched her temple.

'What do you mean?'

'It's the same whether I have a piano or not. I can play without needing the keys. I don't really play with my fingers at all. I play with—' She stopped, then shrugged. 'I don't know. I just turn on the music, and the music comes.'

Katya smiled. 'You are a mystery, Gretchen. A deep, dark mystery.'

But inside, she felt sad and worried. What would become of this girl? With a talent like hers, a career as a concert performer would be within her reach. Except that she couldn't read or write. Brilliant as she was, she couldn't memorise a whole concert repertoire just by listening to recordings. And she was so shy that the idea of getting up on a stage was inconceivable, in any case.

Katya thought of Hans Asperger's contemptuous words: *we can console ourselves in that it is not necessary for her to be able to read and write in order to fulfil a woman's destiny.*

A woman's destiny? Children, church and kitchen? She'd seen Asperger working assiduously with the boys, his face eager. He had hopes for them. They were worthy of his attention. The girls were not. He seemed unable to see any value in Gretchen, and that was heartbreaking. His impatient dismissal of her as lazy and disobedient was infuriating. To shrug, and say that she was a girl, and so it didn't matter whether she improved or not, showed an extraordinary mentality for a paediatrician.

But it was a mentality that seemed to be more and more common. Katya knew – everybody in Austria knew – that across the border in the Third Reich, Hitler was exhorting German women to leave work and make way for men, to stay at home, to put their husbands, sons and fathers before themselves, and to have more children. Those attitudes were swiftly infecting Austria too. They chimed so well with Austrian conservatism. In a country that venerated 'old-fashioned values', and where ninety per cent of the population was Catholic, pushing women back into their box was bound to be popular.

And it was often the women themselves who seemed most enthusiastic about this movement. Women seemed to adore Hitler even more than the men did. Katya thought of the expressions of reverence on Bertha's and Frau Hackl's faces as they listened to the ranting voice on the radio. She thought of her classmates at Glasgow University, their energy, their refusal to be told what they could and couldn't do. The two groups seemed to be a world apart.

When Thor returned from Zürich, Katya explained why she had brought Gretchen home from the clinic early.

'You did the right thing, of course,' he said. 'Brave Katya – and my poor Gretchen!'

'I'm so sorry, Papa,' Gretchen said. 'I really did try.'

'I know you did,' he said, kissing her forehead. 'I'm very proud of you.' He tickled her until her frown disappeared, and she went off to play, laughing. Thor turned to Katya. 'She has made wonderful progress.'

'Not according to Dr Asperger,' Katya replied with a grimace.

'I don't know what his criteria for progress are, but she has just let me kiss her, and smiled. Before you came into her life, she would always push away any kind of affection. I call *that* progress.'

'Unfortunately, that's all I seem able to do for her.'

'She needed love. Desperately.' He drew Katya to him gently, and looked down into her face. 'As did I. You have the gift of love, the greatest gift of all. You've brought me so many precious things, Katya. I bless the day I met you.'

She smiled up at him tenderly. 'I missed you while you were away.'

'I missed you terribly.'

'Come, then,' she said, taking his hand, 'and let's make up for lost time.'

Chapter 11

It was raining swastikas.

The German bombers had thundered low over Vienna a few moments earlier, causing panic. A carter's horse had bolted, automobiles had swerved on to the sidewalk. Children had screamed as their mothers dragged them into the shelter of shop doorways. The busy street had ground to a standstill.

Now the Dorniers were droning away into the distance, and their freight was fluttering to earth: not bombs, but linen squares on sticks. Red, with a white circle and the black, crooked cross of the German Nazi party, the flags were gaudy against the late-afternoon sky.

There were shouts. Eager hands reached up to snatch them from the air. Men elbowed each other out of the way, fighting to seize the emblems. A child was knocked down and trampled in the rush, its thin wail drowned in the jubilant, relieved laughter.

Katya, who had flung her arms around Gretchen as the bombers roared over, now released the girl. Gretchen stared up at the sky in astonishment. The flags were still drifting down on the gentle breeze. An altercation was developing between two women, each pushing a pram and towing toddlers who were bawling for the same flag. Well-dressed and respectable, the women were agitated enough to start screaming insults at one another.

Gretchen felt suddenly afraid. 'Let's go home, Katya.'

'Yes. We'll go and find Lorenz.'

Their shopping trip to buy Gretchen clothes, which had required so much preparation, was well and truly over.

They made their way back towards the square where the chauffeur had parked the Mercedes-Benz.

On a corner, they encountered a jovial policeman who had managed to secure a fistful of the flags. He held two out to Katya and Gretchen. 'You missed out, eh, Fräuleins? Here. Heil Hitler!'

Reluctantly, Katya and Gretchen took them from him and hurried on. There was a carnival atmosphere in the sedate Viennese streets, but Katya knew that much of the excitement was actually relief. Given the increasingly violent threats made by Hitler over the past weeks, those Dorniers might well have dropped something more lethal than cheap flags.

Gretchen was in a state of anxiety, pulling on Katya's arm. She found being in the street stressful enough without this added turmoil. Too many sights and too many sounds still tended to overwhelm her, though she was learning to control her panic.

Katya felt absurd, clutching the flag the policeman had given her. The coarse linen had been so recently printed that the dye was coming off on the fingers of her kid gloves, red and black and oily. She darted to the nearest litter bin and threw the thing into it. Gretchen was glad to follow suit.

But as she hurried away, a loud voice shouted after her. 'Hey, you!'

Katya turned. A fat man in a brown suit had plucked her flag out of the rubbish bin and was waving it at her.

'What do you think you're doing?' he demanded, his face red with indignation.

'I'm sorry,' Katya muttered, and turned to get away. But the man was still shouting, and her path was suddenly blocked with people.

'What's going on?' a stringy blonde woman demanded.

'They threw the swastika in the rubbish,' the fat man called. 'I saw them!'

'Threw it in the rubbish!'

'The dye was coming off on my gloves,' Katya said.

'A Jewess!' someone said with a cynical laugh. 'They hate to get their hands dirty.'

'I'm not Jewish. Let us pass,' she demanded.

'Listen to her accent.' The blonde woman surveyed them through narrowed eyes. 'Foreigners.'

'Communist agitators. Spies.'

'We're not agitators or spies!' Katya snapped.

The fat man stumped up to Katya and held out the swastika. 'Take it.'

'I don't want it,' Katya retorted.

'Take it!'

'I'm not a Nazi, and I don't want it.' Katya's Russian temper was rising. She was tired of being pushed around, tired of the Nazis, tired of human stupidity. 'I'm not going to wave anything dropped out of the sky by Hitler's bombers. Get out of our way.'

'You foreign tart, who do you think you are?' The blonde leaned forward and spat at them. It was more a gesture than anything else, but Gretchen, who hated anything like that, was suddenly sick, bending over to spew a thin stream of vomit on to the paving.

There were exclamations of disgust. 'What's wrong with your brat? Mentally deficient?'

'You're upsetting her. Let us through, please!'

'You're not going anywhere. You should be made to scrub the street!'

'You will take it,' the fat man said aggressively, holding out the flag, 'or suffer the consequences.'

'No. I refuse.'

There was a growl. The threat of violence was suddenly real. After the unbearable tension of the past few months, and the political turmoil that had strained Viennese nerves to breaking point, an explosive release was coming. It could be felt in the air, a dark excitement, a readiness to hurt.

It was the thin blonde who struck first, her arm snaking out and her palm smacking across Katya's cheek.

The blow was not a hard one, but it was shocking nonetheless. Katya flung her arms protectively around Gretchen as the circle closed in. Other hands reached out, fingers pulling her hair, nails scratching at her face. The women began it, then a couple of the men joined in, punching and kicking.

'Jew,' they were chanting, 'Jew, Jew, Jew!'

As the blows thudded into her, Katya's only thought was to protect Gretchen, who was quivering against her. Ducking her head, she managed to push out of the circle and stumbled away. One of the men succeeded in landing a heavy kick to her buttocks. It hurt like hell, but set her attackers roaring with contemptuous laughter, and thankfully, they were content with that, and did not pursue her.

Shaken, they limped on, bruised and starting to ache. But through her shock, Katya knew that they had got off lightly. Violence against foreigners was becoming a daily occurrence in this once gracious and relaxed city, as the tide of Nazism rose inexorably. The rain of swastika flags had produced a kind of mass hysteria.

And before they could reach Lorenz and the car, the cheering all around them became frenzied. The road they had reached was blocked with people. Rumbling along the road was a convoy of military vehicles. German military vehicles. Armoured cars and motorcycles, bearing the cross of the Wehrmacht and flying the swastika, spewing a dark cloud of diesel into the sunshine.

From the top of one of the vehicles, an officer was addressing the crowd through a megaphone.

'The Führer has entered Austria,' the metallic voice proclaimed. 'He has crossed the border at his birthplace, Braunau-am-Inn. The Führer has entered Austria!'

The iron voice was borne away on the growl of engines and the cheering of the crowd. A forest of waving arms and fluttering flags rose up. Katya and Gretchen were carried into the street on the surge of people around them. Excited boys ran alongside the armoured cars. Women were screaming in excitement.

Katya managed to find refuge in the doorway of a shop. Nursing their bruises, they watched the convoy of Nazi war machines. It looked like a giant iron python that was swallowing Austria, inch by inch.

So Hitler had set foot in his homeland. And it was here at last, this thing they had dreaded – the *Anschluss*, the incorporation of Austria into the Third Reich, against all law, crushing all opposition.

War, as Sigmund Freud and others had warned, could not be far behind.

And she, born in Russia, but with a British passport, would soon find herself the prisoner of an enemy state. Today, she had got off lightly. Tomorrow would be different. If she had any sense, she would hurry to the railway station now, and buy a ticket on the first train back to London, before the guns began firing.

The streets of Vienna were crowded as they drove back to the house in the Mercedes, making their progress slow. There was a hysterical carnival atmosphere, with people cheering and waving flags at the roadside.

Lorenz, too, had seen the bombers. He had been talking to people in the square. 'The schools will be shut next week,' he said, edging the big car carefully through the traffic. 'Most businesses will be shut too. They've told everyone to line the streets for the Führer's parade. They want a big show for the newsreels.'

'And so everyone will tamely obey?'

'The children are delighted to have a holiday off school. They'd cheer for the Devil himself. As for the adults—' Lorenz shrugged. 'Half of them are Nazis and the other half are too frightened to say anything.' He glanced at her in the rear-view mirror. 'Are you all right, Fräulein Gretchen?'

'I'm all right,' Gretchen said quietly.

'We ran into a bit of trouble,' Katya said. 'Some people wanted us to carry a swastika. We refused.'

'You were very brave,' Lorenz said, plainly meaning *stupid* rather than *brave*. 'Did they hurt you?'

'We both got a few kicks and punches.'

Lorenz winced and muttered a curse under his breath. 'Everyone is going crazy. You should think about going back to London, Fräulein Katya.'

'Thank God you're back,' Thor greeted her. He took her arms in his big hands and kissed her. 'I heard the news on the radio. Hitler has arrived in Austria.'

'Yes, preceded by half the Luftwaffe. You heard the bombers?'

He nodded. 'They landed at the airport in Vienna. As if they already own the country. Schuschnigg, the Chancellor, has announced his resignation on the radio. God knows what they'll do with him. The same as Dollfuss before him, I suppose. A bullet in the chest.' He poured drinks for them both. 'I was worried about you. Did you have any trouble in the town?'

Katya laughed shortly. 'Other than being beaten up in the street, no.'

Thor paled. 'What are you saying?'

She gulped at the whisky. 'I'm exaggerating. Some stupid Nazis got angry because we wouldn't wave their stupid flag.'

'Katya!'

'Don't be alarmed. I was extremely stupid. Gretchen was terrified. I should have just gone along with it, for her sake.' They could hear her playing Bach in the music room.

He examined her bruises. 'I'm going to call the doctor.'

'This whisky is all I need,' she replied, draining the glass and holding it out for a refill. 'I can't believe it's happening,' she said, draining the glass a second time. 'I never thought it would. I never heard anyone say they wanted it.'

'Of course not.' Thor sighed. 'Our circle is a very particular one. Cultured people, artists, intellectuals. None of those people want to live under Nazism. But there's an Austria you don't know, out in the countryside. People there are poor and less educated. They listen to agitators who tell them that joining the party is a heroic thing. That it's their duty to save Austria from the Jews and the communists. These are the young men who light swastika fires on the mountains, blow up bridges, beat up priests, commit senseless murders. And nobody has been able to stop them. They intimidate anyone who speaks against them, assassinate politicians who oppose them, and then evade punishment – because the courts are sympathetic to them, and let them walk free.'

'But everyone said that was a phase that would come to an end, sooner or later.'

'I'm afraid that hoping evil will go away is futile.' His eyes were dark. 'While the intellectuals have been predicting that Nazism would collapse and fade away, it's just been gathering momentum. And while the politicians were talking, the Anschluss, far from being a matter for discussion, has come down like an avalanche.' He poured another whisky for each of them. 'You'll have to leave, my dear,' he said. And then he added, almost to himself, 'It's going to break my heart to lose you.'

She could see the pain in his face. 'I don't have to go,' she said quietly.

'Yes, you do,' he replied. 'I should never have insisted on your coming. I was selfish. You can't live under Nazi rule.'

'Perhaps not. But it was my decision to come to Vienna. And it'll be my decision if I choose to leave. I love you, Thor.'

'Don't let that cloud your vision,' he replied with unexpected sharpness. 'Hitler is a madman. Nobody can predict what he'll do. There may be war in a week.'

Katya smiled. 'I don't think things are that bad.'

'This time next year, the world will be at war,' he said. He looked so despondent that she leaned forward and touched his cheek.

'I don't want to leave Gretchen, Thor,' she said. In a softer voice, she went on, 'I don't want to leave *you*.'

He kissed her hand. 'We don't have much choice.'

They listened to the cascades of pure notes coming from Gretchen. 'We could all go to England together,' she suggested.

'This is my country. I won't let them chase me out of it.' He sighed. 'Anyway, my work is all here. If I left it behind, I would have to start with nothing, all over again. And there's Gretchen. Moving her to a whole new way of life might destroy all the good progress she's made with you.'

'But what if you're right about war coming?'

'If I am, then I'd be an enemy alien in England. And if you stay, you'll be an enemy alien here.' The telephone began to ring. 'That damned thing hasn't stopped all day,' he said wearily. 'The whole of Vienna is in a panic.' He picked it up and spoke briefly. 'That was Lehár's wife, Sophie,' he reported, replacing the receiver. 'They're all meeting at their apartment tonight to discuss the situation. We'll go after supper.'

During their subdued meal, they could hear the constant, vibrating drone of German aircraft circling Vienna. A point was being made, and it was difficult to ignore.

Frau Hackl served the meal, as always, but suddenly Thor put down his knife and fork with a clatter.

'What are you wearing, Elise?' he demanded.

The woman drew herself up stiffly and squared her thin shoulders. 'You can see very well what I am wearing, Herr Bachmann.'

With a sense of shock, Katya's eyes landed on the enamelled swastika brooch that gleamed on the breast of the housekeeper's starched white apron.

'I won't have that symbol in my house,' Thor said shortly. 'Take it off.'

A flush touched Frau Hackl's bony cheeks. 'I will not take it off. I am proud to wear it.'

'I didn't expect this of you, Elise,' Thor said. 'You've been with me for five years. I thought you were a loyal Austrian.'

'Perhaps more loyal than some who consider themselves so high and mighty,' she retorted.

Thor's thick eyebrows lowered. 'That's impertinent. If you insist on wearing that thing, then you may as well look for employment elsewhere.'

'I would not wish to work in a house where the swastika is not welcomed.' There was a malicious gleam in her eye. 'I have heard things spoken in this house that would be very dangerous for the speakers, if they were repeated in certain quarters.'

'Are you threatening me?' Thor demanded angrily.

'You may take it as you please. Wait and see.'

Thor got to his feet, looking like an angry bear. 'Please leave the house at once.'

The woman unfastened her apron briskly and dropped it with heavy symbolism on the floor. 'I bid you farewell, Herr Bachmann – you and your child, and your foreign woman.'

She said the last words with a hard stare at Katya. Gretchen watched open-mouthed as Frau Hackl stalked out. She got up and hugged her father. 'I'm sorry, Papa.'

'There will be more of this sort of thing, my darling. Much more. Now that we know what Elise is, it's good that she's no longer in the house.'

'Can she really cause trouble for us?'

He shrugged. 'What can she do? Tattletale to the Gestapo? Let's not even think about her any more.'

But Katya could tell that he was angry and upset.

None of them had much appetite after that, so putting on warm coats – the night was bitterly cold – the three of them got in the Mercedes-Benz to go to Franz and Sophie's apartment. The night sky was still loud with German aircraft, their engines reverberating like portending thunder. Lorenz the chauffeur was off duty, so Thor drove.

But getting into Vienna did not prove easy. Traffic on all the roads was heavy. The Lehárs' apartment was in the city, not far from the Opera House. Approaching the centre of Vienna, the streets were lined with crowds of people singing, waving banners and shouting Nazi slogans.

Gretchen looked out of the windows anxiously. The people this morning had been bad enough. It was now something worse, something far darker and more dangerous. Almost every man was wearing a crooked-cross armband. Where had all these thousands of armbands come from? Up to yesterday, you rarely saw them. Now they were everywhere. Perhaps they had come the same way as the flags, dropped from the sky?

Soon, the street was jammed. Progress was almost impossible. Thor edged forward, sounding the horn. But the horn was no use. They were swallowed in the chanting of the mob as figures swarmed around the car. There were thuds as fists pounded the bodywork and boots kicked the doors. Gretchen was rigid with terror. Fearful that the windshield would be smashed at any moment, she and Katya clung together.

Many of the men were carrying flaming torches, as though ready to burn Vienna to the ground. Their faces glistened with sweat, despite the cold night air, and their faces were distorted with rage. There was a demonic quality to this demonstration, a feeling that something bestial had been unleashed, something that had been pent-up in these men for a lifetime.

Menacing faces pressed against the glass, screaming insults and accusations at them. With a curse, Thor was forced to stop the car. Immediately, a youth clambered on to the bonnet of the Mercedes and stood up, stamping on the metal and waving a swastika banner.

Faces full of fury pressed at the window. Their possession of an expensive motor car was enough to make them hated. A man rattled at the locked door and screamed at them. They heard his voice through the glass: 'Jew bloodsuckers! Running away? Come out and get what's coming to you!'

'Come out,' the mob began chanting, rocking the car. 'Come out, come out!'

'Hold tight,' Thor muttered to Katya. He switched off the engine and opened his door.

'Papa, no!' Gretchen called. But he was pushing his way out against the press of bodies. There was a roar from the mob as he confronted them. A wave of hatred filled the car for a moment, the oily smoke of the torches, the acrid sweat of the men. Then the door slammed shut.

They saw Thor raise his arm in the Nazi salute. At once, dozens of arms shot up in response. He addressed the crowd in his deep, booming voice, though Katya couldn't make out the words. He spoke for a minute or so, and it appeared to have some effect, because the mob quietened. Perhaps his sheer size and presence were having an effect. The young man on the bonnet of the car clambered down and handed Thor the swastika banner he had been waving.

Thor got back into the car and started the engine again. Now, when he edged forward, the crowd made way, though many faces were sullen, and the pounding on the car continued.

'What did you say?' Katya asked in a shaky voice.

'To tell you the truth,' he replied hoarsely, 'I don't really remember. Just "Heil Hitler" and that we were Nazis on our way to an important meeting. They didn't all believe me.'

Taking their cue, Gretchen and Katya held the flag to the window so everyone could see it. But they could see the suspicion on the faces that glared in at them.

The wide street in front of the Opera House was milling with gangs, their torches flaring in the cold wind. Gretchen saw that a car had been stopped by the mob. The marchers pulled open its doors and hauled its passengers out.

'Don't look, Gretchen,' Papa said tersely. But it was too late; she saw dark figures close in, beating their victims to the ground with fists and clubs, then kicking the prostrate bodies. Elsewhere along the street, other knots of attackers had formed around other victims, dealing out savage beatings.

Katya pulled Gretchen to her chest and tried to cover her eyes. The majestic bulk of the Opera House – where she and Thor had watched Bruno Walter conduct Mozart's *The Magic Flute* and Puccini's *Tosca* – looked down indifferently on the scene, its ornate facade fitfully lit by the torches. It was as though the gates of hell had been opened.

They managed to find a dark and quiet side street to park the car. 'I hope it'll still be there when we get back,' Thor commented as they hurried towards the Lehárs' apartment.

A group of about a dozen people had gathered in the opulent salon there, huddled around Lehár's piano, at which the composer sat, occasionally fingering a few absent notes on the keys. Katya had the impression of passengers on a sinking ship, the *Titanic* perhaps, waiting for the end. The discussion was about what to do next, and had as its counterpoint the distant shouts of *Sieg Heil, Sieg Heil, Sieg Heil* from the mob in the square.

'We're getting out tomorrow,' a woman said, speaking for herself and her husband. 'We managed to get on a flight to Paris. But we're leaving everything behind. Our art collection! My furs!'

'The flights to Switzerland are all full,' another woman said, her voice tearful. 'We've been trying to get tickets all day.'

'At least the borders are still open,' someone else said. 'We've heard they'll be shut in a matter of days. We could drive through in our cars. If we're going to leave, now is the time – before it's too late.'

'Why the hell should we run away?' Thor demanded impatiently. 'It's the Germans who are foreigners here, not us. We're Austrians. This is *our* country. None of us are guilty of anything.'

'You don't have to be guilty of anything,' Lehár said tiredly. 'You know that, Thor. It's enough to have the wrong name, or look different, or smell different.'

'They'll come for us all, soon,' a man with a despairing face said. 'They'll dig up a Jewish great-grandparent, or remember something we said about Hitler.'

'I've never said a thing against Hitler,' a nervous-looking man ventured.

Thor grunted. 'There's no safety in not having said anything against the Nazis. The crime is in not having joined them.'

'Then it'll be a concentration camp,' the despairing man said. 'Or a firing squad.' He put his face in his hands.

'Calm down, Ernst,' Thor said, putting his hand on the man's shoulder. 'There's no point in giving up yet. We have to fight back.'

'What with?' Sophie demanded.

'Well, I, for one, have my old army revolver at home. I should have brought it with me tonight. I would have used it.'

'Thank God you didn't,' Katya said, alarmed by this line of talk. 'You might have killed someone, Thor, and that would have been the end of us all.'

'We've stood by for years while they bullied us and murdered our statesmen,' Thor said angrily. 'We sheltered behind Mussolini, until he decided to throw his lot in with Hitler. Now we're alone. It's our refusal to stand up for ourselves that's led us to this situation. It's not too late to show some courage and fight back!'

'It's far too late,' Lehár said in a quiet voice. 'Austria is done for. Katya's right. You and your revolver are not going to stop Hitler's Panzers. You will only get us killed.'

'I wish I could get my hands around Hitler's throat,' Thor said, crooking his massive fingers. 'I'd choke the life out of him.'

'Thor the Thunderer.' The ironic comment came from Ludwig Jansen, a successful writer of romances, who was as usual impeccably dressed, with a carnation in his buttonhole. 'I think you're quite mad to take that tone. And you're no better, Lehár. We have nothing to fear from the new regime. I have personal assurances on that.'

'From whom?'

Jansen preened himself. 'I have contacts in the highest quarters. The very highest quarters.'

'That's all well and good for *you*,' the despairing man said. 'We don't enjoy such prestige. *Our* lives hang by a thread.'

'That is mere hysteria,' Jansen said airily. 'I have assurances – from the very top – that Nazism will be applied in the most liberal form here in Austria. There won't even be any measures against the Jews. So you and your Semitic grandmother are quite safe.'

'Nonsense,' Thor said impatiently. 'That's the propaganda they put out. If anything, it'll be worse here than in Germany.'

'We saw people being attacked in front of the Opera House,' Katya said. 'Just ordinary people, dragged out of their cars and beaten up. The mob asked us if we were Jews. They would have beaten us up too, if we hadn't pretended to be supporters.'

Jansen smiled. 'A few initial excesses are to be expected during any revolution. We should not exaggerate a little enthusiasm.'

'Enthusiasm!' Katya exclaimed. 'I'm sure some of those people were murdered in the street!'

Jansen rose, dusting off his perfectly pressed trousers. 'I'm afraid I cannot listen to any more of these preposterous, neurotic outpourings. Speaking for myself, I have no intention of either running away from my homeland, or resisting what is, after all, a perfectly natural unification of the German-speaking peoples.'

After he had left, someone asked gloomily, 'Do you think he's off to the Gestapo to denounce us all?'

'We're his friends. Don't worry about Jansen.'

'Maybe he's right?'

The discussion went on in brittle tones. Gretchen was huddled up under Katya's sheltering arm. Katya wondered what she made of all this. The things Gretchen had gone through today and this evening would be enough to terrify even the boldest of children. The best thing they could do for her was to get her out of Vienna – and preferably out of Austria altogether – as soon as possible.

Thor, infuriated by the day's events, was in a defiant mood, growling like an angry lion, still talking of fighting back against the Nazis. His height and energy filled the room, but Katya knew it was useless. The people here, artists and intellectuals, had no stomach for a fight, and in any case, they were no match for the thugs whose yells could be heard out in the night. One by one, they all declared their intentions to leave Austria as soon as possible, whatever Ludwig Jansen had said.

The meeting broke up in an atmosphere of gloom. Friends shook hands and embraced one another as though they were parting for the last time.

Chapter 12

On the way home, Thor pounded the steering wheel in frustration. 'Why are they so weak? Every time Hitler takes a step forward, the world takes a step back. That's how we've ended up in this mess.'

'They're afraid, Thor,' Katya said. 'And we should be, too. It's too late to talk about standing up to bullies. It's time to get out of Austria while we still can.'

'Would you leave England if fascism rose there?'

'You forget that I was born in Russia,' she said. 'We had to leave there when communism rose. If we hadn't, we'd all have been killed.'

Thor fell into a grim silence. The streets of Vienna were now quiet, although signs of the rioting were everywhere – smashed shop windows, wrecked cars, graffiti scrawled on the walls. An ominous silence had fallen over the city, like the entr'acte in a tragic opera.

When they reached home, they put Gretchen to bed and went to have a nightcap in Thor's study. He poured them each a glass of cognac, and they sat together on the leather sofa beside the fire.

'I hope you're a bit calmer now,' she said. 'I don't like to hear you raving about your revolver.'

'I can't face the idea of living as a slave, humiliated and powerless.'

'And that's why you need to leave Austria.'

'You talk about it as though nothing were easier,' he said bitterly.

'I know it's not easy for a man like you to give up. But you can't stay here to be killed.'

'I could take a few of them with me.'

'You're not a killer, Thor.'

'Are you so sure of that?' he snorted.

'I remember the first day we met here, in this room,' Katya said. 'You reminded me of a bear. A cave bear. The firelight was glowing red on your beard, just as it is now. You reached out to hug me. You were so big. I thought you were going to break all my bones. But your arms were so gentle. You held me as though I were made of porcelain. I think in that moment, I learned everything I needed to know about you.'

Despite himself, he smiled. 'You were a very angry woman.'

'Oh, I still am. I haven't forgiven you yet, believe me.'

'You were absolutely determined to go back to England then. And now, at last, I want you to go. You should be glad.'

'How can I leave without you and Gretchen? You can't ask that of me.'

Thor glanced at her. 'Do we really mean so much to you?'

'Don't I mean that much to *you*?'

He groaned. 'Yes. Yes, of course you do.'

'That day, you told me you'd brought me to Vienna on a whim. I was so furious when I heard that.'

'But I also told you that my whims were not superficial things.' He paused. 'The first time I saw you, in London, I felt something extraordinary happen in my heart.'

'Yes, you told me. Like when you first saw the coffee machine in Milan.'

He ignored her levity. 'I knew you hadn't noticed me. But I couldn't take my eyes off you. You were the only person in the room. What am I saying? At that moment, you were the only person in the world. I stared at you like a fool. My only thought was how I could get you to Vienna. I knew that if I lost you, I would never find anyone like you again.'

'And after that,' she said softly, 'you still ask me to go away now?'

'I can't allow you to stay.'

'I told you, Thor. Staying or leaving is my decision. Just as staying or leaving is your decision.'

'Time is running out.'

'Then we shouldn't lose any more of it,' Katya replied. She put her hand on his. 'There may not be a tomorrow. But we have tonight.'

As they went upstairs to the bedroom together, Katya was thoughtful. If she told him she was leaving Vienna, wouldn't he follow her? Then there would be no more talk of revolvers and strangling Hitler; and they would be safe, whatever happened.

As if to underscore her thoughts, the drone of German bombers had begun again. They were circling Vienna in squadrons, as though trying to cow the city into submission. The threat of their bombs was all too obvious.

Gretchen lay in her bed, listening to their growling. The squadrons were like lions prowling around a tent. It would take so little for them to rip the tent open with their claws and sink their teeth into the people inside. It was warm and cosy in bed. But the illusion of safety was paper-thin.

The next day, Gretchen was due to see Dr Asperger at the paediatric clinic. Katya was hesitant about keeping the appointment, but Lorenz, who had come in that morning, assured her that the city was now quiet, and she wanted some clarity from Asperger. She decided to go after all.

There was a new nurse in the consulting room where they saw Dr Asperger, a rather stern-looking young woman with sharp blue eyes. Knowing that Gretchen wouldn't like the change, Katya asked, 'Where is Sister Rosenbaum?'

'Fräulein Rosenbaum is no longer on the ward,' Asperger replied. 'She has been demoted to orderly.'

Sister Rosenbaum had been a warm, talented nurse, with whom Gretchen had formed a bond, and the news was not welcome. 'I'm very sorry to hear that,' Katya said.

'There's no reason to be sorry. Fräulein Rosenbaum is a Jewess.'

Katya was taken aback. 'And she was demoted because of that?'

'It is now our policy to restrict contact between Aryan patients and Jewish staff. To avoid any contamination.'

'Contamination?'

'Jews are known to harbour lice and infectious diseases.'

'Sister Rosenbaum did not have lice!'

'There is also the question of psychological contamination. Jewish ideas may be extremely harmful to children.'

Katya raised her eyebrows. 'In what way?'

Asperger made a gesture, dismissing the question. 'There will be many changes here,' he replied. 'We will soon have a new regime in Austria, and it will enable us to free ourselves from many undesirable elements here at the clinic.'

'But—'

'We aim to achieve a state of having no Jewish staff with us at all.' He announced this with genuine pride. 'No Jewish doctors, no

Jewish nurses. The clinic will be completely Aryan.' He indicated the new nurse. 'This is Sister Gruber.'

Katya hesitated. This was horrible. Should she walk out now, and take Gretchen with her? But if she did, who else would offer treatment? She accepted the other woman's brisk handshake and turned back to the doctor. 'It will take Gretchen some time to get used to the change.' She couldn't help adding, 'I've heard your opinions, but I didn't think you were such a committed Nazi.'

Asperger frowned. He touched Katya's arm. 'Come. Let's begin the session.'

Katya took the hard wooden chair beside Asperger. The new 'Aryan' nurse started work with Gretchen at a low table, laying out a puzzle composed of wooden blocks of different colours and shapes.

'The essential question of National Socialism,' Asperger said, 'is one of racial hygiene. It is not enough to pursue advancement in the purely medical field. We must see everything in the context of the greater destiny of the German race. Polluted by communist and other Jewish influences, we allowed this vision to slip away from us. From now on, it will be foremost in our minds.'

Feeling depressed by these last few sentences, Katya made no reply. With a sinking heart, she could see that Gretchen didn't like the new nurse's clipped manner. She wasn't engaging with her at all. Tight-faced and pale, she struggled with the blocks, which soon turned from a game into an ordeal – an ordeal that she was failing. Instead of slotting them into the correct places, she had begun stacking them compulsively, the sort of activity she resorted to when stressed. The irritable comments of the nurse only made it worse.

Asperger watched in silence, occasionally making notes on the pad on his knee. Through the open door, Katya could see other children, inpatients of the clinic, in the next room, playing or working at desks. Some of the children were confined to small cages, probably for their own safety, although the sight was disturbing. She noticed for the first time that chalked in capital letters on the blackboard were the words *Wir Österreicher sind deutsch* – 'We Austrians are Germans'. It was yet another shock. She'd regarded the clinic as a haven of safety, illuminated by Asperger's brilliance, even if that brilliance was flawed. To see it welcoming the Anschluss with open arms in this way was alarming.

'No,' the nurse said sharply, knocking down Gretchen's stack of blocks with a clatter, 'that is *not* the way we do it.' Gretchen shrank back and hugged herself, her head bowed. Katya's protective instincts rose furiously. 'How dare you show violence to my child!'

Asperger rose. 'Fräulein Komarovsky, would you come with me to my office?'

Reluctant as she was to leave Gretchen to the new nurse's tender mercies, Katya followed Asperger to his office. She had been in this room before, but there was something new here, too: a coloured portrait of Adolf Hitler, displayed prominently over the desk.

Asperger gestured to a chair, but remained standing after Katya sat down, one hand in the pocket of his white coat, the other resting on his desk. 'I see that Gretchen has regressed still further,' he said, looking down at her.

'The past few days have been very difficult for her. The noise of the aeroplanes, the rioting – and she saw some ugly things. It's upset her a great deal. I hoped you would be able to get her back on track.'

'I am afraid to say that such regressions are a common feature of the condition,' he replied. 'Fräulein Komarovsky, it is time that we spoke frankly, without ambiguity. Gretchen's condition is not curable. She will always regress to an infantile stage.'

'But her piano playing is better than ever—'

'I understand that you regard her piano playing as an accomplishment. But I assure you that, with her condition, it is a mere trick.'

'It's *not* a trick, Dr Asperger.'

'A parrot may recite the poems of Goethe, but that does not mean it understands a word of them.'

Katya was dumbfounded by the cold way he spoke. 'I don't know why you're so negative.'

'She will never be able to work or support herself as a musician. She plays without feeling, without understanding the emotional content. She cannot even read the notes. The idea of her playing with an orchestra is laughable.'

'I think you're wrong,' Katya said, her voice tight with anger.

'You are not a German,' Asperger said crisply. 'As a foreigner – especially as a Russian – it may be difficult for you to understand. The important point with children such as these is that they must not be allowed to contaminate the rest of the German race.'

'Contaminate!'

He ignored the interruption. 'I spoke earlier of racial hygiene. This is where we must focus our attention from now on. Gretchen will never become a productive member of German society. That is a medical fact. She is incapable of forging those bonds with others that are so essential to a strong racial structure.'

'She is just different from other children,' she said.

'Yes. To put it bluntly, she is not only different – she is *inferior*. Incapable of being educated. She has no understanding of what is needed to connect to others. She will never learn to do so. And those who do not connect to others weaken our society.' He cocked his head on one side. 'She is entering puberty, not so?'

'What?'

'I note the development of breasts.'

It was true that two small bumps had appeared lately on Gretchen's chest. Katya nodded. 'Yes. But nothing else has happened yet.'

'No periods?'

'No.'

He nodded. 'Excellent. It is far better that the operation is performed before the onset of puberty.'

'What are you talking about?' Katya asked breathlessly.

He looked at her as though she were being wilfully obtuse. 'I am talking about sterilisation.'

'I can't believe you mean that,' she said, horrified.

'I have explained to you already that in girls, the syndrome is caused by the female hormones. And thus, the symptoms grow worse after puberty. Preventing puberty may be Gretchen's only hope of achieving normality.'

'It will also prevent her from being a mother, which you always tell me is the highest goal of any girl!'

'Yes – but what *kind* of mother, we may ask ourselves. The condition may be hereditary. Even if it is not, she is unfit to be a mother. And her condition is an undesirable trait that may cause untold damage in countless different ways. This is why I am recommending that the operation be performed as soon as possible. Usually, it involves the ligation of the fallopian tubes. However, in Gretchen's case I am recommending complete removal of the uterus and ovaries. Since the organs in question are still small and undeveloped, the operation is a simple one, and recovery is quick. There are no deleterious consequences.'

Katya rose to her feet and faced the man, clenching her fists. 'How dare you suggest such a thing? What kind of doctor are you?'

He frowned. 'Moderate your tone, if you please.'

She was at boiling point. 'I brought Gretchen to you to be helped! Not to be neutered like a stray dog!'

'I assure you, Fräulein, it is the merciful option. Sterilisation will enable her to continue her life almost completely unaffected. She will not even know what has been done to her.'

She was incredulous. 'Do you really imagine that I or her father would permit such a terrible thing?'

'You may have no choice.'

'You can't possibly force us to consent to this!'

He took off his glasses and polished them carefully. Without them, his face looked different, far less boyish. 'False sentimentality is of no use to us here. It will only endanger our people as a whole. If we insist on dragging along such defective material, we hinder the evolution of the race, without giving any benefit at all to the unteachable child. I must make a recommendation to my superiors about Gretchen. They will inform us of their decision.'

Katya felt her knees grow weak, her heart missing several beats. Asperger continued polishing his spectacles as though he had said nothing unusual. He held them up to the light to check for dust. Over his shoulder, the glowering face of the German Führer, Adolf Hitler, stared menacingly at Katya. She was bereft of words.

Sister Gruber came into the office. 'Forgive me, Herr Doktor – the child is crying for her mother. I can do nothing with her.'

Katya turned and ran blindly out of the office. She found Gretchen slumped over the little table, her face crumpled and wet with tears. She threw her arms around the child and clasped her tightly.

'It's all right, Liebchen,' she whispered, 'it's all right, it's all right.'

She and Thor sat together on the sofa in his study, holding each other. Katya's eyes were still wet with tears.

'He called her *defective material*,' she said. 'As though she weren't even human.'

Thor stroked her hair quietly. 'It's the way they've been talking in Germany since 1933,' he replied.

'How can a doctor talk like that, Thor?'

'It's the doctors who invented those ideas. They call it eugenics. The perfection of the race.'

'By sterilising children?'

'And adults.'

'They can't really take her away from us, can they?'

'Not yet. But things are changing, fast. Remember Ludwig Jansen from our meeting? Who had "contacts in the very highest quarters"? He was arrested early this morning. They found his body floating in the Danube two hours ago. He'd been shot. Sophie told me.'

'Oh, no. He was harmless!'

'He was an intellectual who talked too much. They've started arresting people like him. Jews, aristocrats, patriots, artists. Nobody knows what's going to happen to them. And almost everyone who was at the Lehárs' has already left Austria.'

She raised her head to stare at him. 'Thor, we can't stay either.'

'No,' he agreed sadly. 'We can't stay.'

'We have to leave tonight. All three of us. Now!'

'It's not that simple,' he said with a rueful smile. 'I have to tie things up here.'

'Thor, there's no time!'

'I can't just walk out of my life, my beloved. I have to shut down my business, close up the house, transfer money abroad so we can have something to live on. You and Gretchen will go on ahead. I'll join you as soon as possible, I promise.'

'No. I'm not leaving without you.'

'It's not safe for you. And it's not safe for Gretchen. I want you both to leave as soon as possible. Back to London. You'll go on the Orient Express, and I'll arrange a place for you to stay when you get there. It won't take me long to tie things up here. Trust me. In a week or two, I'll join you. A month, at most.'

'What if they arrest you!'

'They have no reason to arrest me.'

'They had no reason to arrest Ludwig Jansen!'

'I am not Ludwig Jansen,' he replied. 'I'm respected in Vienna. I have a position, money, connections.'

'In the highest quarters?'

He smiled. 'In the *right* quarters. Business quarters. Don't worry about me. I'll be fine.'

She could not shake him from this plan. Perhaps because he hadn't been at the clinic and hadn't actually witnessed Gretchen's doctor calmly talking about sterilising her, it hadn't quite come home to him. She had no option but to go along with it, and trust that he knew what he was doing.

An eerie calm settled over Vienna that evening. The German warplanes had stopped circling the city. The telephone, which had been ringing constantly for days, was now silent. The last call was from a friend who told them that their circle of acquaintances was melting away, as people hurriedly left the country. And a loud crackling on the line was evidence, Thor said, that German phone-tappers were now listening to all calls.

They went to bed to take comfort from each other. Their bed was a refuge where they could shut out all fear and doubt, and live only for one another, lost in their lovemaking. It was a golden bubble that enclosed them in joy. Nothing could touch them.

Until morning.

The next day, they went into town to book tickets on the Orient Express. The Wagons-Lits company office was at the railway station. The city was busy today, the streets teeming with hurrying people as usual, but with an atmosphere of great tension in the air. German military vehicles were everywhere, adding to the congestion, and emphasising the impression that Vienna was an occupied city. Katya noted that more and more buildings were sprouting swastika banners, as though a scarlet rash was spreading across the city. Shop windows carried photographs of Hitler. Katya was starting to loathe the glowering face, with its thick nose, glaring eyes and ridiculous little moustache.

The square in front of the railway station had been blocked off, so Lorenz dropped them a few blocks away, and they walked.

Outside the entrance of the station, a crowd had gathered, blocking the way in. As they made their way through the throng, they came to the spectacle that had attracted so much attention: a group of civilians were on their knees, scrubbing the pavement with pails and brushes. All were well-dressed, middle-class people, some quite elderly. Standing over them was a pair of SA men – Nazi stormtroopers – with their thumbs in their belts and grins on their faces.

As Katya and Thor took in the scene, one of the SA men swung his boot and kicked over a pail. The dirty water splashed the only woman in the group, who recoiled, wiping her face. The SA man bent down and screamed in her ear, 'Get back to work, you fat sow!'

Thor started forward with his fists clenched. Instinctively, Katya grabbed his arm in both hands and restrained him. 'No!' she commanded, fighting against his strength.

'They're only Jews,' one of the bystanders said to them laconically. 'It's about time someone dealt with them.' He pointed to an old man with a hat and a long grey beard. 'They say that one's a rabbi. Have you ever seen anything so funny?'

Katya felt sick to her stomach. The display had been arranged for no other purpose than to inflict humiliation on decent people. She could feel Thor vibrating with anger, and prayed he wouldn't try to intercede. Disgusting as this was, there was no sense in trying to come between the SA men, who wore pistols on their belts, and their defenceless prey.

She looked at the people around the circle. The expressions on the faces of the onlookers were neither exultant nor compassionate. They looked like the idlers who gathered at a traffic accident, or to stare at a carthorse that had died in its harness. People at the back were craning their necks for a better view, or hoisting children on their shoulders. By and large, there was silence. Perhaps it was the presence of the stormtroopers that quelled ordinary people. Or perhaps they simply didn't feel anything except curiosity.

The woman who had been splashed with dirty water was crying as she worked. Her shopping bag was beside her. She had obviously been out to buy groceries when these thugs had waylaid her, discovered she was Jewish, and forced her to get on her knees in the filth of the pavement. Katya saw her pale, smooth hands reddening with the lye in the water.

A young man wearing a smart trench coat with a swastika armband stalked around the kneeling woman. Obviously the Nazi party official in charge of this event, he pointed with his highly polished shoes at real or imaginary marks on the pavement. 'There,' he said in a sharp voice. 'And there. Can you not use your eyes? You will keep scrubbing until it is spotless.'

'May I ask what, exactly, she is supposed to be cleaning?' Thor asked in a voice bitter with irony.

Katya's heart sank as the party official turned to look at them with his pale grey eyes. 'Antisocial elements have painted slogans on the pavement. They must be removed.'

'Not everyone wanted the Anschluss. But it seems the Jews are bearing the brunt. By what authority have you forced these good citizens into the task?'

The young man – he could not have been more than twenty-two or twenty-three – frowned. 'By the authority of the National Socialist Party.'

'I'm sorry, I don't recognise that authority.' Before Katya could stop him, he had walked forward and helped the crying woman to her feet. 'Go home, Madam,' he said quietly. Sobbing, she picked up her shopping and stumbled away. The Nazi official and the stormtroopers seemed completely taken by surprise. A couple of them stepped forward, but they didn't try to stop her, and the crowd parted to let her through.

Katya felt that she was frozen with fear. Then suddenly, like a wave of heat, she felt shame – shame at being a bystander, like everyone else, shame at doing nothing. A kind of madness surged through her, melting the ice that imprisoned her. She'd had enough of the fear, the bullying, the threats. She walked up to the elderly man who was said to be a rabbi, and helped him to his feet. Taking out her handkerchief, she tried to wipe the dirt off his hands. 'I'm sorry they did this to you,' she said. He looked dazed, as though unaware of his surroundings. She guided him away, and again the crowd parted to let them through. People stared, but nobody tried to interfere. The party official was standing immobile, his eyes fixed on them.

'You should be ashamed of yourselves,' Thor snapped at the onlookers. He took Katya's arm. 'Come,' he commanded.

They pushed through the gathering and made their way into the railway station, walking as quickly as they could. At any moment, Katya expected to hear the SA men behind them.

'Did we get away with that?' Katya asked.

'I think so – this time,' he replied. 'They're still not sure of themselves. That will change, as their grip tightens. Vienna is becoming a madhouse.'

But the Wagons-Lits travel office was jammed with angry, shouting, would-be travellers – and there were no seats to be had on the luxury train, either going west back to England, or east, towards Prague and Istanbul.

'All booked up,' the clerk shouted, standing on his chair to rise above the hubbub. 'No tickets for this week! No tickets!'

'All the trains are full,' one of the passengers said despairingly, 'not just the Wagons-Lits. Mitropa, Belmond, all of them. It's hopeless.'

The harassed clerks shepherded everyone out of the office, closing and barring the doors after them.

Katya turned to Thor with a wry smile. 'It seems I'm staying.'

'I'll ask Lorenz to drive you and Gretchen to Budapest.'

'Without you?'

'It may be the only choice,' he replied.

'It's not my choice.'

They walked back towards the car, arguing. Looking over her shoulder, Katya noticed the young Nazi official and the two SA thugs behind them. Her heart gave a painful jolt. She said nothing to Thor. But after a few minutes of walking along with her heart in her mouth, Katya couldn't help taking another look back. The three men were still following them, moving with the air of wolves pursuing their prey.

'Those Nazis,' she whispered. 'They're following us.'

Thor stopped abruptly and turned to face them. 'Well, gentlemen? What do you want?'

The young official put his fists on his hips. 'Your names?'

'As I have already told you, I do not recognise your authority. I decline to give you our names.'

'We will find it out, don't worry,' the young Nazi said.

'Is that a threat?'

The youth's eyes narrowed as he looked from Thor to Katya. 'It is a promise. And we will pay you a visit.'

Thor laughed. 'Don't try to frighten me. I was fighting in the Great War while you were still messing your nappies.'

Thor's laughter angered the boy, who stepped forward, tight-lipped. But when he glanced at the SA men on either side of him, he saw that they had remained where they were standing, evidently wary of Thor's size and bearing. His face reddened, and he didn't come any closer.

Thor laughed again. 'Go home. And grow up.'

The three men made no further attempt to follow them. But Katya turned to Thor, frowning. 'You have to stop doing that.'

'Doing what?'

'Provoking these people.'

'Are we supposed to stand by and watch them abuse women and old men?'

'They shot Ludwig Jansen for no reason, Thor. You've got to be careful. You have Gretchen to think of. And me.'

'You're right, you're right,' he said contritely after a few minutes. 'I'll be sensible, I promise.'

Chapter 13

That evening, Sigmund and Anna Freud came to the house with a request for help. Both looked very shaken, Freud even thinner and frailer than before, and Anna with dark shadows around her eyes.

'Anna was arrested by the SS today,' Freud told them without preamble.

'Oh no,' Katya exclaimed, covering her mouth with her hand.

'They marched into our house this morning,' Anna said, 'and took me to the Hotel Metropole, which the Gestapo have made their headquarters. They interrogated me with a lot of stupid questions.' She patted her pocket grimly. 'I carry a lethal dose of veronal with me, hidden in my clothes. If they had taken me down to the torture chambers in the basement, I would have drunk it.'

Katya looked at Thor in shock. His face was grim. 'What happened?' he asked.

'I showed them some letters from people in high places. Thank God, that stopped them from ill-treating me – at least for now. After humiliating me and trying to frighten me, and keeping me there for hours, waiting, they sent me home.'

'I'm not ashamed to say that I burst into tears when she returned safely,' Freud said in a tremulous voice. 'I was certain I would never see her again. It was a dreadful day. From the window,

I could see our respectable neighbours looting Jewish shops and the gangs beating Jews on the street. One man was shot dead on the pavement outside our house.' He was trembling violently, his customary cigar wobbling in his skeletal fingers. 'While Anna was gone, the SS ransacked everything. They confiscated all my banking papers. And they have sequestered my publishing company. They've appointed a commissar, a Nazi, of course, to "run my business affairs". That, I presume, means to plunder me before my final destruction. The time has come for us to leave.'

'But we need help getting funds to England,' Anna said. 'With no control over our finances, we can do nothing.'

'Of course we'll help,' Thor said. 'Just let us know what we can do.'

Both Freuds were in a state of shock. After trying to ignore the threat of the Anschluss – as so many intellectual Viennese had been doing for months – the ghastly reality was like a hammer blow.

They recounted how Freud's house in Berggasse had been turned upside down by the SS, cupboards emptied, Freud's sisters roughly treated, his private papers seized. Freud and his family had been living under virtual siege, afraid to go out. They had got off lightly, but it was clear that deadly danger was hanging over them.

'We are told that Hitler himself loathes psychoanalysis and its principles,' Freud said tremulously. 'He regards it as "Jewish filth". They say he has ordered Himmler to arrest and kill all psychoanalysts – especially Jewish ones, of course. His aim is to exterminate psychoanalysis forever. Not only is my life under threat, but my life's work is facing extinction.'

There was clearly no time to waste. Freud was in the process of applying for visas for the members of his immediate family, but there was no guarantee that these would be granted. And there was still a nightmare of bureaucracy and expense to be gone through.

Freud still did not have the papers he required, including a certificate that he had paid all his taxes, documents certifying that – as a Jew – the police had no reasons for detaining him, that he had completed all the necessary formalities, that he had left no debts to Aryans, and that he had paid the exit tax.

They discussed ways of getting money out of Austria for the Freuds to use, and finally decided that Thor would make a purchase of machinery from Switzerland, which would enable him to transfer funds abroad with the requisite paperwork. The machinery was non-existent, and the funds would be transferred to a bank account in London, and Thor would be repaid in Vienna.

'Austria is finished,' Freud said, refusing the offer of a brandy. The mouth cancer from which he suffered had grown worse, perhaps from the strain, and his voice was thin and faint. 'A history that began in the Holy Roman Empire is now no more. Among all the other sorrows, I grieve for our country. A cultured way of life is coming to an end at the hands of barbarians.'

Katya was filled with pity. After Freud and Anna had left, she turned to Thor. 'That poor old man! He looks so broken.'

Thor nodded. 'I don't know when we will see him again. He's right. A way of life is coming to an end.' He took her hand and led her to his study. 'This is for emergencies,' he said, giving her a thick envelope.

She opened it. It was filled with banknotes. 'Oh, Thor.'

'I took it out of the bank today. Keep it safe. You may need it.'

Katya was dreaming. It was really a memory that her mind was revisiting: skating with Thor in the great square in front of the City Hall, under that velvet sky, spread with diamond stars.

The feeling of that night was so strong, even in her dream, that it enveloped her in warmth and happiness. She drifted across the starry ice endlessly, turning and wheeling, free of all anxiety, lost in peace.

Then, without warning, the ice cracked beneath her skates, splitting open into a black crevasse. Her stomach lurched painfully as she fell into the darkness, limbs flailing against gravity.

Katya sat up in bed, gasping for air. The cracking of the ice had turned into pounding at the front door. The noise was shattering, echoing through the house. She groped for the light and switched it on. Thor was not in bed beside her. The bedside clock said it was four in the morning. The hammering was continuing.

She threw on her robe and hurried down the stairs into the hallway, just in time to see Thor open the front door. A group of a dozen or more men stood outside, most wearing the dreaded black uniforms of the SS. They pushed past Thor and filled the hall, weapons at the ready.

Their leader, an officer in a leather coat and a peaked cap, stalked in and looked around, pulling off his gloves. He had a thin face with a blade-like nose and close-set eyes. He spoke calmly, but his voice carried.

'Thorwald Bachmann. Margarete Bachmann. Katerina Komarovsky. Identify yourselves.'

Thor walked towards the man. 'What do you want with us?' he demanded.

The SS man turned to Thor. The silver skull and crossbones gleamed on the front of his cap. 'You are Thorwald Bachmann?'

'Yes. Who are you?'

'I am Obersturmführer Springer, Waffen-SS. You and the women will accompany us to headquarters immediately.'

'Miss Komarovsky is a foreign national,' he replied. 'And my daughter Margarete is only twelve. I repeat my question – what do you want with us?'

'You are wanted for questioning. Get dressed.'

'Are we being arrested?'

The officer glanced at his wristwatch. 'You have ten minutes to get dressed,' he said in a clipped voice. 'Or you will be taken out in your nightclothes.'

Katya took Thor's arm, afraid that his temper would get the better of him, and that he would say or do something rash. 'I'll get Gretchen,' she said quietly. Her eyes commanded him to stay calm. 'Put warm clothes on, Thor.'

She hurried back upstairs. Gretchen had been awoken by the noise, and was out of bed, trembling and pale. Katya herself felt oddly calm, almost detached, as though she had somehow expected this. She tried to hold on to the warm feeling of her dream as she soothed Gretchen and helped her get ready to go out.

'They're going to ask a lot of questions,' she whispered, pulling on Gretchen's warmest coat. 'Don't be frightened. Just tell them you don't know anything, you don't understand anything. All right?'

Gretchen nodded, her eyes huge.

'Good girl.' She kissed Gretchen's soft cheek. 'And if you get sad, listen to music in your mind.'

They were driven to the Hotel Metropole in the same car. Gretchen huddled in Katya's arms all the way, her silky hair brushing Katya's face. But to Katya's dismay, on arrival at the back entrance, they were all split up and handed over separately to the Gestapo, men in one group, women in another, children in a third group. Seeing

Gretchen's slight figure being hustled away among a gaggle of crying boys and girls almost destroyed Katya's determination not to break down. She had to fight back the tears. She saw the same anguish on Thor's face, as he was taken off in a different direction. Their eyes met for a moment. Then he was gone.

She herself was taken to a crowded waiting room. There were at least three dozen people of all ages already there, all standing, because there were no chairs. A silence hung over the room, enforced by the guards, who carried machine pistols slung at the ready. The window shades were drawn, so there was no view of the outside. The air in the room was already foul, and the doors were kept shut.

The Metropole was a huge neoclassical hotel, overlooking the river. The Nazi secret police had settled in with astonishing swiftness to make it their regional headquarters, like a colony of vampires who had flown across the border overnight. Down in the basement, it was whispered, people were tortured and shot.

The people around her looked for the most part wretched, sick with fear, some with blood on their faces or dishevelled clothes, suggesting they'd been roughed up during arrest. Katya's stomach was churning, threatening at any moment to make her vomit. She was terrified – more for Thor and for Gretchen than for herself. She kept trying to convince herself that even the Gestapo wouldn't hurt a twelve-year-old child. She could only pray that they would be gentle with her, and that she would be released as soon as they saw how innocent she was. She must be so frightened, so confused. Katya had to fight down the impulse to jump up and run through the building, looking for her. She could only hope that the children were being looked after somewhere. Gretchen's fragility would not withstand too much pressure.

And Thor – what if he lost his temper, and told them what he thought about the Nazis? The consequences didn't bear thinking of. His opinions would be a death sentence in the Vienna of today. *Please God*, she thought, *let him keep calm*.

The first hour passed swiftly. The second dragged more slowly. The third was torment. The morning had only just begun; it was not even eight o'clock yet. They were forbidden to sit on the floor. Most of the people in the room must have been there all night, she realised. Perhaps since yesterday. Her own legs were starting to grow weary.

The waiting, she realised, was part of the softening-up process. The longer you waited, the more fear and guilt preyed on your mind. You started to think about everything you had said and done over the past weeks, restlessly wondering where you'd gone wrong, who might have reported you, what you might have to answer for.

And then your mind turned to what they would do to you. The Gestapo's reputation for cruelty was fearsome. They tore out fingernails, people said, beat you with rubber truncheons, gave you agonising electric shocks. Perhaps it was even worse to be innocent, for then you had nothing to confess, nothing to stop the torture. You would end up admitting every crime in the book, just to make it stop. And then they could do what they wanted with you.

More and more people were herded into the waiting room as the morning crawled by. Now and then, someone's name was called, and a shrinking figure would be hustled out. The door would be slammed shut again. The rest was endless waiting.

The noise of the city filtered in through the shuttered windows. It grew steadily louder, a rumble of traffic, punctuated by blaring megaphones and wailing sirens. Then all the bells of all the churches began to toll, the brass voices blending into a medieval cacophony that was half-rejoicing, half-moan. Through the racket, they could hear marching bands, and the constant leitmotif of *Sieg Heil, Sieg Heil, Sieg Heil*, chanted in unison by thousands of voices.

It swelled and faded like a storm. It was evident that Hitler had arrived in Vienna.

Midday came and went. Katya was beginning to feel dizzy with the continued stress. She had been in this airless room for eight hours now, thirsty and afraid. Her legs were aching, her feet starting to swell and grow numb. People close enough were leaning against the walls, and there was no space. She was dying to go to the lavatory, but the guards refused to let anyone leave the room. A dank smell of urine indicated that at least one person hadn't been able to endure.

The door opened and the guards brought in a well-dressed woman of around thirty. Katya caught her eyes in a moment of recognition. It was Winifred Brownlow, the secretary she'd travelled with on the Orient Express last year. She made her way through the crowd to stand beside Katya.

'It's Katya Komarovsky, isn't it?' she whispered, looking straight ahead.

'Yes,' Katya muttered back. 'I'm so glad to see you, Winnie.'

'Likewise. What are you here for?'

'I don't know. They came at four in the morning and dragged us all down here, including our little girl. And you?'

'Turns out my boss is a Jew. His parents converted before he was born, and he was raised Catholic. But that doesn't matter. He's a Jew according to the Nuremberg Laws.'

'What will happen to him?'

'They're confiscating all his assets. He'll probably be sent to a concentration camp.'

'I'm so sorry.'

'I don't care about *him*. He never told me he was a Jew before he made me his mistress, the bastard. Now the Gestapo are after *me*.' Winnie sounded furious. Katya didn't remind Winnie that

166

on the Orient Express Winnie had said her boss was *absolutely wonderful*. 'I just want to get out of this in one piece,' Winnie went on, 'and get back to England. I'll say anything they want me to.' She gave Katya a sidelong glance. 'You should do the same. Sounds like you're in the same boat as me. I take it you're Bachmann's mistress?'

Katya didn't want to talk about that. 'We heard the noise from outside. Has Hitler arrived?'

'Yes. He's making a big speech in the Heldenplatz. He's going to officially announce the Anschluss.' She jerked her head at the people around them. 'That's why they've rounded up so many suspects. In case someone takes a pot shot at him.' Surreptitiously, Winnie grasped Katya's hand. 'Listen, Katya,' she hissed, 'don't let sentimentality get the better of you. If Bachmann's in trouble, dump him fast. Tell the Gestapo you'll sign anything against him. Anything they want. Or you'll go down with the ship. Get it?'

Before Katya could reply, a Gestapo guard shouted, 'Komarovsky! Identify yourself!'

'I'm here,' Katya called.

'Remember what I said,' Winnie whispered as Katya stirred her aching legs into motion. 'He'd do the same to you!'

The children were lined up along the corridor. You had to stand with your shoulders pressed against the wall and look straight ahead. If you slumped because your back was sore, the nurses would dig a pencil into your chest, or take your chin in their fingers and pull you up again.

The SS doctor was walking down the line, pausing at every child to ask questions and take notes. Gretchen called him that in her mind because he was wearing a long white coat like the doctors at the clinic, but he had the SS lightning flashes embroidered on his pocket. He had grey hair and a kind face and a quiet, gentle voice, so quiet and so gentle that you couldn't hear what he was saying to each child. Sometimes he patted the children on the cheek, however, as though he was pleased with them. She prayed that she would get a pat on the cheek.

He was coming closer, but she dared not turn her head to look at him. Her heart beat faster as he approached. He was two children away from her now.

'This boy has high Aryan racial values,' she heard him say. 'Category A.'

'Yes, Herr Doktor.'

There was a rustle of paper.

The doctor moved to the boy next to Gretchen. She heard him sigh. 'Jakob Adler. Clearly Semitic. Nothing to be done here, I'm afraid.' He patted the boy's cheek with a smile. 'Category D.'

'Yes, Herr Doktor.' The nurse pinned a card to the boy's shirt.

Now he was standing in front of Gretchen. He was tall, and he emanated a smell of menthol from the sweet he was sucking. He looked down at her with his mild eyes. 'Margarete Bachmann.'

'We have a note about this one, Herr Doktor.'

'Let me see.'

The nurse handed him a piece of paper. He read it carefully. Gretchen's eyes were fixed on the two black lightning bolts sewn to his pocket. She couldn't look away from them. She was trembling.

'You are Dr Asperger's patient?' he asked her.

Gretchen couldn't answer. Her tongue was frozen to the roof of her mouth. All she could see were the two black Ss on the white cotton. They were writhing like slow snakes.

He bent down to look into her eyes. He had a lined face with a small mouth and little pouches under his eyes. 'Don't be frightened,' he said. 'There's nothing to be afraid of. Can you recite the alphabet for me, Gretchen?'

She couldn't make a sound.

'You can't recite the alphabet? What if I give you a start? A, B, C, D. What comes next?'

Gretchen shook her head infinitesimally. 'I don't know.'

'You don't know? What about your five times table? Can you recite that for me?'

'No,' she whispered.

'Five times two is—?'

'I don't know.'

'This is very sad, Gretchen,' the SS doctor said, as if it really grieved him. 'A girl of your age should know the alphabet and the multiplication tables. It seems our Dr Asperger is right in his diagnosis. An organic problem. Plainly subnormal. Category C.'

'Yes, Herr Doktor.' The nurse pinned the card to Gretchen's coat.

The SS doctor smiled warmly and patted Gretchen's cheek. 'Good girl.' He moved on to the next child.

Gretchen knew now what the pat on the cheek meant.

The interrogation room was small and dark. The curtains were drawn, and the only light came from a lamp on the desk, which shone directly and painfully into Katya's eyes. Behind the desk, four shadowy figures were seated. She couldn't see their faces; she could just make out that they wore uniforms, and that the desk was piled with folders and documents.

They let her stand in silence for a while, as though the interminable wait she'd already endured hadn't been enough. Then she saw a pair of hands move a folder into the light. It bore her own name, in full, and in the Russian format: Katerina Nikolaevna Komarovska. For some reason, that alarmed her. Even more disturbingly, when the hands – which were pale and hairy – opened the folder, it was thick with papers. Had the Gestapo been keeping a file on her all this time? What did it contain?

'You are Russian,' said a flat voice from behind the light, making it a statement, not a question.

'I hold a British passport,' she said, her voice husky with thirst. She waved her passport at them. 'If I am under arrest, I insist that you notify the British consulate immediately.'

'Give me the passport.'

'No! You have no right to take my passport!'

There was no acknowledgement to that. She knew that if she surrendered her passport to these thugs, she might never see it again. They would have to physically take it from her.

She saw the glow of a cigarette in the dark. 'You are Russian,' the same dead voice repeated. 'Why do you lie?'

'I was born in Russia. But my parents fled to England during the Revolution. We no longer have Russian citizenship. We are British subjects.'

'Why are you in Austria?'

'I'm employed as a governess.'

'By Thorwald Bachmann?'

'Yes.'

She caught the gleam of spectacles for a moment in the dark behind the dazzling light. 'Why did you not inform the police immediately of Bachmann's conspiracy against the Führer?'

She couldn't suppress a gasp. 'What conspiracy? That's not true!'

'Don't take us for fools,' a second voice rasped.

'There is no conspiracy!' She could hear her own voice rising, becoming panicky. 'If anyone told you that, they're lying!'

'Who are you accusing of lying?'

'Anyone who told you that there is a conspiracy.'

'And who might that be?'

'I don't know!' she retorted. But she was thinking of Frau Hackl's threat to report 'things spoken in this house' to 'certain quarters' when she had walked out. Had she carried out her threat? Mentioning her name would be tantamount to an admission that Thor was hostile to the Nazis.

'You must have someone in mind, if you make such an accusation,' the first voice replied calmly. 'Give us the names.'

'I don't know any names!'

There was a silence. Then she heard the rasping voice say, 'We must take this one downstairs. She's clever.'

Katya felt her legs grow weak. 'There is no conspiracy!'

The white, hairy hands reached into the light again and picked up a sheaf of papers. '"I will get my hands around Hitler's throat",' he read out. '"I will choke the life out of him." Were you not present when these words were spoken?'

With a squirm of fear, Katya thought of the evening at the Lehárs' apartment, when Thor had urged resistance. Someone there must have repeated Thor's angry remarks. Who? Perhaps Ludwig Jansen, the dapper writer, whose body had ended up in the river the next day. Perhaps before he had died, they had wrung information out of him? Or perhaps he'd felt it his duty to report any criticism of the Nazis?

'No,' she said. 'I never heard those words spoken.'

'"I have a revolver. I intend to use it to end Hitler's life." Did you not hear your employer use these words?'

'No,' she said automatically. 'I never heard him say anything like that.'

'Really?' The voice dripped with sarcastic disbelief. 'Or are you lying to protect the man whose bed you share?'

'I am not lying.' But her voice was shaking. 'Herr Bachmann never said any such thing.'

'Did you and your lover Bachmann not interfere in a public correction meted out to harmful elements by men of the SA?'

'If you mean, did we help an old man and a defenceless woman who were being made to scrub the street on their knees, then yes. That's true.' Katya straightened her back. 'That was not a crime. That was common human decency.'

'So you take it upon yourselves to decide who is an enemy of the state?'

'It was a man of ninety! And a housewife who was out doing her shopping!' Gathering strength, she went on, 'We heard that the Nazi Party took care of the elderly and the vulnerable. But you've separated me from the child I'm protecting. She's only twelve years old! I demand that you bring me to her!'

There was a short silence. Then the spectacles gleamed again as the man leaned forward. 'Do you know the punishment for treason? It is the guillotine. You will be strapped to a board and laid on your back, so that you can see the blade come down on your throat. That pretty head of yours will drop into a bucket. It makes a unique clang, I can assure you. And the blood spouts ten feet. But you will see and hear it all for yourself. Life remains in the severed head for fully five minutes. You will see the world from a new perspective.'

Another man leaned forward, the light just rimming his bony cheeks. 'You had better tell the truth, Komarovsky. Or it will be torn from you.'

'I've told the truth,' she said, feeling that she was going to faint.

'If you continue to lie, you will be taken down to the basement. You will be tortured. And for what? To protect a man who isn't even your husband? You will suffer unbearable pain. It will break your body and your mind. You will never be the same again. Is that what you want?'

'No.'

'Then talk. What else did Bachmann say?'

'He didn't say any of those things. He's a businessman. He's not violent in any way.'

'A little electricity will loosen her tongue,' one of the men said. 'We're wasting our time.'

'Thor didn't say any of those things,' Katya repeated, her voice almost failing her. 'Why don't you believe me?'

There was a curse and the scrape of a chair. A man came striding around the desk. His ugly face was stark with rage. He grasped her arms and shook her. Mama used to shake her when she was a child, but that was nothing compared to the brutality of this. The grip of his fingers was crushing, and the breath was knocked out of her by the violence of the attack. Her head snapped back and forth, her teeth rattling in her head. She felt herself bite her tongue, her mouth filling with blood. All thoughts were obliterated from her mind.

At last, he threw her against the wall. 'Stop wasting our time!' he bellowed into her face, and he stamped back into the darkness behind the desk.

Katya just managed to stay on her feet, but her head was spinning, and she retched with nausea, wiping the blood from her lips.

'Now,' the rasping voice said. 'Repeat word for word what Bachmann said about the Führer.'

'Nothing. Nothing.'

'What is Bachmann's exact relationship to the Jew Freud?' another voice barked.

Bewildered by the sudden change of tack, Katya shook her head. 'They are friends, that's all.'

'Friends! Bachmann appears to be very friendly with Jews!'

She didn't trust herself to make any kind of reply. Now the questions rained thick and fast, taking a different approach each

173

time. What was Thorwald Bachmann's net worth? With whom did he do business? Did he have financial dealings with Sigmund Freud? With other Jews? How much money was in his bank accounts? In whose name were his businesses registered? What did he import? What did he export?

She knew none of the answers to any of the questions, and could only repeat that she was completely ignorant, stumbling over her denials as though she was indeed guilty of some heinous crime.

At last, she broke down. 'I want to see Gretchen,' she sobbed. 'I want to see my girl. What have you done with her?'

With an exclamation of disgust, the man who had shaken her came forward again. She shrank from him. He grabbed her wrist and thrust his brutish face close to hers. 'Find the answers to these questions. You understand? Find them. You will hear from us again,' he promised. 'Next time, I warn you – if you waste our time, you will not be treated so leniently.' He dragged her to the door of the interrogation room and thrust her into the corridor.

Two Gestapo men hustled her back to the waiting room. Trying to control her tears, Katya stumbled through the crowd to her place. Winifred Brownlow was still there.

'God, you look a right mess,' Winifred muttered, passing Katya a handkerchief. 'You were in there for hours. Did they knock you around?'

'A little,' Katya replied wearily.

'They didn't touch me. I was done in fifteen minutes. Told them everything they wanted to know about old Strauss. They patted me on the head. They're after the money. I hope you told them what they wanted to know.'

'I couldn't tell them anything. I don't *know* anything. And even if I did, I wouldn't betray Thor!'

'Don't be a fool,' Winifred hissed. 'Didn't you hear what I said? Forget about your Thor. You have to look after Number One! Tell them what they want, and get out of this godforsaken country!'

Katya was too tired to argue. She closed her eyes and tried to recover her composure. Shortly after that, Winifred's name was called.

'That's it,' she said to Katya. 'I'm off. Remember what I said.'

She waited until late afternoon. Several people in the room fainted, or simply lay down on the floor, despite that being forbidden. The Gestapo guards ignored them. Katya refused to lie down. That would be a sign of weakness, which she was not willing to show. Anger was burning inside her now – anger at the bullying and the brutality, anger at the way people like Winifred Brownlow could be pushed into betraying those closest to them. She was not like Winnie, Katya decided. She was not that weak.

Finally, at around five o'clock, Katya's name was called again. 'Katerina Komarovsky! Identify yourself!'

With aching legs, Katya trudged to the door. An SS officer glanced at his clipboard and then at her. 'You are free to go.'

Her heart jumped. 'Where is Herr Bachmann? And his daughter?'

'I know nothing about that.' He handed her a slip of paper. 'Show this to the officers at the front desk. They will let you out.'

But Katya had no intention of leaving without Thor and Gretchen. She made her way down to the ground floor, struggling through the crowded corridors and stairwells. Could the nightmare really be almost over?

At the main desk downstairs, she queued with her discharge slip in her hand. She felt exhausted. In her almost hallucinatory state, it seemed to her that the German police were large black cats, the detainees small grey mice. The mice scuttled timidly around the cats, freezing when noticed, trembling at every gesture or word.

At the desk, a grim-faced Gestapo man examined her slip, and then pushed a document across to her. 'Sign here.'

'What is it?' Katya asked.

'A statement that you have not been ill-treated by the Gestapo. When you sign it, you can go.'

'I'm not signing it.'

He stared at her, frowning. 'Unless you sign, you may not leave.'

'In the first place, I *have* been ill-treated.' Katya's voice rose. 'And in the second, I refuse to sign until I find out where my employer and his daughter are.'

'If you do not sign—'

'No!' she shouted. 'I'm not signing anything! Where are Herr Bachmann and his daughter?'

Her raised voice caused a shock in the crowded area. Other civilians edged away from her nervously, terrified of being caught up in any kind of resistance to the Gestapo. An SS officer approached.

'What is the matter?' he asked icily.

'I demand to know what has happened to my employer and his daughter,' Katya said. 'I'm a British subject.' She held up her precious passport. 'I've been treated abominably by your bullies, and I refuse to sign anything to the contrary until I see the child again. She is only twelve years old!'

The SS man's face didn't change. 'Come with me, Fräulein.'

She followed him to yet another office. People were staring at her in dread, as though doubting she would ever see the light of day again. In the SS man's office, she was given a chair to sit on, the first she had been offered all day.

The SS officer took the details from her, and picked up the telephone. He rattled some questions down the line, then waited. His eyes were cold as they surveyed her.

At last, he put down the telephone.

'Thorwald Bachmann has been held for further questioning.'

Katya's heart twisted painfully. 'When will he be released?'

'When they have finished with him.'

'And Gretchen?'

'The child has been handed over to the paediatric authorities.'

Katya jumped up from her chair. '*What?*'

The SS officer shrugged. 'She is plainly subnormal. She will be dealt with in accordance with her condition.'

'How can you take her away from us? She's just a child!'

'Why do you care about her?' he asked. 'You are not her mother.'

'I want to see her!'

'She is no longer here. She has been transferred to the relevant authorities.'

'Without my permission?'

'Your permission is not necessary.'

'I am her chief carer!'

'The German Reich has seized control of the state,' he replied unemotionally. 'This means a fundamental change of direction for society, Fräulein. You were employed to care for her because she had no possibility of caring for herself. We National Socialists are determined to create a healthy *Volk*. Principles based purely on so-called compassion and charity are no longer relevant for the national community.'

'You are not human,' she gasped.

'To the contrary,' he retorted. 'We put humanity before every-thing else. Screening the population is an essential task of the SS.

177

The decline of the healthy gene pool means the deterioration of the *Volk*. And that cannot be permitted.'

'Give her to me!' Katya begged. 'I'll take care of her! I promise she won't be a burden on the state!'

'She is not your child. There is nothing to be done. Forget about Herr Bachmann and the child. Go back to Britain, Fräulein. You will find that the principles I have just enunciated will soon reach your own country.' His eyes gleamed. 'And the rest of the world.'

Chapter 14

Katya got home late in the evening. Despite all her protests, she'd been unable to find out anything more about the fates of Thor or Gretchen, and she'd eventually been forced out of the building by the Gestapo, one of whom had sourly commented that she was the first person he'd encountered who was reluctant to leave the building.

Lorenz, who had waited patiently all day, picked her up, and described the day's events on the drive home. Hitler had made a triumphal entry into Vienna at the head of a motorcade, cheered all the way by near-hysterical, flag-waving Viennese. At noon, he had addressed an immense crowd in front of the Hofburg Palace. He had officially proclaimed what everyone already knew – that Austria was no longer a sovereign nation, but was now and for evermore the easternmost province of the Third Reich. The Anschluss had been completed.

The house was silent and empty when she let herself in, trembling and exhausted, but within a few minutes of her arrival, the telephone began to ring. She grabbed at it.

The crackly, distant voice was Papa's.

'Katinka!' He sounded tearful. 'I've been trying to reach you all day! Where have you been?'

'It's been a busy day,' she replied tiredly.

'Your mother and I have been so worried about you. You have to come home!'

'I can't,' she replied flatly.

'Why not, for heaven's sake?'

'Thor has been arrested. And Gretchen is in the hands of the childcare authorities. I can't leave them.'

'Are you mad?' Papa's voice was almost a shriek. 'The next thing you know, they'll arrest *you*.'

'They've already done that. I've spent the day being interrogated by the Gestapo.'

'*Bozhe moy*,' he wailed. 'What did they do to you?'

'They tried to frighten me. But I still have all my fingernails, don't worry.'

There was a scuffling on the phone, and then Mama's voice crackled out of the earpiece. 'You must come home at once, Katya,' she said imperiously. 'You cannot remain in that ghastly place a day longer.'

'Not until Thor and Gretchen are with me.'

'Why on earth? They're nothing to you.'

'I love them both.'

'Don't talk nonsense,' Mama retorted. 'Forget about them. You will never see them again.'

'If I thought that was true, then my heart would be broken, Mama.'

'Have you fallen in love with this man?' Mama demanded.

'I'm afraid so.'

'That was very stupid of you.'

'Yes, you're probably right,' Katya said with a brittle laugh. 'But I didn't mean it to happen, and I can't help it now.'

'There's nothing you can do for them, Katya. Be sensible. These Nazis have taken over, and you have to get out of there, just as your father and I had to do in Russia.'

'I'm responsible for Gretchen. I can't abandon her.'

'These maternal feelings are absurd. You're not her mother!'

'And you're not an expert on maternal feelings, Mama.'

'What?'

Katya felt bitterness well up in her. 'You bullied me into coming here. You've bullied me all my life. You've always told me what to do, always mocked what *I* wanted to do, always had your own way. You've ruled my life.'

'Katya!' Mama sounded shaken.

'I dropped my studies to do what you wanted. I dropped everything. You told me I had to put you and Papa first – and that's what I did. Well, I'm not listening any more. I have to do what I think is right from now on. And I'm not leaving until I have both Thor and Gretchen with me. Goodbye, Mama.'

She put down the phone.

As a rebellion after two decades of tyranny, it wasn't either very violent or very sensible, but Katya felt better. Somehow, it had helped her to control her terror of the situation she was in. It made her feel more in control, at least.

Now she had to find Thor, find Gretchen, and get all three of them out of Austria.

She barely made it to her bed before falling asleep.

The next morning, she made several calls to the Gestapo headquarters, trying to find out information about Thor. None of them produced any results other than a curt dismissal.

The house felt so empty and strange without Thor's big presence. The walls seemed to echo, the spaces felt cold.

What if he was being beaten? Tortured? The thought was too terrible.

Had he already been sent to a concentration camp? Very few people ever got out of those places. Would she ever see him again? She'd had him for only a few weeks, and now he had been taken from her, perhaps forever.

She went to the paediatric clinic at mid-morning, but she did not go directly to Asperger's office. Instead, she went looking for Sister Rosenbaum, hoping that she was still working at the clinic in some capacity.

She met an orderly wheeling a trolley down a corridor, and stopped him.

'Can you tell me where to find Sister Esther Rosenbaum, please?'

The man gave her a strange look. '*Sister* Rosenbaum? You will find *Putzfrau* Rosenbaum down in the mortuary.'

Katya was horrified. 'Is she dead?'

He grinned sourly. 'Not yet. She works there. It's in the basement. But they won't let you in.'

Thanking the man, Katya went down the stairs. This lower level of the clinic had no pretensions of *gemütlichkeit*. There were no pot plants, no paintings. It was harshly lit by naked bulbs; the walls were unpainted brick, covered with wires and piping. Ignoring the NO ENTRY sign on the double doors of the mortuary, she pushed them open.

The bare concrete room was lined with steel cabinets. There were two metal tables in the centre, on which two small figures were lying, draped in sheets. There was a woman on her hands and knees, scrubbing the tiled floor with a bucket and a brush. Katya recognised Esther Rosenbaum, and recalled that *Putzfrau* meant a cleaning woman.

'Esther?'

Esther rose to her feet, dropping her brush in the bucket. 'My goodness, Fräulein Katya! You shouldn't be in here.'

'I know, forgive me for intruding. I'm sorry to see you doing this work.'

Esther Rosenbaum, a pale, slender woman with delicate features, wiped her reddened hands on her apron. 'They're trying to force me to resign, but I need the work. I have a family. So I'll stick it out until they sack me. Two of our Jewish doctors were dismissed this week. One committed suicide the same day.'

'I'm so sorry. I can't believe that everything has changed so much overnight!'

'Oh, it didn't change overnight,' Esther said sadly. 'The change took place a long time ago, slowly, while nobody believed it could happen. Didn't you see the crowds who turned out for Hitler? They had been waiting for years.'

'It's hideous beyond words. Can't you leave Austria?'

Esther arched her back, which was obviously aching. 'We are trying to get out,' she said with a sigh. 'But it's not easy. Nobody wants Jews. Unless they are famous. Or millionaires. The foreign governments criticise Hitler loudly, but they won't take us in. We're trying for Paraguay now.' She smiled tiredly. 'How is Gretchen?'

'That's what I came to see you about. They've taken her away.' She told Esther about their arrest. 'I don't know where Thor is yet, but they told me Gretchen was handed over to the paediatric authorities by the SS.'

The nurse's face changed. 'If the SS took her, they have decided that she is *Lebensunwertes*. You understand the term? Unworthy of life.'

'How can any child be *unworthy of life*?' Katya asked in horror.

'She'll be sent to Germany. They use the children for medical research there. They test vaccines on them. Experimental procedures, new drugs.'

'I can't believe that!'

183

'Unfortunately, it's true. Children like Gretchen are valuable to them because they're healthy. They need them as test subjects. In fact, that's the only value they have.'

Katya was panicking. 'Do you think they've got Gretchen here?'

'I don't see the children any more. Asperger will know. Go and see him – quickly!'

Asperger looked startled when Katya encountered him doing his ward rounds.

'Fräulein Komarovsky! What are you doing here?'

'I've come to talk to you about Gretchen,' she said.

Asperger looked quickly at the group of nurses behind him. 'Continue the round, please.' He took Katya's arm. 'Come to my office.'

She accompanied him to his office, where he shut the door firmly behind them. The photograph of Hitler looked down sternly on them.

'I thought you had been arrested,' he said, gesturing to a chair.

'I was released. Where is Gretchen? Is she here?'

He looked uneasy. 'Why should she be here?'

'The SS told me she had been handed over to the childcare authorities.' She met his eyes directly. 'That's you, isn't it?'

His eyes slid away from hers. 'I don't know why you should think that.'

'Dr Asperger,' she said sharply, 'the question is a simple one. Is Gretchen here or not?'

Reluctantly, he nodded. 'She is transiting through the clinic.'

'Transiting?'

'She is being sent to Berlin.'

'What for?'

'Her father is currently in the custody of the Gestapo. You are not her mother. She has no guardians, and she is a vulnerable child, unable to look after herself. Berlin is now our capital city. The centre of our pan-Germanic state. And it is the duty of the state to care for her.'

'Is it the duty of the state to experiment on her, as though she were an animal?'

His face changed. 'Who made that allegation?' he demanded.

'Your expression tells me that the allegation is true.' Anger and fear were making Katya tremble. 'I want to see her,' she demanded in a tight voice.

'That will not be possible,' he replied.

'As a Christian, how can you condone such cruelty?' she demanded.

'Fräulein Komarovsky—'

'To take a child away from those who love her? To send her far from her home?' Katya's voice was rising sharply. Through the glass pane of Asperger's door, people were glancing in. 'To allow her to be subjected to God knows what pain and terror? And now, to deny her the chance to see a friendly face!'

He looked extremely uncomfortable. 'Please lower your voice. There are sensitive children outside.'

'And how many of these *sensitive children* are also *transiting to Berlin* to be experimented on?'

Asperger winced. 'That is not your concern.'

'I can't understand your mentality, Dr Asperger.'

'That is because you are not a German. You don't belong here. You should return to your own country.'

'Perhaps I should,' she retorted. 'And when I do, I shall tell everyone how the brilliant Dr Asperger treats his child patients – like laboratory rats, to be tortured and murdered. I may be only a medical student, but I'm sure *The Lancet* will believe me – not to mention *The Times*!'

Asperger's eyes narrowed behind his glasses. 'You would be very unwise to do this.'

'Would I?' she said grimly. 'Well, last time we met, you told me that all women are emotional and illogical, so you can expect the worst. You know that you're condoning wickedness. I can see it in your face. You'll never be invited to any medical conferences outside Germany. And certainly, no medical people will ever come to a medical conference here. You will completely lose your international reputation.'

His ruddy cheeks had lost some of their colour. 'My dear Fräulein Komarovsky, an excess of sentimentality would help nobody at this critical juncture.'

'Yes, you've said all that to me before, too. But I assure you, nobody outside the Nazi movement will share your views. Your name will always be associated with the worst kind of medical misconduct.'

He raised his hands. 'Please. There is no need for such language. You may see Gretchen. Briefly. But I urge you – do not upset her in any way. It hasn't been easy to get her to reach equilibrium.'

'I've never harmed Gretchen in any way, Dr Asperger. I'm not going to start now.'

He nodded. 'Very well, very well. Come.'

The ward was one she'd never seen before, behind two sets of locked doors. In contrast to the relatively cheerful atmosphere of the main rooms, with their bright windows and low tables for play, this area was darkened and austere. The only illumination came from small lights set into the walls at floor level.

There were around two dozen beds in the ward. At least half of them were enclosed in cages to prevent the children getting out. A solitary nurse was on duty, sitting behind a desk with a low lamp.

Gretchen was in one of the caged beds. She was curled up with her face to the wall, wearing the stiff linen pyjamas that were given to the poorest children. Katya suppressed her cry of dismay, and waited while the nurse opened the cage. She reached in and touched Gretchen's shoulder.

'Gretchen, Liebchen, it's me.'

At first, Gretchen didn't respond. Then she turned slowly. Her eyes peered at Katya through the tangle of her hair. 'Katya,' she whispered. In an instant, she was in Katya's arms. Her thin body quivered like a frightened animal's, her fingers clutching at Katya convulsively. Katya rocked her to and fro, murmuring her name. At last, she looked up at Asperger and the nurse, who were watching impassively.

'Can I take her out into the light? Just for a moment?'

The nurse glanced at Asperger, who sighed. 'Very well. But don't excite her.'

Gretchen clung to Katya as they made their way back to the main ward. In the bright light there, Katya examined Gretchen carefully for signs of injury. There were none, but the girl looked drawn and pale, and was terribly frightened.

'Where's Papa?' she whispered to Katya.

Katya shook her head. 'I don't know yet, Liebchen. I'm trying to find out.'

'Can we go home now?'

'I'm going to do my best.' Cradling Gretchen in her arms, Katya looked Asperger in the face. 'You can't do this to her,' she said quietly. 'Let me take her home.'

His face was cold. 'I have already told you, Fräulein Komarovsky. The final decision has been made. I can do nothing.'

'You're the one who makes the decisions,' Katya replied. 'You can save her.'

'She will be well taken care of in Berlin.'

'I don't believe that!'

He shook his head. 'I'm sorry. She needs to go back to her bed now.'

'Just a few more minutes,' Katya pleaded. It occurred to her to just take Gretchen now and run for the door. Would they stop her? Looking at the strapping nurses all around, she knew that they would. She'd probably be handed over to the Gestapo again. And that would only make things worse for Gretchen.

Her eyes lit on the old piano that stood in one corner, used to play jolly music for the children's songs and games. Her heart jumped. 'Can she play something on the piano before she has to go? Just for a little while?' As she saw Asperger's face close even further, she quickly added, 'It'll help soothe her.'

He hesitated, then gestured irritably to the piano. 'Very well. But be quick.'

Katya led Gretchen to the instrument. 'Play the Chopin you were learning,' she whispered in Gretchen's ear.

Gretchen sat at the piano and stared at the keys blankly, her hands lying limp in her lap. Her mind was empty. There was no music in her anywhere. She heard Katya whispering, begging her to play. She saw Dr Asperger looking impatiently at his wristwatch, shaking his head with annoyance.

At last, with great hesitancy, Gretchen laid her fingers on the keys. Katya held her breath. Slowly, very quietly, the girl began to play. She had been learning a Chopin nocturne recently, and it was that piece she started now.

One by one, the notes fell, like droplets of water into a dark pool. A silence crept over the ward. Even the patients stopped what they were doing, the children in the caged beds pressing their faces against the bars to listen. The piano was not very well tuned, which gave the notes an eerie, ringing quality, emphasising the melancholy of the piece.

Gretchen was bent over the keys in her customary pose, her hair hanging around her face. Slowly, the melody swelled, yearning, infinitely sad. It seemed to be stretching out, feeling for something that was just out of reach. It rose upwards, with timid hope, slowly gaining volume, then descended again into sorrow.

Katya had never heard Gretchen play with such feeling before, and a lump rose in her throat. She glanced at Asperger and saw that he was watching Gretchen with fascination. The nurses, too, were staring. Despite the poor instrument, Gretchen was somehow coaxing a singing tone from it, her hands reaching for the spreading chords. Katya thought of pale starfish on the bed of some dark sea, finding their way blindly through an impenetrable world.

The music expressed hurt – not angry hurt, or frustrated hurt, but a gentle, deep sorrow. In the repetitions and constant returns to the main theme, there was portrayed the difficulty of escape, of moving on, perhaps of forgetting some painful memory, or an inability to find the right words to express a wound. It was as though, in this piece, Gretchen had found a way of telling the world what she couldn't express in words.

The music soared around the ward. At last, Gretchen stopped playing, the way she always did – in mid-phrase, leaving the silent air begging for more.

Katya saw that some of the nurses had tears in their eyes. Even Asperger looked emotional, his expression troubled. Katya went up to him.

'Do you know how difficult that piece is?' she asked him quietly. 'Do you know how long she has struggled with it? She can't read the notes. And her hands are still too small to play the octaves properly. But she has worked and worked at it. She has it in her head, and she will master it in the end. And this is what you want to send to Berlin?'

Asperger took off his glasses to polish them. 'It is remarkable,' he said, his voice slightly hoarse. 'I had no idea she could play like that.'

'You can't destroy this child,' she said with quiet urgency. 'She has difficulties. Life isn't easy for her. But she finds her way. Let me take her home. Please.'

He sighed. 'I will speak to my superiors. I can promise nothing more than that.'

'No. Give her to me now. Tell your superiors she needs further investigation, whatever excuse you like. Set her free. She deserves to live.'

Asperger swallowed. He looked at his head nurse, the hard-faced Sister Gruber. Sister Gruber alone seemed unmoved by the music, and frowned grimly at him. Then Asperger seemed to reach a decision. 'Take her. Quickly.'

Katya didn't need telling a second time. 'Thank you,' she gasped. She took Gretchen's hand and hurried out of the ward, pulling her along. They made their way through the hospital. At any moment, she expected to hear a shout behind her, hands clamping on her shoulders to stop their escape.

At last, they emerged from the front entrance into the spring sunshine. Lorenz was parked outside. He jumped out of the Mercedes-Benz, wide-eyed, and opened the door. Katya hustled Gretchen into the back seat and climbed in after her.

'Drive,' she said tersely.

Chapter 15

Katya put Gretchen in a hot bath as soon as they got home. It wasn't just that she wanted to wash her clean – she felt as if she wanted Gretchen to be able to wash off the horror of her experience.

Gretchen lay in the bath, too exhausted to move. She looked down at her own pale body in the water. Lately, it was changing. It was not the same as last month, or even last week. The familiar lines were fading, and in their place was something purposeful and alive. What had been gaunt and hollow was now filling. The peaks that the bones had made in her skin were harder to see now. She had once floated in this huge bath like a little leaf. Now she was like a fruit, heavier, more solid, containing something new. She was no longer all ribs and knees and elbows. Yet another Gretchen was coming, a new Gretchen, who looked not like a skinny child, but like a young woman. The changes were taking place without her permission, beyond her control.

Katya sat with her head in her hands. What was she going to do now? Her mind was a blank. There was still no word from Thor. She had no idea where he was, or what was being done to him; and although she had Gretchen, there was no telling whether Dr Asperger would change his mind and send for her again. Even if he didn't, what if some Nazi authority decided that Gretchen should be sent to Berlin after all?

She had to get Gretchen out of Vienna. But how? She couldn't very well abandon Thor to an unknown fate.

But she was completely alone. There was nobody she could trust. Katya now felt that she daren't ask anyone they knew for help.

She went restlessly into the library, where the radio was kept. On the glass disc set into the mahogany, the stations were printed in capital letters: BERLIN, PARIS, LONDON, MOSCOW. She turned the dial to London, and listened to the crackling voice fade in, its tone portentous: '. . . the shadow of the goose-step has fallen over Austria. The eagle and the swastika wave in the breeze. The Gestapo are sweeping across Vienna. Already, thousands of arrests have been made. Thousands have already been sent to Dachau, and thousands more are desperately trying to leave Austria—'

She turned the radio off. She didn't need to hear it. She was living it.

She was going to have to leave Austria. And she was going to take Gretchen with her. She needed to get to the British embassy as soon as possible.

The British embassy, technically a legation, was a nineteenth-century faux-Rococo palace on Metternichgasse, beside the Anglican church. Lorenz had driven them. As Katya and Gretchen arrived, she saw that there was a long line of people snaking all around the block and stretching down Strohgasse as far as the eye could see. Lorenz peered out of the window. 'You will have to queue for hours, Fräulein Katya,' he said. 'But most of these people aren't British.' He pulled the car up on to the kerb and turned to her. 'Give me your passport.' She gave it to him, and he got out of the car. 'Wait here. I'll be back.' He hurried towards the entrance of the legation.

'Why are we here?' Gretchen asked anxiously.

'We're going to see if they can help us.'

They waited in the car, watching the line of people, which didn't seem to move. After half an hour, three trucks came careering down the Metternichgasse, their horns blasting, flying swastikas. Young men in brown shirts were packed into the trucks, some hanging off the tailgates or standing on the running boards, waving rifles. Behind the trucks came a line of taxis, also packed with Brownshirts. Leaning out of the windows, they yelled insults at the people in the line, who shrank back.

At the end of the Metternichgasse, the trucks turned around with much squealing of tyres and came roaring back. This time, dozens of bottles sailed through the air, smashing on the wall of the embassy and showering the people with glass.

Katya and Gretchen huddled down on to the floor of the Mercedes. Something hit the roof. For a few minutes there was a cacophony of shouting and blaring of horns. Then the trucks thundered away. This time, they didn't return.

Cautiously, her heart pounding, Katya looked up. The elegant street was littered with broken glass. The queue of people had broken up into knots of shocked-looking men and women comforting sobbing children.

'Have they gone?' Gretchen asked, trembling.

'Yes. But they might come back. If they do, hide on the floor, like before.'

Lorenz came running across the street towards them. 'They'll see you right away,' he said. 'Come, Fräulein. Hurry.'

The office they were shown into belonged to a harassed-looking ginger-haired attaché called Nigel Bainbridge, who had Katya's passport in his pale, freckled hands.

'Your chap's been telling me all about you, Miss Komarovsky,' he greeted her as she came in. 'But I see absolutely no problem. Your passport's in perfect order. You don't need a visa to return home. You can simply get on to the next train.'

'It's not quite as simple as that,' she replied.

He listened, his greenish eyes flicking from her to Gretchen as she explained their situation. When she had finished, he threw up his hands irritably.

'There's nothing I can do about *this*. All this is well beyond the scope of my authority.'

'Can't you ask the Gestapo about my employer? They won't tell me anything at all, and I'm so worried about him.'

'No, no, no,' he replied. 'Quite impossible. He's not a British subject.'

'Mr Bainbridge, I hoped the ambassador might be able to make official enquiries about Thor Bachmann – where he is, when he's going to be released—'

He cut in impatiently. 'Even if Herr Bachmann was your husband, which I understand he isn't, we would have no authority to make any such enquiries.'

'He's not my husband, but he's my fiancé,' she said boldly. She showed him her hand. She'd put a ring on her engagement finger before leaving the house. She hoped it looked official. 'Are you telling me you can't do anything for him?'

He eyed the ring suspiciously. 'I'm afraid I am.'

'This,' she said, putting her hand on Gretchen's arm, 'is Herr Bachmann's daughter. I'm responsible for her.'

'Yes, I understand that. However, she doesn't concern us either, I'm afraid.'

'But she is in very serious danger. If the Nazis get hold of her again, she'll be sent to Germany. And she will never be seen again.'

Bainbridge winced. 'Ghastly, I agree. Hitler's an absolute blighter.'

'And they might throw me out of the country at any moment. I can't leave Gretchen on her own.'

'No, no, of course not.'

'Then you must, in all conscience, try to do something for her?'

He shuffled his feet, avoiding looking at Gretchen. 'I don't see what I can do, without causing a lot of diplomatic difficulties. You must be aware that our two countries are not now on the best of terms. And this embassy will be closing soon.'

'Are you serious?' she asked, dismayed.

'Force majeure. Since Austria apparently no longer exists as a sovereign state, a fully equipped embassy is no longer required. The one in Berlin is sufficient. And *that's* likely to be shut soon, if things keep on getting worse.' He lowered his voice. 'Between you and me, we've already had an offer for these premises. From the Luftwaffe. Not the sort of offer one can refuse. Sad to think of this beautiful old building being infested with a lot of Nazi louts, but there it is.'

'Mr Bainbridge—'

'My point being,' he interrupted, 'that things are at a very delicate stage right now. The Prime Minister's extremely anxious to avoid conflict with Hitler. So the less we do to rock the boat, the better.'

'You mean we're just going to let Hitler trample all over Europe?'

He frowned. 'The British people aren't keen on another war with Germany. Apart from Mr Churchill, that is. He's always keen on another war, apparently. The general feeling in Whitehall is that as both nations are German-speaking, there's no good reason why Austria and Germany shouldn't unify. It makes sense.'

'It doesn't make sense if you're not a Nazi,' Katya retorted.

'Well, shall we say there's no threat to peace from it.'

'No threat? Don't you know how the Nazis are behaving?'

He shrugged. 'Well, I'm sure you saw the rapturous welcome that Hitler received.'

'As a matter of fact, I didn't. I was being interrogated by the Gestapo that day.'

Bainbridge grimaced. 'Oh, dear.'

'Anyway, I didn't come to talk about politics. Can you give me a visa to get Gretchen to Britain?'

The direct question took him aback. 'Good heavens, Miss Komarovsky. How could I possibly do that without her father's express permission?'

'I've got her passport right here with me.' She laid it on the desk in front of him. 'Austrian children have their own passports.'

He stared at the thing as though it were a toad. 'You can't simply whisk her out of the country!'

'Should I rather let her be whisked off to Berlin to be tortured?'

'She's not your daughter. You can't take her to Britain without her father's consent.'

'If her father were able to speak, he would urge me to get Gretchen to safety as soon as possible.'

'With the greatest respect, that is just your opinion.'

'It's the opinion of anybody with a heart.'

'I have to repeat, it's not embassy business.'

'She's sitting here in front of you!'

He squirmed restlessly in his chair. 'Even if there were no other objections, surely you've seen the queue of people outside, waiting for visas? Why should I give this child preference?'

Katya leaned forward urgently. 'Because you *can*. You can save a precious human life with the stroke of a pen, Mr Bainbridge. You'll be able to get into bed tonight knowing that whatever else you've accomplished today, you've done that.'

Bainbridge, who was the sort of young man she always thought of as chinless, though he actually had a Grecian profile, was growing agitated. 'My dear Miss Komarovsky, you are really putting me in a most difficult position. I beg you not to insist.'

'But I *am* insisting. Look at her! Do you want her suffering and death on your conscience?'

'Of course not! But besides all the rest, we would need financial guarantees for the child. We can't let in people who are going to be a burden on the state.'

Katya drew herself up haughtily. 'Look at my passport.'

'I beg your pardon?'

'Do you see who my next of kin are?'

He examined the passport. 'Oh!'

'My parents are the Baron and Baroness Komarovsky,' she said as icily as she could manage. 'Do you imagine that we are short of funds?'

'I wasn't implying that, of course!' He looked chastened, and for once she was grateful for Mama and Papa's vanity. 'But I could lose my job over this!'

'Haven't you just said that the embassy is closing?'

'Yes.'

'And all the files will be packed up and sent to Berlin?'

'Well, yes, I suppose so.'

'And the Berlin embassy will probably close, too?'

'I don't see what you're getting at, Miss—'

'Nobody will ever know what you've done. You won't lose your job. In fact, one day you'll be proud of helping people escape from the Nazis. You'll go down in the history books as a hero. Not as the heartless bureaucrat who sent an innocent child to her death.'

Bainbridge went very red, then so pale that his freckles stood out stark on his cheeks. 'Damn,' he whispered to himself. He snatched up Gretchen's passport and jumped to his feet. 'I'm not promising anything, do you understand? Wait here.'

Gretchen turned to Katya, her eyes wide. 'Katya, I can't go without Papa!'

Katya took Gretchen's hands, which were suddenly sweaty with anxiety. 'You're in danger here in Vienna. We can't stay.'

'Papa's in danger too!'

'Yes. And Papa would want you to be safe.' She stroked Gretchen's curly hair. The girl was trembling. 'He'll join us when he can.'

'What if he doesn't come? What if he can't find us?'

'He will come. I promise you, Liebchen.' She tried to sound as though she was sure of what she was promising. 'And he'll know exactly where to find us.'

'How do you know he'll come?'

Katya hesitated. She couldn't lie to Gretchen. 'The truth is, I don't know. But we don't have any choice. You know what staying here means. You know what would happen if they sent you to Berlin.'

'Yes,' Gretchen answered in a low voice. Katya could see by Gretchen's expression that she understood fully what danger she was in.

'I don't know where Papa is, or what has happened to him. But I know one thing for sure – he would want me to get you to safety.'

Gretchen didn't answer.

They waited for Bainbridge to return. The street outside was noisy. Vienna had a different sound now, composed of cars driving faster, people talking more loudly, the yells and chants of young male gangs, the incessant drone of aircraft.

Nigel Bainbridge hurried back into the office with the air of a boy who'd just stolen a jam tart off the kitchen windowsill. He thrust Gretchen's passport at Katya.

'There you are. *Please* don't tell anyone what I've done, or the whole of Vienna will be at my door.'

Katya inspected the stamp, half-disbelieving. 'Is it real?'

'Of course it's real,' he snapped. 'I've issued it myself.'

She looked up at him, her eyes filling with tears. 'I can't tell you how grateful I am, Mr Bainbridge.'

He went red again. 'Well, good luck to you, Miss Komarovsky. And to you, Miss Bachmann.'

As they drove through the gates of the house, Lorenz stamped on the brake so hard that they all jerked forward in their seats. At the end of the drive, they could see that there were two German army trucks hulking in the courtyard, as well as a black staff car and a motorcycle mounted with a machine gun. The shock froze them all.

A dozen soldiers in grey uniforms were marching around. It took her a moment to realise that they were loading the contents of the house into the trucks. Katya saw two of them lugging a large Klimt portrait, which she had particularly loved. Others were ferrying books, sculptures, furniture, under the command of an SS officer in black. The house was being ransacked.

'*Scheisse*,' Lorenz muttered under his breath. He slammed the Mercedes into reverse gear, and they shot backwards into the road. Turning the car round with a squeal of tyres, he accelerated away. Her heart racing, Katya turned to look out of the back window. She was certain they would be pursued. But the quiet road remained empty.

Lorenz peered into the rear-view mirror. 'They didn't see us. Or if they did, they don't care.'

Katya was still trembling with fright. 'What are we going to do?' she gasped.

'We wait until they have finished. When they've got what they want, they'll leave. I'll take you to my mother's house.'

Katya started to cry, not because of the plunder of the possessions, but because of the implications it had for Thor. If they were pillaging his house, then they had already decided his fate. And that meant that her worst fears had come true – and that she and Gretchen might never see him again.

Lorenz, grim-faced, drove them to his mother's place, a little house in a village outside Vienna. The old lady, clucking sympathetically, made them a simple meal of bread, ham and cheese. When they'd eaten, Katya spoke quietly to Lorenz.

'I think this is the end, Lorenz.'

'I think so too,' he replied heavily.

'I have to get Gretchen out of Austria as soon as possible.'

'Yes.'

'We can't go through Germany. We'll try to get the train to Zürich.'

He nodded. 'That's a good idea. If there are tickets.'

'Yes, if there are tickets. If there aren't, we'll have to think of something else.'

'I will help with anything I can, Fräulein Katya.'

'Thank you, Lorenz. I don't know what I would do without you.'

He smiled sadly. 'Bad times have come to Austria, Fräulein. I'm ashamed of what my countrymen are doing. It's better that you and the little one are out of the country. When Herr Bachmann is free, he can join you in England.'

Katya nodded. But she knew that any future for all of them was dark and uncertain.

Chapter 16

They drove back to the house as evening was falling. Lorenz parked a hundred yards from the gate, and Katya went cautiously to explore. The courtyard was empty, the place dark.

They went in through the kitchen. There was no sign of Bertha, the cook. A heavy silence lay on the house. Exploring further revealed the devastation the Nazis had inflicted. All the furniture was gone, every stick of it. The walls were bare; the paintings had all been taken. So had the rugs, the silverware, even the beautiful curtains.

With a broken wail, Gretchen discovered that her beloved piano was gone. Katya tried to comfort her, but no words would come.

The library had been gutted. Most of the huge collection of books, some very valuable, had been carried off. Others had been deliberately torn in half. And in the fireplace, a pile of charred paper showed where the Nazis had made a bonfire of the volumes they had considered offensive.

Katya rescued Gretchen's copy of *Grimms' Fairy Tales*, which had been hurled into a corner. The gilded spine of the beautiful old book had been damaged, but it was still intact. It was a small something salvaged from the wreckage.

Thor's study was the saddest sight of all. Everything was gone – the leather sofa where she had sat with him so many times, the desk, the art, even the Italian coffee machine he had been so proud of. Everything was gone. The life that they would have had was now forever lost.

Katya refused to cry. She had already shed too many tears. But she found that she was shaking. The emotion she felt was rage. Rage at what had been done to Thor, Gretchen and herself, rage at the brutal arrogance of men who trampled human dignity under their boots, rage against the man with the funny little moustache, who wasn't funny at all.

If she'd had any doubts about leaving Austria, and taking Gretchen with her, then those doubts had been obliterated now. She knew exactly what she was going to do.

They went upstairs, expecting the worst. The bedrooms, too, had been pillaged, left with bare walls, bare floors and vacant windows. The bed in the master bedroom was one of the few things that had been rejected, perhaps because it was too heavy to bother with. But almost all of the linen had been taken.

Lorenz offered to spend the night, instead of going back to his wife as he usually did, but she made him leave. He did so reluctantly, promising to be back with the Mercedes early the next morning. When he'd gone, they felt more alone than ever.

Gretchen was devastated by the loss of her piano, more than anything else that had been lost. It was as though an intrinsic part of herself had been taken away. She felt sick and empty. They had taken Papa, and now they had taken everything she knew.

As they wandered round the house, trying to take in the desolation, there was a hammering on the front door. Alarmed, Katya peered out of the window. A black car was in the courtyard.

'Don't answer it!' Gretchen pleaded. But the hammering resumed, louder than before.

'Stay up here,' Katya told Gretchen. She went downstairs and opened the door. The man at the door was a taxi driver in overalls and a cap.

'Visitors for you,' he said, indicating the car. Peering through the twilight, Katya saw that the passengers were Sigmund and Anna Freud.

Freud was looking frailer than ever as he limped slowly into the house, leaning heavily on his daughter's arm. 'We have finally been given permission to leave,' he said. His voice was faint and the words barely distinguishable. 'We leave for London tomorrow. There is a chance they may stop us yet, but we live in hope. We have come to say goodbye to you and Thor.'

'You haven't heard, then,' Katya said heavily. 'Thor has been arrested.'

Freud's mouth twisted under his white beard. He closed his eyes. 'They are taking the best. All the best. One by one.'

'I'm in despair. I don't know where he is, or what they're doing to him.'

She showed them how the house had been despoiled. The Freuds peered sadly into the empty rooms. 'They have done the same to my aunt's apartment,' Anna said.

'And to the homes of many of our relations,' Freud added. 'They claim that they have come in friendship, as brothers. But this shows what their real intentions are.' He put a trembling hand on her shoulder. 'You are in grave danger, Katya. You must leave. And take Gretchen with you.'

'I'm arranging it now, Professor. I'm going to get tickets tomorrow.'

'Good, good.' He leaned closer to her. 'Do not use the telephone. You understand? They are listening, all the time.'

'I understand.' She felt a pain in her stomach. Perhaps it had been Thor's furious phone calls, recorded without his knowledge, that had led the Gestapo to him.

Hearing familiar voices, Gretchen had crept down. Freud peered at her. 'Well, child. Can you read yet?'

Gretchen shook her head. She had always been a little afraid of Professor Freud. He asked such strange questions, and his eyes were so dark and sombre. She'd been glad when the sessions with him had ended. But perhaps he had only wanted to help after all. And now that he was leaving Vienna, it was yet another loss, yet another hole torn in the fabric of her life.

'Learn to read,' he murmured. 'If you do not, the world will always be a dark forest for you.'

Gretchen nodded.

The Freuds left soon afterwards. 'Take care,' Freud said, pressing Katya's hand. 'We will meet again – in this world, or the next.'

Katya and Gretchen watched the taxi depart in the gloom. As if to underscore the sombre moment, the German planes were in the air again, the threatening growl of their engines rolling overhead.

'Everyone is going,' Gretchen said. 'We're the only ones left.'

Katya felt as though they were all being hammered into a box, the doors slamming closed around them, even the sky above being shuttered to prevent escape.

They dared not show many lights in case their presence in the house was noted. They made themselves a scanty meal in near-darkness, and then made a bed to sleep in as best they could out of what linen had been left. Gretchen curled up in Katya's arms, trembling from time to time.

'Will you read to me?' she whispered.

Katya retrieved the salvaged copy of *Grimms' Fairy Tales* and opened it to the story of The Six Swans. She read in a quiet voice, and slowly the peace of a tale from long ago stole around them.

Gretchen's shivering stopped. Her eyes, which had been fixed on Katya's face, slowly closed. At last, her body relaxed into sleep. But it was a long time before Katya could join her.

The next morning, Lorenz drove them to the railway station to try to get tickets to Zürich.

Katya had the cash Thor had given her in her handbag. She was prepared for chaotic scenes. In the first days of the Anschluss, the trains had been besieged by people frantic to leave Vienna; the suddenness of the Nazi coup had taken everyone by surprise. But on arrival at the station, she found that an eerie calm was now prevailing. The echoing cavern of the main hall was quiet. Queues of passengers were silent, subdued. The reason was immediately obvious: the German military presence lay everywhere like an iron sword.

Armed *Wehrmacht* soldiers were standing in groups of four or five, watching with grim faces, their weapons slung at the ready. Even more evident were the pairs of men in black leather trench coats, which everyone by now knew was the Gestapo uniform, who took photographs and made notes of everything around them.

The crooked cross and the German eagle glared from every wall. Gretchen shrank against Katya as they walked in. Katya put her arm around the girl and murmured, 'Don't show them you're afraid of them. Best foot forward. Hold your head high, Liebchen.'

They joined the long line to the main ticket counter. The absence of excited conversation and laughter, which were usually present in railway stations, produced the deadening effect of a funeral, rather than of imminent travel.

To her dismay, Katya saw two Gestapo men strolling towards them. Both were burly, with the brutish, battered faces of thugs or ex-boxers. She hoped they would pass her by, but they planted themselves in front of her, scattering others in the queue.

'Where are you travelling to?' one demanded of Katya.

'Zürich,' Katya replied shortly.

He snapped his meaty fingers at her. 'Your papers.'

Silently, she handed over her passport. He glanced at it, then looked her in the face. 'You are Britisher?' he said in heavy English.

'Yes,' Katya replied, trying to disguise her fear of the man and all he stood for.

His heavy brows came down. He tapped his chest, glaring at her. 'Prisoner of war. 1917 to 1919. Lancashire.'

'I'm very sorry,' Katya said, dismayed by the revelation. 'I hope they didn't treat you badly.'

He pointed upward. 'Rain. Mud. Work. Dig potatoes.' He looked down at Gretchen. 'This is your mother, girl?'

'Yes,' Gretchen said without hesitation.

The Gestapo man nodded, obviously relishing showing off the English he had learned. 'You don't like to stay in Vienna any more?' he asked jocosely.

'I like Vienna – very much,' Gretchen replied hesitantly. 'But I must – I must go home now.'

Katya was sweating. She'd had no idea that Gretchen could speak any English. The Gestapo man was apparently unable to tell that Gretchen was not a British child. 'Maybe I come see you in London, *ja?*'

'That will be – very nice,' Gretchen said carefully.

He didn't ask to see her papers, just handed back Katya's passport, and turned to the people behind them. Katya gave Gretchen a squeeze. 'When did you learn English?' she whispered.

'Only a few words. From listening to you.'

'I'm so proud of you.'

The line was very long. She wondered whether there would possibly be enough tickets.

They reached the counter an hour later after shuffling halfway across the station. 'Yes?' the clerk demanded.

'An adult and a child to Zürich, please.'

'Singles or returns?'

'Singles.'

He sneered at the reply, which must have become very familiar to him by now. He put his hand out. 'Travel documents.'

She pushed their passports under the glass. He inspected them, then gave her a sharp glance. He swung in his chair to talk to someone out of sight. Suddenly, Katya's heart was in her mouth. She clutched Gretchen's hand.

The man swung back to face them. 'What day?'

'I'm sorry?' she stammered.

'What day do you want to travel?'

'As soon as possible.'

'There are seats on the Sunday morning train, ten-thirty. Only Third Class.'

'That's fine,' she stammered. She'd been so certain of a refusal that she fumbled stupidly with the money in her purse. She passed the banknotes over. A minute later, they were walking away with the precious tickets to freedom safely in her bag.

They now had four days to wait.

Katya made the last desperate attempts to find information about Thor. The Gestapo rebuffed her. So did the SS. Heedful of Sigmund Freud's warning, she didn't use the telephone for any other purpose.

Bertha, the cook, did not reappear, even though she was owed a week's wages. She obviously thought it prudent to give up the money, rather than come back to the house. Katya gave her wages to Lorenz, who kept faithfully turning up, to give to Bertha at some future date. She also had to make arrangements with him about shutting up the house. She gave him the keys, and told him to keep them – and the Mercedes – until such time as Thor was released.

'I've been thinking,' she said, 'that after we leave, you could use the car as a taxi service.'

'Oh, Fräulein Katya, I couldn't do that!'

'At least you'll be able to earn some money,' she said practically. 'Until we all get our lives back. I'm sure it's what Thor would want.'

He bowed his head. 'Thank you, Fräulein Katya.'

Katya telephoned her parents to say that she was coming home. She made no mention of Gretchen, in case, as Freud had warned, the line was tapped.

'Thank God,' Papa said. 'We'll have you back at last, Katinka.'

They received no visitors other than Lorenz. She and Gretchen went to the shops and bought a few clothes and provisions they would need.

Lorenz had tears in his eyes as they said goodbye at the station on Sunday morning. He kissed Katya's hands and hugged Gretchen. He stood unhappily on the platform, his boots gleaming, waiting for their train to depart.

Their compartment was full. There were six other people packed on the hard leather seats, and their baggage had already filled the overhead luggage racks. Hostile faces looked up at Katya and Gretchen as they entered. Grudgingly, the others made a small space for the newcomers. All of their fellow passengers, Katya saw, were wearing prominent swastika badges. Unpleasant as that was, Katya cursed herself for not having thought to equip herself and Gretchen with similar buttonholes. It might have made their passage a lot easier.

She had very little money. The Nazis had imposed tight restrictions on currency leaving Austria. No one was allowed to take out more than two hundred German marks. It was barely enough to keep them going for a few days of travelling. But she dared not take more. The penalties were severe. For large sums, it was death. She had given all her spare cash to Lorenz.

The train was delayed by half an hour. It sat, sullenly hissing steam, and occasionally giving a jerk, as though it were about to leave, and then changing its mind. When it eventually set off with a huge jolt, bags and bundles rained down from the overcrowded luggage racks. The fat middle-aged couple opposite glared at Katya as though this were her fault. They pulled down the window and waved goodbye to Lorenz.

'Goodbye!' they heard him call over the hubbub. 'God bless you!' Steam enveloped him, blotting out him and the life they had known.

Gretchen wept bitterly. There was a lump in Katya's own throat. Her strange sojourn in Vienna was at an end. She comforted Gretchen. Beneath her sorrow, Katya felt hollow with anxiety. The journey they were undertaking was full of uncertainty, full of difficulties. She could only pray that it would end well.

Chapter 17

The route from Vienna to Switzerland was a long one, taking them through the heart of Austria, bypassing Munich. Spring was now well underway. The countryside was emerging from the drab colours of winter, and a green fuzz covered the trees and hedgerows. Snow still capped the mountains, but the sky was a brilliant picture-postcard blue.

Gretchen had brought only one book with her – her battered copy of *Grimms' Fairy Tales*. Katya saw that Gretchen was making a concerted effort to read the text, rather than just looking at the pictures. She could see Gretchen's lips moving as she silently deciphered the words letter by letter, a deep frown making a V on her forehead.

She found her thoughts returning, as they sometimes did, to Alexei Nikolaevich, the sickly young Tsarevich with whom she had played as a child. There was a strange connection between the two children, both vulnerable, both fighting against innate obstacles. She just prayed that Gretchen was not doomed, as Alexei had been. The thought of her coming to any harm was unbearable.

Now and then, Gretchen would look out at the passing scenery, cupping her chin in her hands. The light profiled her face. It was not as gaunt as it had been when she'd first met Gretchen; the hollows of her cheeks were starting to fill out. She was growing up, Katya thought with a pang. And her father was not here to see it.

Katya missed Thor terribly. The shock of losing him had numbed her for days, and she'd had to focus on Gretchen's safety. But now that they were leaving Vienna, his absence was a dark hole in her heart. She feared for him. Brave and outspoken as he was, he was not a man to try and placate the Nazis. If anything, his arrest would have infuriated him even more, and made him even more stubborn. Like a bear baited by dogs, she feared that he would lose his temper, lash out and say exactly the sort of things that would incriminate him as an enemy of Hitler. And then what would happen to her bear? Would Thor remember that there was a woman and a child who adored him – who waited only for his return? Would that thought cool his hot temper and make him more diplomatic?

At noon, the passengers unfolded packed lunches. The smells of food – especially garlic, ham and beer – filled the compartment. The disapproving couple opposite took turns swigging at a stoneware jug of ale, their eyes never leaving Gretchen and Katya. Katya had stupidly neglected to bring anything to eat, so she and Gretchen went hungry, oppressed by the chewing and stares of their fellow passengers.

Suddenly, the train braked, causing lunches to slide off laps and on to the floor. There was a flood of cursing – until the cause of the stop was revealed. A German military train was rumbling slowly past them, in the opposite direction.

There was an excited scramble to pull down the window and lean out. Howitzers were on their way to Vienna, lashed to flatbeds, accompanied by artillerymen in field grey. The young soldiers, muffled against the cold, were also eating their lunch, spooning up soup and munching bread. Katya and Gretchen's fellow passengers were electrified. They threw up their arms in the Hitler salute, screaming

'Heil Hitler' and pointing to the swastikas they wore. The women blew kisses, the men waved their caps. The German soldiers, by contrast, seemed puzzled or embarrassed by the adulation. Some waved back half-heartedly. Others did not even look up from their food as the train lumbered by. The flatbeds swayed past, one after another, and at last the final one had gone.

'These are our brave brothers,' the disapproving woman said loudly to Gretchen, as she settled back into her seat, 'going to defend Vienna!'

'Who are they defending Vienna against?' Gretchen asked quietly. Katya knew that the question was an innocent one, but the disapproving woman's fat cheeks reddened with anger.

'Insolent child!'

'Don't shout at my daughter,' Katya said sharply. 'She meant nothing.'

'She meant something, all right,' the fat woman retorted. 'You Jews always have smart-mouth kids.'

'You better tell her to keep her trap shut,' her husband added, 'or somebody will shut it for her.'

Katya was too angry to retort that they weren't Jews. What did it matter, anyway? Whether these people really supported Hitler or not, they had plainly chosen to make a very public display, and that inevitably meant finding enemies. She put her arm around Gretchen, who was puzzled and upset by the exchange.

'Did I say something bad?' Gretchen asked.

'You didn't say anything bad,' Katya said. 'In fact, it was a very good question.'

Further outrage followed this remark. Katya tried to shut it out, saying nothing more, just looking out of the window at the beautiful scenery. She was doing the very thing that she devoutly hoped Thor was avoiding. She had to stop. She just had to keep her temper until they left Austria.

The train chugged into Salzburg in the afternoon. To Katya's relief, the fat couple opposite began gathering their things and preparing to leave the train.

Gretchen was very hungry now, and they had two hours to wait at Salzburg, so despite her reluctance to leave their precious train, Katya took her out to get something to eat.

Entering Salzburg station, they found that it was filled with German soldiers, carrying heavy packs and rifles. They were everywhere, camped in groups or standing in orderly lines. Entering the sea of field-grey uniforms, Katya and Gretchen tried to find the exit. It was difficult to move around; the soldiers numbered in their hundreds, and their equipment was piled up in great mounds. Any pretence of a spontaneous Austrian union with the Third Reich was made nonsense by the bombers, cannons and troops that were pouring into the country. There could be not the slightest resistance from Austria in the face of this military might.

The soldiers ignored them. They seemed businesslike and disciplined. But when they emerged into the square outside, a mob of young men – just like the louts they had seen in Vienna – were milling around in a variety of home-made Nazi uniforms, chanting slogans and waving swastika banners.

They were impossible to avoid. They confronted everyone who came out or went into the station, throwing their arms up in the Nazi salute and shouting '*Sieg Heil*' in their faces. The clubs and sticks they carried made it plain what would happen to anyone who didn't respond.

She and Gretchen sketched a salute, and hurried past. Beyond the station square, the streets were noisy with demonstrations. Hitler mania was evidently still raging here, fuelled by proximity to the German border, and perhaps by the hefty military presence.

The first restaurant they came to, in the next street, was called Tuchman's. It was closed. The windows were shuttered, and scrawled on them in whitewash were Jewish stars and the words, 'Don't Buy From Jews!' In case anyone had missed the message, two Brownshirts were posted outside, their fists on their hips.

Similar sights met their eyes further down the street: here and there, shop windows were broken, or daubed with slogans of hate. Brownshirts – many of them evidently old soldiers – prevented shoppers from going into premises bearing Jewish names. From inside some of the besieged shops, frightened faces peered out. But most seemed abandoned.

The restaurants were full of rowdy groups, singing and drinking from tankards. Rather than go into one to eat, they found a *Konditorei* and bought some pastries. They ate them sitting on a bench under a row of lime trees. Gretchen devoured hers hungrily, but the cakes were rich and creamy, adding to Katya's already queasy feeling.

'Mozart was born here,' Katya told Gretchen.

'In Salzburg?'

Katya pointed to a shop window, where portraits of Mozart and Hitler had been posed side by side. 'They're very proud of him.'

'I don't think Mozart would have liked the Nazis,' Gretchen commented, licking chocolate off her fingers.

'Nor do I.' She checked her watch. 'We'd better get back to the train.'

They walked back to the station and boarded their train. The occupants of their compartment had changed. The disapproving couple had been replaced by two well-dressed middle-aged men, both of them perspiring and breathless, as though they'd had to run for the train. There was also a woman in smart Tyrolean loden clothes and a hat with a silver pin, accompanied by a girl a year or two younger than Gretchen. The mother made no attempts at civility, or even to acknowledge anyone else's presence, but the girl immediately struck up a whispered conversation with Gretchen. Katya couldn't hear what the girls were saying, but she was pleased to see that Gretchen, usually so shy with other children, was quite chatty.

The perspiring men were very sociable. They introduced themselves as Herr Schubert and Herr Messner, and said they were in business together. Each wore an enamelled swastika buttonhole, and they vied with each other in praising Hitler.

'Such a great, great genius,' Messner panted.

'Such a wonderful, wonderful day for Austria,' Schubert added, mopping his brow with a silk handkerchief. His nails were beautifully shaped and buffed. He used the fashionable term *Land Österreich*, indicating that Austria was now merely a province of Greater Germany. 'We have been waiting for this our whole lives. The future is truly glorious!'

Bored by the fulsome tributes to Hitler, Katya stared out of the window. A detachment of several hundred German soldiers was being marched along the platform towards a train headed for Vienna. They looked calm, well-organised and very much in control. For the most part they were extremely young, with the clean-cut faces and clear eyes of youth. This was Hitler's new generation, she thought, ready to take on the world and create the 'glorious future' Herr Schubert anticipated.

She was still shaken by the sights they had seen in Salzburg, her nerves jangled and her heart aching. There was still a long way to go on their journey: two hours to Innsbruck and then three more to the Swiss border. The cream cakes she had unwisely eaten sat like lead in her stomach. She hoped she wasn't going to be sick.

Their train was now making great clouds of smoke and steam, and with a long, shrill whistle of warning, it set off out of Salzburg, leaving the old town behind and rattling towards the snowy mountains.

Gretchen and the other girl, whose name was Bettina, were deep in conversation. Katya reflected with some sadness that horrible experiences were helping Gretchen mature.

She heard Bettina exclaim in surprise, 'You don't go to school?'

'My mother teaches me at home,' Gretchen replied. Katya felt a pang. She was all the mother Gretchen had. Indeed, it was unlikely that Gretchen remembered much about her real mother. She must be a ghostly memory by now, dimly perceived in dreams. If only they could be reunited with Thor, and make a family again.

She closed her eyes, concentrating on the end of their journey: Zürich and safety.

By the time they reached Innsbruck, it was growing cold in the train. The two girls had gone exploring, and reached First Class before being turned back by a steward. They reported enviously that First Class was luxuriously warm. However, heating was not bestowed on Third Class passengers. Rugs were handed out by the porter, and these (though threadbare and not very clean) were comforting on chilly legs.

The afternoon was drawing into evening, and the mountains, much heavier with snow than they had looked from a distance, loomed over the town as they approached. The two girls had been asleep for an hour, leaning against each other. They woke up now, and pressed their faces against the window, fascinated by the majesty of the Alps.

The train pulled slowly into the station. This was the last stop before the border – and freedom. But waiting on the platform was an ominous group of Nazi officials and Brownshirts. Katya's heart plummeted at the sight.

The porter hurried up the corridor, shouting 'Nobody is to leave the train until police inspection is complete!' at every compartment.

The officials boarded the train. They sat in silence, listening to the sound of boots thudding closer, and the crash of compartment doors opening. The voices of the police had the harsh tone that was becoming all too familiar, the bark of command that was backed by the threat of immediate violence. Katya held Gretchen's hand tightly. The girl's palm was sweaty.

Herr Messner and Herr Schubert opposite were now panting, as they had done when they first boarded the train in Salzburg. Katya realised they hadn't been out of breath from hurrying then – they had simply been in a state of terror. And they were in a state of terror again.

Her own heart started to thump even harder. She took in their trembling fingers, clutching the briefcases on their laps, their pale faces and glistening foreheads. Perhaps they were Jews, making an escape? She wished with all her heart that they weren't in the same compartment. Pitiful as their state was, they might attract attention, and possibly trouble, and those were the last things she needed.

Herr Schubert jumped suddenly to his feet and crammed his briefcase into the luggage rack over Katya's head. He sat down again, mopping his face and panting, as though the exertion had been immense. He avoided meeting Katya's eyes.

A moment later, their compartment door burst open, and a man in a black trench coat, with two SA thugs behind him, came in. They were all armed with pistols at their belts.

'Documents!'

Silently, the six of them handed over their passports. Katya felt dizzy with fear, as though she were about to pass out. The policeman leafed through the documents, then studied the baggage on the racks.

'Open everything,' he commanded the Brownshirts.

The two SA men unceremoniously hauled the luggage down and began pulling out the contents. Clothes and other personal possessions were dumped on the floor, trampled carelessly under their boots.

'Herr Kriminalinspektor – look!' One of the Brownshirts was holding open the briefcase that had been put over Katya's head. It was stuffed with money; and there was the gleam of gold, too. Everything became very still suddenly.

'Whose is this?' the Kriminalinspektor barked.

Herr Schubert pointed at Katya. 'It's hers,' he said in a trembling voice.

'It's *not* mine!' Katya exclaimed, horrified. 'It's his! He put it up there a moment ago!'

'Nonsense!' Herr Messner shouted. 'It was here when we boarded in Salzburg. Nothing to do with us!'

'She's a foreigner,' Schubert gabbled. 'I saw her looking in it during the journey. It's hers, all right.'

Katya started to protest, but the Kriminalinspektor cut her off harshly. 'You are all under arrest. Take your baggage and get off the train.'

Chapter 18

It was useless to argue. They were all herded off the train and on to the platform, where an icy wind was blowing. They joined a group of other unfortunates who were being assembled, guarded by watchful German soldiers with machine pistols. Gretchen held tightly to Katya's hand, shivering and white-faced. Katya was praying that, once the briefcase full of money had been connected to its real owner, they would be allowed to leave. But it was horrible to see their luggage being unloaded from the train and tossed brusquely on to a disorderly pile. Some of the suitcases were open, spilling out their carefully packed contents, like gutted fish.

The smart lady in the loden outfit was vocal at last. She was spitting with rage. 'I have an urgent appointment to keep in Zürich. I cannot miss it!'

'If you are innocent, then you will be sent on your way,' the Gestapo officer retorted, unimpressed.

'Innocent? Of course I am innocent! May I have your name, please?'

'My name is Kriminalinspektor Sauer.'

'You don't know who I am, Herr Kriminalinspektor Sauer! My husband shall hear of this! He is a very important man!' She continued in the same vein for twenty minutes. Katya wished she had the self-confidence to make the same sort of fuss. Standing dumb and cowed seemed like an admission of guilt. Schubert and Messner stood huddled together, avoiding looking at anyone. They looked older, shabbier and thinner now.

And then their train gave a sudden jolt. The whistle shrilled deafeningly, and it began to pull out of the station. Luckier passengers peered out of the windows at them as it departed.

They watched it leave in despair, the golden lozenges of its lighted windows flickering faster, until they disappeared into the night. It was suddenly very dark and cold. The loden lady ran out of protests and started to cry like a child.

'Get your suitcases! Forward, march!'

The soldiers bullied them into a rough formation, and then trooped them, everyone hauling his or her own suitcases, off the platform. They were herded across the square outside the station. People stared at them as they passed, some pityingly, others jeering. Frost sparkled on the pavement. The vast white bulk of the mountains hung in the night sky, glacial and indifferent. As they climbed the stairs to the police station, several people slipped on the ice that was forming. An elderly woman went sprawling with a cry. Nobody tried to help her get up, though she was obviously hurt. When Katya stopped to assist, one of the soldiers shoved her roughly back. 'March!'

It was even colder inside the police station than out. They were all separated and taken off in different directions. Katya and Gretchen were made to sit on a hard wooden bench in a draughty corridor, waiting for interrogation.

'What if they don't believe us?' Gretchen whispered to Katya.

'They will.'

'But if they don't?'

'We'll make them believe us. Don't worry.' But she knew they were empty words. Muffled shouts and thumps could be heard from other parts of the station, and there was a continuous march of boots to and fro. Photographs of Adolf Hitler, Heinrich Himmler and Hermann Goering hung on the walls. Hitler and Himmler glowered, but Goering wore a sly smile.

A young policeman with his angular head shaved almost to the skull strutted up to them. 'Come.'

They followed him into an office. Seated behind the desk was the police captain who had arrested them on the train. He was leafing through their passports as they came in. He gestured to the chairs in front of his desk. 'So. You insist the money is not yours?'

'It's nothing to do with us. It belongs to Herr Schubert, the man opposite us in the compartment.'

'Strange. If that is true, Herr Schubert is giving it all to you. Over three thousand marks. Most people would seize it with both hands.'

'I know the penalties for currency smuggling.'

He looked up, his blue eyes sharp. 'Do you, indeed? Well, we will shortly find out the truth. A more interesting question—' He broke off, interrupted by appalling screams from the room next door.

Gretchen clutched at Katya in alarm. 'What's that?' she whispered.

'That is Herr Schubert,' the Kriminalinspektor said. 'He is answering a few pertinent questions.' The screams rose higher, becoming unbearable.

'What are they doing to him?' Gretchen asked, starting to cry. Katya put her hands over Gretchen's ears to try and shut out the horrible sounds.

'A more interesting question, I was about to say,' Kriminal-inspektor Sauer went on, 'is who are *you*, Fräulein Komarovsky? And why are you travelling to Switzerland with a German child?'

'I'm Gretchen's governess,' Katya said, trying to keep her voice steady. 'I'm taking her to her father in Zürich.'

'And who is her father?'

Katya tried to ignore the dreadful shrieking coming from Herr Schubert. 'His name is Thorwald Bachmann. He's doing important business for the Reich.'

'So?' He leaned back in his chair, his eyes on Katya. 'What business would that be?'

'He imports machinery.'

'What sort of machinery?'

'I don't know. I'm only the governess.'

'Is he a Jew?'

'No.'

'Any Jewish descent?'

'None.'

'Pure Aryan?'

'Yes.'

'Is he a member of the Party?'

'I – I don't know.'

There was an ominous silence from next door now. The police captain frowned. 'You don't know?'

'He's not – not political.'

'That is the excuse usually made by those who are far too political for their own good.' The screaming of Herr Schubert began again, reaching a pitch of anguish. Then the screams broke down. They could hear him begging incoherently. Kriminalinspektor Sauer cocked his head with a cold smile, listening. 'I think we are getting somewhere with Herr Schubert. Ah, yes,' he said as there was a knock at the door. 'Come!'

A Brownshirt came in. 'He has confessed everything, Herr Kriminalinspektor. The money is his. He is also a degenerate, on the antisocials police list in Salzburg. The other man is his lover.' He held out his hand. Something bloodstained lay in his palm. 'And we found this. Diamonds. Hidden in his arsehole.'

The police captain clicked his tongue. 'Moderate your language. There is a woman present.'

'Sorry, Herr Kriminalinspektor,' the man said with a grin. 'In his rectum.'

'It sounds as though we need to talk to Herr Schubert and his boyfriend a little further,' Sauer said, rising to his feet. 'You will be taken back to the hall, Fräulein. Wait there. Don't attempt to leave the building.'

Shaken by the last few minutes, they were escorted back to their hard wooden bench by the shaven-headed youth. He stood, watching them ostentatiously, as though expecting them to make a run for the street at any moment. They sat shivering in the draught, listening to the distant shouts and screams. Gretchen was distraught.

'It's all right,' Katya whispered. 'We'll be out of here soon.'

Gretchen hugged herself tightly. 'What did they do to Herr Schubert?'

'I don't know.'

'Is he dead?'

'I don't know, Liebchen. Try not to think about it.'

She knew it was useless advice. People were still being brought in from the street, some of them hanging limply between two Brownshirts, disappearing behind one door or another. Gretchen curled up on the bench with her head on Katya's lap. Katya rocked her gently. Soon, Gretchen was asleep.

Two agonising hours crawled past. Katya thought of their train, heading towards Zürich. It would be at the Swiss border by now. And they were trapped in this hellish place. It felt like a nightmare. But it wasn't.

It was dawn by the time they were summoned again. Katya was jerked from a half-sleep by a rough hand shaking her shoulder. They were led, stiff and aching, back to the police captain's office. He was yawning in his chair, stretching his arms above his head. His tunic was undone almost to the waist, showing a stained vest. In front of him on his desk was a plate of scarlet frankfurters and mustard.

'Excuse my appearance,' he said with baroque courtesy. 'It has been a long night. But a rewarding one.' He ate for a while without speaking while they watched, his knife and fork scratching on the cheap plate.

'A nation is like a garden,' he said conversationally. 'The gardener's duty is to cultivate the useful plants and pull out the weeds. Here in Austria, we Germans have acquired a new garden to tend. It has been neglected for a long time by its previous gardeners. So we have to get our hands dirty. The work is messy. The neighbours don't always understand this. You follow me? It would be better not to speak of what you see here.'

'Yes,' she said tensely, 'I understand.'

'Good.' He wiped his hands and opened a drawer. He tossed their passports on to his desk. 'You are free to go.'

Katya was hardly able to believe it. 'Go?'

'Unless you prefer to stay?'

She grasped their precious documents. 'No.'

He picked up his knife and sawed at the sausage. 'Don't come back to Austria, Fräulein.'

Dazed, they walked out into the cold Alpine morning.

'Are you all right?' Katya asked.

'I'm starving,' Gretchen said practically.

'We have to get back to the station. We'll get something to eat there.' But she was mentally calculating their tiny store of money. Their train was long gone. If they had to buy new tickets, they would run out of funds, which would be a disaster. They set off, hauling their suitcases.

The station was busy with people heading for work. She bought Gretchen a poppy-seed pretzel and queued at the ticket office while she devoured it, ignoring her own growling stomach. But when she finally reached the clerk, he was hostile.

'Your tickets have expired,' he said curtly.

'I know. Can't you issue me replacements?'

'Impossible. You missed your train. You must buy new tickets.'

'But it's not our fault! We were taken off the train by the police!'

'Then you must have done something wrong.'

'We didn't do anything wrong,' she retorted angrily.

He was skull-like, with rimless spectacles and a waxy face, upon which a sparse, Himmler-like moustache was failing to thrive. 'I do not believe this. The police do not arrest people for nothing.'

'Well, they did. They kept us all night and only released us this morning. We were completely innocent.'

'You must buy new tickets,' he insisted. 'Or walk to Zürich,' he sneered.

Katya could hear people shuffling and muttering in the queue behind her. Despair made her bold. She spoke louder. 'Is this how you treat visitors to Austria?'

'Don't raise your voice to me, Fräulein.'

'I *will* raise my voice!' Katya pointed at the travel poster beside the cubicle, showing an elegant couple slaloming down a ski slope. 'This is what you tell people it's like. But when foreigners arrive, they are hauled off the train by your police, for no reason, and forced to spend the night in a police station! In the company of criminals! My daughter is twelve years old! Can you imagine what she has seen?' Katya was teetering on the verge of genuine hysteria. 'And now that we have missed our train, you tell me I must buy a new ticket – *or walk to Zürich!* What impertinence! How dare you!'

Her voice had rung around the station, and people were stopping to watch the spectacle. Her belligerence was having an effect. The clerk had grown even waxier behind his desk. He smoothed his vestigial moustache with nervous fingers. 'Please go away from the window.'

'I will *not* go away! I intend to report you for your insolence and uncooperative attitude. And I intend to make sure all foreigners know what to expect in your country. You are a disgrace to your uniform!'

'Shame on you, Herr Müller!' a woman echoed from behind Katya. Others joined in, a chorus of sympathy and indignation.

'What can I do?' the clerk whined. 'I cannot give away free tickets! I would lose my job!'

'You'll lose your job anyway if this lady reports you,' a burly woman called out.

'Give her the tickets, you old mummy,' another woman shouted. There was a burst of laughter.

'Give her the tickets, Tutankhamen!'

The chorus of mockery was too much for the man. Hurriedly, he produced them and thrust them at Katya. 'There – now go away!'

Katya left in triumph, thanking the women in the queue. It seemed that not everyone in Austria was a cowering lickspittle. But their troubles were not over yet. He'd given them Third Class tickets for the last train of the day, leaving at ten that evening. It was now seven in the morning. They had fifteen hours to pass in Innsbruck. Katya put their luggage in the station lock-up for a few pfennigs.

She had promised to call her parents from Zürich today, and she knew they would worry when she didn't, so they walked to the post office, where she spent a couple of her precious remaining schillings on sending a terse telegram:

DELAYED INNSBRUCK OVERNIGHT ARRIVING ZURICH TOMORROW MUCH LOVE KATYA.

Then they wandered around the town. It was a gracious old place, owing its prosperity to visitors intent on winter sports. There were obviously a lot of these visitors still left, enjoying the last weeks of snow on the slopes. They could be seen through the windows of expensive shops and dining in the best restaurants, with bronzed faces and smart clothes, laughing merrily and showing white teeth. Katya envied their happiness. Carefree, well-to-do, they were people who were glad the Nazis had come, people who had made the right choices, and would never find themselves in a Gestapo cell or a concentration camp.

She shuddered as she remembered the screams of Herr Schubert last night. Was Thor suffering similar horrors? Increasingly, she had to face the possibility that he might be dead, and that she might never know his fate.

She had told that dreadful police captain that Thor was not political, and that was true. He was too warm and human to be enslaved by any political dogma. Nazism seemed to her to be a philosophy of punishment, a worship of death. It ran counter to the best impulses of human nature. But perhaps its appeal to the worst impulses was what made it so strong? Perhaps there was a sizeable part of the population that just wanted an excuse to unleash their cruelty?

She couldn't bear to think of Thor being ill-treated. He was so kind and sensitive. All his strength wouldn't help him in the hands of Nazi officialdom. She prayed that these thoughts hadn't also occurred to Gretchen; but Gretchen had a penetrating, instinctive intelligence.

Gretchen suddenly seized her hand, jolting her from her dark thoughts. 'Katya! Look!'

Across the street was a large piano shop. It was just opening up. Assistants could be seen inside, turning on the lights, dusting the instruments. Gretchen pulled Katya across the street and pressed her nose to the window. Pianos of every size, in a variety of woods, glowed under the spotlights, with their lids temptingly upraised.

Gretchen turned imploringly to Katya. 'Please? Can we go in? Please, please!'

Reluctantly, because she didn't want to draw any further attention to themselves, she followed Gretchen into the shop. The smell of new pianos enveloped Gretchen, composed of lacquer, furniture oil and exotic woods. Dreamily, Gretchen wandered between the instruments, until she reached the biggest of all, in the centre of the room, a gleaming black concert grand that was twice the size of her piano at home. She stared at it yearningly.

The manager walked up to them. 'Isn't it magnificent?'

Gretchen nodded, her eyes fixed on the instrument. 'Can I play it?'

He chuckled indulgently. 'This is the best piano we have in the shop, young lady. It's a Steinway Model D. It costs thirty thousand Deutschmarks.'

Gretchen nodded. Figures were not her strong point. 'Can I play it?' she repeated. The man looked at them both shrewdly. Katya could tell that he didn't think they were the sort of people who might have thirty thousand Deutschmarks lying around. He was an oily, mannequin-like man in his forties. He shrugged. 'We have a young lady who demonstrates the pianos. I will call her. Wait here, please. And in the meantime, don't touch!' He glided away.

Gretchen couldn't take her eyes off the piano. Katya's heart went out to her. She was so young, tossed in a stormy sea of troubles that threatened to overwhelm her; and the Steinway was like a great ship, offering refuge, if only she could clamber aboard it.

The manager returned, accompanied by a woman of about Katya's own age, who had a sheaf of music tucked under her arm. She was brushing crumbs hastily off her mouth. She had evidently been interrupted in her breakfast. But she had a pretty face and a ready smile, with rounded pink cheeks and dark hair and eyes.

'This is Fräulein Hildegard,' the manager said. 'She will play for you.'

Fräulein Hildegard shook hands with them briskly, then studied Gretchen with an intelligent gaze. 'You are the pianist?'

Gretchen nodded. 'Yes.'

'What grade have you studied to?'

'I – I don't know,' she answered in a small voice.

'Grade Six? Grade Seven?'

Gretchen was baffled. 'Gretchen hasn't studied at all,' Katya said, rescuing her. 'She plays by ear.'

'I see.'

The manager, not hiding his contemptuous smile, oozed away, clearly certain that he wouldn't be selling the most expensive piano in the shop today. But Fräulein Hildegard merely nodded. 'It's a great thing to play by ear,' she said gently. 'Not everyone can do it. What would you like me to play for you?'

'Anything,' Gretchen said.

'All right.' Fräulein Hildegard lifted the lid of the piano carefully and removed the crimson felt. Gretchen couldn't suppress a little gasp as the gleaming ivory keys were revealed. She was like a starving child looking in a pastry-shop window. Fräulein Hildegard opened a score and put the music on the stand. 'I'm studying at the Tyrolean State Conservatory,' she said, 'and I have an examination coming up. This is one of the pieces I'm preparing. It's by Brahms.' She began to play.

Gretchen edged closer and closer, watching the young woman's hands intently. She was so used to seeing her own hands on the keys. She had very seldom seen another pianist playing, at least not up close like this. It was fascinating. At last, she had crept so close to Fräulein Hildegard that she was pressed against her chair. The young woman broke off with a merry laugh, and turned. 'You don't like my playing?' she asked.

'You play very nicely,' Gretchen said awkwardly.

'But *you* want to play.'

Gretchen was blunt. 'Yes.'

Fräulein Hildegard looked around quickly to see if anyone was watching, then slid along the stool. She patted the place next to her. 'Sit beside me.'

Gretchen didn't need a second invitation. She slipped eagerly into the place beside Fräulein Hildegard, who watched indulgently as Gretchen slowly caressed the keys with her fingertips. 'Do you want a score?' Hildegard asked.

Gretchen shook her head. 'I can't read music.'

Fräulein Hildegard raised her dark eyebrows. 'Really? Not at all? You should learn.'

'I'm trying.'

'All right. Play what you want.'

Gretchen's face was pale and tense now. She depressed one of the keys and played a single note and listened to it ring, until the sound faded away. Then she played a second note, and stared into space, as though watching it fly away.

'Perhaps the action is a little heavy for you?' Fräulein Hildegard suggested kindly.

'What does that mean?'

'You have to press hard to get the notes. Perhaps you prefer a smaller piano?'

'No, it's all right. This one is beautiful.' Without another word, she started to play. The piece was one Katya hadn't heard her play before, but she recognised it as a Beethoven sonata, one that Gretchen had often listened to at home, but had never attempted. It began with some slow, sad phrases that seemed to be asking a question, and then searched for an answer.

Fräulein Hildegard's face changed. Her lips parted as she listened. She glanced up at Katya, then at Gretchen's face, as though looking for some kind of explanation.

The music developed steadily into a torrent under Gretchen's pale hands, the chords reverberating with growing strength. The huge piano responded, like a powerful horse obeying a slight but masterful rider. Cascades of wonderful sound surged around them.

Fräulein Hildegard got up quickly and lifted the top board of the Steinway, so that the music swelled out even more loudly. Katya saw people all around the shop stopping to turn their heads and listen.

It was an extraordinary performance. Gretchen was pouring all her sorrow, all her fear and anguish, into the music. The horrors of the past weeks, the suffering she hadn't been able to articulate, were now throbbing in every note. Her eyes were shut tight, her mouth compressed into a white line. She swayed slightly on the stool, a small figure against the great, black expanse of the piano, intense and yet almost unmoving, like the eye of a cyclone that was whirling around the shop.

Fräulein Hildegard was staring at her with an expression of puzzled awe. The oily salesman came hurrying back, his eyes wide. Others in the shop were coming to look too. People were even coming in from the street outside, attracted by the performance. Soon there was a crowd around the Steinway, but Gretchen was oblivious. She was lost in the music, lost in a way that only she could understand.

At last, the piece came to an end. Gretchen's hands dropped to her sides. She opened her eyes slowly, and then started to cry. They were broken, jerky sobs of release. Katya helped her get up and hugged her tightly. As soon as she could, she led her away from the crowd.

'Wait!' Fräulein Hildegard had hurried after them. She took Katya's arm. 'Is it a trick?'

'No, of course not. How could it be a trick?'

'I don't understand how she could learn a Beethoven sonata without lessons, without reading music. And then, to play like that – like a grown woman, with so much expression, so much feeling! If I could play like that, Fräulein, my career would be assured. I've never heard anything like it in my life before.'

'She learns by listening to the gramophone.'

'You're joking.'

'No.'

Fräulein Hildegard peered into Gretchen's tear-stained face. 'Is it true?'

'Yes,' Gretchen whispered. She pressed her face against Katya's breast. Katya just wanted to get Gretchen somewhere quiet, so she could master her jangled emotions, but Fräulein Hildegard was not ready to let them go. 'You played the first movement of that sonata. Can you play the second?'

Gretchen shook her head. 'I haven't learned it yet.'

'Learned it? How, learned it?'

'I play it in my thoughts. And when I know it, it will come out.'

Fräulein Hildegard looked at Katya for an explanation. 'The music gets into her head in strange ways,' Katya said. 'She spends hours curled around the gramophone, playing one record after another. Sometimes she'll play a piece immediately after hearing it.

Sometimes pieces need to mature in her mind before she attempts them. I don't know how it happens.'

Fräulein Hildegard sighed. 'That explains your fingering, Gretchen. It's all wrong. It sounds wonderful, I don't mean that it doesn't – but there are better ways to do it. With some lessons you could—' She drew a deep breath. 'Well, I don't know *what* you could do.'

The oily salesman had joined them. 'There's a man interested in the Steinway,' he said. He patted Gretchen on the head as though she were a clever little dog. 'How would you like to come in here and play every day?'

Gretchen shrank away from him. 'No, thank you.'

'You could earn some good money. We would pay you well.'

'Are you giving my job away, Herr Zimmermann?' Fräulein Hildegard asked ironically.

'I didn't say that.' He tapped his fleshy nose. 'But a child prodigy always brings a crowd. And that is very good for sales!'

'Thank you for letting Gretchen play,' Katya said, moving towards the door. 'It was very kind of you. Goodbye!'

'Where are you going now?' Fräulein Hildegard demanded, following them.

'I'm not sure,' Katya admitted. 'Gretchen just needs to go somewhere quiet.'

'The Tiroler Café,' Fräulein Hildegard said decisively. 'It's just down the street. It's very quiet. I'll join you there in half an hour.'

'I don't think—'

'Here.' She pressed a five-schilling note into Katya's hand. 'Take this. Buy yourself a coffee, and Gretchen something to eat.'

'I can't take this!'

'I don't mind paying to hear a great performer. And I don't think you have much money, yes? Wait for me there. I won't be long, I promise. And please – don't run away!'

The Tiroler Café was as quiet as Fräulein Hildegard had promised. They found a table in a corner. Katya ordered a much-needed
cup of coffee, and Gretchen chose a doughnut and a glass of milk.
She was recovering her poise.

'That piano was so beautiful,' she said wistfully. 'It sounded
like a whole orchestra.'

'You certainly made it sound like a whole orchestra. Are you
feeling better now?'

'Yes. I was only crying because the music was so sad.'

Katya smiled. 'You've heard it many times before.'

'Yes, but today, I understood what it was saying. Before, I
didn't, really.'

'Oh, Gretchen.' Katya put her hands over Gretchen's. 'You've
gone through so much. You've seen and heard things a little girl
shouldn't see and hear.'

'I'm not a little girl any more.' Her eyes were grave and dark.

Katya nodded slowly. 'I suppose you aren't.'

'Will we ever see Papa again?'

'I don't know.'

'What if we don't ever see him again?'

'At least I will always be with you. If you want me.'

Gretchen gave Katya one of her rare luminous smiles. 'Yes, I
want you. Even if we get Papa back. You'll marry him, and we'll
all be together.'

'That sounds like a good idea,' Katya said.

Fräulein Hildegard came bustling into the café. She unfastened
the belt of her coat and sat down with them. 'You got something
to eat. Good.'

'This is very kind of you, Fräulein Hildegard.'

'Shall we drop the Fräulein business? I'm just Hildegard.'

'And I'm Katya.'

Hildegard rested her rounded chin on her clasped hands, and stared at them both with her bright black eyes. 'There is a big mystery here, and I want to know all about it. Tell me everything.'

Hildegard listened without interrupting as Katya told her everything – or as much of it as she thought was safe. Even though she felt instinctively that she could trust Hildegard, the experiences of the past few weeks made her cautious.

When she'd brought the story up to date, Hildegard's cheeks were indignantly flushed. 'Well,' she said, 'the first thing I have to say is that I am *not* a Nazi. In fact, I detest the lot of them. They are nothing but a bunch of criminals who trample on everything that is beautiful. What they've done to your family is outrageous,' she said hotly. 'You've nothing to fear from me. I'd like to help, if I can.'

'Thank you, Hildegard, but I don't think there's anything you can do.'

'May I say something? Gretchen has an astonishing talent. There are sometimes young musicians who play far beyond their years. As Herr Zimmermann said in the shop, people are amazed. But it's almost always mechanical. There's no feeling. Gretchen plays with real passion, real feeling. That's rare. However, there's only so far she can go without training. She should be at music school. She should be taught the right technique. She should—'

'I know,' Katya interrupted unhappily. 'And so does Gretchen. But we need to be safe before any of that is possible.'

Hildegard leaned forward urgently to Gretchen. 'Once you get to England, Gretchen, promise me you'll go to the best music school you can find.'

'I promise,' Gretchen nodded.

'Learning to read music is not as hard as you think. It's easier than learning to read words. And learning the right fingering is even more important.' She took out a little notebook and a pen, wrote on a page, and tore it out. 'This is my address,' she said, handing it to Katya. 'If you get into any trouble before you leave Austria, come to me.'

Katya was touched. Kindness was a rarity these days. She felt her eyes mist over. 'Thank you.'

'I hope you find Herr Bachmann soon. I never thought I would feel ashamed to be Austrian. But these days—' She shook her head. 'We can only hope for better times. I'm afraid I have to run back to the shop, or Herr Zimmermann will fire me. Although whatever I play now is going to be a bit of an anticlimax.' She kissed them both formally on each cheek as she left.

And then they were alone again.

Chapter 19

They were back on the platform before ten. It had been a long, cold day with nothing to do but count the hours as they passed. The railway station was quiet at this late hour, and their train was very late, so it was past one in the morning by the time it arrived.

It came in painfully slowly. They could see at once that it was heavily guarded. Brownshirts were standing on the footplates of each carriage, rifles slung over their shoulders. It was also jammed to capacity. They had to push their way into a carriage that was already full, and find somewhere to stand among the jumble of baggage and people. The air was stifling. People were smoking, despite the prohibition signs. Underlying the tobacco was a smell of sweat and fear.

Katya looked around. Their previous train had been full of prosperous middle-class burghers. This one seemed to be carrying people with the hunted air of animals making a final, desperate run. Listening to the half-whispered conversations all around, she could hear people discussing what would happen at the border. They spoke of it as though it terrified them.

A bearded young man who was seated a few yards down the carriage got up and made his way towards them. He lifted his hat politely. 'Please,' he said to Katya, 'take my seat over there.'

'That's very kind, but I don't mind standing.'

'This is a slow train,' the young man warned. 'It stops at every station, and there are endless checks, as you'll see. It will be three or four hours before we reach the border.' He glanced at Gretchen. 'Perhaps your daughter would like to sit down? She looks tired.' When Katya hesitated, he added, 'That lady in the seat beside is my wife. She'll keep an eye on her.'

It was true that Gretchen was worn out. She looked peaky and hollow-eyed. Gratefully, Katya accepted. Gretchen went to sit next to the young woman, who welcomed her with a smile and began talking to her.

'We have no children,' the young man said to Katya, keeping his balance as the train jerked into movement. 'My wife wants them badly, but I tell her, no. Not until the future is better.' He had a cut lip and a black eye, as though he'd been in a fight. As if to make up for his injuries, he wore a bright yellow bow tie. He put on a pair of horn-rimmed spectacles and looked into Katya's face. The lenses made his black eye look even more lurid. 'May I ask – are you perhaps Jewish?'

'I'm afraid not.'

'Don't be afraid. It's a good time not to be Jewish. I only ask because your face seems . . .'

'Un-English?' Katya smiled tiredly. 'My parents are Russian.'

'Ah, that must explain it. My name is Reuben Schwartz. My wife is named Rachel. We're Jews. From Vienna.' He paused, as though waiting for her to draw back in disgust. When she didn't, he leaned closer confidentially. 'And may I ask what passport you're travelling on?'

'Mine is British. My daughter's is Austrian.'

He closed his eyes, as if inhaling some precious scent. 'You're very lucky. You will have no problems at the border. We're travelling on three-week permits. That's all the Nazis will issue us. And we don't know whether they'll let us out . . . or whether it's just a way of gathering up Jews for the concentration camps.'

'I'm sorry,' Katya said. 'It's horrible.' She saw that Reuben Schwartz's wife now had her arm around Gretchen, who had fallen asleep on her bosom.

'Your husband isn't with you?' Reuben asked, following her gaze.

Katya hesitated. 'He was arrested by the Gestapo. We don't know where he is, or what's happened to him. We're praying that he'll come to find us in London.'

His angular face drooped into melancholy lines. 'May he live a hundred years. His crime?'

'Being human.'

'Yes, that is a serious offence these days.' He turned as a commotion broke out in the carriage. Four uniformed men were pushing through the crowded aisles, shouting commands. Reuben grimaced. 'The Brownshirts,' he muttered. 'Looking for money or jewellery. I hope you haven't got anything like that tucked away.'

'We haven't.'

Everyone in the carriage had fallen silent. The SA men were making all the noise, bawling insults and barking orders. They opened suitcases at random, emptying the contents on to the filthy floor of the carriage and kicking them around with their boots, looking for anything valuable. It was exactly the way they had behaved at their house. Katya felt sick. They were clearly taking a cruel delight in the fear and distress they were causing.

'They have already searched this carriage twice since Vienna,' Reuben said bitterly. 'They get a bonus for catching anyone hiding currency. And of course, they enjoy it.'

Katya felt every muscle of her body tensing as the guards approached. It was a purely physiological reaction, which she could do nothing about. The proximity of SA or Gestapo men filled her with terror.

A woman began screaming as the men pulled off her clothes, yanking at her underclothing. Everyone looked rigidly ahead, nobody stirring a finger to prevent them. They found nothing but the satisfaction of exposing some female flesh. One of the men made a joke and laughed raucously, his hand in her underwear. She was left crying hysterically as they moved on. Katya felt her stomach heaving. She had eaten nothing since Hildegard's cup of coffee that morning, or she would have vomited. If they did that to her, she felt she would die. She prayed they would pass by Gretchen and Rachel Schwartz. For some reason, they did, choosing to harass some people on the other side of the carriage.

There was more shouting, more women's screams. Katya couldn't bear to look. The Jewish man put his hand on her arm to calm her. 'Hold fast,' he whispered.

At last, they reached the place where she and Reuben were standing. They guffawed at Reuben's split lip. 'You'll be getting some more of that before long, Jew-boy,' one said.

'Passport,' one of the others barked at Katya. The words came on a reek of alcohol. She realised that the Brownshirts were all very drunk – both with the beer they had swallowed and the power they had been given. She forced herself to stay calm, handing him her passport. He peered at it, his face red and sweaty.

'Britisher?'

She nodded, not trusting herself to speak. He turned and shouted to his companions. They clustered around, looking from Katya to her passport and muttering among themselves. One of them laughed quietly. Another took out a notebook, and laboriously copied information down into it from the document. He gave her a sneering grin when he returned the passport and a mock salute. They moved on to their next victim.

'What does that mean?' she asked Reuben.

He shook his head. 'I don't know. But they've noticed you. Be careful at the border.'

'What can I do?' she asked helplessly.

'What can any of us do?'

Reuben stayed with her for the rest of the night, talking quietly. His calm, resigned presence was comforting and distracting, for which she was grateful. He had been a student in Vienna, he told her, supported in his law studies by his wife's work as a secretary. But the day after the Anschluss, he had been beaten up in the street, and told that the university was barred to him and all Jews.

'We decided to leave quickly, before it gets worse. In a way, we're lucky. We're young, and we have no property to leave behind. My wife's employer managed to get travel documents for us. And here we are, making our way in the wide world.' He seemed to have no idea what he and Rachel were going to do once they had reached Switzerland; she felt that he didn't really expect to make it across the border.

The slow journey towards Switzerland grew increasingly chaotic. Everything was falling apart. The train, as Reuben had warned her, stopped at every station on the way. Each time, the Brownshirt guards were changed, and each time, the new influx of ruffians, drunker and more violent than the last, brought fresh misery as they rooted through the luggage for prizes, scattering the contents, assaulting any Jews they found, molesting the women; until the carriage looked like a shipwreck, a hopeless muddle of clothing and pathetic possessions belonging to God knew whom, with crying women trying to sort it all out and men wiping blood off their faces.

Katya felt like crying herself. These thugs had been unleashed on the population of Austria by the Anschluss. There was no protection against them. They were backed by the full might of the German military machine. Their task was to terrify and humiliate the civilian population, to enforce complete obedience to the new regime.

As the train pulled into Feldkirch, the last station before the border, banks of searchlights flared into life on either side of the train. The white light stabbed into tired eyes, making the passengers cover their faces and shrink away.

The men who boarded the train here were not drunken louts but German Gestapo officials. They were deadly serious.

'Everyone off the train. Take your luggage and assemble on the platform. The train is being cleared. Everyone out! Out! Now!'

Silently, exhausted and cowed by the terrible journey, the passengers gathered their possessions and moved out of the carriage. Katya kept her arm tight around Gretchen.

'What are they going to do with us?' Gretchen whispered.

'I don't know,' Katya answered. 'Try not to be frightened.'

It was vain advice. Gretchen was blank-faced with shock. Each day seemed to bring new terrors for her.

A Gestapo sergeant came down the line, taking all the passports. He disappeared into an office, leaving them to the tender mercies of the customs officers.

Tables had been set up all along the platform. Every bag had now to be heaved on to them and searched yet again, though it seemed inconceivable that the Nazi troopers could have missed anything on the train. But this time, the search was more professional – and more brutal still.

The police went to work grimly, dumping out the contents of every suitcase, then slashing open the linings of each one with razors, looking for false bottoms. After that, they cut open the handles to look inside those. The soles and heels were prised off shoes. Teddy bears and dolls were ripped apart. Books were torn out of their spines. Jackets and coats had the seams slit open and the padding pulled out.

And every third or fourth passenger was taken off for a physical search. A more complete humiliation would be hard to imagine.

Katya and Gretchen waited among the huddled, silent troupe of passengers, shivering in the icy wind. She didn't know where Reuben and Rachel had got to. The cold glare of the searchlights was relentless. She'd never felt so tired and despairing in her life. She tried as best she was able to keep Gretchen from breaking down.

The knowledge that the Swiss border, and freedom, were only a mile or two down the track made this final check all the more agonising.

At last, they reached the inspection tables. Their suitcases were opened and subjected to the same ruthless search as all the others. The linings were cut out, the handles sawn in half, rendering them all but useless. Thank God, she thought, they hadn't tried to smuggle out any money. But Gretchen couldn't hold back a cry of misery as her beloved copy of *Grimms' Fairy Tales* was torn apart, the spine split open to look inside. The police ignored her.

The inspection was over in a few minutes. The customs man threw their defiled clothes back at them. 'Pack it all up. Move! Quick! Quick!' The constant shouting was dazing them. You wanted to cover your ears and shrink to the ground. They stuffed their possessions back into the cases as quickly as they could. Now they were pushed towards the office to get their passports. Let this be the end of it, Katya prayed. Let us get our passports back and be in Switzerland by tomorrow.

In contrast to the chaos outside, the SS officer sitting across the desk was immaculate and quiet. His uniform was pressed, the silver lightning flashes and death's heads gleaming against the black serge. His face was expressionless, his high cheekbones and thin nose giving him the remote air of a Baltic aristocrat. He had their passports in front of him. He examined the documents carefully, turning the pages delicately in his white fingers.

At last, he looked up at Katya. His eyes were slanted, a pale, cold green, like glass. 'Why are you taking this German child out of our country?'

He had spoken in perfect English, taking her by surprise. 'I'm her governess. She has no mother. I'm taking her to see her father.'

'Where is her father?'

'He's in Zürich, on a business trip. We're going to stay with him for a week.'

His eyes seemed to look straight through her. 'Where is he staying?'

Katya had prepared the lie. 'At the Hotel Schweizerhof, in the Bahnhofplatz.'

'His name?'

'Thorwald Bachmann.'

He reached out and picked up the black telephone on his desk. Her heart felt as though electricity had jolted through it. Then it sank down into her shoes. His eyes didn't leave Katya's face as he made the call. It took only a few minutes before he replaced the receiver. 'There is no Thorwald Bachmann staying at the Hotel Schweizerhof.'

'He must have moved to another hotel.' Her voice was papery.

'Which hotel might that be?' His manner was polite, in stark contrast to the roughness of the Brownshirts, and all the more chilling because of that. He indicated the telephone. 'I have a direct line to Zürich. I can call them all, if you wish.'

'No. I – I can't imagine where he is. Perhaps he hasn't arrived yet. I'm sure he'll be there tomorrow.'

He picked up his pen. 'Herr Bachmann gave you a letter, of course, permitting you to remove his daughter from Germany?'

'No.' Her throat was bone dry. She tried to swallow. 'We didn't know that was necessary.'

'Did you not know that it is a crime to take a child out of Germany without written consent from the father?'

'No,' she said. 'I didn't know that.'

'It is also a crime to lie to the authorities. I am sure you knew *that.*'

'I'm not lying!'

'Everything you have said to me so far is a lie. I suggest you start telling the truth now, before you make things worse for yourself. Where is Thorwald Bachmann?'

'I don't know.'

'You don't know? And yet you have his daughter with you?'

'We were supposed to meet in Zürich! I – I don't know what's happened. Some silly mix-up, I'm sure!'

He considered her for a long while. At last, he spoke. 'Miss Komarovsky, you are under arrest for the crime of child abduction. I advise you not to tell any further lies. You have already committed a serious offence.' There were two Brownshirts at the door already. He nodded to them. They marched forward and grasped Katya and Gretchen by the arms, hauling them to their feet. Katya felt as though the breath was knocked out of her lungs. She tried to plead with the SS officer, but he was already writing in a ledger. He didn't look up as they were pushed out. Her mind was whirling.

In the corridor outside, they passed Reuben Schwartz. He was being dragged, limp and unconscious, between two burly SA men, his toes trailing along the linoleum floor, his face a pulped mask of blood. She was only able to identify him by his bright yellow bow tie.

They were put in a cell, together with two dozen other people who had been detained. The mood was very sombre. Many of the women were sobbing quietly, the men sitting silent, staring at the floor. Some had been beaten, a few so badly that they could not stand, and they lay on the cement floor.

Gretchen felt that she had entered the terrible world of the Grimms' fairy tales, or the Brueghel and Hieronymus Bosch paintings that had frightened her as a child. It had all become real and had enveloped her: the grotesque cruelties, the dark beings that loved to torment, the black sky that lowered over the innocent victims and the lost children. Why would people deliberately create such a world? It bewildered her.

Katya held her close, rocking her gently. She didn't know how else to comfort her. What was going to happen to them now? Her imagination tormented her. Perhaps she had been terribly stupid. Perhaps it would have been better for them to have lain low, stayed quiet, and waited for Thor's release – instead of drawing attention to themselves by trying to leave Austria. She recalled Papa telling her about the shooting parties he joined on the moors with his wealthy friends: it was only the birds that took flight who were shot by the sportsmen. Those that hid sometimes escaped.

She felt a deep ache of failure.

It was now dawn. The early light that slanted in from the high barred window was steel-blue. The station had quietened; earlier there had been the sound of beatings, screams and groans from adjacent cells. Now there was silence.

Then the rumble of trucks approached. A man looked up, his face swollen and bruised. 'They've come for us,' he said.

They listened to the sound of the trucks manoeuvring outside. The toxic stench of diesel fumes filled the cell. With a crash, the door was opened, and Brownshirts came in.

'Out! Out! Everybody out! Form an orderly line! Women to the left! Men to the right!'

They were hustled out into the cold air. Three canvas-backed trucks were waiting for them. A squad of soldiers with guns had lined up to ensure nobody escaped.

Also there, watching the proceedings with folded arms, was the black-clad SS officer who had arrested Katya during the night. When he caught sight of Katya, he turned to the soldier beside him and gave an order. The man ran over to Katya and pulled her out of the line. 'The Sturmbannführer wants to see you. Come!'

Taking Gretchen with her, she followed the man.

The Sturmbannführer's face was as expressionless as before. 'I have received information from headquarters. Your employer, Thorwald Bachmann, is under arrest for crimes against the state. You concealed this information from me.'

'I said I didn't know where he is,' she replied, her heart thudding, 'and that's true. I don't know what you've done with him.'

'He is in custody. He will be tried shortly, and is facing a lengthy sentence.'

Katya felt the tears flood her eyes. 'He did nothing wrong!'

'His crimes have implicated you,' he said coldly. 'Your loyalty to him is misplaced, I assure you.'

'He's a good man!'

The Sturmbannführer ignored that. 'Since you are a foreign national, we are prepared to be lenient in this case. You may proceed to Zürich. But the child remains here, and will be handed over to the National Socialist People's Welfare.'

Her heart, which had risen wildly, now plummeted again. 'I can't accept that!'

'You have no choice.'

'I'm not abandoning Gretchen!'

A slight crease appeared between his eyebrows. 'You are trying my patience, Miss Komarovsky. You have heard of Dachau?' He nodded towards the trucks, which were rumbling like hungry monsters. 'That is where this transport is headed.'

'If Gretchen is going to Dachau, then I'm going with her.'

'Don't you understand? You're guilty of a serious offence. Yet you are being offered your freedom. Proceed to the platform, and be grateful to the Nazi state for its leniency.'

'I am not leaving my child.'

'You are not her mother.'

'She's as much mine as if I were her mother. And if you try and separate us, then I will tell the world what your illustrious regime is really like. I'll go straight to the newspapers and tell them how I've seen your bully boys beat innocent people half to death, how you lock up children, how you commit horrible crimes with nobody to stop you.'

'Don't be a little fool.'

'You get away with it because nobody says anything,' Katya went on furiously. 'It's all glossed over. People don't know the truth. But I've seen what Nazism really means, and I'll make sure everyone listens to me!'

There was a glare of anger in the glassy green eyes now, the first emotion he had shown. 'Is that your last word?'

'Yes.'

'Then you must face the consequences of your criminal action. You will live to regret this day.' He turned to the soldier beside him. 'Put them both on the truck.'

Chapter 20

The truck was packed full with wretched humanity. Once the tailgate had been roped shut, it was nearly dark inside, illuminated only by a few spears of light that pierced through the eyeholes in the canvas, illuminating a face here or there. Katya thought of cattle, on their way to the slaughterhouse.

'Papa's alive,' Gretchen whispered. 'That man said so.'

'Yes,' Katya replied tiredly, 'at least we know that.'

Gretchen squeezed her hand. Whatever grim sentence might be imposed on Thor, they had the knowledge that he hadn't been murdered out of hand, like so many others. He was alive, and where there was life, there *was* hope.

The journey was unspeakably comfortless and dreary. Each one of them now had a number on a card, pinned on their chests. Katya's was 147. Gretchen's was 147A. Katya prayed that meant they would be kept together, and not separated. But there was no guarantee of that.

Crammed on wooden benches, they were jerked against one another, spines jolting, heads sometimes cracking painfully together. The hours passed. Nobody spoke. The only subject of conversation would have been what lay in store for them at the other end, and that was too terrible to talk about, although it hung over them all.

Dachau! The name struck dread into every heart. The Nazis had built the place as a labour camp to 're-educate' political prisoners; but everyone had heard of the cruelty that reigned there, a regime of brutal labour and savage punishments that few survived for long.

How was little Gretchen going to endure a place like Dachau? Katya, trying to shelter Gretchen from the worst of the truck's jolting, could feel how slight the girl's body was in her arms, how delicate. They had so nearly reached safety. Now they might both die behind the barbed wire of Dachau, and nobody would ever know their fate.

Katya had fallen into a fitful doze, haunted by cloudy nightmares, when she was awoken by a surge of bodies crashing into her. She tried to hold on to Gretchen, but Gretchen was gone. People were tumbling over her, hard and soft bits of bodies slamming into her. The world was turning upside down, and there was nothing to hold on to. The screams of the people around her were drowned out by a grinding roar, like a huge tree uprooting itself.

Over and over she rolled, battered by unseen limbs, calling for Gretchen. The maelstrom seemed to last forever, but at last it slowed into stillness. There was silence, broken only by the groans and whimpers of people around her. She was lying on a pile of bodies, some limp, some squirming. She opened her eyes. There was a fissure of light in the darkness. She groped towards it, and realised it was a rent in the canvas tarpaulin of the truck – in the *roof* of the truck, because the truck was now lying on its side.

The rent had been made by a tree branch that had ripped through the fabric, and it was just wide enough for Katya to crawl through. She grasped at something outside for support, a leathery shrub, and struggled into the daylight.

There was dust everywhere. Choking on it, she tried to make sense of what had happened. The truck had rolled off the road into a ravine. The cab was jammed against a rocky bank, but already she could see the driver inside trying to force the doors open.

Something warm and wet was running down her face. She touched it and found she was bleeding copiously from a cut on her head. There was no pain yet, but the sticky blood was getting in her eyes. She wiped them as best she could and tried to get her thoughts in order.

Other survivors were crawling out of the torn canvas, looking dazed and battered, some of them bleeding, as she was. She stumbled back to help. She and some others grabbed the edges of the canvas and ripped the hole wider. Inside the truck was a tangle of bodies, some moving brokenly, others ominously still.

'Gretchen!' she called, coughing and choking on the dust. 'Gretchen, where are you?'

Others were calling for relatives or loved ones. And now she could hear shouts from higher up in the ravine. The other trucks had stopped on the road, and the soldiers were picking their way down the steep bank, between the trees.

Suddenly it dawned on her that this was the only chance of escape she would ever have. If she didn't seize this moment, then both she and Gretchen would be dead soon. Her stunned senses were galvanised into action. Frantically, she crawled back into the truck and hunted for Gretchen. The carnage inside was appalling; skulls had been cracked and limbs broken as people had been thrown against one another, or on to the steel ribs supporting the canvas. She had been extraordinarily lucky to have escaped a more serious injury. All around her, hurt people were crying out for help, but she was focused only on finding Gretchen.

They had been sitting on a bench near the back of the truck, having been among the last to board; but everything was confused now, and she struggled to locate the spot in the welter of limbs.

She was disorientated for a few sickening minutes; then she saw a mass of dark curly hair, and dug her way towards it, clambering over bodies and broken seats.

'Gretchen!' She grabbed an arm and pulled. Gretchen rolled out from under someone else, her eyes closed and her face white. Gasping with the exertion, Katya lifted Gretchen's limp upper body and hauled her towards the exit. She'd been terrified that Gretchen was dead, but as they emerged through the tear in the canvas, Gretchen suddenly gasped into semi-wakefulness, her eyes opening.

'We have to run, Gretchen,' Katya said, shaking her. 'Wake up! Get on your feet!'

'Katya? I thought I was dead—'

'You're not! Now, Gretchen! Come!' She pulled Gretchen to her feet. The girl was groggy, her legs giving way under her like a newborn colt's. But the shouts of the soldiers were coming closer, and already the survivors of the accident were starting to flee among the trees. The sound of a shot came rolling down.

Pulling Gretchen with her, Katya scrambled downwards, further into the ravine. A young woman with long blonde hair joined them.

The ravine was deep and dense. The vegetation was increasingly thick, and the going was difficult. Gretchen, who was still dazed, whimpered as Katya dragged her along, but it was a question of life or death, and Katya couldn't afford to let her slow down.

As if to underline that point, there were more shots from behind them. They could hear the soldiers shouting orders to halt, but they kept running. Rather die here in the open, Katya thought, than perish in the horror of a concentration camp.

The three of them slid on loose rocks that rolled out from under their feet, rattling down into the valley below. Another shot, and a bullet that whistled over their heads, showed they were giving their position away. The blonde woman stopped, terrified. 'They'll kill us!'

'They'll kill us anyway,' Katya panted. 'Don't stop. Run!'

The blonde woman, like a panicked animal, ran off in another direction. They lost sight of her.

Then came the most frightening sound of all – the rattle of machine guns, accompanied by the screams of people in their death agonies. Bullets slashed through the trees around them, scattering leaves and twigs.

'Keep going,' Katya urged Gretchen, 'don't stop!'

But Gretchen's foot hooked on a tree root, and she went sprawling on to the ground, her hand jerking out of Katya's. And at the same instant, they heard the bark of a soldier, terrifyingly close: 'Halt! Or I shoot!'

He was crashing through the undergrowth behind them, moving fast. In a moment, he would be upon them. Katya threw herself down next to Gretchen, behind the scant shelter of a bush on the edge of a glade. Holding each other tight, they hid their faces against one another. 'Don't make a sound,' Katya panted.

The soldier was shouting commands. His voice was taut. Katya looked up through the leaves. He was ten or fifteen yards away, holding his machine pistol at the ready, looking around him. He looked young and very nervous. 'Where are you hiding?' he shouted, his voice cracking. 'Come out!'

What Papa had said about the birds that took flight flashed through Katya's mind. She held tight on to Gretchen, to stop her moving.

The soldier moved forward, shouting. Abruptly, a second figure rose from the scrub. It was the woman who had fled with them. She had been hiding, like Katya and Gretchen. She ran desperately for cover, screaming, her long blonde hair fluttering behind her. Before she had run more than a few paces, the soldier opened fire on her, his machine gun stuttering smoke. She went down on her face, her arms outflung, without making another sound.

The young soldier walked cautiously towards her. Katya realised that she had clamped her hand over Gretchen's mouth, but Gretchen's eyes were wide and staring, seeing it all.

The soldier seemed not to know what to do next. He stood over the body of the woman he had shot, looking down at her. For a long time, he didn't move. Then he knelt down and touched the blonde hair, which was spread out, gleaming in the sun.

Someone shouted from higher up in the ravine, 'What's happening?'

The young soldier lifted his head. 'I shot one,' he called. 'A woman.'

'Dead?'

He rose and rolled the body over with his boot. 'Yes.'

'Any others down there?'

'No. What do I do with her?'

'Take her number and come back.'

'And leave her here?'

'Yes, you idiot. At the double.'

The young soldier took the cardboard number off the dead woman's chest, then reloaded his weapon. He looked around the glade. He was talking quietly to himself, but Katya couldn't hear what he was saying. Then she realised he was praying. He crossed himself, turned and made his way slowly back up the incline.

They remained frozen until he was out of sight. Intermittently, shots were ringing out around the ravine. The prisoners who'd made a break for freedom were being exterminated without mercy.

As quietly as she could, Katya got to her feet and helped Gretchen up. 'He just *killed* her,' Gretchen said shakily.

'Yes.' There was no time to talk about it. That could come later. If there *was* a later. After the shock of the last fifteen minutes, Katya's mind had reached a crystalline clarity. She was no longer confused. Everything had condensed into a single, burning focus – staying alive. She wasn't even afraid any longer. Seeing that woman die a few feet away had removed fear. 'Move quietly. But don't stop.'

They climbed down the bank, which grew steeper and steeper, until they had to cling to saplings to keep from sliding all the way down. The shooting from above had slowed, and then fallen silent.

Katya had been given an insight into the Nazi mind by now. She knew what they would be doing. They would count the bodies and match them to their list. Soon enough, they would realise that she and Gretchen – and possibly others – were missing. Then they would come looking.

She and Gretchen had to get as far away from here as possible.

As she was thinking that thought, the ground gave way beneath them. They tumbled the last twenty feet down an almost vertical gulley, landing on the edge of a stream that snaked between banks overgrown with ferns. It was dark and sheltered down here, and for a moment, Katya was tempted to just huddle among the ferns and hope the soldiers wouldn't find them; but she knew that would be a vain hope. If they had a chance, then it was now.

Upstream or downstream? She had no idea where they were. Perhaps it didn't matter which way they went, so long as they got away from here.

'Take off your shoes,' she said to Gretchen. 'We'll wade in the water.'

'Why?' Gretchen demanded.

'In case they look for us with dogs. If we walk in the stream, we won't leave any scent for them to follow.'

They took off their shoes and woollen stockings and tied them round their necks. Gingerly, they entered the water. It was shallow but bitterly cold. The stream bed was pebbly, and at first painful on their bare soles; but the cold soon numbed them.

They waded upstream for two hours, hearing nothing but the ripple of the water and the scrunch of pebbles underfoot. Katya began to feel that they might have got away. But it became clear they were going deeper into the ravine. The banks were getting steeper and rockier, and they were starting to encounter little waterfalls that needed to be climbed. Katya cursed herself for not having worked out that going upstream would naturally lead them to higher ground, and eventually, the mountains.

It was also beginning to get darker in the ravine. The sun was starting to go down. Soon, it might be too dark to risk going any further. It would have been better to have walked downstream, and have come out into some valley, where they might have had a chance of finding shelter for the night.

Her thoughts were interrupted by a sudden cry and a splash. Gretchen had slipped on a boulder and fallen into the stream. When Katya helped her out, she was soaked, shivering, and near tears.

'My feet ache so much with the cold,' she whimpered. 'Can't we rest for a little while?'

Katya would have preferred to keep going, but she could see that Gretchen was completely exhausted. She helped Gretchen take off her wet things, and sat her in one of the few patches of sunlight that remained. She knelt in front of Gretchen and gently rubbed her bare feet, which were blue with cold.

Gretchen was shivering. 'I don't think I can go much further.'

'I've made a mistake. We should have gone downstream. This way, we're going to end up in the Alps.'

'What are we going to do?' Gretchen asked, through chattering teeth.

'The sun's going down, and you're wet. Maybe we should rest for tonight, and decide what to do tomorrow morning.'

Gretchen nodded. 'Yes. You look awful.'

'Thanks.'

'No, I mean your face is covered in dried blood. Let me wash it off.' Katya hadn't been aware of it until now, but Gretchen was right; the skin of her face was tight with crusted blood from the wound on her head. Gretchen scooped water from the stream and washed it off carefully. There was comfort in tending to one another in these small ways. But now that they had stopped running, both were covered with cuts and bruises that would hurt even more once the adrenalin faded away.

'What are we going to eat?' Gretchen asked.

The question revealed their utter desolation. They had nothing. Their passports had been confiscated. So had the small amount of money they had prepared for the crossing. They were helplessly exposed to the world. 'We'll have to go hungry.' Katya smiled crookedly. 'But there's plenty of cold water to drink.'

It started to get cold long before the sun was gone. They made a shelter out of dead leaves and burrowed into it, holding on to each other for warmth.

Gretchen began to drift into sleep almost immediately. 'That soldier was praying after he shot that woman,' she murmured.

'Yes. I heard him.'

'How can someone murder someone else, and then say prayers over them?'

'I don't know,' Katya admitted. 'He didn't hesitate about killing her. Perhaps he thought he was only doing his duty.'

'He knew it was wrong. I heard him saying "forgive me". Did you see him stroking her hair?'

'Yes, I saw.'

'Why did he do that?'

'I suppose he felt sorry for what he'd done.'

'I think he saw that she was the same age as him. And he was thinking that if they'd met somewhere else, they might have fallen in love, and got married. Instead of – of what he did.'

Katya thought of the wisdom in Gretchen's words. Her strange insights were always surprising, sometimes startling. And the violence she was witnessing would inevitably leave scars, which she would have to deal with somehow over the coming months.

They both fell into a deep, exhausted sleep for some hours. The penalty was that they both woke up again before midnight, freezing cold, wide-eyed and frightened. It was impossible for either of them to get to sleep again after that, and there were hours of darkness left.

The night was filled with the rustling of animals and birds. A fox yelped nearby, startling them, and an owl called, monotonously and endlessly. Katya's mind was filled with the shocking events of the past days, memories playing and replaying over and over again. She'd run instinctively from the overturned truck. But had that been the right decision? And what was their next move? To live like hunted animals, until they starved, or were caught? Or gave themselves up? No, not that. If there had ever been any chance of mercy from the Nazis, it was gone now. They would probably mete out the same justice that the blonde woman had received.

In the darkness of the night, the odds overwhelmed her.

'Can you hear that?' Gretchen hissed.

'What?'

'Listen!'

The night was silent now. Katya strained her ears. Then she heard it too – the distant rumble of a truck. Her heart began to beat fast.

'Are they looking for us?' Gretchen whispered.

Katya didn't answer. They listened, alert as wild things to the sounds of danger. But the truck's note faded away without stopping. After a silence, the sounds of another vehicle filtered faintly down to them through the trees. A car, changing gear with a crunch, and fading into silence. Then, a few minutes later, another.

'The road must be up there,' she said. Birds, perhaps awakened by the traffic sounds, were singing sleepily. It was starting to get light. Soon it would be dawn. 'We should go up and walk along it.'

'But the soldiers!'

'We can't keep climbing blindly into the mountains,' Katya said practically. 'God knows where we'd end up. But the road will at least take us somewhere. And if we see Nazis, we'll hide.'

Gretchen was sceptical, but she could see the sense of Katya's reasoning. They made themselves as presentable as they could, although they were a very bedraggled sight, their clothes crumpled and dirty, their hair matted. The climb up to the road was horribly steep and rocky, and all the more difficult in the dim light. Eventually, they emerged from the scrub and found themselves on a hairpin bend in a narrow, winding road.

Dark, forested mountains rose all around, with the line of the snowy Alps in the distance. Other than the road itself, and a sweep of electricity power lines that ran over the road, there was no sign of human life anywhere to be seen. Had they already entered the

Third Reich? But there was a small metal sign with a state road number and the word *Österreich*. 'We're still in Austria,' Katya said.

'Which way do we go?' Gretchen asked.

'Down,' Katya replied without hesitation.

'Back the way we came?'

'Yes.' She smiled at Gretchen's expression. 'Life's like that.'

They set off, walking along the verge, on the other side of the wooden railing that ran beside the road. The path was lush with fresh spring growth. The pine trees were releasing a rich, resiny smell into the cold air. Katya had been thinking. 'If people ask us,' she told Gretchen, 'we're English tourists, touring the beauties of the Tyrol. We had an accident in our car, and that's how we got hurt. We're waiting for the car to be fixed.'

'Okay.' Gretchen nodded.

They had walked for ten minutes before the first car approached. They huddled into the bushes in case it was military. But it was an old-fashioned saloon car, and the people inside didn't pay them any attention as it passed. It sputtered on down the road, disappearing around the next bend. The sun was rising, and the warmth was welcome. Ahead of them, the road snaked in a series of tight curves; around each turn, new Alpine vistas came into view. Now they could see a village, down in the valley below, four or five miles off, with a church spire and fields around it. They walked slowly, both aware of aches and pains from yesterday's ordeal.

A deep rumble from behind them presaged heavy vehicles coming along the road. This time, they grabbed each other's hands and clambered down the bank to get out of sight. They huddled together, peering anxiously through the undergrowth. With a chill of fear, Katya saw that the approaching vehicles were German army trucks. They rolled past in convoy, their weight shaking the ground, each one packed with soldiers and equipment. Katya lost count, but at least twenty vehicles must have passed them. They didn't emerge until the rumbling had faded away.

A small signpost came into view on the side of the road up ahead. Eager to see what it said, Gretchen ran to it.

'Innsbruck!' she called. 'It says fifty-two kilometres to Innsbruck!'

Katya felt a surge of hope. Thank God, the road from Feldkirch to Dachau had taken them via Innsbruck. And in Innsbruck they had at least one friend. 'Hildegard!'

'The lady from the piano shop?' Gretchen asked.

'She promised to help us if we ever needed it.'

'Do you think she really meant it?'

'Yes. Didn't you?'

Gretchen nodded hesitantly. 'She seemed really nice. But we weren't in such bad trouble then. She'd be risking her life. She might just call the Gestapo.'

'She hates the Nazis. She said so. Something about her tells me she meant what she said. I'm sure she'll help. At least she might give us a meal. We haven't had anything to eat for days.'

The mention of food made Gretchen push her fists into her belly with a woeful face. 'I'm so hungry,' she wailed. 'I could eat a whole pot of boiled potatoes – mashed with butter – and cream – and salt—'

'Stop!' Katya begged, her own stomach twisting inside her.

'There has to be something to eat around here,' Gretchen groaned.

'Like what?'

Gretchen hunted in the undergrowth at their feet. 'I used to eat this in the garden when I was little,' she said, pulling up some weeds.

'Dandelions!'

'They're quite tasty,' Gretchen said humbly, offering Katya the green stuff. 'So long as you don't eat the stems. They're tough, and taste bad. You just eat the leaves and the flowers.'

'Are you sure they're not poisonous?'

'I survived, didn't I?'

More to please Gretchen than anything else, Katya took the dandelions resignedly and munched on them. The taste was bitter and wild, but better than she had expected. 'If you tell yourself it's chicory, it's not that bad,' she admitted.

They walked on, experimenting with other weeds that they found – lamb's lettuce, chickweed and purslane. 'If you call them wild herbs, they taste better,' Gretchen advised. But after one particular experiment, she had to bend over and retch; and the green stuff didn't do anything to fill their empty bellies.

A few cars passed them, and each time they withdrew into the bushes. Katya's earlier mood of optimism was fading. Fifty kilometres was a long way to walk. Especially without any proper food or anywhere to sleep.

The sparse traffic increased by mid-morning. Around noon, the clop of a horse's hooves and the rattle of cartwheels came down the road from behind them. This time, Katya stayed on the side of the road, waiting.

The wagon, pulled by a big white carthorse, was being driven by an elderly man with his wife. The man wore a moleskin jacket and a floppy hat, the woman a dirndl and a wide-brimmed bonnet. They were a couple from a former age. It was the woman who nudged the man to stop the horse. He reined it in, and the couple stared at them.

'*Grüss Gott*,' the woman called, looking them up and down.

'*Grüss Gott*,' Katya answered. The wagon was loaded with large round Austrian cheeses and knobbly hams. The rich, smoky aromas wafted intoxicatingly to them.

'Where are you headed?' the woman asked. Her Tyrolean accent was so strong that Katya found her hard to understand.

'We're going to Innsbruck,' Gretchen replied.

'On foot?'

'We're motorists, but our car is broken.'

'You have troubles, eh?' the woman asked shrewdly.

'Yes,' Gretchen said, before Katya could stop her. 'We have troubles.'

The couple's eyes were astute. 'With *them*?'

'Yes,' Gretchen said again. 'With *them*.'

The old man jerked his head. 'Get in the cart. We're going as far as the railway station at Martinsbühel. You can walk to Innsbruck in a couple of hours from there.'

'If you get under the canvas,' the old woman added, 'you'll be out of the sun.'

'Thank you!' Gratefully, they clambered on to the wagon and crept under the hood. The horse set off with a jolt. The cheeses and hams were sweating slightly in the sunshine, and the oily smell was almost overwhelming. In their hungry state, Katya felt dizzy. Gretchen rolled her eyes to show she felt the same way.

The old lady reached back to them with something wrapped in cloth. It was a hunk of bread and two thick slices of ham. 'From our own pigs,' she said. She waved away their thanks. 'Eat, and praise God.'

They did exactly that. Katya saw that Gretchen's eyes were full of tears. 'Are you all right?' she asked.

Gretchen nodded, wiping her cheeks with a greasy hand. 'Yes. I just feel like I'm alive, for the first time in my life.'

Chapter 21

They reached Innsbruck late that evening. The elderly couple had dropped them at a small town two or three miles away, and they had plodded wearily the rest of the way in the dark. Gretchen was dropping with exhaustion, and Katya herself was aching all over. But she still had the scrap of paper on which Hildegard had written her address.

The address was an old apartment block, facing the river. As she reached out to press the button next to Hildegard's name, she had a sudden attack of anxiety, for all her exhaustion, and hesitated.

'We've come all this way,' Gretchen sighed. 'And we don't have anywhere else to go.'

'You're right.' Katya pressed the bell. After a few moments, they heard a reply from the speaker.

'Who is there?'

'Katya and Gretchen. The girl who played the piano in your shop.'

They heard a muffled exclamation. 'I knew it!' Hildegard's voice said. The door clicked open. 'Third floor. Be quiet. And don't put on the lights.'

They climbed the stairs in the dark, reaching the sliver of light from Hildegard holding her door open. She drew them in, putting her finger on her lips. When the door was closed, she stared at them in shock.

'Oh, my God. What has happened to you?' she hissed.

'We were arrested at Feldkirch,' Katya said tiredly. 'They put us in a truck going to Dachau. But the truck overturned on the road, and we escaped. We got a lift to near Innsbruck with a farmer and his wife. I know this wasn't what you meant when you offered to help,' Katya said, feeling as though she were about to cry. 'But we have nobody else to turn to—'

'This is *exactly* what I meant,' Hildegard interrupted in a low voice.

'We'll just stay for a night—'

'Hush,' Hildegard cut in. 'Never mind all that.' She took their hands. 'I'm so sorry that good people like you have seen the worst of us.' She looked more closely at Katya. 'You have blood in your hair, Katya!'

'It's just a cut from the accident. I'm fine.'

'You both need a bath, but you can't have one tonight. Nobody is allowed to use the bath at night in this block. It's full of Nazis, and they complain about every noise. Even if you flush the lavatory. They spy on everything everybody does. So we have to be quiet, like mice. Yes?'

They nodded to show they understood.

'Are you hungry?'

Gretchen shook her head. 'Just some water, please.'

Hildegard poured them glasses of water. 'You look absolutely exhausted. Don't worry about anything tonight. Sleep now. We'll talk in the morning. Yes?'

Without any fuss, Hildegard took them to a little bedroom that had two single beds. They were too tired to thank her properly as she made the beds and offered them nightdresses. After she'd left them, they lay facing each other in the dim glow of a nightlight.

'I didn't think we'd be alive tonight,' Gretchen whispered.

'Nor did I.'

'I wouldn't be here without you.'

'I wouldn't be here without you, Gretchen. You've been so brave. So grown up.' Gretchen's face was smooth in the soft light, only the shadows under her eyes betraying what she'd been through. 'I'm so proud of you.'

'Brave? You don't know how frightened I've been!'

'Being brave doesn't mean not being frightened. Being brave means carrying on even though you *are* frightened.'

Gretchen's eyes were closing. 'If we'd gone to Dachau, we might have seen Papa.'

'I thought that too. But we'll see him somewhere, Liebchen, I promise you.'

Gretchen nodded, though they both knew that was an empty promise. She pillowed her cheek on her fist and slept.

Katya didn't know that she had fallen asleep too, until she felt herself violently tumbling over and over, arms and legs and heads thudding into her, the tearing of metal in her ears.

The nightmare shot her up in bed, gasping for air. It took a long time for her heart to stop racing. She checked on Gretchen, who was snoring faintly. After that she rolled over and slept like the dead.

They awoke early the next morning to an empty flat – and a sense of dread.

Hildegard was gone. Going to the window, they saw the river flowing fast down below, and a spectacular, if wild, vista of forest and snowy mountains beyond. The sounds of doors opening and closing and other activity in the apartment block reminded them of Hildegard's warning that it was 'full of Nazis'. The thought was not comforting.

'Do you think she's gone to the Gestapo?' Katya asked. 'We could get out now, and run.'

'Where would we go?' Gretchen asked. 'We'll just have to trust her. Stop worrying.'

Katya smiled inside at Gretchen's adult tone. They had fallen into a pattern of reassuring one another, each one expressing a fear, the other soothing. Gretchen was indeed growing up, and more than that, she was becoming something that she had not been before – a friend.

The apartment was small and crowded with books, most of them about music. They covered every wall. But what drew Gretchen like a magnet was Hildegard's piano, a small upright that occupied pride of place in the parlour. Katya could see that Gretchen was itching to play, but they dared not make any sound.

They didn't have long to wait. Hildegard came in after half an hour. She had gone out early and had bought fresh, hot rolls for their breakfast from a bakery around the corner. She put the coffee pot on the stove. The smells were dizzying – both Katya and Gretchen had woken up starving.

'Some of my neighbours heard you coming in last night,' she said. 'I got some questions this morning. I had to say something. So I said you were my cousins from England, mother and daughter. Mrs and Miss Smith.'

'The Gestapo might be looking for an Englishwoman and a girl,' Katya said in alarm.

Hildegard nodded. 'I know. But there's a chance you might meet the neighbours – and the minute you open your mouth, people will know you're not Austrian. So it's better to say you're foreign. Tourists come to Innsbruck in their thousands, which is lucky. Local people are used to them. We'll just have to hope we can get you away from here before anyone puts two and two together.' They sat down to eat breakfast. 'But until we can work out how to do that, the best thing you can do is lie low here.'

'We've got no money,' Katya said.

'Katya, please.'

'But I'll pay you back somehow, as soon as I can—'

'I don't want money. Stop, before I get angry.'

'It's so kind of you to take us in,' Katya said. 'We don't want to put you to any trouble – let alone put you in danger.'

Hildegard had apple cheeks and merry eyes, but they now had a hard glint in them. 'Let me tell you something, Katya. I am a proud Austrian. I love my country. I love the Tyrol, where I was born. But we're an independent people.' She gestured at the window. 'There's a rabble out there who claim to be delighted that Germany has invaded us, but I'm not one of them. I was happy with the way things were. I hate the Nazis, and I always will. They've started rounding up Jews, you know. Even here in Innsbruck. They're shutting down Jewish businesses and confiscating Jewish people's passports. I'm afraid for my grandfather. He's Jewish. He converted, but that's not going to protect him – or my mother – or me. He's in his seventies now. What's going to happen to him? I would do anything to stop what they're doing to my country. So if there is any trouble, or any danger, I face it willingly. Do you understand?'

'Yes.'

'And there's something else. I will never forget hearing Gretchen play, that day you walked into the shop. She is a true musician, and we musicians help each other. That goes beyond politics, or nationality, or anything like that. We speak the same language, and it needs very few words. Isn't that true, Gretchen?'

Gretchen blushed to the roots of her hair, and nodded. 'Yes,' she whispered.

'So you see, for me, it's a privilege to help.' Hildegard looked at the little gold watch on her plump wrist. 'I have to go to the Conservatory. Your clothes are in a sorry state, so I'll take them to the laundry on my way. Please wear anything of mine you like in the meantime. I'll be back this evening, and I'll bring something to eat. And if you want to play the piano, Gretchen, you are more than welcome. You're my cousin, after all! The apartment rules are that you can play between ten and twelve in the morning and between four and six in the afternoon. Tomorrow morning I'm free – so maybe we can have a lesson, yes?' She laughed at Gretchen's expression. 'I promise it will be enjoyable. Trust me. And now I must fly.'

It was still early, and Gretchen had to wait almost two hours before she could touch the piano. On the stroke of ten, she was in the chair, and starting to play. Katya leaned on the windowsill, listening, gazing up at the white peaks that seemed so impossibly far away. Beyond them lay Italy and Switzerland, and safety. How would they ever get there?

She was still tired from the events of the past few days, and so she went back to bed and dozed for a while, floating on Gretchen's music. She hadn't noticed that the music had stopped until she was awoken by Gretchen shaking her arm. Gretchen's face was pale and tearful.

'Katya, I have to go to the hospital!'

Katya sat bolt upright, her heart in her mouth. 'Why? What's wrong?'

'I must have hurt myself in the accident. I'm bleeding!'

'Where from?'

'Down there,' Gretchen said wretchedly. 'It's awful. It won't stop.'

Understanding dawned on Katya. 'Oh, Gretchen. Let's go to the bathroom.' As she comforted the weeping girl, Katya remembered Hans Asperger's words about 'the onset of puberty'. Puberty had certainly chosen its moment – and like a fool, she had completely neglected to prepare Gretchen for it. A real mother, she berated herself angrily, would have done so long ago. She had let Gretchen down yet again.

Explaining everything to a girl who hadn't had a mother, and who had no friends of her own age, indeed who had hardly been to school, was difficult at first. Nobody had told her what to expect, and she was convinced that she'd sustained some grave internal injury. But as Katya gently explained, she brightened.

'So it happens to you too?'

'It happens to all women. And I'm so sorry I didn't tell you. I should have done. I wasn't thinking. I feel terrible. I've failed you so badly!'

'As long as it's normal—'

'It's not just normal, Liebchen, it's a wonderful thing. It means you really are growing up now.'

'It's awfully messy,' Gretchen commented ruefully. 'Can't it be stopped?'

'Not like turning off a tap.' Katya smiled. 'It won't last long, but in the meantime, there are some easy ways to cope.' She thought about looking through Hildegard's closets to see if she could find something, then rejected the idea as an intrusion. 'I'll have to go out and get what we need. Wait here and don't open the door to anyone.'

She slipped out of the apartment block, using the key Hildegard had given her and taking some of the money Hildegard had left for emergencies. She walked along the riverbank until she found a shop. There she bought what she wanted. Being outside was somewhat nerve-racking. She expected at any moment to feel a heavy hand on her shoulder. But nobody seemed to notice her particularly. It was evident that Innsbruck was, as Hildegard had said, a cosmopolitan place, used to foreign tourists.

Returning to the apartment block, however, she encountered a middle-aged woman emerging from the building. She gave Katya a sharp up-and-down glance. 'It's Frau Smith, isn't it?' she said.

It took Katya a moment to remember the alias that Hildegard had given her. 'Oh! Yes, that's right.'

The woman stuck out a bejewelled hand. 'I am Frau Hagler. I live in the apartment above you. I have lived there twenty-two years.'

Katya shook the ring-encrusted fingers uneasily. 'How do you do?'

'They are beautiful, are they not?'

'I beg your pardon?'

Frau Hagler was a bleached blonde whose generous proportions strained her expensive and tightly buttoned sealskin coat. Her fat cheeks and chin were plentifully powdered and rouged, but her nose, thin and beaky, was sharp, like her eyes. 'The Alps,' she said, gesturing to the white-capped mountains with a proprietorial air. 'You have come to see our Alps, not so?'

'Oh!' Katya said again. 'Yes, that's right.'

'You have no such mountains in your country.'

'No, we haven't. The Alps are very beautiful.'

'And you have come to witness Austria's finest hour,' Frau Hagler went on, with a gleam in her pale blue eyes. 'In our country's long history, this is the greatest moment!'

'You mean—?'

'I mean the Anschluss.'

'Yes, of course.' Katya could hear Gretchen playing the piano upstairs, and was eager to get up to her. But Frau Hagler was

271

blocking the way, bobbing from side to side like a peroxide seal on an ice floe.

'He is, without doubt, the greatest human being who has ever lived,' she said excitedly.

'Hitler?' Katya responded, trying not to sound incredulous.

'The Führer. Adolf Hitler. Yes, he has genius. Yes, he has nerves of steel. Yes, he has compassion, a heart brimming with love. He has all these. But do you know why he is so great, Frau Smith? It is because he gives himself completely to his people.'

She paused with her head on one side, waiting for Katya to respond. Given her experiences of the compassion and love of Hitlerism over the last weeks, Katya was unable to summon up the enthusiasm that Frau Hagler obviously wanted. 'Yes, I see,' she said in a neutral tone.

Frau Hagler raised her finger. 'He gives himself to his people without stinting. He is not interested in money, or young women, or anything like that. He cares only for his people. He gives everything to us. Everything! He is truly the saviour of the German *Volk*. Other nations must understand this, Frau Smith. Understand, and admire!'

Katya had finally managed to edge her way around Frau Hagler. 'It was very nice to meet you,' she said, backing away. 'I must go to my daughter.'

'She is playing the piano, yes?'

'Yes.'

'She plays well for a child. Tell her she must stop at twelve sharp.'

'I will.'

Frau Hagler raised a pink palm. 'Heil Hitler!'

'Good morning,' Katya replied, unable to bring herself to give the Nazi salute. She hurried up the stairs. Katya glanced back at the door to Hildegard's apartment and saw that Frau Hagler was watching her with narrowed, speculative eyes. Were they still safe?

'Camelia!' Gretchen exclaimed when Katya gave her the familiar blue box, with its oval portrait of a nineteenth-century beauty. 'I've seen these in the shops. I always thought it was soap, or something.'

'We have different brands in England. I've used these ever since I came to Austria. They're called "Camelia" after a courtesan in a famous French play by Alexandre Dumas, *La Dame aux Camélias*. That's her on the box. You can see she's wearing a red camellia. She wore a white camellia to show she was available, and a red one when she had her period.'

'What's a courtesan?' Gretchen asked, intrigued, 'and what was she available for?'

That opened a new line of discussion on subjects that Gretchen had only the sketchiest understanding of. She listened to Katya's explanations gravely.

'So I could have a baby now?' she concluded.

'Technically, yes. But your body isn't really ready yet, and won't be for a few more years. When you're old enough to get married, you'll be old enough to have children. If you want to.'

'I don't think I'll ever want children. It's difficult enough just being me.'

Katya smiled at Gretchen's rueful tone. The arrival of adolescence had confirmed that Gretchen was becoming a young woman, with a young woman's innate poise. The curves of her face were rounding. Her movements, once gawky and brusque, were becoming instinctively graceful. The otherworldly strangeness that had been such a dominant trait in her was now maturing into

273

something else, unique, as though the hardships she'd been through had forced Gretchen to evolve.

She felt a deep stab of pain that Thor was not here to see it. Gretchen was growing up without a father. And he must think of her every living minute, wondering if she was safe.

I will keep her safe, she promised him in her mind, and willed the thought to travel through the ether to him.

Katya just prayed that there would be a happy ending to the story – and not a tragic, premature end.

Hildegard came home in the early evening, bringing groceries. The three women congregated in Hildegard's tiny kitchen to prepare the evening meal, a bowl of hearty soup with a loaf of black bread and smoked cheese. There was a lot to talk about. Hildegard frowned when Katya told her about meeting Frau Hagler in the lobby.

'That one is the gossip of the neighbourhood – and the biggest Nazi in Innsbruck, into the bargain. She thinks Adolf Hitler is a divine being.'

'So I gathered.'

'I could wish you hadn't bumped into *her*, of all people.'

'I had to go out on an urgent errand.' Quietly, she took Hildegard aside and told her about Gretchen.

'Oh, but that's wonderful! We'll have to celebrate. But you didn't need to go out – I have plenty of Camelia in my cupboard.'

'I didn't want to rummage through your things. You're being so kind, and you have exams coming up. I feel we're intruding.'

'Not at all! But it's true the exams are looming. I spent most of the day on the piano in the auditorium. But do you know, I think I am improving. I think Gretchen has taught me something.'

'What could I possibly have taught you?' Gretchen asked, wondering.

'I will tell you, Gretchen. But first, I hear we have something to celebrate today, so—' Hildegard opened a bottle of wine and poured them all a glass, including Gretchen. 'To the red wine of life!' When they'd clinked glasses and drunk, Hildegard went on. 'When you left Innsbruck, I felt sure that our paths would cross again. I've thought about you two a lot. Especially you, young Gretchen. When I heard you play in the shop, so instinctively, without knowing a note of music, I realised something about myself – that although I was technically accomplished, there was something missing. That something was *feeling*. You play with so much true emotion, Gretchen, that you made me ashamed of putting so little of myself into my music. Studying music at a conservatory, one can get very caught up in technique, and forget that music has a soul. Today, my tutor complimented me on my interpretation! So thank you, Gretchen. One day I hope to be in the audience when you give your debut performance.'

The praise, together with the red wine – the first that Gretchen had ever drunk – filled Gretchen's cheeks with a pink blush. She looked quite radiant.

'Thank you for making it so special for her,' Katya said later on, when they'd finished clearing and washing up. 'You're an angel. But we can't stay here. We have to get out of Austria. I need to go to the British consulate and arrange for a new passport for myself and some kind of travel documents for Gretchen.'

'We'll go tomorrow,' Hildegard promised. 'I know where it is.'

But the British consulate was to prove a bitter disappointment. It was a tiny bureau on the first floor of an office block, and it was closed.

The stolid porter who opened the door to their banging was surly. 'Don't you see we are shut?'

'Can't we speak to the consul?' Katya begged. 'We need help urgently.'

'The honorary consul has been recalled. All enquiries must go to the embassy in Vienna.'

'But that's three hundred miles away!'

'I can't help the geography, Fräulein.' With a thick finger, he tapped the notice pasted to the door. 'All enquiries must go to the embassy in Vienna.'

'But—'

'Times have changed,' he cut in. 'I can't help you.'

He slammed the door shut in their faces.

Katya was in despair. 'What are we going to do?' she asked Hildegard.

'I don't know,' Hildegard admitted. 'You can't show your faces at the border without papers. They'll arrest you at once. We have to think of something really ingenious.'

'I'm running out of ingenuity,' Katya said.

'Something will turn up,' Hildegard declared. 'In the meantime, you and Gretchen both need rest, more than anything else.'

In the afternoon, as she had promised, Hildegard gave Gretchen a piano lesson.

It seemed bizarre, in the midst of their troubles, and with death and danger all around them, to bother with a music lesson, and yet Gretchen took it as seriously as she had taken everything else that had happened lately; and somehow, making music felt like a light glowing in the darkness all around.

She listened carefully as Hildegard explained the basics of body posture at the piano, the best angles for the arms, wrists and hands, the way to achieve the best spread of the fingers. She performed the exercises diligently for a while, under Hildegard's critical eye. It was strange to hear Gretchen, who could play Bach and Beethoven by ear, solemnly plodding through the most basic of exercises – and eventually, frustrated by the repetition, she broke free, and raced off into a full-blown piece from her head.

Laughing, Hildegard got up from the stool and went to Katya. 'I thought that would happen, sooner or later. Your Gretchen is not gifted with patience. But my God, listen to that!'

They listened to the music exploding from Gretchen's swiftly moving hands; the notes were like flocks of birds bursting from a cage, soaring into the sky.

'Yes,' Katya said. 'It never ceases to astonish me.'

'Well, I think she's learned something,' Hildegard said, watching Gretchen's hands with a critical eye. 'Any problems with the you-know-what?'

'She was complaining of a tummy ache this morning, but so far, nothing too painful, thank God. I'm praying that she's spared miserable periods.'

Hildegard studied Katya's face with shrewd black eyes. 'You really see her as your daughter, don't you?'

'Yes, I do.'

'You're risking your life for her.'

'I know.'

'You could just leave her, and go back to England.'

Katya smiled. 'No, I couldn't.'

'Because you love her?'

'Yes.'

Hildegard was quizzical. 'Is it possible to love someone else's child like your own?'

'I don't have any of my own, so I can't say. All I know is that when she's hurt, or when she's in danger, it feels like my insides are being torn out.'

'I can't imagine how it must feel to be so committed to someone else.'

'I'm all she has, but that's not the reason I love her. I love her for who she is.'

Hildegard nodded. 'And the father?' she asked gently.

Katya sighed. 'We were deeply in love. He's a wonderful man. But I don't know whether he's alive or dead – and I have to accept the fact that I'll probably never see him again.'

'That must be very painful for you.'

'He's strong and sensitive and just such an *honourable* man. I can't bear to think of him in the hands of those monsters. If I didn't have Gretchen to take care of, I would probably just break down,' she admitted. 'But I have to stay strong for her.'

'Were you planning to get married?

Katya winced. 'Thor did propose to me.'

'Don't tell me you turned him down!'

'I told him I couldn't be his wife,' she replied, 'but that I could very happily be his lover.'

Hildegard's eyebrows went up. 'That was very modern of you.'

'I was in love with him, but I didn't want to give up all my hopes of being a doctor. Now, though . . .' Katya sighed. 'I rather regret not saying yes. It might be easier for him, wherever he is, to think that I was completely committed to him.'

'I understand,' Hildegard said gently. 'But he knows you love him.'

'I just hope he knows I'm doing everything I can to protect Gretchen. I know he'll be worried sick about her.'

Gretchen finished playing, and came to them, flushed with triumph. 'It's all so logical! I don't know why I never worked it out – your thumb and little finger play the white keys, and the long fingers play the black ones. And if your wrists are in the right place, you can reach everything. Thank you for showing me, Hildegard.'

'There's a lot more to learn.' Hildegard smiled. 'But that's a good start.' She checked her watch. 'It's nearly noon, and if we play any longer, we'll have Frau Hagler banging on the ceiling. But how about starting to learn to read music?'

'Do I have to?' Gretchen asked, pulling a face. 'It's so hard for me.'

'I've got something for you.' Hildegard presented her with a black-covered exercise book. Gretchen opened it, to find that the pages were covered with blank music staves.

'There's nothing in here,' she said.

'You're going to fill it,' Hildegard replied. 'I believe that if you learn to *write* music, *reading* it will come naturally.'

Gretchen looked at Katya, bemused. 'Is that true, Katya?'

'I don't know, Liebchen,' Katya said with a smile, 'but it's worth a try, isn't it?'

The next days passed in an uneasy limbo. The thunderous knock at the door that they had anticipated with such dread did not come; the memories of the horrors they had been through surfaced in turbulent dreams, but faded in the morning light. Gretchen worked diligently at learning to write music. The task was painful at first, but Katya saw that as she began to associate the marks on the page with the sounds they represented, her interest was kindled. Hildegard had hit on a clever way of engaging Gretchen's attention.

Getting out of the country, however, remained Katya's chief preoccupation. Welcome as this musical refuge and rest were, they couldn't stay with Hildegard for long. It wasn't fair on Hildegard to expose her to the risk – nor was it safe for them to remain in Innsbruck. An escape route had to be found.

Hildegard went to the Tyrolean State Conservatory three days a week. The examination for her Performance Diploma was coming up, and she was increasingly nervous about it.

She had just left one morning when the door buzzer sounded. Assuming that Hildegard had forgotten her key, Katya pressed the button to let her in. She opened the front door of the apartment to wait for her.

But the tread ascending the stairs was not the light tap of Hildegard's heels. It was the heavy thud of military boots. Katya's heart froze. She almost slammed the door shut in terror, but realised how foolish that would be.

A burly figure in a black leather trench coat came into view up the stairwell. With a nightmare sense of disbelief, she met the sharp blue eyes of the Kriminalinspektor who had interrogated them at the police station a few days ago. He was followed by a Brownshirt – the same man who had beaten and tortured Herr Schubert in the next room.

'Ah,' Kriminalinspektor Sauer greeted Katya. 'Fräulein Komarovsky. I thought it must be you.'

Chapter 22

The two men marched into the apartment, filling it with dark menace. Katya was struggling to accept that their sanctuary had been invaded with such terrible swiftness. She had a fleeting wish that they were still in the forest, even if starving to death, rather than here, now.

The Kriminalinspektor faced Katya, his hands on his hips, his face impassive. 'Your neighbour, the excellent Frau Hagler, was quite correct, as usual. She has been an invaluable source of information from the start. There is apparently nobody she is not prepared to denounce, even close members of her family. Her devotion to the Führer is most commendable. If there were more Austrians like the good Frau Hagler, our task would be a far easier one.'

Katya was silent. There was nothing to say.

He swung round to face Gretchen, who was standing, white-faced, by the piano. 'And here is the child. Excellent. Your name?'

'Gretchen,' she whispered.

'They say you are a prodigy. That you can play any piece by ear, after hearing it once. Yet you cannot read or write. Is this true?'

Katya reached for Gretchen protectively. Gretchen pressed against Katya's body like a much younger child, trembling.

The man smiled thinly. 'Cat got your tongue? Can't she speak?'

'Yes,' Katya said in a low voice, 'she can speak.'

'What is her age?'

'She is twelve.'

Sauer indicated Hildegard's piano. 'Play something, girl.'

Gretchen just shook her head slightly, feeling terrified.

'Don't be a fool,' the man snapped, his voice hardening. 'I have no time to waste on you. *Play*.'

Afraid of the consequences if the officer lost his temper, Katya gently pushed Gretchen towards the piano. 'Play something,' she whispered. 'Please, Liebchen.'

Painfully slowly, Gretchen sat at the piano and lifted the lid of the instrument. She stared at the keys, unseeing. The Gestapo man folded his arms, frowning.

In the lengthening silence, the thug behind him muttered a curse in disgust. 'Want me to give her a slap, Herr Kriminalinspektor?'

Sauer shook his head impatiently. 'Not yet.' Katya's heart was in her throat. If they touched Gretchen, she thought, she would tear their eyes out with her nails.

At last, Gretchen laid her right hand on the keyboard. Her fingers looked as pale as the ivory keys themselves. A soft note sounded, fading away. Then another. Slowly, the notes coalesced into a Bach melody. Her left hand fluttered like a moth on to the keyboard, and began playing another melody, the counterpoint to the first. The isolated sounds became music, melodies playing against one another, inverting, contrasting, opposing, weaving a spell. Gretchen's eyes closed, as though her own playing was transporting her away from the frightening present to some remote, safe place.

The piece, one of the *Goldberg Variations* that Gretchen loved to play, was a short one, lasting only a couple of minutes. When it ended, Gretchen remained immobile at the piano, as though unable to return to reality.

The Hauptmann grunted. 'So it's true then. An idiot savant. Incapable of normal tasks, yet with one extraordinary talent.' He turned back to Katya. 'I require a demonstration before I decide how to deal with you.'

'I'm sorry,' Katya stammered. 'I don't know what you mean.'

'This is a rare condition. My colleagues in the Gestapo will be interested. We have an officers' club. We like to arrange entertainments – concerts, informative lectures, and so forth. It helps to provide relaxation. This child will provide a stimulating demonstration.'

'Demonstration!'

'Our next soirée is on Friday evening. I will send a driver for you at seven-thirty.'

'I don't think that will be possible!'

'It must be possible,' Sauer replied calmly. 'There is no obstacle. The child can prepare a short programme. Our members may suggest variations, *ad libitum*. You agree?' He was smiling lightly, but his eyes were implacable.

'I don't think it's a very good idea,' Katya replied miserably.

'Nonsense. Would you prefer that I arrest you immediately?'

'No.'

He turned to his sergeant. 'Arrange a driver for Friday.'

'*Jawohl*, Herr Kriminalinspektor.'

The Kriminalinspektor glanced around the apartment. 'You have found a nice little nest. You are our guests here in Innsbruck. And guests owe their hosts some return for their hospitality, not so?' He raised his hand. 'Heil Hitler!'

'Heil Hitler,' Katya heard herself reply.

He turned on his heel and left.

'Oh, Hildegard, I'm so sorry to have involved you.'

Hildegard shook her head angrily. 'I knew what I was doing. I'm just ashamed of being the same nationality as Frau Hagler. For myself, I have no regrets, Katya.'

'But I do,' Katya said. 'I wish we'd never come to you and mixed you up in this.'

'Never mind about that. You should run, right now. Get out of this place.'

'Where would we go? They're obviously watching us,' Katya replied. 'We wouldn't get a mile away. And even if we did, they would come for you.'

'I can take care of myself.'

'We've seen what these people do,' Katya said with a shudder. 'There's no defence against them. I just hope they won't make any reprisals against you. How did that man know Gretchen was musical?'

'Innsbruck is a small town,' Hildegard said. 'After Gretchen's performance at the piano shop, the manager was telling everybody about this remarkable child. That old brute Hagler put two and two together. It wasn't hard.'

'I don't understand why Sauer doesn't just arrest us.'

'I suppose he wants you cooperative for his damned Gestapo club.' Hildegard grimaced. 'My God – a Gestapo club! Who could imagine that such a thing existed! What if it goes wrong? What will they do to the two of you? They're such hideous monsters, they're capable of anything.'

'We'll be all right,' Katya said, with a confidence she was very far from feeling. 'You need to focus on your exam. You mustn't let anything distract you now.'

'I've lost interest in my exam. Nothing's normal any more.' Hildegard's face was set. 'I hate seeing these German gangsters on every corner. I hate people like Frau Hagler, who welcome them with open arms and turn on their fellow Austrians.'

'Forget her.' Katya laid her hand on Hildegard's arm. 'My dear, I hope you don't mean it when you say you've lost interest in your exam. Whatever happens, you've got to get your diploma.'

'Should I work on something with Gretchen, to prepare her?'

'I don't think so. She's almost hysterical as it is. I don't want to put any more pressure on her.'

Gretchen was indeed wound as tight as a watch spring. 'What do they want with me?' she asked Katya tensely. 'Do they want to put me in a zoo, like a wild animal?'

'I'm so sorry,' Katya said.

'I *hate* that man,' Gretchen said vehemently. 'He likes to hurt people. *He's* the one who should be in a cage, like a savage beast, for people to stare at. I can't do it. I *won't* play for those people!' She turned to Katya, her face passionate. 'They don't deserve to have music.'

'No, they don't deserve to have music. But I don't think we have any choice, Liebchen.'

'Why should we always give in to them?' Gretchen demanded fiercely. 'They killed Papa. Let them kill us too.'

Katya hadn't heard Gretchen articulate the thought that her father might be dead so clearly before, and she was shocked in some strange way. 'We don't know that Papa is dead,' she replied slowly. 'But whatever has happened to him, he wouldn't want you to die. Living is the best thing you could do for him. Do you understand what I'm saying?'

Gretchen was crying. 'Don't leave me, Katya.'

'Leave you! Why on earth do you say that? I'll never leave you.'

'I'm so afraid that you will. I would be nothing without you. What would happen to me if you left? And you should leave! You shouldn't stay here with me. You should go back to England, and be safe, and—'

Katya put her arms around Gretchen. 'Hush. I'm not going anywhere. You belong to me, and I belong to you.'

Gretchen clung to her. 'I love you, Katya.'

'I love you, Gretchen.'

They rocked together in silence.

The Gestapo car arrived for them on Friday at exactly 7.30 p.m.

It was a black Mercedes, very like their car in Vienna – except that this one sported swastika pennants on the hood, and was driven by a squat Brownshirt with a battered face.

They were driven to town, under an archway, and into a tight, narrow street that was filled with similar black cars and heavily dominated by a large stuccoed building with barred windows. Over the door was a bronze eagle grasping a crooked cross in its claws.

In the lobby, their names were taken and written in a ledger. Then they were put under the charge of a burly guard, who escorted them up several flights of stone stairs. Gretchen was trembling and silent. Katya could only pray that she would withstand whatever these men chose to inflict on her.

They could hear the noise of loud male laughter and con-versation as they arrived at the top floor of the building. Their guard opened double doors and pushed them into a room that was crowded with people, mostly men in evening dress. The air was acrid with the smoke of cigars and cigarettes.

The room was comfortably appointed, like a gentlemen's club, with leather sofas and armchairs. At the far end of the room was a bar, manned by a steward in white, over which hung a swastika banner. A lot of drinking was going on, a full glass in almost every hand. The few women present were smartly dressed and well-groomed. The men's suits were crisply pressed. They were not spattered with blood, like the thugs they'd seen at the police station, but they had the confident, relaxed air of a conquering race, the arrogance of unquestioned power.

Katya and Gretchen were largely ignored by the men, although a few women turned to glance at them curiously. They stood by the door, waiting to be commanded. Gretchen had a tight hold of Katya's hand. Katya could feel Gretchen's palm cold yet sweaty against her own.

At last, one of the men shouted boisterously, 'Well, Heinrich! What have you got for us tonight?'

Kriminalinspektor Sauer appeared from the throng, carrying a pewter tankard of beer. His cheeks were flushed. 'Something very interesting,' he shouted back. 'You will see. Clear a space!' The members of the club made space in the middle of the room as two Brownshirts hauled in a baby grand piano. Gretchen's grip on Katya's hand grew even tighter. The Brownshirts opened the lid of the piano, and then brought in the piano stool, a small table, a gramophone and a stack of records. They set everything up under Sauer's barked commands. When everything was ready, he turned to Gretchen. 'Come, girl.'

Gretchen was frozen, unable to move.

Sauer stalked up to Gretchen with lowered brows. 'Don't embarrass me,' he growled quietly. 'Or I will make you both regret it.'

'Please, Liebchen,' Katya whispered, hating herself. She felt like a traitor for pushing Gretchen, but she was terrified of the reprisal that might fall on disobedience.

Like a sleepwalker, Gretchen allowed herself to be led to the piano. She sat on the stool, surrounded by a sea of dress suits.

All smiles again, Kriminalinspektor Sauer addressed the room. 'The child you see here before you is twelve years old. Unlike other German children of her age, she cannot read or write. She can barely speak her mother tongue.' There was some loud laughter at that. Sauer raised his hand. 'But, my friends, she is what is called an idiot savant. A great rarity. Although she is deficient in other regards, she has an unusual gift. She is able to play any piece of music that she hears. She will now demonstrate.'

He took a record out of its sleeve and placed it on the gramophone.

Katya felt sick. She'd had no idea that Sauer had been planning something like this. It was a test far more demanding than anything Gretchen had ever been given. It was true that Gretchen played by ear – but only after hearing music several times, and only when it surfaced from the strange labyrinth of her mind.

If she failed now, and humiliated Sauer in front of his colleagues, the consequences could be terrible.

The record began to turn. In the silence, they heard the plop of the needle landing on the shellac. The speaker hissed for a moment. Katya was unable to breathe, her eyes fixed on Gretchen's small figure. The music that came out of the speaker was the tinkling sound of a lounge piano, the sort of musical piece that was played in cafés and tea rooms all over Austria while Sachertorte and cream cakes were being gobbled. It was nothing like anything Gretchen had ever played before.

Sauer let the music run for a minute or two, then lifted the needle off the record.

'Play it,' he ordered Gretchen.

Gretchen didn't move. She sat staring at the keys blankly, with her hands in her lap. Katya had to force herself not to run over to her and throw her arms protectively around her. Sauer's smile darkened into a frown. 'Play it!' he commanded loudly. When Gretchen still didn't respond, he walked up to her, bent down, and shouted in her ear. 'Play it, or I will have you flogged.'

Gretchen flinched away from the man. Jerkily, her hands lifted out of her lap, and moved to the keys. The opening chords of the music materialised from her fingers. She played the banal, hackneyed tune exactly as they'd just heard it, ending at the point where the needle had been lifted. Katya felt relief flood her.

'She just needed a little encouragement,' Sauer told the audience. There was laughter.

'This is a hoax, Heinrich,' a fat man said with a shrug. 'The girl has rehearsed the piece beforehand.'

Sauer smirked. 'You think so? Then I invite you to choose any record you please and put it on the gramophone.'

Katya's relief froze into horror. The possibilities for disaster were now infinitely multiplied. The fat man, his belly straining his white shirt front, rifled through the records and chose one. He put it on the turntable and stood back. 'Let's hear her play *that*,' he sneered.

This was very different, Mozart's 'Alla Turca', a popular concert piece, and not something Gretchen had ever tried to play. After a couple of minutes, Sauer lifted the needle off the record.

'Play,' he ordered.

This time, Gretchen didn't hesitate. She began to play the piece fluently. But her face was pale and strained. The music sounded perfect, and she stopped playing exactly where Sauer had stopped it.

One of the women, in an emerald-green evening dress, walked forward and poked Gretchen sharply in the back with her finger. Gretchen flinched and cried out.

'I just wanted to see if she's human,' the woman said, to laughter. 'She's like some kind of machine. Do you notice how she stops exactly where the music stops? It's uncanny.'

'It's unnatural,' one of the other women said. 'It gives me the creeps, as a matter of fact. She should be put in a museum of curiosities.'

'She should be taken out and a bullet put in her head,' a man said. 'It's an aberration.'

'There's some kind of trick, isn't there, Sauer?' an older man with grey hair said to Sauer. 'Come on, man. Tell us how it's done. Is there another gramophone hidden in the piano?'

'Look for yourself, Herr Kriminaldirektor.'

The senior man peered into the bowels of the piano, then took Gretchen by the elbow, yanked her to her feet, and looked in the piano stool. 'Nothing there.'

'There is no trick, Herr Kriminaldirektor. The girl is a *lusus naturae*. A prodigy.'

The Kriminaldirektor stared into Gretchen's white face. 'What's your name, girl?'

Gretchen could not reply, just stared over his shoulder.

'An idiot,' the man said contemptuously.

'Exactly,' Sauer said complacently. 'An idiot savant, as I said.'

'I still think it's a trick of some kind.' A man laughed. 'Maybe she's a dwarf – and really forty years old!'

The Kriminaldirektor grasped Gretchen's jaw in his fingers and forced her mouth open. 'No,' he grunted. 'The teeth are a child's. The molars are barely out.'

'Get her to play something else,' a woman called out. 'Put another record on!'

Their interest now piqued, the women shuffled through the record collection and chose something new – this time, a selection of Chopin's waltzes. 'Go through them all,' the woman in green demanded excitedly. 'That way, we'll catch her out, sooner or later!'

A record was put on the gramophone. The steward was called to bring fresh drinks. He went around serving the alcohol as the performance got underway.

This time, the pieces followed one another in quick succession. The first minutes of each number were played, and Gretchen was commanded to repeat them. She obeyed, with the same blank look on her face. Each time, there were exclamations of surprise or scepticism at the accuracy with which she could repeat the music. But Gretchen seemed to be shrinking into herself, as though dwindling into nothing.

She felt as though she had become so small that she had been placed on the gramophone herself, and was being spun in ever faster circles, like the playground roundabout she had loathed as a child. She was sick and dizzy, but there was no time to get off and vomit.

The women, oblivious to the cruelty they were inflicting – or perhaps enjoying it – kept playing new tracks, determined to make her stumble, or to uncover some trick by which she was performing these little miracles.

Katya could only stand helplessly by and watch. She could see that Gretchen was swiftly growing dazed, exhaustion draining the colour from her face, until she was as white as bone, her head starting to droop.

'Well, my dear wife,' a bald man said to the woman in green, 'our daughter has been taking lessons from the best teacher in Berlin for ten years, and she can't do this. I think we'll have to stop those lessons, eh?'

'I don't believe it,' the woman in green spat. 'It's a hoax.'

'Perhaps she simply has a wide repertoire.'

'At twelve? She can't possibly have learned all those pieces beforehand,' someone said. 'It's remarkable.'

'Nonsense. It *has* to be a hoax,' the woman in green insisted excitably. 'Remember years ago, there was that horse – Clever Hans – who could do arithmetic, or so they said. He would tap out the answer to sums with his hoof. But it turned out his trainer would give him secret signals. This must be something similar!'

'Except that this is not a horse, Elfriede,' a stout, soft-looking woman said, 'and she is doing rather more than tapping a hoof.'

'Someone is giving her a signal!'

'What kind of signal can make a child play the piano with all ten fingers?' The stout woman smiled.

'It's the mother.' Elfriede's sharp eyes had landed on Katya. 'The mother is doing it somehow.' Shimmering in green, she strode over to confront Katya. 'How is it done? What's the trick? I demand to know!'

'There's no trick,' Katya said quietly.

'Of course there is a trick.' Her breath was laden with alcohol. 'Don't lie to me!'

'She simply plays what she hears.'

Elfriede's palm cracked across Katya's cheek, leaving it burning. 'Foreign bitch! Do you know where you are? Don't give me your insolence.' She struck Katya again, this time backhanded, on the other cheek. One of her rings cut the skin, and Katya felt the wetness of blood. 'Tell me how it's done!'

The men were laughing. 'Your wife's a tiger, Ulrich,' someone called to the bald man.

'Really, Elfriede,' the stout woman said quietly, 'you can be remarkably stupid sometimes.' She came forward and gave Katya a handkerchief. Katya took it and dabbed her cheek, feeling numb.

'I'll get to the bottom of this,' Elfriede vowed. She marched back to the piano. 'Give me something really difficult. You people that know about music – find me something *hard*.'

Grinning, a man passed her a record. 'This one's a challenge.'

Elfriede pulled it out of the sleeve and put it on the gramophone. The music rolled out – one of Brahms' *Hungarian Dances*, a fast, glittering, gypsy csardas. 'You will play the whole thing this time, you hear?' she shouted at Gretchen. 'And if you get a note wrong, my husband will put a bullet in your head!'

'Elfriede, you're going too far,' the stout woman protested.

'Shut up, Ursula. You're always too soft.' Elfriede turned back to Gretchen. 'I mean it, you little freak!'

The men, who had been looking rather bored up until now, were taking an interest, leers on many faces, malicious eyes fixed on Gretchen. The Brahms gypsy dance whirled from the speaker, a bravura piece of music that was complex and technically demanding. It would be a difficult piece for any pianist, let alone Gretchen. Did Elfriede mean what she had threatened? Her heart beating fast, Katya edged closer to Gretchen, ready to throw herself in the way of any danger.

The Brahms lasted only two or three minutes, but it was a pyrotechnic display of virtuosity. Nobody would be able to repeat that by ear alone. Gretchen would surely be hopelessly lost, on top of everything else she had heard tonight. It was the end.

'Now,' Elfriede hissed, coiling her slender emerald body around the curve of the piano like a viper, 'play *that*.'

Gretchen had been staring blindly at the keys while the music played. Now, she raised her head slowly and looked Elfriede in the face for a moment. There were dark shadows under her eyes, and her teeth were clenched.

Then she began to play. There were gasps as the first chords rang out, then exclamations of astonishment as the music developed.

Gretchen was playing the piece as though she'd been rehearsing it for weeks, with passion and brilliance.

Elfriede reared up, her face a mask of fury. Then, before Katya could stop her, she had brought the heavy keyboard lid crashing shut on Gretchen's hands.

Chapter 23

'So,' Sauer said laconically, 'you have broken your toy, Elfriede.'

'I hope you're pleased with yourself,' Ursula, the stout woman, echoed bitterly.

Elfriede turned her back, laughing, and rejoined her friends. Someone had put some dance music on the gramophone now, and couples had started foxtrotting around the piano, as though nothing had happened. The show was over. Nobody was interested in Gretchen any more.

Ursula was sniffing back tears as she helped Katya get Gretchen out of the room. Gretchen had screamed as the heavy lid slammed down on her hands, but she was now completely silent. She hadn't shed a tear, but she was in shock, stumbling as though her legs were rubber. Katya was terrified.

'I need to get her to a doctor,' she said desperately. Gretchen's wrists had taken the brunt of the blow, and both were swelling rapidly, and turning purple. She was certain that bones had been broken.

'You won't find a doctor at this time of night,' the stout woman said. 'I'll take you to the hospital myself. Come.'

Halfway down the stairs, Gretchen stopped and vomited. They had to hold her hair out of the way. They got her down through the lobby and into the narrow street. 'Wait here,' Ursula said. She hurried away to get her car.

In the light of a streetlamp, Katya looked into Gretchen's face. 'I'm sorry, I'm sorry, I'm so sorry,' she blurted out. 'I should have protected you. I failed!'

Gretchen didn't respond. She didn't seem to know where she was.

There was a footstep behind them. Kriminalinspektor Sauer had come down, puffing on a cigar. 'It was my intention to arrest you both at the end of the evening,' he said. 'The SS in Feldkirch have ordered that you be detained.' He stretched and yawned, looking up at the moonlit mountains that towered over Innsbruck. 'We in the Gestapo do not always do what our colleagues in the SS tell us to do, surprising as that may seem. But you cannot remain here, Fräulein Komarovsky. You understand me? If I come across you again, I will have to arrest you and hand you over to the SS. You and the child need to disappear.' He took a last puff of his cigar and tossed it across the street. It hit the road with a shower of sparks. He turned without another word and went back into the Gestapo headquarters, leaving Katya in despair. What was to become of them now?

With a squeal of rubber, a car came around the corner and raced down the street towards them. Ursula was wedged behind the wheel. She peered out of the window at Gretchen and Katya. 'Get in!'

Katya helped Gretchen into the car. As soon as they set off, Ursula began gabbling. 'They asked my husband to join the Gestapo. I didn't want him to. He was doing well in the Ordnungspolizei. But he was so proud to be chosen. He said it was a promotion. And now everything has become detestable.' She drove fast and erratically through the darkened streets, peering short-sightedly from side to side. 'I don't like these people. They're drunk with their new power. I'm frightened of what they're going to do.'

'Is this the way to the hospital?' Katya asked anxiously. She was sitting in the back seat. Gretchen was curled up with her head in Katya's lap, her eyes closed.

'Yes, yes. We'll be there soon. Elfriede says I am soft. I *am* soft. I don't like to see people get hurt. Is that so wrong? You can see what they're going to do, these people, can't you? You can see what they're going to do. Everyone can see what they're going to do.' She was driving into the hospital grounds now, and a minute later, pulled up at a building marked 'Outpatients'. 'Here we are. Goodbye!'

'Aren't you coming in?' Katya asked.

Ursula turned to look at her unhappily. 'I can't. My husband is in the Gestapo. I can't be mixed up in this.'

'I don't have any money.'

'Oh, I see.' The woman rifled in her handbag and thrust a fistful of notes at Katya. 'This should cover it. Don't mention my name.' She reached over and opened Katya's door. 'Goodbye!'

There was nothing to be done but accept such help as the stout woman had given her. 'All right. Thank you.' Katya got out with Gretchen clinging to her. Ursula set off at speed, leaving them standing there.

'The right radius and ulna are both fractured,' the young doctor said. 'I suspect the left wrist is fractured too. But I'm only going to plaster the right arm. Two casts make life very difficult for a child.' He got busy with the bandages and the plaster mix. He'd given Gretchen a spoonful of morphine syrup against the pain, and she was drowsing on the bed, her face very pale. He spoke excellent English. 'The cast will have to stay on for at least six weeks. It's an unusual injury. May I ask how it happened?'

'She was playing the piano,' Katya said tensely, 'and someone slammed the lid shut on her hands.'

'That was very careless.'

'It was done deliberately.'

His face changed. 'I see. And may I know who was the perpetrator of this crime?'

Katya looked at his name, which was embroidered on his white coat: David Turteltaub. 'It was the wife of a member of the Gestapo,' she said.

He stopped what he was doing, and went to shut the door quietly. 'Are you Jews?'

'No.'

'I am. That is why you find me here on the night shift in Outpatients, instead of on my wards. Before too long, they will dismiss me. And after that, the concentration camp. What was this child's offence?'

'She played the piano better than the woman's daughter.'

'Ah, yes. To be beaten at anything does not suit the master race.' He was expertly plastering Gretchen's arm as he spoke. 'In my opinion, one is best to leave them to it. They are very good at certain things, after all. Breaking children's arms, for instance.'

Katya had been shaken to the core when the heavy piano lid had crashed on to Gretchen's arms. 'Will there be any permanent damage?' she asked, holding back tears.

'To these little wrists, most likely not. They will heal. The girl is young. But in here—' He touched Gretchen's forehead. 'In here, who can say? You will have to be the doctor there.' This comment set off the avalanche of pent-up emotion in Katya, and she started crying. He peered at her in concern. 'Are you also injured?'

'No. It's just been a difficult few days. I love her so much. I wish it had been me instead of her. I wanted to be a doctor, too. I gave it up. It seems – seems a long time ago now.'

'Ah. How far did you get?'

'Only to the end of my second year.'

'Which university?'

'Glasgow.'

'I did part of my degree at Edinburgh. Well, fractured dreams, like fractured wrists, may knit up again.' He had a sensitive face, with eyes the colour of faded denim, as though they were much older than the rest of him, and curly straw-coloured hair. 'Certainly, there will be no piano for a couple of months. Even after the cast comes off, she will need to strengthen the muscles before she can begin to play. Don't let her start too soon.' He had moulded a cast that covered Gretchen's palm. Her thumb and fingers, which were both turning blue, poked out forlornly. 'I've made it as light as I can. It will start to set in twenty minutes, but it won't really be hard until tomorrow. And she will have to wear a sling. I will make her one.' He began washing his hands in the basin. 'Where are you staying?'

'With a friend. But we'll have to find somewhere else. We're on the run from the SS.'

He sighed. 'A lot of us are on the run from the SS. I'm thinking of starting a cross-country club. The Schutzstaffel Harriers.' He dried his hands, and perched on the table, considering Katya thoughtfully for a long time. 'You are too young to be the girl's mother,' he said at last.

'I'm her governess. Her father has been arrested in Vienna. We've had no word from him in weeks.'

He grimaced. 'The fear and uncertainty are among their most effective weapons. People vanish without trace. Those who love them are left to dread the worst. It ensures compliance. Tell me, how exactly do you come to be here?'

He listened as she told him briefly how everything had unfolded. He was interested to hear that she had met Freud.

'I am a great admirer. He and his daughter have arrived safely in London,' he said. 'There was a big fanfare. It was on the World Service. So, I take it you are rather more than the governess – to both father and daughter?'

'I don't know what I am,' she said tiredly, brushing the hair gently away from Gretchen's face. 'I'm failing them both. I'm useless.'

Turteltaub's prematurely faded eyes were smiling. 'Not quite useless. As a matter of fact, you're not doing so badly.' He opened a wall cabinet and took out a little brown bottle. He poured two measures into medicine cups. 'Here. It's medicinal.'

They both drank. She emptied the measure in one gulp. 'Every time I close my eyes, I see that woman smashing the piano lid down—'

'Don't dwell on it. And now we must admit Gretchen to the children's ward, at least overnight, for observation, and to make sure the cast sets well.'

Katya was alarmed. 'What if the Gestapo find her here?'

'It's true that they check patient lists every day. But I will make sure to change the name and the reason for admission. And there are arrangements for mothers to sleep beside the children. What else are you going to do, Katya? You had better not go back to your friend tonight. Sauer may have someone waiting for you there. And you can hardly sleep under a bridge, or in a ditch, with an injured child. Tomorrow, in the light of day, you can consider your options.'

'I don't have very much money to pay for this.'

'My dear, money is the least of your problems. Put that out of your head. I am an Austrian, and you are my guest. You'll be safe here for a while. Some of the staff are still sympathetic to me. Others—' He shrugged. 'Well, be careful. But this is the best course, in my eyes.'

He was gentle but insistent, and she allowed herself to be carried along by him. He wouldn't let her telephone Hildegard, warning her that the telephones were most likely tapped. 'It's better that she doesn't know where you are, even if she does worry. I'll go and speak to Admissions.'

The children's ward was in semi-darkness, lined with small, motionless figures in beds and cots. Dr Turteltaub had arranged a bed in a secluded corner, with a curtain that could be pulled around it. A nurse brought a hospital shift for Gretchen to sleep in. Katya helped her put it on.

'Where are we?' she mumbled, half-waking from the drugs.

'In hospital. We're safe,' Katya said.

The roundabout had stopped at last. Gretchen was no longer spinning. But there were echoes and rustlings in her ears, and a terrible pain in her arms. She felt as though a thousand radios were playing somewhere in her head, disjointed fragments from a thousand pieces of music, some so fast they twittered like birds, others so slow they groaned like forest trees.

Mercifully, she sank into the blackness like a stone, slipping into oblivion.

They put her carefully in the bed, her injured arms laid at her sides, over the blanket. She was asleep again in a few moments. There was a mattress on the floor next to the bed for Katya. 'It's the usual arrangement,' Turteltaub said apologetically, 'but at least you're close to her. Remember, Gretchen is now called Charlotte. Your family name is Kuberich. I've admitted her for suspected diphtheria. It's very infectious, so that should deter any inquisitive visitors.'

'You're being so kind,' Katya said. 'I don't know how to thank you.'

He patted her arm. 'I'm afraid I won't see you again until I come back on duty tomorrow afternoon. Try to find Sister Ludmila, if you can. She's one of the few on my side. Say as little as possible to anyone else. Keep the curtain closed as much as you can. And good luck, Katya.'

Katya had slept no more than an hour all night, worrying about Gretchen. She was jolted into alertness by the bustle of the early morning shift. The sun was just rising. She got up and checked on Gretchen. The girl was sleeping peacefully; she hadn't moved all night. Katya was relieved to see that there was a little colour in her cheeks now.

With a sudden rattle, the curtain was pulled aside, revealing a tall nurse with her greying hair pulled back from a bony forehead. She wore a matron's cap. Her piercing eyes shot from Gretchen to Katya. She frowned and folded her arms. 'What's going on here? This is supposed to be a diphtheria patient.'

Another nurse, smaller, younger and plumper, came over. 'That's Dr Turteltaub's patient, Matron. He's left some special notes about her.'

'Special notes? What special notes?'

'I'll get them.'

While she was away, the matron stuck a thermometer under Gretchen's arm, and took her pulse. Waking, Gretchen began to whimper with pain. The matron's sharp eyes were unfriendly as she looked at Katya. 'How did she get these injuries?'

'It was a – a motor accident.'

'So she does not have diphtheria?'

'Not – not exactly.'

'Not exactly?'

Katya was stuck for an answer. Luckily, the young nurse returned with the notes on a clipboard. The matron read through them, and snorted in disgust. 'Always some funny business with Dr Turteltaub.'

'Always some funny business with all Jews,' the young nurse called over her shoulder as she left.

'Well, we shall soon be rid of them – and all their schemes,' the matron said, giving Katya a hard look. 'Are you one of his little friends?'

'I don't know what you mean.'

'I mean that you have been billing and cooing with our Dr Turteltaub.'

'I met him for the first time last night.'

'Did you, indeed.'

Katya turned her attention back to Gretchen, who was crying. 'My daughter's in pain,' she pointed out. 'Can she have something?'

'What sort of something?'

'Dr Turteltaub gave her morphine last night, but it's worn off.'

'Morphine is contraindicated for diphtheria,' the woman said spitefully. 'It will suppress the breathing.'

Katya bit back her angry retort. There was no point antagonising the matron. 'An aspirin, then. Anything.'

'You will have to speak to Dr Turteltaub tonight.' She didn't bother saying goodbye, and snapped the curtain shut as she left.

'It hurts so much,' Gretchen moaned.

'I'm so sorry, Liebchen. I'll go and get something,' Katya vowed.

Gretchen gave Katya a tiny smile through her tears. 'But it was a good thing that woman broke my arm.'

'Why?'

'Because I was just about to stop playing. My mind was blank. I couldn't remember any more! And then she would have shot me. I'd rather have a broken arm than be shot.'

Katya couldn't suppress a laugh. 'That's what I love about you. You always look on the bright side.'

Katya went out circumspectly to look for Sister Ludmila, as Turteltaub had advised her. The ward was already busy; there were nurses and doctors everywhere. By dint of asking, she finally located Sister Ludmila on a neighbouring ward. Unlike the other nurses, she was in a nun's habit, with a cross hanging on her snowy apron. She was in her sixties, her coif framing Slavic cheekbones and slanting eyes.

'Dr Turteltaub told me to look for you,' Katya blurted out. 'My daughter was admitted last night with a broken arm. She's in pain, but none of the nurses want to help her, and—'

Sister Ludmila laid a finger on Katya's lips. 'Hush, child. Don't talk so loud.' She took Katya aside and went on in a low voice, 'Are you Jewish?'

'No. But I'm in trouble with the Gestapo. It was one of them who broke my daughter's arm.'

The nun's green eyes flashed indignantly. 'Take me to her,' she commanded.

Katya took her to Gretchen's ward. Sister Ludmila drew the curtain to shut them in, then examined Gretchen. 'Little bird,' she said sorrowfully, 'you have a broken wing. Why did they do this?'

'Because she's different,' Katya said.

'Ah, the great crime, to be different from *them* – as if it were a sin not to be cruel and evil, as they are.'

'It hurts so much,' Gretchen whispered. 'I'll never play the piano again.'

'You will play, little bird.' Sister Ludmila laid her hand on Gretchen's brow gently. 'I will get you something for the pain.'

She returned shortly with the morphine syrup, and within a few minutes Gretchen was drowsy and peaceful again. 'Thank you, Sister,' Katya said quietly.

'It was a wicked deed. But I am afraid that wicked deeds are being done all the time in Austria now – and that an even greater wickedness is to come. When I came to this country from Yugoslavia fifteen years ago, it was a good Catholic nation. But they have turned their backs on God, and God will turn his back on them.' Gretchen was asleep now. She folded her hands and prayed quietly over the girl, then crossed herself. 'You were very lucky to come across Dr Turteltaub,' she said to Katya. 'He has a tender heart. He will give treatment to those whom society has cast out – and forgets to charge his patients sometimes.'

'He doesn't seem popular with the staff.'

'Of course not. He is a Jew. They have all been taught to hate Jews. The management will dismiss him sooner or later.'

'The matron accused me of flirting with him.'

Sister Ludmila smiled slightly. 'He has a weakness for a pretty face. Well, there are worse crimes than that, aren't there? The Nazis say that the Jews are devilishly cunning. For my own part, I have often found them to be simple, innocent people. And that applies very much to Dr Turteltaub.'

Sister Ludmila left, promising to return in the afternoon. Katya kept the curtain closed around Gretchen's bed, and even managed to snatch a little sleep now that Gretchen was quiet again.

She was awoken at mid-morning by the sound of men's voices. Pulling the curtain aside a little, she was alarmed to see two men in the unmistakeable black trench coats of the Gestapo, conferring with the matron. She saw the matron pointing towards Gretchen's bed.

She shut the curtain hastily and retreated, her heart beating fast. There was nowhere to go, nowhere to hide.

Shortly after, she heard footsteps approaching. 'Frau Kuberich!' demanded an authoritative voice. It took her a moment to remember that this was the name Turteltaub had given her.

Trying to stop herself from trembling, she emerged from the curtain. 'Yes?'

The men had hard faces, felt hats pulled down over their brows, like Chicago gangsters in the movies. 'Your papers, please.'

'I don't have them.'

'Why not?' one asked sharply.

'All our clothes and possessions have been sent to be disinfected,' Katya said, not knowing where the inspiration for this had come from. 'They think my daughter has diphtheria.'

They retreated hastily a few paces. 'Don't come any closer,' one of the men said. Despite his broken nose and scarred face, he looked suddenly apprehensive. Somehow, this lie passed muster for the time being, though she knew it would soon be uncovered. They asked a few more questions, wrote down the answers, and hastily left. Katya was aware of the matron's eyes watching the whole proceeding. When the Gestapo men had left the ward, she came over to Katya.

'You are clever, eh?' she sneered. 'I wonder what your story is, *Frau Kuberich*?'

'Whatever it is, we've done nothing wrong,' Katya retorted. The adrenalin was still running through her veins, making her brave – and angry. She was tired of being bullied and threatened. 'This is supposed to be a hospital,' she went on briskly, looking the other woman in the eyes, 'but it feels more like a prison to me. What's happening in Austria, that the secret police make a habit of marching into the children's ward?'

'We need the cats,' the matron replied meaningfully. 'There are too many rats.'

'If you ask me, the cats are the problem here.'

The matron flushed. 'If you don't like it in this country, you should go back to your own!'

'Do you know, that's damned good advice,' Katya retorted. 'I just wish I could take it.' She went back to Gretchen's bedside, seething.

She had a long, slow afternoon to think. Gretchen was exhausted after her ordeal, and slept for hours without stirring. Katya had time to reflect on the past weeks. One thing was clear – they couldn't go on like this, terrified to death, stumbling from disaster to disaster. They'd had a succession of very narrow escapes, and a bit of good luck here and there, but sooner or later they were going to be caught, and that would be the end of them both.

She had to come up with a real plan. But the master stroke evaded her. Knowing that the SS were waiting for them at the border meant that trying to get to Switzerland was impossible. Perhaps there was a way to escape to Italy.

The matron and the other nurses studiously avoided them all day. The glances that were cast their way were hostile. A tray of food was silently brought at lunchtime, which they shared, but otherwise it was plain that they were not welcomed, or even considered as patients.

'I want to get out of this place,' Gretchen whispered to Katya. 'They hate us here.'

'I know, be brave. We'll go as soon as we can,' Katya said, brushing Gretchen's hair from her face.

Dr Turteltaub arrived at four, much to Katya's relief. He examined Gretchen in his careful way and pronounced himself satisfied with the way the cast had set. He was less pleased to hear that the Gestapo had spoken to Katya, and that the matron was suspicious.

'That's not good. It's only a matter of time before one of the staff betrays you. It's best that you come to us now.'

Katya was taken aback. 'To you?'

'I live close by, with my sister, Shulamit. We have a spare room. I've told her that you'll be coming for a night or two.'

'Oh, that's so kind. But – I don't—'

'You don't have anywhere else to go,' he said gently. 'Get ready to leave in an hour.'

Chapter 24

Shulamit Turteltaub was waiting for them in the twilight, at the garden gate. She was a diminutive figure in a wheelchair.

'Welcome, welcome,' she murmured, as she led them quickly into the house, speeding along the garden path on her glittering wheels. She closed the door behind them as they came in, and took them to a small sitting room. She drew the curtains, and only then turned on the light, which revealed her to be a small, delicate-featured woman in her twenties, with her brother's light blue eyes, though her hair was nearly black, whereas his was blond. Her back was severely curved, her childlike legs tucked up beneath her. 'David didn't tell you what to expect, did he?' she said. 'I can't walk any more. But when I am in my carriage, I am a queen. David told me what happened to you. I'm so sorry. This is not Austria. Not the Austria we knew.'

Katya saw in Shulamit a brightness of spirit that was rare. For all her small size, she was clearly the mistress of the house. The kitchen, and much else, had been adapted so that she could reach everything from her wheelchair.

David wouldn't be home until much later, so they began to prepare supper. As Shulamit worked, she told them that their parents were both dead, and that she and her brother had been living together for several years. 'I look after him,' she said with a little laugh, 'although he's convinced that it's he who looks after me. We're very happy together.'

The future, however, was not so rosy.

'I'm afraid of what will happen to us now,' she said, her smile fading away. 'It's not just that we're Jews – that's bad enough. My spinal condition makes it much worse. The Nazis want to exterminate everyone who doesn't fit their ideal of human perfection. They call it euthanasia, constructive killing. They've already begun destroying those they say are a burden on the state. I'm so afraid that one day they will knock on the door. They want to take away the little time that I have left to live.'

'Unworthy of life,' Gretchen said in a low voice. 'That's what they say about me.'

'You!' Shulamit looked at Gretchen quickly. 'Why?'

'Because I am strange.'

Shulamit smiled slightly. 'In what way are you strange?'

'If I knew that,' Gretchen said ruefully, 'I wouldn't be strange any more.' They told Shulamit about Gretchen's experiences with Hans Asperger and the paediatric clinic. Shulamit listened with sad eyes.

'You and I are the same, then,' she said at last. 'You are a musician, and I am an artist. That's something else David didn't tell you about me, perhaps?'

'What do you paint?' Gretchen asked.

Shulamit put down the bowl she was using and dried her small hands. 'Come, leave this. I want to show you.' She took them down a corridor. 'I have the biggest room in the house for my work,' she said over her shoulder as she wheeled herself along. 'David is very kind. We sleep in shoeboxes so that I can daub canvases all day long. Here we are.' She pushed open the door.

Katya couldn't suppress a gasp. Nor could Gretchen. The room was crowded with portraits, some half-finished, others already dry. But they were all of one man.

'It's—'

'Yes,' Shulamit said. 'I only paint Hitler. But I take away the moustache.'

Gretchen and Katya walked into the room, staring around. Hitler's face glowered at them from all sides, in all his iconic poses. The quality of the painting was superbly lifelike, the skin seeming to be so alive that it would be warm to the touch. But without the bushy toothbrush moustache, each image was somehow shocking. The Hitler faces were obscenely naked, the pouchy eyes looked outraged at the exposure of the secret upper lip.

'He's so ugly!' Gretchen said wonderingly.

Shulamit nodded. 'Exactly. Take away the famous moustache and look what is left: an ugly man with a sour little mouth, malignant eyes, a nose like a slab of clay. A man who sleeps badly, who has constipation, whose breath smells bad. A bank manager who wouldn't give you a loan.' She laughed quietly. 'I've been painting these for two years now, while we waited for the Anschluss. One day I hope to have an exhibition of them. I'll call it "The Hitler Nudes". What do you think?'

'I think if the Gestapo see these, they'll send you straight to Dachau,' Katya said.

'They're probably going to send me there anyway. But if they do ever come in here, I have one painting to save my life with. I've done one Adolf with a moustache. Would you like to see it?'

'Yes, please,' Gretchen said cautiously.

Shulamit went to a corner and, with an effort, turned a large canvas around. It was a half-length, life-size portrait of Hitler, in brown uniform and swastika armband, with folded arms and frowning brows. The moustache was in place under the broad nose.

Gretchen walked up to it, and then exclaimed aloud. 'Look, Katya! It's a rat!'

Katya looked closer. The moustache was indeed a rat, with matted black fur, clinging to Hitler's upper lip with its claws. Its snout was nuzzling into one nostril, and the thin, hairless tail lined the pouting mouth.

Shulamit enjoyed their reaction with a malicious gleam in her eyes. 'Do you think the Nazis will notice?' she asked slyly. 'I'm sure they won't. After all, we're surrounded by millions of rats, aren't we – but you hardly ever see them.'

'Until one day they swarm out of their holes,' Gretchen said, 'and then they're everywhere.'

Shulamit nodded. 'The doctors are right. You *are* strange. We're going to be great friends, I can see that.' They went back to the kitchen to continue preparing the evening meal. 'These Nazis,' Shulamit said with a quiet laugh, picking up the bowl she was using. 'I wonder what has made them so bitter, so arrogant? They say they were betrayed in the Great War, and that somehow the Jews are to blame. But our father fought in that war, and was wounded twice in Serbia. We still have his medals. It's better that he's not here to see this.'

Gretchen looked at Shulamit's hands, so small and yet capable of producing such powerful images. She thought of Georg in the clinic, and wondered what had happened to him. Perhaps he had been taken away, as the orderlies had always threatened. Perhaps he was already dead, all his knots finally untied. The thought made her want to cry.

David Turteltaub came home later in the evening. They ate a simple meal together. 'Did Shulamit show you her clean-shaven Hitlers?'

he asked with a smile. 'Interesting, isn't it? You think the man has a face that you would recognise anywhere. But all you really see is the ridiculous moustache. If he were to shave it off, nobody in Germany would be able to pick him out of a police line-up of bag snatchers.'

After they'd finished the meal, he took Katya out into the garden, leaving Shulamit and Gretchen to talk in the dining room.

'I have bad news,' he said quietly. 'Those two Gestapo men came back this evening, asking about you and Gretchen. They interrogated me for an hour. I tried to put them off the scent, but I don't know what Matron may have said to them. She's on their side, of course. And she's like a dog with a bone. I was hoping to be able to give you somewhere safe to rest for a couple of days, but they will come knocking on my door before long.'

'I was thinking of walking to Italy,' Katya said.

'Italy!' He stared at her with wide blue eyes. 'You're talking about crossing the Alps to Italy?'

'It must be possible.'

'For experienced hikers, who know the way, and have the right clothing and equipment, perhaps. For you and Gretchen? It's suicide, Katya.'

Katya felt her heart sink like lead. 'It might work.'

'For Gretchen? With one arm broken and the other badly bruised? Impossible. There is still snow in the higher areas. And there are Alpine border patrols in the mountains. The Nazis are extremely vigilant, far too vigilant for that plan to work, even if the physical obstacles weren't immense. And if somehow you managed to reach Italy, what then?'

'I'll ask my parents to wire money to us. We'll get train tickets home from there.'

He shook his head. 'With no travel documents? Mussolini will send you back to Germany. You might as well hand yourselves over to the Gestapo right now.'

'Then what can we do?'

'Go east, not west.'

'How?'

'The Orient Express to Budapest.'

Katya laughed sadly. 'I'm afraid that's a little beyond us, Dr Turteltaub.'

'Please. Call me David.' He got up abruptly and walked around the garden for a moment, deep in thought. Then he returned to his chair opposite her. 'Take Shulamit with you.'

'What?' she asked, startled.

He leaned forward urgently. 'Take her with you. Take her with you, and I will help you get to Budapest.'

'David, I don't see how we can!'

He put his hand on the arm of Katya's chair. 'My sister is doomed if she stays here, Katya. She's not only a Jew, she's also what the Nazis consider "*unworthy of life*". And she mocks the Nazis to their faces. They'll come for her one of these days. She would never survive a concentration camp. It doesn't bear thinking of.'

'No,' Katya said in a low voice, 'it doesn't.'

'We have relations in Budapest, good people, who will take care of her. The Hungarians are accepting Jews now, but nobody knows for how long. I have to get her out of Austria and to our relatives as quickly as possible. Listen to me. I have been planning this for a year, since long before the Anschluss. I've set aside money. I can get false papers for her and for you. I just need someone to go with her.'

'What about you?'

'I must stay here and try to get other family members out of Austria. There are elderly aunts and uncles, cousins. They all depend on me. And I have to rescue what I can of our family's fortunes. I must sell properties, and somehow smuggle the money abroad. It won't be easy, but I will join Shulamit in Hungary at the last minute.'

'What if things become impossible?'

'If the worst comes to the worst, I can do what you proposed, make my way to Italy over the mountains. I'm fit and strong, and I know the mountains well. I can take my chances. But for Shulamit, there can be no delay. She is the first on the list.'

'Of course.'

'I don't say there's no risk, Katya. But the Gestapo are less likely to challenge passengers on a luxury train, with wealthy foreign observers around. The Arlberg Orient Express passes through Innsbruck three days a week. You will travel together. I'll get the train tickets and the travel papers for you all. I know a man who is helping numbers of Jews to get out of Austria. He can also produce forged passports and travel documents. He's expensive but very good.' He smiled briefly. 'A career banknote forger. And he's never been caught.'

'I don't know what to say.'

He laid his hand on hers. 'I know it's not ideal for you. Budapest is a long way east, and you will have to travel back to London from there. You'll go through Italy on the way home – Trieste, then Venice. After that, through Switzerland to Lausanne, then Paris. A long journey. But I will get the tickets. Think about it. Yes? Think about it tonight. Talk to Gretchen. And tomorrow, decide. But remember that there is not much time.'

'I'm deeply grateful.'

'Not one-thousandth as grateful as I will be if you help Shulamit to escape.' He rose. 'Now, let's go back to the girls.'

Katya's heart was thudding heavily as they went back into the house. A strange destiny had opened so many doors for her and

315

Gretchen. Could this be the last one? Could this be the one that let them finally escape from the nightmare?

Gretchen and Shulamit were laughing together in the kitchen. Katya realised that she hadn't seen Gretchen's face so happy for weeks. Shulamit turned her bright sparkling eyes to them as they came in. 'Thank goodness you're back. Gretchen has been terribly critical of my art all evening.'

'I haven't!' Gretchen exclaimed.

'She's pointed out the fatal monotony in my work.'

'I did not!'

'And I have to admit that she is absolutely right,' Shulamit went on solemnly. 'All those moustache-less Hitlers! You can't write a symphony with one note – as Gretchen has so trenchantly pointed out.'

'You are awful,' Gretchen giggled. 'I said nothing like that.'

'And so, my friends, I have decided to expand. More than expand. Diversify! What do you say to a series of emaciated Goerings? *There's* a picture worth seeing – our glorious Field Marshal without the great belly straining at his uniform, hollow-cheeked and hungry-eyed. Perhaps naked except for a loincloth, like dear Mahatma Gandhi. Would anyone recognise him? Or what about Himmler with a big black beard and long mustachios, holding a smouldering bomb? Would you be able to distinguish him from a mad Moravian anarchist?'

'I think these are excellent projects from the artistic point of view,' David Turteltaub said gravely, 'but not perhaps conducive to our immediate safety.'

'We artists don't care about our safety, do we, Gretchen?' Shulamit said with a smile. 'They broke Gretchen's arm for playing the piano too well, and they may do the same to me for leaving a moustache off a painting. Who knows? While there's life, we'll be gay and kick up our heels.' She laughed merrily. 'Well, I shan't kick up *my* heels, but the rest of you are commanded to do so.'

Katya's mind was whirling with David's proposal. It had come like a lifebelt thrown into a raging sea. It would be madness not to seize it. Passports, travel money, tickets – all were suddenly on offer.

But there were grave difficulties. The most obvious was taking on responsibility for Shulamit. Gretchen's plaster cast would already attract attention. A young woman in a wheelchair was even more noticeable. Despite David Turteltaub's assurances that the forged documents would be of the highest quality, there was a very strong chance of being identified and arrested.

The far lesser problem, of getting home from Budapest via a very long train journey, could be dealt with in due course; but the danger was real.

Katya's eyes drifted to Shulamit's bright laughing face. Considering the danger they were all in, it was one of the happiest evenings Katya could recall since they'd lost Thor. Gretchen had been in a state of shock following her broken arm, silent and withdrawn. Now she was emerging.

She had taken instantly to Shulamit, something that was unusual for Gretchen, who was usually so shy with new people. But there was a subtle affinity between Gretchen and the young woman in the wheelchair. Of course, both were artists. More than that, perhaps each recognised something of herself in the other person – of being different from others, of seeing the world from a special angle.

Katya's mind was suddenly made up. She could no more leave Shulamit behind than she could leave Gretchen behind. She felt a wave of guilt at her previous doubts. Helping Shulamit escape the Nazis was a duty, a privilege, not a burden.

At the end of the evening, she spoke quietly to David. 'Of course I'll do it,' she said. 'I'm ashamed that I hesitated.'

Relief swept over his face. 'Don't you want to consult Gretchen?'

'I don't need to. I know what her answer will be.'

He touched her arm. 'God sent you to us.'

'And you to us,' she replied. 'I'm so grateful, David.'

'I'll get started tomorrow,' he said. 'The sooner we get things moving, the better.'

Now that an escape route was in sight, Katya's fear grew unbearably intense.

What if they were betrayed before the arrangements were in place? What if that hammering on the door came in the middle of the night? What if they were arrested on the platform, just as they were boarding the train, their lives snatched away? To have the cup of hope dashed from their lips at the last moment would be the cruellest stroke of all. She tried to control her nerves.

In the meantime, David Turteltaub was busy. He produced four suitcases, well-used, but of good quality, with the stickers of international hotels plastered on them.

'A traveller with no luggage attracts immediate attention,' he said. 'With these, you will look much less suspicious.'

He also brought clothes for her and Gretchen to put in the suitcases, toiletries and other possessions, everything used, but everything of good quality. 'Where did you get all this?' Katya asked, astonished by his ingenuity.

'My family are having a whip-round. Everyone is contributing something. We are all grateful to you for what you're doing.'

One evening, towards midnight, he took them out on a mysterious errand to the Altstadt, the oldest part of Innsbruck. The streets were empty at this hour. They went down darkened, narrow alleys, their shadows lengthening and shrinking as they passed under the streetlights, and turned on to a steep flight of damp, crooked stone stairs that led to the river. Halfway down, David knocked on an arched doorway. The door opened cautiously, and they were beckoned inside. The place was a cellar, reeking of photographic chemicals and full of photographic equipment.

They were received by a shocking apparition – a man without a face. For a moment, the illusion persisted, until Katya realised that he was wearing a black silk mask, with cut-outs for eyes. He was also wearing a white laboratory coat and white gloves.

'I've never seen his face,' David whispered to Katya. 'Those are his rules.'

This was the photographer who would take their pictures for the forged passports. Silently, he directed Katya and Gretchen in turn to sit in front of a grey screen, surrounded by bright lights. Dazzled by lamps, Katya had a stomach-churning memory of being interrogated by the Gestapo at the Hotel Metropole in Vienna. She pushed the panic back down into its dark lair.

Using an old-fashioned camera on a tripod, the masked man took several photographs of Gretchen and Katya, after which he carefully weighed both of them on a scale, and measured their height, writing down everything in a notebook.

When it was done, David handed him an envelope. It was thick with banknotes. The man ruffled through them quickly, then put the money in his pocket. Just as silently, he gestured towards the door. They left, their mission accomplished.

'This is costing you a lot of money,' Katya said to David as they ascended the dark stairs. 'I'm so sorry.'

'Think nothing of it. Money is meaningless where life is concerned. The passports will be ready in a few days. I'm afraid you won't be able to choose your new names.' He smiled. 'He uses real passports that unlucky tourists lose while on holiday.'

'Do so many tourists lose their passports?'

'Well, let's not enquire too deeply into how he gets them. As I said, he's expensive, but he's very good.'

Shulamit and Gretchen spent hours together each day. Gretchen was the only person allowed to help Shulamit with physical tasks – Shulamit hated to have her wheelchair pushed, or even touched, or to be given assistance she hadn't asked for. And although she talked freely and irreverently about her own condition, others referred to it at their peril – she could be very snappish.

'I know just how she feels,' Gretchen told Katya. 'All my life, I've felt that I wasn't a person, just a problem. People don't really see me. They just see what they think ought to be fixed, and expect me to be grateful when they explain how wrong in the head I am. I've been pushed around and shoved into corners and locked in cupboards, and stuck with needles, and analysed, and tested, and always, always found wanting. The nurses at the clinic used to call me *die Kaulquappe*, the tadpole, because I wasn't one thing or another. It humiliated me terribly. I've never felt that I was good enough. I've always been a freak. It's so demeaning.'

'Oh, Gretchen, I'm so sorry if I made you feel that way!'

'Don't be silly! You were the first person who didn't treat me like that. You made me feel that I was a human being, not a patient, not a crazy thing who didn't know what was good for her. Everyone else has always made assumptions about me, instead of asking me what I felt. Even Papa was like that. He always treated me as though he knew more about me than I did. He never really listened or looked.'

'When we meet him again, we'll tell him that,' Katya promised.

'He didn't mean to be hurtful,' Gretchen said, her eyes sad. 'He loved me. He wanted to help. He just always assumed I was sick and weak.'

With deep sorrow, Katya noted Gretchen's use of the past tense. 'You're not weak, Gretchen.'

'I know. I've learned that now. And Shulamit's not weak either. She's so strong.'

'Yes, I'm very strong,' Shulamit said, having overheard the last words as she came into the room. 'I only look small and helpless to lure in my prey.'

Gretchen burst out laughing. Laughter had been such a rare thing with her. Lately, despite everything, she was laughing more; but her laughter came in odd, breathless bursts, as though she were still learning how to do it.

'No, Gretchen and I aren't weak,' Shulamit went on, 'but we're easily hurt. That's different. And we're bad-tempered and spiteful. All in all, we're damned difficult people, aren't we, Gretchen?'

'Yes,' Gretchen said, 'we are. We get angry when people try to help us.'

'And we get angry when they don't.'

Gretchen smiled. 'Yes.'

'But our perspective is different from yours.' Shulamit's eyes sparkled merrily. 'I see the world from three feet off the ground, and Gretchen sees the world from a hundred feet up in the air.'

When she discovered that Gretchen still couldn't read or write, Shulamit made a concerted effort to teach her. She got out her childhood copy of *Struwwelpeter* and set to work reading it with Gretchen. The violent tales and grotesque illustrations captivated Gretchen in the same way that the Brothers Grimm had done.

Gretchen was drawn to the violent and the grotesque. But it was the jog-trot poetry and rhyming couplets that really seemed to intrigue her. She was fascinated by the rhythms of the verse, and Katya could see that she was making a real effort, for the first time, to learn what the letters on the page meant.

'Bravo,' Shulamit said, when Gretchen managed to decipher a line all on her own, without too many mistakes. 'Now you are going to be a princess, and princes will come from all over the world to ask for your hand in marriage.'

Gretchen pulled a face. 'I'm never getting married.'

'And why not, pray?'

'It's a horrible idea!'

'You seem very certain.'

'I'd rather be like you.'

'Oh?' Shulamit cocked her head. 'You think that because I'm scrunched up in a wheelchair, I can't find a husband?'

Gretchen flushed a deep red. 'I didn't mean that!'

'I'll have you know that I have had suitors, despite my ill temper and bad disposition.'

'Really? Why didn't you accept them?'

'Someone like me can afford to pick and choose,' Shulamit said with a sniff. 'I'm not going to accept the first fellow who comes along.' She frowned. 'Also, my suitors both wanted children. And the doctors say that having a child would probably kill me.'

'Oh! I'm so sorry!'

'Don't be. I have no intention of remaining single all my life, I assure you. Do you know what the English word for an unmarried woman is? Spinster. Isn't that ugly? It sounds like our word for a spider, *Spinne*. Well, that's me, spinning my little web to catch a shiny, fat fly.'

'Ugh.'

322

'Sooner or later, the right man will come along. I'll know him when I see him.'

'How will you know?' Gretchen asked.

'I suppose he'll take off his boots and throw them at me. That's what husbands do, I hear.'

'Seriously, Shulamit.'

'Well . . . he'll see me for what I am. He'll love me madly, and tell me I'm the greatest painter since Raphael, and we'll have a wild time in bed – with no children.'

'How can you have a wild time in bed with no children?' Gretchen demanded, interested.

'You're much too young to discuss such things.'

'I've had my first period!'

Shulamit smiled. '*Mazel tov*. Perhaps I'll explain when you've had your second period. But for now, back to reading and writing, young lady.'

Struwwelpeter was the perfect choice for Gretchen to finally get to grips with reading. Every day with Shulamit, the words started taking on a meaning for her, until she could decipher a whole verse of poetry. The little book fascinated her, with its tales of childhood crime and punishment. 'It's like another world,' she said to Shulamit. 'It's funny, but it's also so cruel. A little boy won't stop sucking his thumbs, so someone runs in and cuts them off with giant scissors. Another one doesn't like soup, so he starves to death. It's all children falling in the river or burning alive.'

Shulamit laughed. 'I think a lot of Nazis were given this book in their childhood. It explains how they are today.'

'I was given the Brothers Grimm. Maybe that explains how *I* am.'

Shulamit's smile faded. 'And how are you?' she enquired.

'Oh . . . I suppose I'm the maiden in the tower, or the princess in the thicket of thorns.'

'That sounds very lonely.'

'Actually, I can't remember my childhood,' Gretchen said. 'I don't think I ever was a child.'

'Nor was I. I was born an adult.'

'I think I was too,' Gretchen said. 'There was always this grown-up inside me, looking out. They used to bring children to play with me, but it never worked. I was always much better on my own. I don't think I knew how to be a child. I only knew how to be me.'

'I was the same. I didn't ever have children around me. Just doctors. Our house was always full of them. I think David became a doctor partly because of that. So that he could look after me.'

'That's so lovely.'

'Well, I'm glad he qualified, but I never wanted him to shape his life around me. I want him to find his own happiness.'

'I think he's very happy being with you.'

'A man has to be more than a brother. I see the way he is with women. There are so many who flock around him. Nice girls, lovely girls. They fall in love with him all the time. But he never lets them get too close. He always closes the door just when things start getting serious. And I know why – because he's afraid that if he marries, he won't be there for me any more. I hate feeling that I'm stopping him from living his life. I don't mind anything else about being the way I am. But that's the most miserable thing. And it will all be wasted, anyway.'

'What do you mean?'

'I live on borrowed time, my dear. One of the first memories I have is hearing a doctor tell our parents that I wouldn't live very long. I stopped being a child in that moment. You can't have a childhood when you're expecting to die. So I didn't bother with one. I just became an adult straight away – so I would get as much life as I could.'

Gretchen threw the book aside. 'You're not going to die!' She kissed Shulamit's smooth cheek. 'You're going to come and live with us, and we're going to be together, and live forever. And I'll play for you every day!'

Shulamit didn't respond, but her eyes filled with tears.

'Did I upset you?' Gretchen asked in dismay.

'No, my dear. But I don't get many kisses, so they have to be savoured.' Then she put her own arms around Gretchen's neck. 'I wish I could have seen you play,' she said quietly. 'But I think I know what it would sound like. I hear your music all the time.'

The next day, their new passports arrived. As David had promised, they were real British passports, with navy-blue board covers and gold-stamped coats of arms. The names in the cut-out boxes were Mrs Phyllis Wilkinson and Miss Jeanette Wilkinson, mother and daughter. But the solemn-faced photographs on the front pages were of Gretchen and Katya. The alterations had been expertly done, the stamps covering the corners of the photos as they should.

Fascinated, they looked through the well-thumbed pages. Mrs Wilkinson and her daughter, of Bolton in Lancashire, had been regular travellers. They'd been to France, Greece, Norway and Belgium. Mrs Wilkinson's marital status was listed as 'Widow'. Katya hoped that wasn't a bad omen. When they were safely back in England, she vowed to herself, she would contact the Wilkinsons and tell them what had become of their missing passports.

They were now much closer to the hour of their departure, and Katya's heart was constantly trembling, her stomach so full of butterflies that she could hardly eat. Her anxiety that something would happen to stop them at the last minute haunted her, and at night produced terrifying dreams of pursuit and capture.

Neither Gretchen nor Shulamit seemed to feel that tension. They were so happy in each other's company that they seemed not to feel anxiety. For the first time, Katya felt lonely. Happy as she was that Gretchen had found a friend, she couldn't help feeling that she was losing Gretchen to someone who understood her better, someone who had an instinctive bond with her.

She tried to dismiss the unworthy feeling of jealousy, but the enduring pang was there. In a few crisp words, Gretchen had given her an insight into her deepest feelings, her resentment against a world that had patronised, marginalised and demeaned her all her life.

And she, Katya, was part of that world. Shulamit was not. Shulamit had understood Gretchen from the first moment. They were, as the currently fashionable saying went, on the same wavelength. Both were outsiders, both artists, both strangely and richly gifted.

Not for the first time, Katya felt that she had let Gretchen down from the start. Her own prejudices and preconceptions had got in the way of seeing Gretchen as she really was. And that hurt.

When David remarked, 'It seems my sister and your daughter have formed a bond,' she knew that he had the same feelings.

'It's very rare for Gretchen to take to someone like this,' she replied.

'And very rare for Shulamit.'

'It seems they share a lot.'

'Yes. And whatever it is, you and I don't share it with them.'

She smiled ironically at him. 'No, we don't. Do you feel shut out?'

'A little,' he confessed. 'Do you?'

'A little. But I'm so happy for them both at the same time.'

'Of course.' He nodded. 'But one can't help feeling some-how – rebuked.'

'That's exactly the right word,' Katya exclaimed. 'I feel so clumsy and stupid.'

'If it's any consolation,' he said gently, 'I doubt whether anyone could have done better than you.'

'It's not any consolation. I should have done better myself!'

'I suspect that all parents feel the same way. Even foster parents.'

'I just wish I had been more understanding from the start.'

'How could you, Katya? You had no experience whatsoever. But I have to say that I think choosing you was a stroke of genius on Gretchen's father's part.'

Katya felt a lump rise in her throat. 'Gretchen seems to have accepted that he's dead. But I can't. She can be very logical some-times, very hard-headed. She's tougher than I am, in fact.'

He sighed. 'Shulamit is certainly tougher than I am. I've wor-ried about her ever since she was born. But I think I'm going to miss her more than she will miss me.'

'You can't leave it too late to get out of Austria, David.'

'I know. I thought I could do some good by staying. But Hitler has lit a bonfire that is going to spread. There is nothing any of us can do except try to survive it somehow.'

The next day, Gretchen brought up the subject of her friendship with Shulamit.

'Does it upset you?' she asked Katya.

'No, Liebchen. I just realise how little I've understood you.'

'I don't understand myself,' Gretchen replied. 'Shulamit's right. Most of the time, I'm not really here at all. I'm up in the air. I look down on myself, and I have no idea what's going on down there. Sorry if that doesn't make sense. I didn't mean to hurt you.'

'I'm so glad you've started to talk about your feelings.'

'I suppose I'm just finding out who I am,' Gretchen said.

'Yes, you are.'

'And you've helped me so much with that, Katya. You're patient and you listen. That means everything to me.'

It astonished Katya to hear Gretchen talk like this, like an adult. 'The truth is that I'm in awe of you, Gretchen,' she said quietly.

Gretchen's brown eyes met hers. 'Don't be jealous of Shulamit,' she said. 'Nobody can ever take your place. I love you forever.'

Chapter 25

'Gretchen is very special,' Shulamit said to Katya. 'She has a great deal to offer the world.'

'So have you,' Katya replied.

Shulamit laughed. 'I? Oh, I am terrestrial, a crawler. Gretchen was born to soar. You'll see. You must take good care of her. Watch her until she has flown so high that she's out of sight.'

'I'll do my best,' Katya said, smiling.

'It won't be easy.'

'It hasn't exactly been a stroll in the park up to now,' Katya commented wryly.

'It's a wonderful thing that you're doing, whatever it costs. We're all responsible for each other in this world. One tries to believe in a God, but even if He's there, He's not always listening. Perhaps He's on the telephone a lot. In the end, it's up to us to take care of the people around us.'

'I agree.'

'Gretchen has a wonderful capacity for love. I don't mean shallow love. I mean real love, deep love, true love. That is very rare.'

'I know it is.'

Shulamit rocked her wheelchair to and fro a few times, something she did when thinking. 'What will you do,' she asked suddenly, 'if Gretchen's father never comes back?'

'I'll take care of her as long as she needs me.'

'But you want to return to your medical studies.'

'Yes. That won't stop me. I'll work it out. We'll find somewhere to live together. Gretchen will go to school, I'll go to lectures. As you said, it won't be easy. But we'll manage.'

'You won't put her into an orphanage?'

Katya was shocked. 'Never!'

'Do you mean it?'

'We trusted a paediatric clinic with her. The result was a catastrophe. After that, I knew I would never do anything like that again.'

Shulamit nodded. 'Good.'

'She's mine, Shulamit.'

Shulamit nodded again. 'For the time being. Just make sure you know when to let her go.'

And then David came home, bringing their train tickets.

'Your train leaves tomorrow at ten minutes past noon,' he announced.

'So soon!' Shulamit exclaimed. 'I hadn't quite believed it was going to happen.'

'We may never get this chance again. I was only able to get these tickets because I know someone at the travel office. There's no time to lose. We need to start packing now.'

'Perhaps it's better to be quick,' Shulamit murmured. 'I hate goodbyes. If there was more time to say them, I might not be able to leave you, my dear boy.'

'Oh, it will be a great relief to have you out of the house. No more smell of turpentine, no more linseed oil getting into the salad.'

The brother and sister smiled at each other sadly. 'Well, it won't be for long, will it, David? You will come to me soon?'

'I promise,' he said. 'You can count on me.'

'I do count on you. I shall be at the window every day, looking out, like Sister Anne in *Bluebeard*.'

'And one day, you will see me come riding along the road.'

In some ways, the proximity of their departure made it easier, as Shulamit had said. From Katya's point of view, there was less time to feel fear. But her hands were shaking as she packed the suitcases for herself and Gretchen, and her stomach seemed to have an iron cannonball in it.

What if they encountered Sauer and his men at the station? He had warned her that if he saw them again, he would arrest them on the spot. And that would be the end of all their hopes.

There was nothing to be done but pray.

Once again, they were on the platform at Innsbruck railway station.

Although there were police around, there was no sign of Kriminalinspektor Sauer. In fact, the station wore an air of carefree celebration. The first time they had been here had been at night, among a crowd of angry and frightened passengers, some of whom were already doomed. The second time had been under the cruel eyes of Brownshirt thugs and Gestapo goons, with hunted passengers making a final, desperate run. Now, the station was a postcard picture of flags and flowers.

She recalled the smell of tobacco, sweat and fear that night. Today, brightly coloured tubs of tulips, anthuriums, carnations and sweet peas were stationed along the platform, perfuming the warm air and overlaying the greasy smell of fresh paint. Katya realised with some astonishment that it was already May. The cherry trees that had been in flower were now making leaves, their pink and white petals blowing in the wind, creating the illusion of snow. Roses were starting to bloom in the immaculately tended borders. There were rows of lilac trees in blossom on the other side of the tracks, and beyond, the Alpine meadows shimmered with wildflowers as they rose towards the white peaks.

And the station had just been painted in cheerful colours and hung with crisp flags. The old Austrian flag was gone. The crooked cross hung everywhere, red, white and black, drifting in the light breezes. The passengers who crowded the platform were in summer clothes, the women in new hats, the children in shorts or frilly frocks. Laughter and chatter were everywhere. No face was worried or depressed, no eye failed to sparkle. These people were content with life. They had nothing to fear. There was instead an atmosphere of jubilee, of celebration.

Among all this festivity, the four of them were silent, standing together beside their luggage, which was in the charge of an elderly porter, like a sorrowful island in a sparkling sea. There seemed to be nothing to say. Katya felt as though this was a dream. As though the sunlight and the warmth would fade at any moment, and she would wake – to what? To the dark of a prison cell?

The tannoy crackled into life, announcing the arrival of their train. The tracks began to hum. Passengers crowded expectantly forward, and the porters hefted the handles of their trolleys. In the distance, they could now see the billowing clouds their train was making.

A short while later, the big, dark-green locomotive came into sight, spewing black smoke and white steam from various funnels. It rumbled up to the station, hissing, its brakes squealing as it slowed down. Now the carriages were in view, each one bearing the proud legend, ARLBERG ORIENT EXPRESS, PARIS—BUDAPEST.

The bustle of boarding the train swept Katya out of her trance-like state. The problems of getting Shulamit out of her wheelchair and through the doors, of managing their luggage, of finding their compartment, were all too pressing to allow for distractions.

Their compartment was First Class, with seats for six. There were already three other passengers settling in, a middle-aged Austrian couple and their teenage daughter. They stared with a mixture of contempt and disgust as Shulamit was carried in by two porters and settled into the window seat opposite. Katya covered Shulamit's legs with her plaid travelling rug, and tucked her in. Gretchen took the middle seat.

As she was getting their hand luggage stowed away, Katya heard the Austrian woman arguing with the porter in the corridor outside, not bothering to lower her voice.

'And we must travel all the way, looking at *that*?'

'I'm afraid there is nothing I can do, *gnädige* Frau,' the man said apologetically.

'We have paid a lot of money for our tickets!'

'She has bought a ticket too, *gnädige* Frau. I am sorry.'

'Where is she travelling to?'

'Budapest, I believe.'

The woman exclaimed angrily, 'Now our whole journey will be spoiled. It's most disagreeable to have to look at such a person. Instead of enjoying the scenery, we will be staring at *her*. And she even looks Jewish to me. If she is travelling to Budapest, then it is certain she is a Jewess!'

'Her passport is Aryan, however.'

'I don't believe a word of it. It turns my stomach!'

In the compartment, Katya met Shulamit's eyes. They were calm. She shook her head slightly, warning Katya not to get upset, or engage in any argument.

'Can't she be moved to another carriage?' the woman was demanding.

'The train is full, *gnädige* Frau. Besides, she has reserved her seat. Try to ignore it, that's my advice.'

She snorted. 'Ignore it!' She marched back into the compartment, grim-faced, and plumped down next to her husband in a wave of lavender scent and aggravation. 'It seems there is nothing to be done,' she said to him loudly.

He shrugged. 'These things happen. We must put up with it.'

Their daughter ostentatiously took out a guidebook and buried her sharp-featured face in it.

Katya felt breathless and dizzy. David Turteltaub had come to stand on the platform outside their window, looking in at Shulamit. Although the window was down, they were not speaking, just holding one another's gaze silently. The expression on his face was difficult to interpret. He was smiling, but his lips were tight, and his eyes were forlorn.

A long, shrill whistle from the locomotive announced their imminent departure. He stepped back from the train, waving. A gush of smoke and steam swept down the platform from the locomotive, obscuring him. And then he was gone.

The train set off with such a jolt that Shulamit, who was sitting with her back to the engine, almost slid off her seat like a child. Gretchen and Katya grabbed her. The woman opposite drew back her feet with an exclamation of revulsion.

Then they were moving, clattering steadily down the track, picking up speed, heading towards their destiny.

The train settled into a rhythmical, swaying progress through the Austrian countryside. The Alpine views from the windows would have been exhilarating under other circumstances; in the brilliant sunshine, the snow-lined peaks were dazzling. The beauty was somehow unreal, like an overexposed tourist photograph.

Inside the walnut-panelled compartment, the daughter of the couple opposite had put on a pair of sunglasses. Her father had draped his newspaper over his face and was snoring gently. The mother remained vigilant, as though ready for Shulamit to sprout fangs and claws at any moment.

Shulamit, for her part, seemed serenely indifferent to the hostility radiating from the plush seats opposite. Katya could only marvel at her coolness. They spoke as little as possible to one another, so as not to attract any more suspicion.

An hour after their departure, a moustachioed steward came down the corridors, announcing that lunch would shortly be served in the dining car, and distributing menus. The three of them had purposely not made any reservations, to avoid crowds, but the family opposite seized the menus, and discussed the options with great seriousness among themselves. After the bell had sounded, they got up and went up the corridor.

'I want to scratch out that woman's eyes,' Gretchen said tightly.

'Keep your nerve,' Shulamit said, patting Gretchen's hand.

'Aren't you angry with her?' Gretchen demanded.

'No more than I would be with a little yapping dog,' Shulamit replied. 'I've known such people all my life. Their own unhappiness is their punishment.'

'Their unhappiness can be dangerous,' Katya commented. 'I wish we had more agreeable fellow passengers.'

'Perhaps a meal of roast pork and mashed potatoes in the dining car will sedate them.' Shulamit checked her watch. 'We'll arrive at Kitzbühel shortly. It's a very pretty place. David and I went skiing there last season.'

'You went skiing?' Gretchen asked.

'Yes, with Prince Franz Josef and his party.'

'Really?'

'Oh, yes. The prince was rather a nuisance, really. He was absolutely infatuated with me, and determined to marry me. At every opportunity, he would drop down on one knee and beg me to be his bride. I managed to escape him by strapping skis on to my wheelchair, and went whizzing down the most difficult slope of all. He couldn't keep up, of course. It was then he realised that our union was not to be. In his disappointment, he tried to impale himself on his sabre, but went off and had a large dish of sausage goulash instead.'

Gretchen was laughing her odd, breathless giggle. 'And I almost believed you!'

'You have no reason not to believe me,' Shulamit replied with dignity. 'He was the most eligible bachelor in Europe, and I the most eligible spinster.'

'Why didn't you accept him?'

'Two reasons. One was that awful moustache of his. It tickled dreadfully. The other was his names. Franz Josef Maria Aloys Alfred Karl Johannes Heinrich Michael Georg Ignaz Benediktus Gerhardus Majella. I knew I would get them wrong during the wedding ceremony, and then all our children would be illegitimate.'

In the absurdity of the tale, Gretchen had quite forgotten her upset at their vicious fellow passenger. Her tension had evaporated. Katya reflected that Shulamit Turteltaub was a clever young woman.

They got out the sandwiches they'd prepared, and made a light lunch.

The train arrived at Kitzbühel towards two o'clock. The station was small and rural, overshadowed by the vastness of the Alps all around. But the platform was festive. A Tyrolean band in lederhosen and feathered caps was thumping out folk tunes. Every member of the band wore a Nazi armband. The brass of their instruments gleamed in the sunlight.

The family opposite – who, they had learned, were named Bichler – threw open the window eagerly. The music was deafening and discordant, but the Bichlers appeared to be enchanted by it.

'These are the traditions we have missed,' Frau Bichler exclaimed. 'Orchestras on the platforms to welcome the trains! That is the real, old Austria!'

'Which the communists wanted to destroy,' Herr Bichler said.

'Oh, yes!' His wife nodded emphatically, her jowls wobbling. 'Well, God be thanked, that danger is past.'

The band paused briefly to refresh themselves with tankards of dark beer. Though the air was crisp at this altitude, their faces were red and sweaty. The audience on the train applauded enthusiastically. The band leader, a clarinettist, trotted along the platform with a velvet bag on a stick, collecting money.

When the bag was thrust in through their window, the Bichlers dropped a fistful of change into it. Gretchen and Shulamit ignored the thing, though the man jingled it aggressively in their faces.

'You don't give them money?' Frau Bichler demanded.

'I don't really want to encourage them,' Shulamit said mildly.

The band resumed, fortified by beer and money. The music was even louder now. They had to endure it for a full hour while passengers boarded or left the train. Katya's head was starting to ache. The crash and thump of the playing was a kind of assault on the senses that left one dazed.

At last, the train set off again. The jarring music was left behind. As they left Kitzbühel, they passed a ramshackle Tyrolean house, built close to the railway track. A dozen or so children of various ages were sitting along the balcony among pots of geraniums, dangling their bare feet. They all jumped up and raised their right arms. Their shrill voices could be heard calling, 'Heil Hitler! Heil Hitler!'

The Bichlers responded by bawling eager 'Heil Hitlers' of their own out of the window. Slightly out of breath after the exertion, Herr Bichler turned on Shulamit. 'You don't give the Hitler greeting?'

'I don't really want to encourage *him*, either,' Shulamit replied, and went back to her book, a Thomas Mann novel.

The Bichlers resumed their seats, looking at one another in silent outrage.

It was a long, hot afternoon. The next stop was at Zell-am-See. It was much quieter than Kitzbühel, though German flags hung languidly in the warm air. The platform was almost empty. Here, it seemed that summer had properly arrived. The mountains were green, swathed with wildflowers, and the lake gleamed like topaz in the sun. It was warm enough for Herr Bichler to open the window for some fresh air.

The train stood immobile and inert for a long while. As Shulamit had predicted, the rich lunch soon put the Bichlers into a postprandial coma. Gretchen, too, fell asleep, with her head on Katya's shoulder. Shulamit read her book peacefully, sometimes making notes in the margins with a little gold pencil. Katya listened to the locomotive hissing like a sleepy snake in the silence.

The sound of youthful female voices percolated into the tranquillity. A group of teenage girls had come trooping on to the platform, wearing white vests and black shorts. One of the girls held aloft a banner with a diamond-shaped swastika on it.

'The BDM!' Frau Bichler exclaimed to her daughter. 'Look, Ottilie!'

Ottilie jumped up to look out of the window. The girls had evidently been on a cross-country hike; it was a parade of bare, tanned limbs, swinging braids and thudding boots. They were singing the by now all-too-familiar Horst Wessel song as they marched along.

Herr Bichler was captivated by the adolescent breasts under the flimsy white vests. 'They will soon be women,' he said appreciatively.

Gretchen, who had woken up, asked, 'Who are they?'

'The girls' branch of the Hitler Youth,' Shulamit answered dryly. 'The League of German Maidens. An import from our new masters.'

Frau Bichler turned on Shulamit. 'It is such a pity for you,' she said venomously, 'that you cannot go out into the fresh air like those healthy girls. It would do you the world of good.'

'Do you think so?' Shulamit replied.

'I'm sure you don't even know what a beautiful country it is out there.'

'I have some idea. But perhaps it is becoming a country I don't want to live in any more.'

The BDM girls marched away, their piercing voices fading, the sun glancing off blonde heads of hair. Herr Bichler craned out of the window to watch them out of sight.

There were no stops after that for almost four hours.

In the late afternoon, they approached Salzburg. The sun was lowering towards the horizon. The valleys were beginning to pool with long shadows. When Salzburg came into view, it was as a city in a fairy tale, its castles and towers and spires soaring into the hazy air against a backdrop of majestic mountains. Everyone in the compartment was awake now, and the beauty of it silenced them all.

The train snaked into the town. As at Kitzbühel, a band was playing on the platform. But it did not consist of jolly Tiroleans in lederhosen. This was a *Wehrmacht* military band in full uniform. The standards of their regiment had been set up in front of them. Behind them was row upon row of swastika flags, making zigzags of black and crimson, as though each one were a great shout, an iteration of the fact that Austria was no more. And the music they played consisted of military marches, the bass drum pounding with a force that seemed to penetrate into the cosy First Class compartment.

Even the Bichler family seemed momentarily taken aback by the display. There were no comments about the real, old Austria. The train edged past the band, and now the reason for the band became clear: columns of German soldiers came marching past the carriages, their jackboots crashing in time to the marches, iron-grey uniforms formidable in the evening light. They carried large packs, and were heavily armed, with mortars and machine guns mounted on wheels.

Frau Bichler had rallied. 'Yes!' she exclaimed, her eyes gleaming behind her spectacles. 'Look at that! Magnificent! Now the world will learn to be afraid of us once again! Look at those young men! Aren't they so handsome, Ottilie!'

'I knew a pretty girl once,' Shulamit said conversationally. 'She fell in love with a soldier. He was a big, handsome fellow, and she couldn't wait to be in his arms. So she opened her door to him. But once he was inside, he declared himself the master of the house, and began to put his muddy boots on her furniture, and eat everything in the kitchen, and steal all her nice things – and generally make himself very disagreeable indeed. So she asked him to leave. But he just laughed, and drew his sword, and said that if she opened her mouth again, he would cut her pretty head off.'

Herr Bichler bridled. 'What the devil do you mean by that?'

'It's just an old story,' Shulamit said, opening her Thomas Mann again.

'The girl is mad,' Frau Bichler said to her husband.

'Quite mad,' he agreed. They all stared out of the window at the endless rows of grey uniforms.

Chapter 26

Their next stop was Linz, the city Adolf Hitler called his home town. Here, the station was hung with banners, like a pagan banqueting hall in some fortress of the Dark Ages.

Once again, the steward brought menus, and once again the Bichlers pored over the offerings intently, discussing each dish in lip-smacking detail.

'I'm so hungry,' Gretchen whispered to Katya.

'There are a few more sandwiches,' Katya whispered back. 'We'll have them when those people go off to the dining car.' Gretchen nodded. Katya looked at her watch. The train would be in Linz for another hour. The next stop was Vienna – where they would change trains, and there would be a long wait. At eight in the morning, they would set off again. They would reach the border after a few hours; and then an unbroken all-day run to Budapest, arriving late in the afternoon. She dared not let her mind dwell on that. There was such a long way to go yet. And the border loomed, like an abyss in a nightmare, to which they were inescapably being pulled.

At length, the dinner bell sounded, and the Bichler family, having made their decisions, left the compartment to go to supper. It was always a relief when they were gone. Katya stretched out with a sigh. 'Gretchen's right. That woman is unbearable.'

'At least she looks one in the face when she's being poisonous,' Shulamit said. 'It's the daughter I object to. She hasn't met my eyes once since we got on the train. She just stares at my legs. I think she's jealous of them.'

There was a knock at their door. It slid open, and a waiter they hadn't seen before came in. 'Supper menu,' he said, holding out the leather-bound folder.

'No, thank you,' Katya replied, 'we won't be going to supper.'

The man, who was younger than the other stewards, bowed and pushed the menu towards her. 'Take a look. You never know, *meine Damen*. You might find something you like inside.'

Reluctantly, she took the menu, and he disappeared.

Shulamit looked out of the window at the barbaric flags. 'When I see all this, I feel despair. I feel that a shadow has fallen over the world, and there is no light anywhere.'

Gretchen's eyes filled with tears. 'Shulamit, don't talk like this. I don't like it.'

Shulamit put her hand over Gretchen's. 'Forgive me. I shouldn't be so gloomy. Ignore me, Gretchen. I get these black moods.' She smiled.

But the words she had spoken hung in the air.

It was dark by the time the train set off again for Vienna. There was nothing to be seen from the windows except their own reflections. Herr Bichler drew the blind down. The Bichlers had returned to the compartment bringing the smells of their dinner with them. Now Herr Bichler lit a cheroot, oblivious to the discomfort he caused everyone else. The air in the compartment was soon blue with acrid smoke. Katya got up and went out into the corridor for some fresh air.

She found an open window, and leaned on the rim, looking out into the night, feeling the cold air buffet her face. Twinkling lights showed the presence of houses and towns out there, but the rest was impenetrable darkness. She thought of what Shulamit had said. The sensation of being on the brink of a chasm, of looming catastrophe, was now stronger than ever before. She had been focused on their own survival; but now she felt that the survival of much more was at stake. She was not a person who generally thought in grand ideas – Europe, the world – but the deepening of Nazi power was threatening everything and everyone it touched. Like an abyss, it seemed to suck you into it inexorably.

Gretchen came hurrying up to her, interrupting her thoughts. 'Have you seen the waiter who left that menu?' she demanded.

'No, but I'm sure he'll come to collect it.'

'I opened it. There's something inside.'

Katya turned. Gretchen, very pale in the dim light of the corridor, was holding out a slip of paper. Katya held it to the lamp. Written on it were two terse lines:

DANGER!

INTENSIVE GESTAPO CHECKS AT BORDER!

She felt the shock run through her.

'Who wrote it?' Gretchen asked.

'I don't know. Someone trying to warn us.'

'Do they know who we are? Has someone betrayed us?'

'I don't know,' Katya repeated. 'Perhaps they're warning everybody.'

'But why us? We must look suspicious!'

'Perhaps.'

'What are we going to do?'

344

Katya folded the note carefully. She felt sicker than ever. 'I don't know what we can do.'

'We could get off the train at Vienna,' Gretchen said urgently.

'And then what?'

'Go back home. To our house.'

'There's no going back, Liebchen.' Katya drew her close. 'Somebody else is in the house now, I'm sure. And we would soon be caught.'

'But—'

'We're going to have to face the border police again, whatever happens. The person who sent that note is just warning us to be prepared. But it's our only way out. And it's a chance we have to take. There's no other option.'

Gretchen nodded. 'All right.'

'And keep your nerve, Liebchen. We all need to be brave. We'll tell Shulamit.'

They got Shulamit's wheelchair from the guard's room and took it to the compartment to help her into it. Every time this happened, the Bichlers would mutter and complain as though it was the greatest inconvenience to have to move their legs aside. When they got to the bathroom, Katya showed Shulamit the note.

Shulamit read it. She raised her eyes to Katya's. 'Did this frighten you?'

'I'm a little disconcerted that we so obviously look like fugitives.'

'Oh, we outlaws know how to recognise one another,' Shulamit said wryly. 'We're quite a secret society. We have all sorts of secret signs. Since the Nazis came to power in Germany, people pass these little notes to each other.' She crumpled the piece of paper and flushed it away. 'It's good to be forewarned. But there's nothing we can do about it, is there?'

'No,' Katya agreed, 'there isn't.'

It was strange to be back at the station in Vienna again, where their journey had started, weeks ago. It was now approaching midnight, and the station was quiet. They disembarked from the train and made their way through the cavernous, echoing hall to the waiting room. There they found a corner where they could rest; there was to be a long wait until morning. But at least they had parted company with the Bichlers.

The waiting room was a restless place. People came and went all night. It was also very cold. Shulamit and Gretchen curled up on a bench, wrapped in their coats and covered with their travelling rugs. Katya stayed awake, on guard duty. Her mind was full of fears and anxieties, going round and round on the same track. They had travelled from one end of Austria to the other, and still they were not free.

Where was Thor now? Was there any chance that he was still alive? After the stress of the past weeks, she found to her dismay that she couldn't really remember his face, or the sound of his voice. All she recalled was a large, protective presence that wasn't there any more. She didn't even have a photograph of him. It was as though he had hardly existed at all – except for the girl who slept beside her. That thought brought a hard lump into her throat. Her world had been well and truly torn apart. How would she ever get back to the person she had been before Thor and Gretchen had come into her life?

After several dreary hours, an announcement came on the tannoy: the Orient Express to Budapest was now ready for passengers.

She woke the other two, and they made their weary way towards the platform. Their train, resplendent in blue and gold, was waiting in the cold light of dawn. This Orient Express was bigger, the compartments more luxurious. Theirs was an intimate four-seater salon, inlaid with precious woods, like the one she'd left London in. A little enclosed basin and toilet gave them privacy, which was especially convenient for Shulamit.

Two assiduous porters helped transfer their suitcases on board and got them settled. The heating was on in their compartment, and there was a warm current of air, faintly perfumed with diesel, around their ankles. They were able to take off their coats at last. A steward brought coffee in a silver-plated pot, served in delicate Limoges cups, with croissants and little pots of jam. There was even a pretty arrangement of rosebuds in a crystal vase. Being in the lap of luxury helped create an illusion, however thin, of safety. They sat in silence, trying to get their breakfast into stomachs tense with fear.

They were among the first to board the train. The platform slowly got busier as passengers boarded. Most looked very prosperous, fashionably dressed and accompanied by expensive luggage. One woman came with a set of seven matching suitcases in violet-dyed crocodile skin. Another arrived dramatically with two sizeable and hollow-ribbed borzoi dogs that snapped ferociously at everyone and had to be accommodated in a cage in the guard's van.

There was one empty seat in their compartment, and they waited uneasily to see who their fellow traveller might be. He arrived at last: a tall, middle-aged man wearing an impeccably tailored grey suit, matching spats and gloves, with a Homburg hat and a malacca cane. He surveyed them all coldly, looking like a figure in a fashion plate, and then turned to the steward who had accompanied him.

'I prefer not to travel with a cripple. There is invariably a smell.'

The steward rubbed his hands anxiously. 'I am sure that won't be the case, Count.'

'I demand that you provide me with an alternative berth.'

347

'But sir—'

'The count is quite right,' Shulamit said. They turned to look at her. 'I always have an accident while travelling,' she went on. 'Regrettable but inevitable. I have no control, you see. I just have to let go. The smell, of course, is not pleasant. The only thing one can do is to open the window. And then, unfortunately – the soot from the engine – on one's clothes, you know – so hard to remove—'

The count backed away, pushing the steward ahead of him, and slammed the door. They could hear his indignant voice raised in the corridor outside.

'That got rid of *him*,' Shulamit said with satisfaction. 'Now we shall all be cosy together.'

The train set off punctually at eight o'clock. As it rolled through the centre of Vienna, Katya was choked with emotions. She was saying goodbye to a city that would always have deep meaning for her; the city of her first love, her first sorrow, where her heart had been forged and then broken.

They all had similar thoughts, and were silent as the Orient Express picked up speed through the industrial suburbs and then cleared the city and made a straight line through the green countryside towards Hungary.

Unbearable though the tension had become, Katya somehow fell asleep. The wretched night and all its attendant terrors had worn her out. She was not only asleep, but dreaming. In her dream, everything was all right. They had crossed the border without incident. They were out of the shadows at last, and gliding into the sunlight. The relief was exquisite. She wanted to laugh and dance through the golden landscape that unfolded before them.

The harsh voices broke her dream into a thousand pieces.

'German Reich border control! All passports, please!'

Hours had passed. The train had stopped. They were at the Hungarian border. It was upon them suddenly, the crossing they had dreaded.

Katya clawed her way into wakefulness. All three of them had fallen asleep, and all were in the same confused, frightened state. The door of their compartment slid open with a thud, and two German police officers pushed their way in.

'Passports,' the first repeated, holding his hand out to Shulamit, who was sitting, as before, with her back to the engine. 'Quickly, please, Fräulein.'

Her face impassive, Shulamit handed over her passport. The man took it. He and his companion leafed through it carefully, examining every part of the document, holding each page up to the light of the window. They cracked the spine and looked inside the seam with a pencil torch. The checks seemed endless.

Katya found she couldn't breathe, as though a steel band had clamped around her lungs.

'You are at present residing in Maria-Theresien-Strasse, Innsbruck?' the man demanded.

'Yes,' Shulamit answered. If she was afraid, she gave no outward sign of it.

'Why are you leaving the German Reich?'

'To go to Budapest,' she replied with a little shrug.

The man was angered. 'I am asking you what is the purpose of your visit to Budapest.'

'Oh, I see. I am undergoing medical treatment for my spinal condition there.'

He grunted. 'What is wrong with your spine?'

'A congenital deformity.'

'What kind of deformity?'

'I don't see that that is any business of yours.'

He glared at the little hunched figure before him. 'Everything is our business, Fräulein.' But he didn't pursue the issue. Instead, he rifled through Shulamit's bags, pulling out everything and inspecting it as though expecting to find gold bullion among her clothes. In the meantime, the other policeman was examining her passport all over again, from cover to cover.

At last, they seemed satisfied. They gave the passport back to Shulamit and turned to Katya and Gretchen. 'Documents!'

Katya's hands were shaking so badly as she handed the passports over that she almost dropped them. Once again, the intense scrutiny began. Her mind flashed back to the dark, damp cellar in Innsbruck. Was the forger really as good as David Turteltaub had said he was? The slightest error, the smallest mistake, would be found now, and would mean death. They must have been mad to take this chance. She dared not look at Gretchen, feeling sure they would both break down if she did.

The other official had taken the passports now. He drew a jeweller's loupe from his pocket and fitted it into his eye, peering at the paper through the magnifying lens. Katya felt faint. She tried not to show the terror she felt. Surely they could hear her heart beating in her chest?

There was a long silence, broken only by the sound of pages being turned.

'Everything in order.'

She looked up blankly. The official was holding the passports out to her, looking bored. She reached for them, her heart surging with relief.

Then the other officer said, 'Wait.' He was looking in a small black shiny notebook.

The first officer drew the passports back. 'What?'

His colleague was leafing through the pages. 'There was an alert a few days ago. Referring to a foreign woman travelling with a child who has an injured arm. It's in here somewhere.'

Katya felt a black tide rise around her, blotting out everything. She felt that she was sinking into darkness, and could do nothing to save herself or Gretchen.

'You gentlemen aren't very good at your job, are you?' It was Shulamit's voice.

The policemen turned. 'What do you mean?' the man with the notebook growled.

'You haven't been able to tell that my passport is a forgery.'

'What!'

Shulamit went on calmly, 'Or that I am a Jewess.'

They stared at her incredulously. 'Are you trying to be funny, Fräulein? We will see how humorous you are in a Gestapo cell.'

There was a slight smile on her face. 'Oh no, I am not trying to be funny at all. I am a very dangerous Jewess. A malignant cripple. My real name is Shulamit Turteltaub. I am travelling to Budapest to foment a Jewish plot to assassinate the so-called Führer, Adolf Hitler.'

'You are mad.'

'Not at all. But Adolf Hitler is. Mad and vile. A mad dog who should be shot like one.'

'Shut your mouth, Jew!'

'Not until Hitler is dead in the gutter he crawled out of.'

'You are under arrest,' the man snapped.

Gretchen's body started violently with shock. But Shulamit's eyes met hers for a moment with a dark intensity, and Katya's fingers bit into her arm to stop her from moving.

The policeman tossed their passports at Katya, the alert forgotten. The two of them hoisted Shulamit roughly out of her seat.

She weighed very little, and she looked like a child as they carried her out.

They heard voices in the corridor, barked commands, the slamming of doors, the rattling of metal. There was a silence, broken only by the sleepy, snakelike hissing of the locomotive.

Katya and Gretchen sat frozen in their seats, Katya's fingers still clamped around Gretchen's arm.

Then they saw the police, outside on the platform. They were pushing Shulamit along in her wheelchair, something she hated. But her head was held high, and she looked straight ahead, like a queen.

A huge pressure was swelling in Gretchen's chest, building like a wave that refused to break.

A long scream burst from the engine.

The train lurched into movement. It picked up speed, the wheels clattering as it left Shulamit behind, drove past the border post, rumbled over the bridge, sped onwards towards Budapest.

'We didn't say anything.' Gretchen's voice was trembling. 'Why didn't we say anything?'

'Because we were afraid.'

'We let them take her instead of us!'

'Yes. She gave her life for us.'

'And we let her!'

'Yes, we let her.'

'Why did she do that?' Gretchen had been crying for hours – not the sobs of a child, but the silent, rending tears of a grown woman. 'Why? Why?'

Katya wiped her own eyes. 'I think she had planned to do it all the way along, if she saw you were in danger. I think she felt

352

something special for you. She wanted to save you any way she could.'

'I can't even thank her.'

'I think she knows that you will thank her with everything you do in your life, Liebchen.'

But it did not console Gretchen to be alive, even when they reached the beautiful city of Budapest, which is linked to Vienna by the River Danube, flowing through its heart, and breaking it in two forever.

Epilogue

The Musikverein building, the heart of Viennese music, had survived the war better than most other public buildings in the Innere Stadt. Like a great, pink Greek temple, it stood proudly amid the wreckage. Under the leadership of the greatest conductor of the day, Wilhelm Furtwängler, the Vienna Philharmonic had given concerts throughout the war, right up until the day a Russian bomb had sailed through the window of the Goldener Saal, scattering the orchestra.

Furtwängler had been suspended by the Occupying Powers while he was investigated for cooperation with the Nazis, but was now declared clean, and had been made musical director once more; and concerts had resumed within months of the German capitulation.

Katya walked into the building, lost in thought. The elderly concierge leaned over his counter to greet her.

'Have you been walking around Vienna on your own, Fräulein?' He wagged his finger. 'Didn't I tell you it's not safe?'

'You did tell me. I wanted to see what has become of the places I knew.'

'*Alles im arsch*,' he said crudely, using the language of the old soldier he was. 'But we asked for it.'

'Nobody wanted *this*, Herr Hufnagel,' she said dryly.

'We will rebuild it. Come back in the summer and you will see a change, I promise you. We Viennese know how to make life beautiful.'

He was ready to chat, but she could hear the piano in the Brahms Saal, and she wanted to get there now. She waved to him, and crossed the lobby quickly.

The Brahms Saal was as far removed from the devastation she had seen that morning as could be imagined. Here, where every inch was gilded and painted and carved and ornamented, the war might not have taken place at all. In fact, you were still in the age of Johannes Brahms and Clara Schumann, who had both played here in the nineteenth century.

Gretchen was at the piano on the stage, rehearsing the Schubert she was to play tonight, but Katya didn't disturb her. She went up the stairs to the balcony at the far end of the hall. Mama was there, huddled in her overcoat behind one of the golden caryatids that supported the canopy.

'It's freezing,' she greeted Katya querulously. 'Why don't they put the heating on in this place?'

'The oil is rationed, Mama. They'll put the heating on for the concert tonight.'

'I'll have pneumonia by then.' Mama was going to be sixty this year. She complained constantly about the cold, and Katya worried about her. Since Papa's death during the war, and her stroke, she had aged. She'd let her hair, once jet black, turn grey. Her clothes were dowdy, and the rings that had encrusted her fingers had long since all been hocked. The fierce energy that had once driven her seemed to have sunk away. The past nine years had been hard: the war, the London Blitz, the stripping away of all her pretensions, the loss of Papa. At times, she seemed broken by it all.

Katya sat beside her. Gretchen's playing soared up to them from the distant stage. Furtwängler had provided her with a lovely Bösendorfer grand piano, which had been put in storage during the worst of the bombing and had been brought out and tuned for Gretchen's debut. She was fussy about her instruments, but she had declared herself satisfied with it. Katya thought of the Steinway in the piano shop in Innsbruck, remembering the look on Gretchen's face when she'd seen it.

'Isn't this hall magnificent, Mama?' she said, partly to get Mama's mind off the cold. 'And the acoustics are excellent.'

Mama looked around disparagingly. 'It's nothing to the Mariinsky in St Petersburg.'

'No, of course not,' Katya agreed, hiding a smile. Along the side galleries, she could see several people listening to Gretchen's rehearsal – journalists writing in their pads, some Russian and French officers, a tall figure muffled in a coat and hat that was Wilhelm Furtwängler himself.

Furtwängler's invitation to Gretchen, who had been forced to flee Vienna in 1938, who had been adopted by the British, and who had become one of the most brilliant young musicians of her generation, had caused a sensation. It was seen as a first gesture of reconciliation, a plea for sanity in a world that had gone mad.

Gretchen was already being hailed as 'a Viennese prodigy', though this was the first time she had set foot in the city since 1938. Vienna, which had once been so unkind to her, was ready to reclaim her. The concert was a sell-out. Not a single seat remained unsold, even the rows above stage, where you saw nothing at all of the performers.

'I've never heard her play better,' Katya said to Mama. 'She hasn't shown the slightest trace of nerves.'

'I wish you had married and had a child of your own,' Mama said in that petulant way she had developed.

'Gretchen *is* my child,' Katya said gently. 'As for marrying – I'll be thirty-six this year. I don't think I could put up with a husband, even if I could find one who would put up with *me*.'

'You've given your life to that girl. And she's not even your blood.'

'It has been worth it. Besides, you know you love her too.'

Mama glanced at her with a touch of her old malice. 'Do you remember how angry you were with me and your sainted father for making you give up medicine? And now look – you could have gone back to university, but you never did. Everything has been for Gretchen, Gretchen, Gretchen.'

'There was the small question of the war, Mama. And I didn't just have Gretchen to care for.'

Mama grimaced. She touched the side of her face that always drooped now, checking that saliva hadn't trickled from the corner of her mouth. Her stroke, and Papa's heart condition, had come on after his bankruptcy. They had both been severely debilitated, and there had been nobody else to care for them. If Katya hadn't been there, God knew what would have become of them. Like so many women, it had fallen to Katya to mother a child and support ailing parents at the same time.

But Mama was right. In the end, it had all really been for Gretchen. Bringing her to England so young had confronted her with huge challenges. Katya's idea of starting university again had proved an impossible hope. Gretchen had needed her. And she had been there for Gretchen.

Katya leaned on the rail now and watched her at the piano. Perhaps nobody would ever know the effort that Gretchen had put into her education, the struggles she had faced. And she had never given up. Nobody but she knew what it had cost: the gruelling years of study with teachers who had broken her and put her together again, the fierce competition to win the bursaries and scholarships, the isolation at a time when the Luftwaffe were raining bombs on London, and people didn't want to hear a German name spoken. Gretchen had triumphed over it all. She was twenty-one, and people were already comparing her to Myra Hess and Moura Lympany.

She stopped playing now, and made a note on the score in front of her. Katya caught the gleam of gold in her hand. She always used the little gold pencil that Shulamit had left on the carriage seat the day they had taken her away. It was her talisman.

Katya could still hear Gretchen's voice: *We didn't say anything. Why didn't we say anything?* And her own response: *Because we were afraid.*

Those words had come to haunt the whole of Europe.

And that was another reason she had given up her studies for Gretchen's sake. Others had made sacrifices far greater. Compared to that, what were a few years? Didn't all mothers make similar sacrifices in their time?

She had made promises and she had kept them.

Katya went up to the stage. Wilhelm Furtwängler was talking to Gretchen, a gaunt figure towering over her.

'No more rehearsing, child. It's enough. Stop now.'

Gretchen looked up anxiously. 'But Maestro, I want to be perfect tonight.'

He laid a bony hand on her shoulder. 'You have been told that the more you rehearse, the better you play?'

'Yes, Maestro.'

'They all teach this. It's not true. With my orchestras, I rehearse as little as possible. Leave room for the music to blossom tonight. The pieces you have chosen are great music. You cannot make them any more perfect than they are, because they are dreams, not mathematical formulae. Do you understand?'

'I think so,' she said doubtfully.

He smiled, the old scar at the corner of his mouth puckering. 'You will understand tonight. You have to be more than an interpreter. You have to be a creator as well. Music is a dream, as life is a dream. It is never finished. It is always becoming. It is not your task to play every note with arithmetical precision. It is your task to allow the music to flow through you and become what it wants to become. Close the piano, child. Go with your mother and rest.'

Obediently, Gretchen rested in the afternoon in their hotel room. They were staying at the Sacher, once the epitome of old-world Viennese charm and luxury, where long ago they had eaten the famous chocolate cake on Sundays among dukes and duchesses. It was now a billet for British intelligence officers, who hurried in and out at all hours of the day and night, crowding the elegant street with their Jeeps. Vienna was only an hour away by tank from what Winston Churchill had called the Iron Curtain. The geography of the city had made it a nervous place.

She and Gretchen had been given the quietest suite, at the very top of the building. Gretchen didn't sleep, but lay on the bed with her eyes closed, motionless. Katya sat in the armchair, wrapped in a rug, reading Proust by the wintry light from the window.

'Did you understand what Herr Furtwängler was talking about this morning?' Gretchen asked after a while, without opening her eyes.

'About music being a dream?'

'Yes. What did he mean by that?'

'I suppose he meant that you can't plan too much. Things happen that are beyond your control. You and I both know the truth of that.'

'Yes, we do. But I think he meant something deeper.'

'Well, you're the artist, not me.'

'Sometimes I feel it's all a dream. We try to pretend that everything is logical. But it isn't. Sometimes our dreams are truer than real life is. And when you listen to great music, you understand that.' She opened her eyes and looked at Katya. 'What did you see on your walk?'

'*Alles im arsch.* That's how the doorman put it.'

'Awful?'

'Awful.'

'I didn't want to see it.'

'It's better not to, perhaps.'

'Do you think I'm a coward?'

'You're not a coward, Liebchen. You're the bravest person I know.'

'I've never felt brave.'

'Nor have I,' Katya confessed. 'Are you nervous about tonight?'

'No. Because I know you'll be in the audience. I just wish—'

She fell silent, but Katya knew what Gretchen was thinking. The confirmation that Thor had died in Mauthausen concentration camp had only come to them at the end of the war, when the camp had been liberated. The SS had destroyed most of the archives as they fled, but there had been witnesses who had confirmed that Thor Bachmann had perished there, worked to death, like so many of the Viennese intelligentsia, in the most brutal conditions, in the winter of 1940. The Red Cross had relayed the information to them.

Thor's body had been incinerated by the Nazis in the crematorium, like the others. There was no grave, not even a memorial yet, and visiting the camp was forbidden until it had been properly excavated. But they had agreed that they would make a journey there as soon as it was possible.

They had both accepted the fact of his death long before the news had come, but the blow had still been dreadful, and they were both still recovering from it.

She had loved Thor with all her heart. He had been torn from her almost before she had been able to know him fully. And nobody had ever taken his place. The thought of his suffering was terrible to her. People said it was better to know than to remain in doubt; but perhaps there were some things it was better not to know.

Of the fate of Shulamit they had never known anything. She had been taken off the train by the border police, and had vanished into the sprawling machinery of death that the Nazis had constructed across Europe. Nothing more had ever been heard of her, and all enquiries had come up empty-handed.

Frail as she was, it was impossible that Shulamit could have survived imprisonment at the hands of the Gestapo. The best they could hope for was that her end had been quick, and that she had not suffered pain or degradation before it.

The vastness of her self-sacrifice had shed both light and shadow on the years that had followed. She had given herself up to their enemies so that Katya and Gretchen could go free.

There had been no way to repay that sacrifice except to live each day as what it was – a precious gift, bought dear.

They were back at the Musikverein in the evening. Katya wore a plain grey suit. Gretchen had chosen black. She looked achingly lovely in the dress, Katya thought, her bare arms and throat pale as ivory. She had grown into a striking young woman with a willowy figure, her face framed by a mass of curly chestnut hair, her eyes burning with an intense gaze. She was extremely photogenic, something that would not hinder the career upon which she was embarking. Dramatic good looks were an asset in this new age of mass media. A beautiful face sold records and made good newspaper and magazine copy. And then there was the new medium of television, which people said was going to bring classical music to vast new audiences around the globe.

Not that Gretchen cared about success. For her, it had always been the music that mattered, nothing but the music. And it would always be the music that mattered. But success meant a degree of safety, and keeping Gretchen safe was what had preoccupied Katya for the past decade.

In her dressing room backstage, surrounded by flowers, Gretchen was astonishingly calm, looking through her scores and chatting to Katya. 'Did you know that Schubert and Beethoven were both members of the Musikverein? Isn't that incredible?'

'Yes, it is.'

'To be playing here, where they played! It's like a dream!'

'A very strange dream,' Katya said with a touch of dryness. 'Some of the people who'll applaud loudest tonight are the same people who broke your arm in 1938, and would have sent you to be exterminated. Doesn't that strike you as ironic?'

Gretchen's eyes darkened, and a shadow passed over her face. She touched her right arm for a moment with her fingertips; then the shadow was gone. 'That's just how the world turns. It doesn't matter, you know. You can't live in the past.'

'Certainly you can't live in the past at twenty-one. At my age, the past is a somewhat heavier burden.'

Gretchen jumped up from her stool and threw her arms around Katya. 'Don't be sad, darling,' she said, kissing Katya's cheek. 'You're not so very ancient. And we're alive, and we have each other. And it's Vienna, and it's my first big concert. We'll have champagne tonight, the director has promised us!' She laughed. She had never lost that odd, breathless laugh, as though she were still learning how to do it. 'I've never had champagne. Do you think I'll like it?'

Katya smiled. 'My guess is that from now on, you'll have to get used to it.'

There was a tap at the door. A stagehand brought in yet more flowers, a large arrangement of hothouse lilies. There was a note from Furtwängler pinned to them. As she found a place for them among the others, Katya wondered where, in this devastated city, lilies or champagne could be found. Probably on the flourishing black market. It didn't matter. Gretchen was right. The world turned, and one had to turn with it. One couldn't afford to be left behind. Yesterday was always leaving and there was always tomorrow, waiting at the door.

The hall was starting to fill. Whatever happened, the Viennese took their music seriously. The men were in evening dress, the women in long gowns. Perfume and cologne were in the air. There were military uniforms among the civilians too: a couple of Russian colonels, an English general there to stake the British claim on Gretchen, some dozen American and French officers. They congregated in the lobby, talking affably to each other through their interpreters, as though the world were not already divided into rival camps yet again, and the sabres rattling in their scabbards.

In the corridor outside Gretchen's dressing room, Katya heard someone call her name. She turned. It was Hildegard.

They hugged each other, swaying to and fro in delight. 'I'm so glad you made it,' Katya said. 'It's absolutely wonderful to see you again, Hildegard. Come and see Gretchen!'

'Not until after the performance,' Hildegard said. 'She has to get herself focused now. I'll only distract her. Trust me, I know. She's chosen a fiendishly difficult programme. But if she pulls it off, she'll be a sensation.'

'She'll pull it off,' Katya said.

They found a quiet corner to talk. In appearance, Hildegard had changed very little since 1938. She was as glossy as a berry. She'd got her degree and had become a music teacher. But the war years had been hard for her. She'd married in 1939, on the eve of the outbreak. Her husband had been called up in 1942, had been captured, and was still in a Russian prisoner-of-war camp. In 1944, a heavy Allied bombing raid on Innsbruck had destroyed her home. She'd had to evacuate to her parents in the country.

'But things are getting better now,' she said. 'The Russians have said that Anton will be released next year. I hope it's true. And I'm working again. Life will get back to normal in the end.'

'I suppose it will,' Katya sighed.

'You don't sound very certain.'

'I've forgotten what normal is,' Katya replied. 'In fact, I wonder whether my life was ever normal.'

Hildegard squeezed Katya's hands. 'I was so sorry to hear about Thor.'

'Thank you. I don't think we were expecting anything else. We were braced for it, or so we thought. But when it came, it was crushing. We realised that, despite everything, there had been that little scrap of hope left. Like a chink of light in a dark place. And now it was gone.'

'Nobody else?'

'Nobody.'

'I'm so sorry,' Hildegard said again. 'None of you deserved what they did to you.'

'There were millions who suffered worse. At least we survived. I'm very grateful for that.' Katya smiled. 'And you know, my life has been a love story after all. A love story with a difference.'

'I understand. You must be happy tonight.'

'I am.'

'Remember how I asked you whether you can really care for someone else's child like your own?'

'Yes, I do.'

'Well, you've proved you can. You've done an astonishing job with Gretchen. I admire you so much for that. And for the way you took care of your parents. But now it's time you started thinking of yourself, my dear.'

'I'm a bit out of practice with that.'

'Get back in practice. This life – it's not a rehearsal, you know. You can't live for others. It has to be your show.'

The rumble of conversation in the concert hall was very loud now. Nearly all the guests had taken their seats. The first bell was ringing.

'I have to run, or I'll be locked out,' Hildegard said, kissing her. 'See you inside!'

She gathered her long gown and hurried away. Katya went back to Gretchen's dressing room. Gretchen was on her feet now, breathing deeply and slowly with her eyes closed. It was the preparation routine one of her professors had taught her, based on yoga. Katya watched her slowly raise her arms and fill her lungs. She looked to Katya like a beautiful gull, lifting its wings to catch the wind, about to take flight and soar. She opened her eyes and smiled at Katya. 'Why are you looking at me like that?'

365

'I'm just so proud of you.' Katya's voice was husky. 'So proud, Liebchen.'

'Wait until I've finished my performance before saying you're proud!'

'I'm not proud of your playing. I'm proud of *you*.'

'I would be nothing without you,' Gretchen replied. 'Now don't make me cry. Go and take your seat.'

Katya kissed her on both cheeks, and went to find her seat in the hall. Mama would be there already, and she hated to be left alone in public places. The second bell was ringing now to warn concertgoers that the auditorium doors would soon be closing.

She slipped into the hall through a side door. They'd been given four front-row seats. Hildegard had taken her place, and was sitting next to Mama. But the fourth place was still empty. Her heart faltered. Perhaps he wasn't coming.

But as she settled into her seat, she felt him sit down beside her. She turned. 'David!'

He was in evening dress, *comme il faut*. He smiled at her and kissed her hands. 'Katya. You look wonderful.'

'I thought you might not come!'

'I wouldn't have missed it for the world.' David Turteltaub was greying, looking more like the distinguished paediatrician he was now than the young houseman he had been in 1938. Katya knew he had escaped to Hungary before the war, then to Shanghai. He'd returned to Europe and had spent the war in Switzerland, where he worked in a large teaching hospital and had a thriving private practice. He consulted the gold watch on his wrist. 'Sorry I'm late. My taxi got a flat tyre going over a bomb crater. This town has gone to the dogs somewhat.'

She laughed. 'Welcome to Vienna.'

'Thank you. How is Gretchen? Nervous?'

'Not a bit of it. Cool as a cucumber.'

'She was always a brave girl.'

'Yes, she always was.'

'I can't wait to see her.'

'I can't wait for you to see her either.' She put her hand over his and looked into his gentle blue eyes. 'We owe you so much, David. One day, I hope—'

He shook his head to silence her. 'No thanks. No apologies. Shulamit did what she wanted to do. Just as you've done what you wanted to do. Nobody forced either of you. If you had a debt to her, you have paid it. She would be satisfied. Tell me how you are.'

Katya hesitated. 'I suppose I feel at a bit of a loose end now,' she confessed. 'Gretchen has engagements lined up for the next year. I'll go with her to most of them, of course. She needs me, and she's still a bit too young to travel on her own. But I feel I'm getting less and less useful. And I remember Shulamit telling me to be sure I knew when it was time to let Gretchen go. I think of that a lot lately.'

'You gave up your studies for her. You must go back to medical school.'

Katya shook her head. 'Oh, please. It's too late for that.'

'Not at all,' he said seriously. 'I don't believe in "too late". Nothing is ever too late.'

'I'm rather long in the tooth, David.'

'I know exactly how old you are. After qualifying, you would have thirty years ahead of you. Maybe more. Some of the best physicians I know qualified late. It makes them special. Come to Zürich. I can do a lot to help you there.'

'That's a very kind offer.'

'I told you – fractured dreams, like fractured bones, may knit up again.' He smiled. 'It'll be good having you there with me. We have shared history. Nobody else knows the things we know. That gets important as life goes on.'

'I'll think about it,' she promised. And she realised that, inside, she felt it might really come true.

The lights were dimming. The hall became dark. Conversation subsided to murmurs, then whispers, then an expectant silence. The only lights were on the stage now, illuminating the sweeping black prow of the grand piano, which seemed like a great ship about to set sail.

When Gretchen walked on to the stage, there was a tumult of applause. Following the protocol of the Brahms Saal, it did not last too long. This was an audience accustomed to the very best. They would judge, and they would save their real applause for a truly memorable performance – and they would know it when they heard it.

Gretchen seemed about to sit at the piano, then stopped. She turned, and walked to the front of the stage, and gazed out over the audience. The spotlight bathed her, making her uplifted face glow like a pale flame. Katya felt yet again, but perhaps more intensely than ever before, how her love for Gretchen – the purest, most unselfish love she had ever known – had illuminated her life.

Gretchen spoke quietly, but her voice carried clearly to the hundreds of people gathered there.

'Thank you for having me in this beautiful place. This used to be my home, once.' She paused, looked around the hall, then went on. 'I am only here tonight because certain people gave up a great deal for me.' She lowered her eyes to Katya and David in the front row. 'Some gave up their dreams. Some gave up their lives. None of them ever asked for thanks. But I thank them now. And tonight, on my debut, I dedicate this music, and all the music I will ever play in my life, to those people.'

There was an absolute hush as she walked to the piano. Katya found that she was gripping David's hand tightly in her own. She could feel her eyes burning with tears.

Gretchen took her seat at the piano. She laid her fingers on the keys. And the dream began.

ACKNOWLEDGMENTS

I want to thank my brilliant editors, Victoria Pepe and Mike Jones, who have been wonderful, as always.

And once again, I want to thank my readers, who give me so much support and admonition, and who teach me so much about the art of storytelling. Don't stop telling me what you think.

ABOUT THE AUTHOR

Photo © 2021 Ahmad Abdulkawi

Marius Gabriel was accused by *Cosmopolitan* magazine of 'keeping you reading while your dinner burns'. He served his author apprenticeship as a student at Newcastle University, Britain, where, to finance his postgraduate research, he wrote thirty-three steamy romances under a pseudonym. Gabriel is the author of thirteen historical novels, including the bestsellers *The Designer*, *The Ocean Liner* and *The Parisians*. Born in South Africa, he has travelled and worked in many countries, and now lives in Lincolnshire. He has three grown-up children.